continued . . .

"Anne Bishop does not disappoint. I have not read a book of hers that did not immediately captivate me and draw me immediately back into her world. . . . [She] weaves her spell so well."
—SFRevu

"If you are a fan of high fantasy with some romance and a limited amount of spell casting, Bishop is a good choice for you."
—BookSpot Central

"Bishop tackles surviving various horrors head-on. . . . It's a difficult subject, but one that Bishop writes about sensitively, with compassion and without blinking or pulling punches."
—Romantic Times

Tangled Webs

"Bewitching. . . . With feverish pacing and terrifying twists, Bishop's surefire spellcraft will leave readers' hearts pounding."
—Publishers Weekly (starred review)

"An excellent action-packed tale that grips readers . . . and never slows down. . . . The story line is fast-paced and the cast seems real."
—Midwest Book Review

"Bishop is one of those wonderful writers who get steadily better as they grow more experienced, and I have no problem saying this is the most enjoyable of her books to date, but I doubt it will stay that way for long."
—Critical Mass

"Reading Tangled Webs was like meeting up with an old friend. . . . The humor brought a smile to my face . . . and I will always appreciate how Bishop can make even the most superpowered characters seem like those eccentric neighbors next door."
—Dear Author

Queen of the Darkness

"As engaging, as strongly characterized, and as fully conceived as its predecessors . . . a perfect—and very moving—conclusion."
—SF Site

"A storyteller of stunning intensity, Ms. Bishop has a knack for appealing but complex characterization realized in a richly drawn, imaginative ambience."
—Romantic Times

"A powerful finale for this fascinating, uniquely dark trilogy."
—Locus

Heir to the Shadows

"Daemon, Lucivar, and Saetan ooze more sex appeal than any three fictional characters created in a very long time."
—The Romance Reader

"*Heir to the Shadows* isn't as dark as its predecessor. . . . All the other elements that made the first book such a gripping read are present: vivid and sympathetic characters, a fascinating and fully realized magical system. . . . It's a terrific read, and I highly recommend both it and *Daughter of the Blood*." —SF Site

"Bishop seems to delight in turning fantasy conventions on their heads . . . still darkly opulent, often exotic." —*Locus*

"Ms. Bishop's striking magical concepts and powerful images are wonderfully leavened with unexpected dash and humor, creating an irresistible treat for fantasy fans." —*Romantic Times*

Daughter of the Blood

"A terrific writer. . . . The more I read, the more excited I became because of the freshness of [her] take on the usual high-fantasy setting, the assurance of [her] language, all the lovely touches of characterization that [she slips] in so effortlessly."
—Charles de Lint

"Darkly mesmerizing . . . [a] fascinating, dark world." —*Locus*

"Vividly painted . . . dramatic, erotic, hope-filled."
—Lynn Flewelling

"Lavishly sensual . . . a richly detailed world based on a reversal of standard genre clichés." —*Library Journal*

"Intense . . . erotic, violent, and imaginative. This one is white-hot." —Nancy Kress

"A fabulous new talent . . . a uniquely realized fantasy filled with vibrant colors and rich textures. A wonderful new voice, Ms. Bishop holds us spellbound from the very first page."
—*Romantic Times* (4½ stars)

"Dark, intricate, and disturbing."
—Josepha Sherman, author of *Forging the Runes*

"Has immense appeal for fans of dark fantasy or horror. Most highly recommended." —Hypatia's Hoard

"A high-voltage ride through a new realm. Bishop draws her characters with acute emotion [and] leaves the reader lusting for her next novel."
—Lois H. Gresh, coauthor of *The Termination Node*

"Dark, morbid, sinister, and yet it holds you completely fascinated and spellbound by its beauty. Once I'd begun reading . . . I couldn't bring myself to put down the book and leave the world that Anne Bishop had magically spun around me . . . one of the most original and readable books in the fantasy genre." —The 11th Hour

ANNE BISHOP

TWILIGHT'S DAWN

A *Black Jewels* Novel

A ROC BOOK

ROC
Published by New American Library, a division of
Penguin Group (USA) Inc., 375 Hudson Street,
New York, New York 10014, USA
Penguin Group (Canada), 90 Eglinton Avenue East, Suite 700, Toronto,
Ontario M4P 2Y3, Canada (a division of Pearson Penguin Canada Inc.)
Penguin Books Ltd., 80 Strand, London WC2R 0RL, England
Penguin Ireland, 25 St. Stephen's Green, Dublin 2,
Ireland (a division of Penguin Books Ltd.)
Penguin Group (Australia), 250 Camberwell Road, Camberwell, Victoria 3124,
Australia (a division of Pearson Australia Group Pty. Ltd.)
Penguin Books India Pvt. Ltd., 11 Community Centre, Panchsheel Park,
New Delhi - 110 017, India
Penguin Group (NZ), 67 Apollo Drive, Rosedale, Auckland 0632,
New Zealand (a division of Pearson New Zealand Ltd.)
Penguin Books (South Africa) (Pty.) Ltd., 24 Sturdee Avenue,
Rosebank, Johannesburg 2196, South Africa

Penguin Books Ltd., Registered Offices:
80 Strand, London WC2R 0RL, England

Published by Roc, an imprint of New American Library, a division of Penguin
Group (USA) Inc. Previously published in a Roc hardcover edition.

First Roc Mass Market Printing, March 2012

FOR ALL THE READERS

WHO MADE THIS JOURNEY WITH ME

ACKNOWLEDGMENTS

My thanks to Blair Boone for continuing to be my first reader, to Debra Dixon for being second reader, to Doranna Durgin for maintaining the Web site, to Nadine Fallacaro and Julie Green for answering questions about things medical, to Jennifer Jackson and Anne Sowards for their continued enthusiasm for the *Black Jewels* stories, to David Rapkin and John Sharian for bringing the characters to life in the audio book, and to Pat Feidner just because.

CONTENTS

JEWELS

WHITE
YELLOW
TIGER EYE
ROSE
SUMMER-SKY
PURPLE DUSK
OPAL*
GREEN
SAPPHIRE
RED
GRAY
EBON-GRAY
BLACK

*Opal is the dividing line between lighter and darker Jewels because it can be either.

When making the Offering to the Darkness, a person can descend a maximum of three ranks from his/her Birth-right Jewel.

Example: Birthright White could descend to Rose.

AUTHOR'S NOTE

The "Sc" in the names Scelt and Sceltie is pronounced "Sh."

BLOOD HIERARCHY/CASTES

MALES
landen—non-Blood of any race
Blood male—a general term for all males of the Blood; also refers to any Blood male who doesn't wear Jewels
Warlord—a Jeweled male equal in status to a witch
Prince—a Jeweled male equal in status to a Priestess or a Healer
Warlord Prince—a dangerous, extremely aggressive Jeweled male; in status, slightly lower than a Queen

FEMALES
landen—non-Blood of any race
Blood female—a general term for all females of the Blood; mostly refers to any Blood female who doesn't wear Jewels
witch—a Blood female who wears Jewels but isn't one of the other hierarchical levels; also refers to any Jeweled female
Healer—a witch who heals physical wounds and illnesses; equal in status to a Priestess and a Prince
Priestess—a witch who cares for altars, sanctuaries, and Dark Altars; witnesses handfasts and marriages; performs offerings; equal in status to a Healer and a Prince
Black Widow—a witch who heals the mind; weaves the tangled webs of dreams and visions; is trained in illusions and poisons
Queen—a witch who rules the Blood; is considered to be the land's heart and the Blood's moral center; as such, she is the focal point of their society

WINSOL GIFTS

This story takes place after the events in Tangled Webs.

ONE

Daemon Sadi, the Black-Jeweled Warlord Prince of Dhemlan, crossed the bridge that marked the boundary between private property and public land. On one side of the bridge was the drive leading to SaDiablo Hall, his family's seat; on the other side was the public road leading to the village of Halaway.

Fluffy snow dusted the bottoms of his trousers as he walked toward the village in blissful solitude. Of course, he'd had to sneak out of his own home in order to *have* that solitude, and he recognized that there was something not quite right about the most powerful male in the Realm of Kaeleer sneaking out in order to avoid three snoozing Sceltie puppies. But whether he was allowing little bundles of fur to dictate his actions instead of using his rank and power to do as he pleased wasn't the point. At this moment, here and now, he was alone on a crisp winter morning, and *that* was the point. No one was whining about having cold paws. No one was complaining that he walked too fast. No one was grumbling because he wouldn't stop every few feet so interesting smells could be properly sniffed.

And no one was going to sulk because he refused to carry someone with wet fur under his coat and up against his white silk shirt.

Solitude. Bliss. And, if his mother had created the gift he'd asked her to make, fun.

Winsol was almost here. Those thirteen days were a

celebration of the Darkness—and they were a celebration of Witch, the living myth, dreams made flesh.

It would be his first Winsol as the ruler of the Dhemlan Territory, his third celebration since he'd come to live in Kaeleer. The first year, he'd still been mentally fragile from the years when he'd wandered the roads in the Twisted Kingdom, lost in the insanity of guilt and grief. And in that first year, he'd also been lost in the wonder of finding Jaenelle Angelline again, alive and well—and still able to love him.

The second year, she had been the one who had been so terrifyingly fragile. She had unleashed her full power to prevent a war between Kaeleer and Terreille that would have destroyed both Realms—and had torn her body apart in the process. She shouldn't have survived—wouldn't have if the kindred and the Weaver of Dreams hadn't done the impossible and remade the living myth, the Queen who was Witch.

But this year he and Jaenelle were together, they were married, and the worst thing looming over their heads was how many invitations to parties and public gatherings they needed to accept in order for him to fulfill his duties as Dhemlan's ruler.

He made his way through Halaway's quiet streets, noticing lights in the windows of most of the houses. The snow wasn't marred yet by many footprints or cart wheels, but soon the merchants would open their shops, people and carriages would fill the sidewalks and streets, and the small village would bustle through another day of holiday preparations.

As he approached the cottage where his mother, Tersa, lived, he studied the walkways up to her cottage and the neighboring one that was occupied by Manny, an older woman he considered a friend rather than a former servant. Then he smiled and, using Craft, dealt with the snow as he glided up the walkway and knocked on the cottage door.

He waited a minute, then knocked again.

The third time, he put a bit of temper and Craft into the act of applying knuckles to wood, which guaranteed the sound would roll through the cottage like thunder.

A few seconds later, the door swung open as the young woman on the other side growled, "If someone doesn't answer the door, you could take the hint that it's too early for com—"

She blinked at him. He smiled at the journeymaid Black Widow who lived with Tersa as part of her training.

"Lady Allista," he said politely.

"Prince Sadi." Her tone was much less polite. Since he was who and what he was, she couldn't shut the door in his face.

But she wanted to.

Obviously, Allista was one of those women who did not wake up cheerful. That was all right. A few months of marriage to Jaenelle had taught him the value of having a few tricks when it came to dealing with a witch who woke up grumpy—and he had become an expert at all of them.

"Tersa asked me to come early," he said, slipping past Allista. "Since my timing is a bit off, why don't I make breakfast for the two of you?"

He shrugged out of his overcoat and vanished it as he continued down the hall to the kitchen, not giving Allista time to answer.

All right. Tersa hadn't told him to come *this* early, but she would be awake—and he wanted to slip out with his requested gift before too many people were up and about.

"Good morning, darling," he said as he walked into the kitchen.

Tersa turned away from the counter and studied him for a moment. Then she smiled. "It's the boy. It's my boy."

Her boy. His mother was a broken Black Widow lost in the madness the Blood called the Twisted Kingdom. Lost in the dreams and visions—and the shattered pieces of her mind. She remembered him as the child he had been before he'd been taken from her. She remembered him as the youth who had met her again but didn't know who she was.

And sometimes she remembered him as the man he was now. But however she saw him on any given day, he was always the boy. Her boy.

"I've come to cook you breakfast," Daemon said. He gave her his best-boy grin. "And to talk about gifts."

She narrowed her gold eyes as if she was about to argue. Then she shrugged and turned back to the counter. "There are bacon and eggs and bread for toast."

"That sounds like breakfast," Daemon said. "How would you like me to make the eggs?"

She hesitated—and he wondered if she would be able to answer or if her mind had turned down another path too far removed from such mundane things as bacon and eggs.

"I like them scrambled," she finally said.

He put an arm around her, brushed his lips against her temple, and felt all his love for her well up and squeeze his heart. "Me too."

Lucivar Yaslana backwinged and landed lightly on the walkway in front of Tersa's cottage. He looked at the cottage directly in front of him, then at its neighbor.

Manny had spent most of her life as a servant, was used to working with her hands, and didn't shun physical labor. Even now she'd taken on the duties of housekeeper for Tersa and Allista, an arrangement that satisfied all three women. But Manny wasn't a young woman by any stretch of truth, and it seemed a bit early for her to have been out sweeping the walkways.

Not swept, he realized as he studied the sharp, perfect edge that divided the snowy lawn from the cleared walkway. Not even a hearth witch could get that kind of edge. Not with a shovel or broom, anyway. So someone had used Craft to remove the snow.

He crouched, held out a hand, and felt warm air.

And then someone had put a warming spell on the flagstones to keep them clear of snow.

The cottage door opened and the *someone* walked out.

Lucivar rose and looked pointedly at the walkways,

then at Daemon. "You know, Bastard, using Craft is all well and good, but it wouldn't hurt you to sweat once in a while."

"If I'm going to work up a sweat for a woman, I'm going to be doing something besides sweeping the walk," Daemon replied.

Lucivar grinned.

They were brothers. Half brothers, but they had never made that distinction. They both had the coloring of the three long-lived races—the black hair, light brown skin, and gold eyes. They had inherited much of their looks from their Hayllian father, who was the High Lord of Hell. Daemon's face was a more refined, beautiful version of Saetan's, while his own face was more rugged than their father's. But the real distinction between him and Daemon came from the other side of his dual heritage. He had the dark, membranous wings that set the Eyrien race apart from the Hayllian and Dhemlan Blood.

They studied each other for a moment before Lucivar's mouth curved in a lazy, arrogant smile.

"You're up early," Lucivar said, taking the few steps that separated them.

"You're up even earlier, since you had to come in from Ebon Rih," Daemon replied. "You must have left at dawn."

Lucivar shook his head. "I'm farther east; sun rises earlier. But I was up at dawn."

"Was that by choice?"

"Hell's fire, no, but the little beast is up with the sun, and I feel less guilty about Marian holding the leash most of the day if she gets a little extra sleep."

"How is my darling nephew? Counting the days until Winsol?"

"One of us is," Lucivar muttered. He smiled grimly in response to Daemon's laugh. "Last year, Winsol was something that just appeared and dazzled him. This year he's figured out that Winsol is *coming*."

"Ah."

"Ooooh, yeah. So every morning, he climbs into bed

with us, pries my eyes open, and says, 'Papa! Is it Winzel yet?'"

Daemon's lips were curved in a smile, but his golden eyes were full of sharp understanding. "Can you put a shield around the bed?"

"Tried that. Unfortunately, one that will keep him out also keeps Marian out. She didn't appreciate smacking into a shield when she wanted to get back into bed after getting up to pee."

"Lucivar."

He heard Daemon's concern wrapped around that single word.

"I've got a light shield around Daemonar's room that will wake me if he starts wandering," he said. That shield was a necessary precaution now to keep his son safe—from him. A Warlord Prince was a born predator, a natural killer. A Warlord Prince startled awake didn't think; he attacked. The first morning Daemonar pounced on him, the boy's physical scent and psychic scent had penetrated his sleep-fogged brain fast enough that he managed to pull back what might have been a killing blow.

Marian's presence didn't bother him. He was so steeped in the feel of her, she could touch him, mount him, do just about anything to him before he was fully awake without provoking that lethal rise to the killing edge. But Daemonar was male, he was a Warlord Prince, and he'd matured just enough over the past few weeks that Lucivar's aggressive instincts now recognized caste before son.

So even though he let the boy have the fun of prying his eyes open, Lucivar was always awake and aware before Daemonar entered the room.

He looked into his brother's eyes and knew he didn't need to say anything more.

Then Daemon looked pointedly at Tersa's cottage and raised an eyebrow as if asking a question—or demanding an explanation.

"None of your business, Bastard," Lucivar said.

It wasn't, and they both knew it. They also knew that

Daemon was protective of Tersa and, in the past, had been brutally efficient when it came to dealing with men who had taken the wrong kind of interest in her.

And they also both knew that, in Terreille, Lucivar Yaslana had earned his reputation for being unpredictable, uncontrollable, and explosively violent toward women, so Daemon's concern about his brother spending time with his mother was not without reason.

"Well," Daemon said after an awkward moment. "I'd better get back to the Hall before the rest of the household is up."

Lucivar nodded. "We'll be coming in at the end of the week to help you and Jaenelle get the Hall ready for Winsol."

"Get what ready?"

Lucivar blinked, decided Daemon wasn't being a smart-ass, and gave his brother a pitying look. "Since I've been married longer than you, here's a piece of advice: Never ask questions like that. They'll only get you into trouble."

Daemon huffed out a breath. "There are servants at the Hall. *Lots* of them. They're the ones who are getting things ready."

The pitying look changed to a wicked grin. "You *do* have a lot to learn."

"No, really. They haven't put up any of the fresh greenery because that's done on the first day of Winsol, but yesterday Helene hauled out a century's worth of decorations from the Hall's attics. Hell's fire, one of the young maids even put bells on the Sceltie puppies."

"Did the puppies jingle into your study to complain?" Lucivar asked.

"Of course they did. Until the wolf pups decided the bells sounded fun. So now I have Sceltie puppies prancing up and down the great hall wearing bells while the wolf pups howl."

"Your guests are going to be greeted by a jingle howl?" Correctly interpreting Daemon's look, Lucivar added, "If you try to whack me upside the head, you'll end up on the ground."

Daemon squeezed his eyes shut and muttered, "Maybe I can run away from home."

"We're not allowed to do that. Trust me. We're allowed to hide for an hour or two at a time, but we're not allowed to run away from the festivities."

"Says who?"

"The women we married."

Daemon sighed. "Was life simpler when we were slaves in Terreille?"

"Simpler in some ways, yes. But not as much fun. See you in a few days."

Lucivar stepped aside to let Daemon pass. Choosing to be cautious, because the Sadist had earned his reputation too, he watched until Daemon was out of sight, that gliding walk and feline grace covering a lot of ground. Then he approached the cottage and knocked on the door.

Allista, looking like a cat who had been dunked in a tub of water and then stroked the wrong way, hesitated before letting him into the cottage.

"The witchling is still sleepy," Tersa said when he walked into the kitchen. "But boys start the day early in order to do all their boy things."

On another day, it would have been interesting to find out what Tersa considered "boy things," but one of them needed to stay focused, and it had to be him.

Her mind had shattered centuries ago, but Tersa was still brilliant in her own way, still powerful in her own way. She had given up sanity in order to regain the Hourglass's Craft and could draw power out of madness in ways that even Saetan didn't understand.

Lucivar loved her. It was that simple. He had begun these twice-monthly visits for the same reason he had visited his own mother, Luthvian—as a family duty. But unlike Luthvian, who had hated her son because of the heritage she had given him, Tersa had accepted the wings and the fact that he was an Eyrien warrior down to the very marrow of his bones. She didn't criticize him for what he was—or for what he wasn't. She didn't lash out at him physically or verbally. He could sit in her kitchen and enjoy her company, and she seemed to enjoy his.

He should have told Daemon about the visits. Maybe not when Daemon had first arrived in Kaeleer, since Sadi had had enough things to deal with, but he should have said something soon after, instead of having that nugget of information come out a few weeks ago while they were dealing with that damned spooky house that had been built to trap, and kill, some of their family. He wasn't sure why he hadn't said anything. Maybe because he'd been afraid he would be asked to step aside? After all, Tersa was Daemon's mother, not his, and when the real son was present, a surrogate wasn't needed. Or maybe, like his father, he had gotten into the habit of not mentioning any relationship that would have given Luthvian an excuse to feel neglected or cast aside. Even now, when his mother was a whisper in the Darkness and truly gone, he had continued to keep his visits to Tersa private. Either way, by the time Daemon came to Kaeleer, the visits were a long-established habit that he didn't discuss with anyone.

"Do you want food?" Tersa asked. "There are some scrambled eggs and toast left. The boy made them."

In that case, he wasn't going to refuse. No one made scrambled eggs better than Daemon—including his own darling hearth witch wife. Which was something he would never ever admit to anyone. Especially Marian.

Since Allista hadn't joined them, he figured she had already eaten or would fend for herself, so he got a fork out of the drawer, hefted the bowl, leaned a hip against the counter, and began to eat.

"You should sit at the table," Tersa said.

"I can eat just fine where I am." She looked like she was about to scold, so he added casually, "Did you eat?"

"I ate."

He caught the hesitation before she answered. She would have eaten something. Daemon wouldn't have left if she hadn't. But she still had the skinniness of someone who had been half-starved for too many years, and even now, when there was plenty of food, she sometimes became too distracted by something only she could see and forgot to eat.

So he never wasted an opportunity to feed her.

Scooping up another forkful of scrambled eggs, he held it in front of her. "Open up."

Her mouth remained stubbornly shut.

He sighed—but his eyes never left her face and his hand remained steady. "Am I going to have to embarrass myself by making funny noises like I do with Daemonar?"

Her mouth fell open in surprise, and he slipped the fork in before she realized what he was doing.

She scowled at him. He grinned at her. And prudently ate a couple of forkfuls of egg himself before offering her another.

Tersa waved him off and got her own fork.

They polished off the eggs—and he made her work to claim the last bite—then he finished off the toast while enjoying a mug of coffee.

"Were you able to do it?" he asked as he rinsed off the dishes and set them in the sink.

Tersa frowned at him. "I was able to do it, but . . ."

Grinning, he wiped his hands on a towel. "Let's see."

Using Craft, she called in a small wooden frame and set it at one end of the kitchen table. The carefully constructed web attached to the frame held the illusion spell. She triggered the illusion spell, and they watched as a small black beetle appeared and headed for the other end of the table. It grew and grew with every step. When it got as big as his palm, it burst open with enough gore and green goo to delight a small Eyrien boy.

"You have the box?" Tersa asked.

He called in the long wood-and-glass box he'd had made to hold the illusion web and keep the entire illusion contained. He valued his skin—and his marriage—enough to make sure the bug remained in the box.

After she placed the illusion web into its part of the box, they watched the beetle once more. Lucivar grinned at the way the gore and goo splattered all over the inside of the glass before it all faded away. "Darling, this is *perfect*."

Tersa looked uneasy. "Maybe I should ask your father."

Not quite a statement, not quite a question. More a tentative testing of an idea.

He shifted his weight from one foot to the other, not quite sure if he was troubled or intrigued by the words. "Why?"

"I made little surprises for my boys before, and it caused trouble. Almost hurt them. I don't want to cause trouble for my boys. Your father will know what to do." She nodded, as if she'd made a decision. "Yes. Your father will know."

Lucivar vanished the box and decided this would be a good time to give her something else to think about— *before* she contacted his father.

Boys. My boys.

The ground shifted under his feet. His breath caught. He felt like he was riding a current that could be a very sweet wind or have a cutting edge.

"What boys, darling?" he asked.

"My boys." She glanced at him, suddenly shy and hesitant.

Painfully sweet words, and a possibility he hadn't considered about why Tersa had welcomed him from the first time he'd knocked on her cottage door.

"Am I one of your boys, Tersa?" he asked.

She was Daemon's mother. She would have been around during the childhood years he couldn't remember. She had known him as a child—and he must have known her. That hadn't occurred to him before.

"The girl," Tersa said hesitantly. "Luthvian. So angry because she wanted what couldn't be. So angry because she wanted to deny what was."

She reached out, not quite touching him, her eyes caressing the very thing his own mother had always pretended not to see.

"Sails to the moon," she said softly. "Banners unfurled

in the sun. She was always so angry about something as natural as an arm or a leg. Such a foolish reason to hate a child."

"Tersa?"

Her eyes had that unfocused look. She was no longer seeing the room she stood in, wouldn't know where she was physically if he asked. She was looking at a memory seventeen hundred years in the past. Seeing Luthvian. Seeing him when he was Daemonar's age. Maybe even younger.

"She wanted the boy, but did not want the boy to *be* the boy," Tersa said. "But what else could he be? Cuddles and hugs. Their father's love is strong, and they need him, but they want softer love too. Cuddles and hugs. And little surprises." She smiled. "They pick flowers in the meadow. The boy brings his flowers to me. I tell him the names of the ones I remember as we arrange them in a vase. His father tells him the rest. Tells both boys. But the girl doesn't want flowers from the meadow. That is too simple, too Eyrien. She will not take the flowers, so the winged boy brings them to me. There is so much fire in his heart, so much laughter. And trouble. That gleam in his eyes. Oh, yes, he is trouble. But there is no meanness. He is a boy. He will be a strong man. She will not look, will not see. So he comes to me for cuddles and hugs and little surprises."

Tears stung Lucivar's eyes. He blinked them away. Swallowed them with his heart.

He took a step closer, touched her shoulder with his fingertips. "Tersa? Am I one of your boys?"

She looked at him, her eyes full of uncertainty. But she nodded. "My winged boy."

He took her in his arms and held her gently as he finally understood why spending time with her mattered so much to him. He hadn't remembered those early years of his childhood; he hadn't remembered her. But his heart had recognized her and knew what she had been for him.

"Thank you," he whispered into her tangled hair. "Thank you." He added silently, *Mother.*

*   *   *

Jaenelle leaned back from the breakfast table and stared at the object in front of her. "It's a mousie in a glass dome."

"Yes." Daemon smiled at the illusion he'd talked Tersa into making for him.

"It's a mousie wearing the formal dress of a court official."

"Yes."

"And you intend to give this to Lucivar? The Warlord Prince of Ebon Rih? The man who has said that the only reason for paperwork is to have something to wipe your ass with after taking a crap?"

"Oh, yes."

As they watched, the mousie began squeaking emphatically while gesturing with one paw and waving a scroll held in the other. Of course, the squeaking could barely be heard through the glass dome, but the tone was still clear. Especially when the mousie began jumping up and down in a tantrum.

"He's capable of leaving this out on the desk without a sight shield so that court officials see it," Jaenelle said. "You know he's capable of doing that."

"I know. But I figure having this just might keep him from strangling some pompous ass from a Queen's court."

Jaenelle pursed her lips and studied the mousie. Then she sighed. "You have a point. There have been a few times when he's come too close to strangling a pompous ass."

"All the more reason to give him something to laugh about." Daemon kissed the top of her head and reached for the glass dome. "I'm heading up to the Keep to show this to Father, so I'll—"

"You can't go today."

He stopped, his hand frozen over the dome. "I can't?"

"*Daemon.* You have to help me get ready. This will be our first Winsol when we're officially hosting the family. You can't just shrug off the details."

Sure, he could.

"Marian is coming later in the week to help out," Jaenelle continued. "And Winsol begins next week. We have to go over the lists."

"Lists?"

His wife stiffened. Then she turned in her chair and looked at him.

The bones in his legs turned to jelly—and not in a good she's-looking-for-hot-sex kind of way.

"I'll be in my study," he said meekly.

"Good," Jaenelle replied sweetly. "I'll join you there after I finish breakfast. I hope you didn't have anything scheduled for this morning."

Hell's fire, Mother Night, and may the Darkness be merciful.

"Only my Lady's pleasure," he said.

Jaenelle reached up and tugged on his jacket. Obeying the unspoken command, he leaned over and touched his lips to hers.

"Your tone lacks sincerity, Prince," Jaenelle said. "But since this is your first Winsol as a husband, you're forgiven."

Then she kissed him—and he hoped she would have reason to forgive him for a lot of things over the next few days.

TWO

Prince Sadi,

Your presence is requested at your mother's cottage. Please join me there after dinner.

SaDiablo

Daemon banged once on the cottage's front door.

It couldn't be *too* serious, since he hadn't been asked to respond immediately. But a command like this from his father was unusual—and "your presence is requested" was a phrase in Protocol that amounted to a command.

And just because it wasn't "too serious" didn't mean it *wasn't* serious.

Hell's fire! What could have happened since his visit yesterday morning that required the High Lord to come to Halaway? And why hadn't he been told about it *before* Saetan had arrived?

He banged on the door again, then opened it himself, almost clobbering Allista, who had been hurrying to reach it.

"Where?" he snapped, too worried about why he'd been summoned to be polite.

"The parlor," she replied.

He opened the parlor door—and froze.

His father sat in one of the chairs by the fire, his legs crossed at the knees, his fingers steepled, and the black-tinted nails of his forefingers resting against his chin. His mother stood in front of the other chair, twisting her fingers and looking anxious.

The room looked wrong. He kept his eyes on his father, but he *knew* the room looked wrong. Then he realized why. He didn't have an actual memory of the situation, but he was certain that the last time he'd seen his parents positioned like this, he had been much, much younger and much, much shorter.

"Come in, Prince. Sit down," Saetan said. He looked at Tersa. "Darling, could you bring in some coffee?"

Tersa nodded. "And nutcakes. Boys need something sweet after a scolding." She gave Daemon a distracted smile as she scurried past him.

Scolding? he thought as his heart settled back to a regular beat and his mind adjusted to the fact that his mother wasn't hurt or ill. *Oh, no. There is not going to be a scolding.*

He looked his father in the eyes and said, "I'm an adult."

Saetan met his look with steely calm. "When you walk out that door, you're an adult. Right here, right now, you're a son. *Sit.*"

He sat. It was humiliating that his body had obeyed that voice before his brain made a decision.

Saetan took a deep breath and let it out slowly. "Your mother is concerned about her boys."

"We didn't do anything."

Where in the name of Hell had *those* words come from? And why had there been a flash of amused panic in Saetan's eyes before the High Lord regained that steely calm?

"When you and Lucivar were little boys and one of you said that to me, I *knew* we had something to talk about," Saetan said. "And we would sit for as long as it took to discuss it."

Meaning for as long as it took the boy to start squirming beneath the weight of that stare and blurt out whatever it was he had done.

And damn it, that stare *still* worked.

"It's nothing," Daemon said.

"Tersa didn't summon me here for 'nothing.'"

Daemon considered the alternatives. There were none. Reminding himself that he'd intended to show the gift to Saetan anyway, he called in the globe and set it on the table next to the chair. As the mousie went through its routine, he watched the fingers that had been resting on Saetan's chin creep up until they were pressed hard between the High Lord's eyes.

When the spell finished with the mousie squaring its little shoulders, ready to begin again, Saetan lowered his hands and said in a strangled voice, "You're going to give this to your brother?"

"Yes."

"I see." Saetan shook his head and sighed.

Daemon heard the chuckle under the sigh and felt woozy relief wash through him.

"Put that away," Saetan said, pointing at the globe.

He did, with alacrity.

"You came because of this?" Daemon glanced at the still-closed parlor door. Was Tersa waiting for some kind of signal before coming back into the room?

"Because of what happened in the spooky house, your mother was concerned about making surprises for her boys and wanted my opinion."

"Boys?" Daemon asked as the significance of the word sank in.

A flood of . . . Not memories. Not exactly. More like he was riding a wave of remembered *feelings*.

"We were hers when we were young, weren't we?" Daemon said slowly. "Both of us."

"Luthvian birthed Lucivar, but Tersa was the one who loved him." Saetan looked at the fire burning in the hearth. "That was fitting in a way. If Tersa hadn't insisted that I see Luthvian through her Virgin Night, Lucivar wouldn't exist. She had as much to do with that conception as the two people who were in the bed that night. So in a very real sense, he is her winged boy."

Daemon stared at the carpet, trying to sort through feelings that were more elusive than memories. Trying to sort through the tangle of his bond with Lucivar. They had loved each other, hated each other, fought with each other, and fought for each other. There were things he might have done—and things he wouldn't have done—if Lucivar hadn't existed, but none of those things would have been worth the price of not having a brother. Especially *this* brother.

An aftertaste of bitterness filled him. He looked up to find his father watching him.

"Since Tersa was willing to take the cast-off boy, I'm surprised Luthvian . . ." He trailed off.

"The way your mother is now is about how she was then," Saetan said softly. "Walking the roads of dreams and visions, yes, but not walking so deeply in the Twisted Kingdom that she couldn't find the borders of sanity. If Tersa could have been persuaded to trade, Luthvian would have taken you in a heartbeat, because even then you were everything she wanted—and everything your brother wasn't."

Daemon stiffened, and the air chilled in response to his temper.

Saetan smiled. "Same response, all these centuries later."

"She didn't try to talk Tersa into trading?" The word choked him, sounding too much like the years of slavery that would never be forgotten.

"Luthvian didn't like your brother, so you didn't like her. Hell's fire, Daemon. Sometimes you took my breath away when Luthvian tried to coax you into doing something with her. Just you and her. You were barely old enough to string words together in a complete sentence, and you were still so coldly and cuttingly polite that there was no doubt how you felt about her."

Good.

Saetan studied him. "Being Warlord Princes, the two of you are bound to feel territorial about anyone who matters to you, and subtle challenges and bristling are not unexpected when those territories overlap, especially when the individuals are still getting used to sharing. But for Tersa's sake, I need to know if it's more than that. So I want an answer to a question: Do you have a problem with Lucivar spending time with your mother?"

"Our mother." The moment Daemon said the words, something in him settled. Things that were the most precious, the most important, were shared cautiously, if at all. Their years of slavery had taught him and Lucivar that hard lesson. Sooner or later, Lucivar would have told him about visiting Tersa. Of that he was certain. "Tersa is our mother."

"Fine, then. We'll all have coffee and nutcakes, and I'll reassure Tersa that making these little Winsol surprises won't get her boys into *too* much trouble."

"Wait." Daemon held up a hand. "What did Lucivar ask her to make? Aren't you going to tell me?"

His father just looked at him—and laughed.

THREE

After giving the door to the butler's pantry a perfunctory knock, Daemon walked into the room and wasn't sure who was more flustered—himself or Beale.

Good manners dictated that he walk out of the room as if he'd seen nothing. Curiosity had him closing the door and asking, "Are the acoustics good in this room?"

Beale lowered the flute and said, "It's a private place to practice."

There was enough emphasis and bite to the word "private" to tell Daemon that if he'd been a boy instead of a grown man—regardless of being the High Lord's son—he would have been booted out the door, and that boot would have had the strength of Beale's leg behind it.

"Beale . . ." Daemon looked around the pantry. Two rolltop desks, side by side, shelves of the best silver, the bottles of wine that were anticipated to be needed for the next few days.

Hell's fire, the Hall had at least one music room. Why was the man hiding out here to practice?

"I suppose this is a practical place to practice whenever you have a few minutes between your duties," Daemon said, feeling a sudden need to choose his words with care. In no way did he want to imply that Beale might be shirking his duties. "But surely you have some free time in the evenings, even with all the preparations needed because the Lady and I will have a more demanding social calendar than usual."

Beale gave him a measuring look. Daemon wasn't sure against what standard he was being measured—and he was even less sure that he measured up to that standard.

At last Beale said, "We do have free time, even with the increased activity at the Hall. The High Lord always insisted that everyone working here have some time for their own lives. Since there are so many who work at the Hall, and so many who reside here as well, we are our own community and have our own entertainments. Several people play musical instruments, so we have a musical evening each week and give a performance once a season. Those who enjoy reading have literary discussions. There are also weekly card games. Since the Hall allows several beginning positions to be used as a training ground for Blood who have chosen to work in domestic service, such activities provide the younger staff with opportunities to enjoy society without needing to go to the village. And because the rules at the Hall are so strict—and strictly kept—the penalties for mistakes while playing cards are not so great."

"Like a youngster gambling away all his wages," Daemon said.

"Exactly."

Feeling awkward, Daemon looked away. "I've owned the Hall for a year now. Should I have known about this?"

Beale laid the flute in its case. "Taking care of the interests of the SaDiablo family is not a small task, Prince. Neither is taking care of Dhemlan. And you've also had the equally demanding—and more important—task of helping the Lady regain her health. I don't think last Winsol you were able to think much beyond those things."

Astute assessment, Daemon thought, nodding.

"This year the Lady is well and you've settled into the routine of ruling Dhemlan, so your own view of the world can now widen."

He started to agree. Then he noticed a look in Beale's

eyes and rocked back on his heels to reassess all the information he'd been given during this little chat.

"So what duties am I ready to assume?" he asked warily.

Beale smiled. "The servants' Winsol party is held on the first evening of Winsol. There is dancing later, but the evening begins with a short musical program. The High Lord and the Lady would join us for that part of the evening before going on to their own engagement. And they would sing one of the traditional Dhemlan songs for Winsol, a lovely one about the warmth of family on the darkest night. Last year, the High Lord came down and sang it for us."

"Is the Lady coming down this year to sing it for you?" Daemon asked.

"Yes, she's already said she would."

He nodded. His singing voice wouldn't hold up to professional standards, but he could carry a tune and read music, so he did well enough for at-home entertainment. "Do you have the music?"

"I do." Beale opened a drawer in his desk and pulled out a small stack of sheet music. "The top one is the Dhemlan song. The next one is a song the Lady and the High Lord used to sing for guests. It is in the Old Tongue."

Daemon groaned. The Old Tongue was a liquid kind of language, beautiful to hear and damned difficult to learn.

"Perhaps if you learned the music, you could accompany one of them?" Beale suggested.

"That would be better." Much better. "Thanks for the music." Daemon opened the door, ready to retreat.

"You're quite welcome, Prince."

Having a suspicious feeling that his list of things to do before Winsol had lengthened more than he thought, Daemon hurried toward his study—and stopped short when he saw Lord Marcus, his man of business, handing a coat and hat to Holt, the footman on duty in the great hall.

"Did we have an appointment?" Daemon asked.

"Not exactly," Marcus said. "I came in the hopes you could spare an hour or two for me to review some things."

An hour or two. Mother Night.

"Of course," Daemon said. "Holt? Please ask Mrs. Beale for a tray of coffee."

"There's some fresh baking," Holt said. "I'll ask if she'll add a bit to the tray."

"Thank you." He'd been lured to that part of the Hall because he'd passed a stairway and caught some delicious scents rising up from the kitchen. But when he got to the doorway and heard Mrs. Beale snarl about "them who try to snitch the treats before the pans were cool," he decided he liked his balls better than nutcakes. Realizing he needed some excuse if his presence near the kitchen was discovered, he had ended up in the butler's pantry—and now had his musical assignment for the festivities.

Which made him wonder if the scents coming up from the kitchen had been a Craft-enhanced lure. And damn it, he'd swallowed the bait without getting a taste of anything else.

"Have you come to add to my list of things to do?" Daemon asked as he led Marcus into his study and settled into one of the chairs on the informal side of the room.

"Afraid so." Marcus set a bulging leather case near his feet. "I was informed, discreetly, by both Beale and Helton that the bonuses traditionally given at Winsol are usually distributed on the first evening so that the servants who are spending a few days with their families at the beginning of the holiday have some extra spending money."

"I see." He'd presented the envelopes on Winsol Day last year, and no one had said anything to him. Apparently this was another part of his duties he was ready to assume in the correct way. "All right. Do you have the lists of people working at each SaDiablo residence or estate?"

"I have them." Marcus hesitated. "May I make a suggestion?"

"This seems to be the day for them," Daemon said dryly. "Go ahead."

"You should hire a secretary."

"Feeling overworked, Marcus?"

"A bit, but that's not the point. I take care of your invest-

ments and check on the property you personally own here
in Kaeleer, and you have the firm that worked with your
father looking after the rest of the investments for the
SaDiablo family, but I think you need someone who can
help you take care of day-to-day business. Someone with
sufficient rank and polish to be your representative at the
SaDiablo estates or at a Queen's court. The High Lord, I
believe, had your elder brother, Mephis, working in that ca-
pacity. You should consider hiring someone for the position."

Daemon almost dismissed the idea out of hand. Then he
realized he already had someone working for him who
would fit the criteria—if Prince Rainier was willing to take
on that kind of work.

"I'll think about it."

Marcus looked surprised and pleased—until they heard
the jingling and howling outside the study door. Then he
looked like he'd swallowed something sour.

"Is there something else I should be aware of?" Daemon
asked.

Marcus shook his head and wouldn't meet his eyes.

Concerned now, he pushed. "Your wife and daughter?
They're well?"

"Yes." Marcus glanced at the study door and winced.

Daemon weighed what he knew about Marcus's girl
against what was outside the study door and asked innocently, "Have you finished your shopping for Winsol? Gotten
all your gifts?"

Marcus shifted uncomfortably. "My daughter wants a
puppy, but we haven't decided on the breed—or if we're
going to get one at all," he added hurriedly.

Fortunately, Holt brought in the tray of coffee and
baked goods. Daemon focused his attention on the tray
and hoped his expression would be mistaken for eagerness
to indulge in the treats.

"You'll be coming by again before Winsol Night, won't
you?" he asked, working to keep his voice neutral. "Why
don't you bring your daughter with you the next time?"

Apparently he hadn't kept his voice neutral enough, because Marcus's hand froze over the plate and he looked up, alarmed.

"No," Marcus said. "She's been hinting that she'd like to have a kindred Sceltie live with us, but I don't need a bundle of fur that could end up being the highest-ranking member of the household."

Considering the Sceltie pups who were still in residence, that was a distinct possibility.

"Think of the advantages of having a playmate who could also be a good protector," Daemon soothed. "And I would consider it a personal favor if you brought her with you to look at the pups. Consider it a gift from you to me. Besides, just because your daughter sees the puppies doesn't mean she'll take to any of them." *Or that any of them will take to her.*

Marcus said words that were not in keeping with the spirit of the season. Then he ate two fruit tarts and a nut-cake, wiped his hands on a napkin, and opened his leather case, a clear indication that they were changing the subject.

They worked steadily through the lists of people employed by the SaDiablo family, with Daemon mostly confirming the amount Marcus suggested for each bonus. Neither said a word when Daemon doubled the amount of Marcus's bonus. After all, at this time of year, it would be rude to call a bribe a bribe.

Marcus sighed as he put all the papers back in his leather case. "I'll send on the packets to the other houses, and bring the packet for the Hall myself."

"And you'll bring your daughter?"

"I'll bring her." Marcus sighed again. "You drive a hard bargain, Prince."

Daemon smiled. "It could have been worse, Marcus."

"How?"

"She could have asked for a cat."

FOUR

"Come in," Daemon said, glancing up from the paperwork on his desk as the study door opened. Leaning back, he crossed his legs at the knees and steepled his fingers, resting two of his long black-tinted nails against his chin as he watched Rainier limp to the visitor's chair and sit down with exaggerated care.

That autumn Rainier and Surreal SaDiablo, along with seven landen children, had been caught in a trap meant to kill members of the SaDiablo family.

The spooky house. Daemon still wasn't sure whether it was arrogance or a kind of madness that had led a writer who had discovered his Blood heritage to try a pissing contest with the darkest-Jeweled Blood in the Realm. Realizing how close they'd all come to being caught in that trap had been a sobering lesson. If Lucivar hadn't been an Eyrien warrior backed by the strength of his Ebon-gray Jewels, Surreal and Rainier wouldn't have gotten out of that damn house. As it was, three of the children were killed, not to mention all the other people who had been killed so that they would be the predators in the game. Surreal had been wounded, and the poison still hadn't worked its way out of her body completely. And Rainier . . .

He was a dancer, Daemon thought sadly. Then he added, *Everything has a price.*

"How's the leg?" Daemon asked, even though anyone could see the healing wasn't going the way it should. Hell's fire, Rainier had been walking better a few weeks ago when he'd joined them for a viewing of Jaenelle and Marian's spooky house, an entertainment for children that had been one of the reasons Jarvis Jenkell had created a deadly version of the place.

Rainier shrugged, but his face was pale and strained despite his effort to smile, and there was a fear in his green eyes that he couldn't quite hide. "Some days it's better than others. I wanted your opinion of something."

Trying to change the subject, boyo? All right, I'll let you lead this dance. For the moment.

Using Craft, Rainier called in a rectangular box and floated it over to the desk, placing it directly in front of Daemon.

Jewelry box, Daemon decided, leaning forward to study the flowers and leaves carved into the top. The box itself was excellent in craftsmanship and sufficient as a Winsol gift, so when he opened the lid, he whistled softly.

A gold metalwork gauntlet. Delicate-looking, if you ignored the talons on the ends of the articulated fingers. A weapon disguised as a pretty.

"It's a Winsol gift for Surreal," Rainier said. "Do you think she'll like it?"

"It's beautiful and deadly," Daemon replied. "She'll love it." He closed the box and returned it to Rainier before offering the man a brandy.

Something was wrong here. Very wrong.

Rainier had been a dance instructor for years. Hell's fire, he'd been Jaenelle's dance instructor—a young Warlord Prince who had been able to hold his own with Jaenelle and the coven of young Queens who had been her closest friends.

Now Rainier worked for him, and he paid the man a generous salary. But he recognized Banard's work. The jeweler made some pieces that wouldn't beggar an ordinary man's pocket for a year, but that custom-made gauntlet wasn't one of them.

What was Rainier trying to prove?

"What are your plans for Winsol?" Daemon asked.

"I'm going to Dharo to spend some time with my family," Rainier replied, his smile looking sicker than before.

Why? Daemon wondered. *They usually prefer that you keep your distance.* Hadn't Rainier made a family visit a few weeks ago? Right around the time when something began to go wrong with the healing of his leg?

"Unless there's something you need from me," Rainier added.

"No, I don't—" A thought occurred to him, and he didn't think he'd get an honest answer without inflicting some pain. So he would inflict the pain.

"It's come to my attention that there is a traditional Winsol dance. It would be prudent for me to learn it."

"Don't look to me to teach you," Rainier said. "I'm crippled."

At least he didn't have to dig for the bitterness festering inside the other Warlord Prince.

"And who do you blame for that, Rainier?" Daemon asked too softly, leaning back and steepling his fingers again.

"I don't blame anyone," Rainier snapped. "It happened."

"Yes, it happened, because you did what you were supposed to do—defend and protect."

"Not well enough. Three children died and Surreal got poisoned. I didn't protect them well enough, and I lost . . ." He swallowed, obviously fighting not to say more. "I was a dancer. It's all I've ever been. All I wanted to be. I'll never be that again."

"Are you sure?" Daemon asked.

"Yes, I'm sure!"

Daemon hesitated, but it had to be said. "Everything has a price, Prince Rainier. An escort's life is always on the line."

"I know that."

"Do you? You were wounded in battle. It doesn't matter what the battleground looked like; that's the truth of it. You're not the first man who's had to rebuild his life because of battle scars. You won't be the last." Knowing that he wasn't getting through to the man, Daemon unleashed some of his own frustration. "You could have lost your leg instead of losing some mobility. Hell's fire, Rainier, *you could have died in that place*."

"Maybe it would have been better if I had," Rainier said softly.

Daemon felt his temper rise from the depth of his Black Jewel—sweet, cold, and deadly. Rainier wasn't stupid. He knew who would be waiting for him if he got maudlin enough to commit suicide. The boy thought he had troubles now? Wait until Saetan got done explaining things to the fool—especially a fool who had helped himself become demon-dead sooner than he should have.

But it might explain Rainier's buying a gift he really couldn't afford. And Lucivar needed to be aware of that possibility.

"What's the state of your finances?" Daemon asked.

Rainier blinked. Then color stained his cheeks. "Frankly, Prince Sadi, that's none of your business."

"I just made it my business. Do you want to find out how fast I can acquire every scrap of private information about you, or are you going to answer the question?"

Rainier squirmed. "I'm doing all right. I have some savings."

"Your salary will continue, paid quarterly as usual," Daemon said.

"For what?" Rainier let out a pained laugh. "There's not much I can do."

"I have some thoughts about that, but right now you can make some effort to heal." Daemon put enough ice in his voice to have Rainier's eyes fill with wariness. "I'll take care of the rent on your apartment in Amdarh, as well as any other necessary expenses like food."

"I don't need your charity, and I don't want your pity," Rainier snapped.

"You're not getting either, so shut up." But it was becoming clear that someone was giving Rainier heavy doses of both, and those things could become more crippling than a damaged leg.

Daemon huffed out a sigh. "You're going to have to come to terms with what you can do physically and what you can't. I can't help you with that, but I can make things easier for a while so that you can concentrate on healing. You're a good Warlord Prince, Rainier, and a good escort. Too good to lose because you're having trouble finding your balance."

Another pained laugh. "That's a good way of putting it."

"After Winsol, you'll be spending a few weeks in Ebon Rih with Lucivar." *And may the Darkness have mercy on you.* "So I suggest you visit your family in Dharo and enjoy the festivities."

"Am I dismissed?" Rainier asked, his voice a shade too polite.

"Yes, you're dismissed. Happy Winsol, Rainier."

Rainier pushed himself to his feet, then leaned on the cane. "Happy Winsol, Prince."

Daemon suspected that he and Rainier were both wishing each other a lot of things at that moment, and "happy" wasn't one of them.

He waited until he was sure he'd given Rainier enough time to leave the Hall. Then he left his study—and didn't have to go far, since Beale was waiting for him.

"Lady Karla requests your presence," Beale said.

He'd known when the Queen of Glacia had arrived. It was hard to miss that particular psychic scent—and hard to miss the presence of a Gray-Jeweled witch in his home.

"She's waiting for you in her suite," Beale added.

"And Lady Angelline?"

"The Lady has gone to the Keep. She intends to be back in time for dinner, but said if she was late, you should start without her."

Not likely, but he didn't need to say it, since it was already understood by the household staff.

Daemon made his way through the Hall's corridors to the section that held the family's suites of rooms. When

Jaenelle was fifteen, the coven came to spend a summer, reuniting with the special friend they thought had been lost. The coven—and the boyos who also came for that afternoon tea and never quite went home again—had been given suites. Even now, when those Ladies were the Queens of their own Territories, those suites were still theirs, a second home and a place where they still gathered as friends and Sisters.

Karla's suite looked out over Jaenelle's courtyard. He knocked on Karla's door and didn't get an answer. His hand hovered over the door's handle, but he tried another approach before reacting as if something were wrong.

Karla? he called on a psychic thread.

Come on through, she replied. *I'm down in the courtyard.*

He entered her sitting room and hurried to the glass doors that led out to the balcony. He paused then, reassured when he saw her standing near the drained fountain, her face raised to the sun. Moving more leisurely, he went down the nearest set of stairs and joined her.

"Kiss kiss," Karla said, giving him a wicked smile.

Raising the hand she offered, he kissed her knuckles.

"Darling, isn't it a bit cold out here?" he asked.

"Your blood must be thin if you think this is cold. Which you wouldn't notice as much if you put on a coat."

At least he had put a shield on his shoes to keep his feet dry and protect the leather.

She linked her arm in his and sighed. "Glacia's winter has too much bite for me a lot of days, so I wanted to take advantage of spending a little time outside in softer weather."

"Meaning a *little* snow on the ground and air that doesn't freeze your lungs?" Daemon asked dryly.

"Exactly."

He felt her shiver and led her to the stairs. "Enough."

"Bossy."

"Protective."

"Bossy."

He bared his teeth and said, "Kiss kiss," which made her laugh.

He didn't know if it was proof of Beale's uncanny timing or if Karla had made the request earlier, but they entered the sitting room moments before Holt brought a tray of coffee and pastries.

"You look good," Daemon told her as he poured coffee for both of them.

And she did, despite her face having thinned and aged a decade more than her years. Whether that aging was due to the task of ruling Glacia or a result of the poisoning she'd survived two years ago, he couldn't tell.

"Flattery will not get you the last nutcake," Karla said, taking the cup he offered. "I do feel good most of the time. Oh, my legs feel the weather, so there are uncomfortable days, but unlike people whose brains are attached to their penises, I've actually done what I was told to do in order to get better and keep my legs as healthy as they can be."

Shit. "So this isn't a social call?"

"Jaenelle asked me to come and look at Rainier. Provide a second opinion as a Healer."

Daemon stiffened. "*Jaenelle* asked for a second opinion?"

"Tells you something is wrong, doesn't it?" Karla sipped her coffee. "Doesn't matter what Jewels she wears; Jaenelle is the most brilliant Healer in the entire Realm. If she can't heal something, it can't be healed. I'm testimony to what she can do. I shouldn't have survived that brew of poisons I was given when my uncle Hobart tried to regain control of Glacia. And having survived, I shouldn't be as healthy as I am."

"Do you . . . ." Daemon swallowed some coffee to wet a suddenly dry throat. "Do you sometimes wish she'd let you die? You wouldn't be walking with a cane, wouldn't have weak legs, if you'd made the transition to demon-dead."

"That's your cock talking," Karla said.

"It is n—" He stopped. Thought. "Rainier."

"Yes. Rainier."

He set his cup down on the table in front of the sofa. "He won't come all the way back, will he?"

"No, his leg will never be what it was. It will never support him the way it did before that Eyrien war blade cut through all that muscle and half the bone. If he'd gone down and stayed down, any of us—Gabrielle, me, Jaenelle—could have healed him and brought him almost all the way back. Maybe so close to all the way back he could do whatever he wanted to on that leg as long as he gave it some care. But he slapped shields around his leg and kept fighting."

"He did what he had to do."

"I know. But that leg will never be the same because of it, and he knows that."

"Does he?"

"Yes, he does. He's fighting it, Daemon. I don't know what he's doing or why, but I can see the results. Jaenelle has had to rebuild that bone and muscle so many times, there is almost nothing left to work with. Something is riding him, and riding him hard, but if he doesn't stop damaging that leg, he really will be crippled."

"He's not a fool," Daemon said.

"No," Karla said quietly. "He's scared. That's worse."

"Anything I can do?"

She shook her head. "No, there's nothing you can do. And there is nothing I can do that Jaenelle hasn't done."

"Maybe having a leg so damaged there is no possible way to dance is easier for him than a leg that is almost whole but not whole enough."

"Maybe, but I wouldn't have thought Rainier was that much of an ass." Karla selected a pastry. "Is he still going for this extra training with Lucivar?"

"He's going. And he's already been told if he doesn't show up on his own, Lucivar will hunt him down and drag him all the way to Ebon Rih."

"Well, then. I'm sure things will get sorted out—one way or another."

Since he could imagine how things would get sorted out

if Rainier started a pissing contest with Lucivar, he changed the subject. "How is Della? Is she excited about Winsol?"

Karla laughed. "She's more excited that I've agreed to let her start learning basic healing."

Daemon took a nutcake. "Training doesn't usually start so early, does it? She's still a girl." A girl who had lost her mother when her entire village had been slaughtered by Eyriens working for Dorothea and Hekatah SaDiablo. A girl who had been rescued by Arcerian cats and spent months with them, living wild, before being adopted by Karla.

"She's not a natural Healer—wasn't born to that caste—but she has good instincts and a keen interest. She wants to specialize in healing kindred."

He tried to keep a straight face—and couldn't. "Does she practice her bedside manner on KaeAskavi?"

"Every chance she gets. Which is another reason I'm here today. If you want to know about kindred, you ask Jaenelle. Of course, Della and KaeAskavi are only together these days when we're at the country house. The house in Sidra is too frustrating for him."

"City streets would be hard for a cat that size."

"Oh, it isn't the confined space," Karla said, a wicked twinkle in her glacier blue eyes. "It's the frustration of having all that prey wandering around and not being allowed to catch and eat any of it."

"We're talking about horses, right?"

"You know better than that."

Mother Night.

"So," Karla said, "we have a plate of goodies and a pot of coffee, and I have another hour to visit before I have to be heading back home. Why don't you tell me all the things you don't want the coven to know?"

Since he'd rather chew off his own hand than get backed into *that* particular corner, he took the easy way out—he put the nutcake back on the plate and gave her all of the goodies.

"Coward," Karla said.

"Damn right."

She laughed. "Even if you are a cock, you're all right, Sadi." She held out the plate. "Here. We'll share. No gossip required."

"Why do you need to go back so soon? Glacia is on the other side of the Realm, and that's a long way to come to spend so little time here. You and Jaenelle haven't had an evening together in quite a while." Putting a touch of persuasion and a hint of seduction in his voice, he purred, "Stay. You can head back early in the morning. I'll arrange for a driver and Coach so you can work or nap on the way home. Stay."

She blinked at him. Then blinked again. "Hell's fire, you're good. I could feel my bones starting to melt."

He smiled at her and let the spells fade.

"I had said I *might* stay over," Karla said. "But I didn't want to make it a certainty."

"Are you worried about Della being home alone?" Would any of the Blood who had supported Karla's uncle and survived the fighting two years ago try to hurt the girl?

"Yes, but not for the reasons you may be thinking. You've got that look in your eyes, Sadi. The 'I'm ready to bristle and attack—where's the enemy?' look."

"So what is the concern?" he asked too softly. Because she was right—he wouldn't think twice about going to Glacia and eliminating any problems that might be plaguing Karla or a young girl.

"Prince Hagen, my Master of the Guard, likes children but has none of his own. So Della has found a surrogate father and he has found a daughter."

"Then what's the problem?"

"Rules have a way of getting . . . lost . . . when I'm gone for more than a day. It's the most amazing thing. No one can remember why vegetables are supposed to be part of a meal. No one can tell time to figure out when a girl Della's age should go to bed. On the other hand, the man can be so strict about other things, I'd swear he took lessons from Uncle Saetan."

"So while Auntie Karla is away . . ."

"They'll have a good time." She sighed with too much drama. "Fine. I'll stay."

"And I'll be more than happy to entertain you with gossip." *Just not about me.* He took the nutcake. "Why did Jaenelle go to the Keep?"

Karla hesitated before answering. "I think she wanted a second opinion."

"Witch-child." Saetan leaned against the blackwood table in the Keep's private library and crossed his arms. He hadn't known what would cause it, but he'd known this day would come. And because he'd known, he tightened the leash on his temper a little more. It was almost Winsol. He didn't want a fight to smear the celebrations.

But there was going to be a fight. He could read that truth in the way she moved and the look in her eyes.

"Should I start sorting books?" he asked.

She looked at the empty table and smiled as she shook her head.

It had been a useful ploy, pretending to sort old books while some member of his extended family eased into talking about whatever the trouble was. Useful until he'd discovered the coven knew it was a ploy and were pretending right along with him.

None of the boyos, including his own sons, had figured out the deception, which embarrassed him a little on behalf of his gender. On the other hand, with them it was still a useful tool.

"No, there's no need to sort books," Jaenelle said. She hesitated. "Papa, there's something I want to ask you."

"Subject?"

"Rainier."

Not what he'd expected. He relaxed a little.

"He's not healing the way he should."

She grabbed her golden hair and pulled hard enough to make him wince.

"Maybe it's because I can't . . . because I'm not . . ."

"No," he said softly, a clear enough warning to anyone who knew him. And Jaenelle, his daughter and Queen, knew him.

She lowered her hands and looked him in the eyes. "Maybe if I took back the power—"

"*No.*" Saetan straightened, then lowered his arms so that his fingers rested lightly along the edge of the table. "That part of your life is done."

"I didn't lose the Ebony like everyone thought. Maybe I can—"

"Damn you to the bowels of Hell, *you will not do this.*"

He saw the change in her and recognized the instant when it was Witch staring at him through Jaenelle's sapphire eyes.

"You don't know why things are different, High Lord," Witch said in her midnight voice.

"Yes, I do, Lady. I went to Arachna. I met the Weaver of Dreams. I saw the tangled web that made dreams into flesh. And I saw that one slender strand of spider silk that changed the dream when she came back to us. There was another dreamer. You."

She stepped back, wary now. "How long have you known?"

"A while now. Before you and Daemon married." He paused, then added dryly, "Well, between the secret wedding and the public one, anyway. The point—and I hope you believe I will do what I say—is that my daughter has the life she wanted for herself, and taking back the Ebony would ruin that life." And there was no certainty—none at all—that Jaenelle could still be a vessel for that much power, that taking back the Ebony wouldn't kill her. "So you need to understand that I will fight my Queen into the ground in order to protect my daughter's life. Witch-child, you never wanted that kind of power, so the only way you will take it back is by going through me. You'll have to destroy me completely, because I will fight you with everything I am."

Her face turned alarmingly pale. "You mean that."

"Yes, I mean that. Everything has a price, Lady. That will be the price if you try to reclaim the Ebony."

A heartbeat. Another. Then he was no longer facing Witch. It was Jaenelle studying him with haunted eyes.

"But . . . Rainier," she said.

"I'll remind you of a few things you've obviously forgotten." His voice slipped into that tightly controlled scolding tone that could intimidate *any* child. Even this one. "When you were seventeen, you put Lucivar back together. Considering the condition he was in when Prothvar brought him to your cottage in Ebon Rih, he shouldn't have survived at all. But you not only healed the broken bones and internal damage; you rebuilt his wings out of the few healthy scraps that were left."

"I wore the Black then and had a reservoir of thirteen Jewels to tap," Jaenelle said, her voice full of frustration. "And Lucivar was all-or-nothing. Systemic healing. He came out of it whole or he died."

"The Black isn't Ebony," Saetan said. "You've never used Ebony for healing because it was too dark, too powerful. You used the Black."

"Well, Twilight's Dawn isn't the Black," she snapped.

"No, but there is a Black thread in your Jewel. Compared to a true Black, you've got a thimbleful of power at that level, but it's there. You also have two Black-Jeweled Warlord Princes and an Ebon-gray Warlord Prince who would have given you whatever power you needed for a healing web. And if you'd needed that kind of strength to add to a healing brew, Daemon or Lucivar would have given you the blood. The power was available, witch-child. This has nothing to do with the Jewels you no longer wear."

"Then why isn't Rainier healing?" Jaenelle paced, circled—and began snarling in a way that made Saetan wish he could put a shield between them without insulting her. "He was healing. He *was*."

"Could he dance again?"

"Yes!" She paused. Thought. "Not everything. Not the

demanding dances he and I used to do sometimes as a special performance. His leg muscles will never be able to support that kind of demand. But all the social dances, yes. All the kinds of dances he taught." She looked cold and bitter. "But he's done enough damage to those muscles now that he won't be able to do that."

"Then whatever is wrong with Rainier has nothing, or little, to do with the healing itself," Saetan said quietly. "I don't think it's his leg that needs to heal so much as his heart."

He opened his arms. She stepped into the embrace and held on.

"Would you like some advice?" he asked.

She nodded.

"Let Lucivar deal with Rainier."

She raised her head and narrowed her eyes. "Why?"

"Because I think Lucivar will be able to figure out the right motivation to help Rainier heal."

"Lucivar will scare the shit out of him."

"Precisely."

She laughed and rested her head on his shoulder.

He savored the embrace. Since the day he'd met her—a seven-year-old girl who had walked through Hell without fear—he'd had to share her with so many others. Quiet moments when it was just the two of them had been rare, and he cherished every one.

"Papa?"

"Witch-child?"

"I won't destroy the life your daughter dreamed of having."

His breath caught. "Is that a promise?"

"Would you see a promise like that as a gift?"

"Yes, I would."

She looked at him and smiled. "Then it's a promise."

FIVE

Surreal looked at the fat, fluffy, lazy flakes of snow, then at the fire in the sitting room's hearth, and decided the fire had more appeal. Especially after she coughed and felt the burn in her lungs.

All right, she should have mentioned the burning sensation and continued shortness of breath weeks ago when Jaenelle was first healing the poisoned wound in her side. But she'd thought she'd shaken off the effects of the back-lash spell that had trapped her and Rainier in that damn spooky house and that the shortness of breath was because of the poison.

You can take care of this now or you can flirt with pneumonia all winter, Jaenelle had told her.

She didn't want to flirt with anything at the moment, and since the "cure" was drinking a healing brew three times a day, limiting her time outdoors when the air was bitter cold, and stopping physical activity before she became fatigued, she wasn't about to argue.

Especially since she planned to have Jaenelle put those instructions in writing so she could wave them in front of Lucivar when she went to Ebon Rih after Winsol. She couldn't get out of everything he had planned for her, but even Yaslana wouldn't challenge Jaenelle as Healer.

Maybe she could take up knitting or something.

She tried to picture herself sitting on the sidelines making a badly knit blanket while everyone else was doing something interesting.

Maybe not.

A quick knock on the sitting room door announced Helton, the butler at the SaDiablo town house. Entering with a full tray, he said, "I've brought the hot water for your healing brew, and a piece of berry pie still warm from the oven."

There was also a sandwich and a small plate of cheese and grapes. After all, it had been at least two hours since she'd eaten the broth he'd insisted she have to "warm her up" when she returned from shopping that morning.

Everything has a price, Surreal thought. And the price for not being completely well was having her butler fussing over her more than his duties would normally allow.

She settled on the sofa and called in a small hourglass timer and the glass jar that held the healing mixture. After filling a tea ball with the mixture, she put the ball in the pot of hot water and turned the timer.

Helton started to leave, then stopped, his head turned in a way that indicated he was talking to someone on a psychic thread.

"Prince Rainier is here," he said.

"Send him in." She glanced at the tray.

Helton studied the tray too. "I should bring in another serving."

"Just another piece of berry pie." Surreal bared her teeth in a smile that had Helton shifting a little closer to the door. "I'll share the rest, but not the pie."

A twitch of his lips. A twinkle in his eyes. "Very well, Lady."

"Are you all right?" Rainier asked sharply as soon as Helton ushered him into the sitting room and closed the door.

Better than you are, boyo, Surreal thought as she watched Rainier limp to the chair nearest the sofa. "I'm all right."

"The footman said he had to check and see if you were feeling up to seeing visitors today." Rainier winced as he got himself settled.

"Should I ask Helton to bring in some coffee for you?" Surreal asked. "Or there's brandy if you prefer."

"What are you drinking?"

"Healing brew." She watched the timer. Almost done.

"Then you're *not* all right," Rainier snapped.

She removed the tea ball and put it in the little bowl on the tray. She poured a cup of the brew and sat back—and wondered how much of the anger suddenly filling the room was on her behalf.

"Turns out my lungs are more vulnerable to cold weather because of that backlash spell. Or the backlash spell made them more vulnerable to the poison, which has made them more vulnerable to cold weather." She shrugged. "So after Jaenelle got done snarling at me for not mentioning that my lungs still burned, she made up this brew, which I'm drinking three times a day for a few more days. Then it's once a day for the rest of this winter."

"You also fatigue easily, don't you?" Rainier said. "That's why there was a question about whether you wanted visitors."

It was tempting to make light of all of this. After all, she *was* healing. But he had been in that house with her, and he deserved better than a light answer.

"Yes, I still fatigue easily. And it's humiliating to admit, but I'll need to take a nap this afternoon because I was out most of the morning shopping."

"Does Lucivar know about this?" Rainier asked.

She grinned. "Not yet. But I'm going to make sure he does. In fact, I'm going to make sure *everyone* in the family knows I fatigue easily."

"Why . . . ?" He thought for a moment, then huffed out a laugh. "Well, I guess he'll back down a *little* bit if he knows he'll get his ass chewed by Jaenelle every time you start wheezing."

"I hope that will be enough incentive, but you can't

count on it with Lucivar." She wasn't looking forward to spending the winter months in Ebon Rih. For a lot of reasons.

She drank her brew, and they sat in companionable silence for a few minutes.

When she caught Rainier eyeing the piece of berry pie, she snarled, "Mine."

"Greedy," he muttered.

"I'll share the sandwich, grapes, and cheese."

His expression told her plain enough he didn't consider that a fair exchange, but he perked up when Helton returned with another tray that was a duplicate of her own "tray of nibbles."

Draining her cup and setting it aside, Surreal studied the tray—and sighed. "I guess I'll eat myself into a stupor and let Helton roll me up to my room."

"When you're drinking healing brews, your body burns even more fuel," Rainier said. "You actually do need that food."

She looked at him, her unspoken question filling the room.

He held her eyes for a moment, trying to bluff. Then he looked away, snatched his plate off the tray, and began to eat.

"Leave it alone, Surreal," he said after the silence became strained. "As a favor to a friend, leave it alone."

For now. But she was going to have a chat with Jaenelle and find out how bad things really were with Rainier.

"So were you just out wandering today?" Surreal asked.

"Actually I stopped by to bring you this." Rainier called in a wrapped package and handed it to her.

She narrowed her eyes at him. "You finished your shopping?"

"Yes."

"And you've got all the damn presents wrapped? Hell's fire. If I don't have more luck finding things to buy—and how do you buy things for a family like mine?—I may be wrapping the presents moments before I hand them out."

His smile was brittle. "I'm usually run off my feet just before Winsol and don't have time to shop. There's a traditional court dance that's only performed during Winsol. There's always a group of people who want to brush up on the steps—and there are the young men each year who figure out that males who know that dance get a lot more attention at the parties, and they want lessons."

"You'll teach them again next year."

The brittle smile turned bitter, and he said nothing.

"So you're delivering packages early because . . . ?"

"I'm going to spend Winsol with my family."

"Why?"

A pained laugh. "Because they felt obliged to ask me, and this year I didn't have the excuse of being too busy to come until the last days of Winsol."

"You can still be too busy. I'll get some paper. We'll make a list."

"Surreal."

I don't know how to fix this, Surreal thought, hurting for him. *Does anyone know how to fix this pain that's killing the heart of who and what he is?*

"Well," Rainier said, getting to his feet. "I'd best be on my way. I have some things to do before I head to Dharo."

She met him at the sitting room door and hugged him.

"Happy Winsol, Surreal," he said, his voice husky.

"Happy Winsol, Rainier," she replied, wishing she could say something more.

SIX

The day before Winsol began, Daemon walked into a sitting room in the family wing of the Hall and stopped abruptly.

"Mother Night," he said. "Where did you find such a magnificent—and perfect—evergreen tree?"

Jaenelle grinned at him. "It did turn out well, didn't it?"

It dazzled his eyes and tugged at his heart. Little balls of color shone among the branches, which looked like they had been given a light dusting of gold on the tips of the evergreen needles. Crystal icicles hung from the branches. And the smell . . .

Daemon frowned and walked toward the tree, baffled. The evergreen scent should be filling the room.

He touched a branch. His fingers went right through it.

"If it fooled you, it will fool anyone," Jaenelle said.

"It's an illusion?" He tried to touch another branch, unwilling to believe.

"Yes. I made it. Marian and I decided to limit the number of trees that the family would cut down for Winsol."

Lucivar and I didn't get a say in this?

He caught the tip of his tongue between his teeth. He hadn't participated in a typical Winsol celebration here at the Hall, so maybe he wasn't supposed to make many—or any—decisions.

"We took a couple of trees whose elimination would benefit the surrounding trees," Jaenelle said. "We'll use the branches to create wreaths or other decorations. That will add the scent to the room." She edged toward the door, then stopped as if listening to something beyond the room. "Oh, good. Marian is here."

Which meant Lucivar was also here. *Prick?* he called on a psychic spear thread.

Let me stash the little beast and I'll meet you, Lucivar replied.

"All right," Daemon said to Jaenelle. "Since Marian is here, I'll—"

"Stay here," Jaenelle said, heading for the door. "I need to pee, and someone needs to guard the gifts until they're all properly shielded."

Daemon looked at the gifts stacked around the tree. "Huh?"

"I'll be back in a few minutes. Don't leave the room. When I get back, Marian and I will sort the gifts and put on the appropriate shields."

"What are you figuring is going to happen to them?"

She just looked at him.

"Fine," he said, trying not to grumble. "I'll guard the gifts."

She was almost out the door when she stopped and looked at him over her shoulder. "Papa arrived a little while ago, but I haven't seen him yet."

Then she was gone, and he felt as if he'd been shuffled to a back room and given a senseless task just to keep him out of the way. Hell's fire, his father and brother were in the Hall. He should be spending time with them instead of guarding boxes. Or he should be in his study, working. He still had some work to do. Not much, but some. And even if he didn't have work and just stretched out on the couch and read a book, he wouldn't feel like a stray puppy that someone had forgotten. Not if he was in his study.

A quick knock on the door. Before he could say anything, a maid and two footmen entered the room, their arms full of boxes.

"Excuse us, Prince," the maid said. "We were told to bring these gifts here."

Daemon smiled at them and stepped aside.

"Are you going home for Winsol?" he asked.

"We're drawing lots tonight to see who's working which days," the younger footman said.

They stacked the packages in front of the tree. Moments after they walked out the door, Lucivar walked in.

"Hiding already?" Lucivar asked. "Winsol hasn't officially started."

"I'm guarding the gifts," Daemon replied.

"From what? You didn't put any food under there, did you? You never put food gifts under the tree. I did that one year, and the younger kindred found the boxes of fudge and the boxes of rawhide strips. What a mess."

"If there's food under the tree, I didn't put it there."

"Good. There's something I want to show you. I had it made for Daemonar and—"

A quick knock on the door, and another maid entered the room.

"I was told to put these packages under the tree," she said.

"They're going to be in and out of here for the rest of the day," Lucivar muttered as soon as the maid left. "Let's find another room. We need a couple of minutes in private."

"I'm supposed to guard the gifts," Daemon said.

"*Tch.* The little beast is in the playroom, enthralled by jingling puppies, so the room will be fine. We won't go far. Besides, he doesn't know which room has the presents."

Since Daemon thought guarding the gifts was a pointless exercise anyway, it didn't take much persuasion. He and Lucivar hurried along the corridor, sneaked around the corner, and slipped into another sitting room.

"Do we ever use this room?" Daemon asked, looking around.

"Male sanctuary," Lucivar replied. "Used to use it when the coven lived here most of the time. Gave the boyos breathing room to talk among themselves while still being close by if they were needed." He waved a hand, dismissing further interest in the room. "Look at this." He called in a rectangular wood-and-glass box.

Daemon obediently leaned over to look into the box.

"It's a bug-in-a-box," Lucivar said, grinning.

From one end of the box, a little black beetle emerged. As it made its way to the other end, it grew and grew and grew until . . .

Pop!

There were sounds. Daemon wasn't sure a beetle actually made sounds that were a cross between insect noise and cranky grumbling, but it added to the appeal. Or the disgust. He had a strong suspicion the emotion of the person viewing this little toy would depend on whether that person had a penis or breasts.

"You have that box shielded, don't you?" he asked.

Lucivar made a huffy sound of disbelief. "I've got it triple shielded. There is no way Daemonar is getting that bug out of the box."

"If he does . . ." Daemon looked at his brother.

Lucivar sighed. "The only question will be whether Marian tries to kill me before she divorces me or after."

"As long as you know the risks." He grinned. Couldn't help it. "Daemonar will love it."

"Yeah, he will."

Picturing Daemonar's face when the boy opened that gift reminded him of where he was supposed to be. "I'd better get back to guarding the gifts."

Lucivar vanished the box. "I'll go with you. If I look like I've got something to do, maybe I won't get cornered into doing something."

They hurried back to the other room, opened the door—and froze just inside the doorway.

Hell's fire, Mother Night, and may the Darkness be merciful.

"He wasn't anywhere near this room when we left,"

Lucivar said. "I swear by all I hold dear, he wasn't anywhere near this room."

Well, the little beast was in the middle of it now, sitting on the floor surrounded by various-sized boxes and drifts of torn wrapping paper.

"Papa!" Daemonar cried. "Unka Daemon! Lizzen!"

Bang bang bang. The sound of box on floor.

And the sound of something delicate—and no doubt expensive—breaking inside the box.

Daemon felt his face muscles shift into a tight smile—or maybe it was a grimace. Must have been the appropriate response, because Daemonar grinned at him and went back to banging the box on the floor.

"Whatever is inside is already broken," Lucivar said. "No point taking it away from him now. He'll just grab for something else."

"We'll have to figure out who brought it and get it replaced." *Sweet Darkness, please don't let it be something that was commissioned and was one of a kind.*

Lucivar stared at the boy and the mess, looking more and more baffled. "Marian wants another one of those."

"Another one of what?"

Lucivar lifted his chin. "Those."

Daemon looked at the little winged boy who was the reason Jaenelle was going to rip him into chunks and feed him to somebody, then back at his brother. *"Why?"*

Lucivar sighed. "I don't know." Then he narrowed his eyes. "But I'm pretty sure it's your fault."

He completely lost the ability to speak. He just stood there with his mouth hanging open, staring at Lucivar.

Lucivar nodded. "Yeah, I'm pretty sure it's your fault."

"Bt. Dt. Zt." The sputtering sounds fired up his shocked brain. "Since I am *not* the one sleeping with your wife, it is *not* my fault."

Lucivar was looking grimly pleased. "Yeah, it is. Marian's been mentioning lately how much I value having a brother the same age."

Daemon usually valued having a brother too, but that was beside the point.

"You can't do this," Daemon said.

"It's not that hard," Lucivar replied. "Just don't drink the contraceptive brew during a woman's fertile time, and it isn't hard at all." His voice changed when he added, "Besides, it might not be another little beast. It could be a cuddly little witchling. A miniature of her mother."

There was a dopey look on Lucivar's face.

"Ah, no," Daemon groaned. "No, no, no. You're being seduced by the possibility of a daughter."

"Maybe."

"Then let me remind you that our father had four children, and all of them had cocks." Five, actually, if they counted the boy who had been murdered shortly after birth.

Lucivar slanted a look at him. "So you're saying I shouldn't count on getting a cuddly little witch?"

"I'm saying the odds aren't in your favor, so before you pour your contraceptive brew down the sink, consider what it will be like having two of *those* in the house."

Lucivar winced and muttered, "One of them would probably end up living with you half the time."

It was a distinct possibility—and it was exactly what he was afraid of. Not that he didn't love Daemonar. He did. But most days he loved him much better knowing he could send the boy home.

Suddenly, Lucivar tensed. "How long are you supposed to guard this room?"

Daemon felt all the blood drain out of his head. "Mother Night. Jaenelle is going to be back any minute now."

They sprang forward at the same moment Daemonar gave the box one last *bang* on the floor before throwing it and reaching for another.

"You get the boy away from here, and I'll do what I can to clear up—or hide—this mess," Daemon said.

Lucivar grabbed Daemonar and swung him around as

they twirled toward the door, distracting the boy from the fact he was being taken away from the presents.

Once brother and boy were safely out of the way, Daemon dropped to his knees and began gathering up boxes and wrappings.

He could vanish everything and sort it out later—if he could figure out an excuse Jaenelle would accept for why the packages had disappeared.

Of course, these boxes had arrived after she'd left the room, so maybe she didn't know about them. That would be good. That would be wonderful. That would—

The door opened—and he froze. When there was no outraged shriek, he dared a look over his shoulder.

Saetan stood in the doorway, clearly amused. The bastard.

Daemon said, "If you love me at all, don't ask how this happened. Just help me fix it."

Saetan walked toward Daemon, the door closing silently behind him. "I know how it happened. As a reward, and to give you a break from the festive chaos going on in the rest of the Hall, your wife asked you to guard the gifts. And you, not having brains enough to get comfortable with a brandy and a book, decided guarding the gifts was foolish. So you left 'for just a few minutes,' and when you returned, you learned how much of a mess can be made in a short amount of time."

Daemon closed his eyes and hunched his shoulders. Right now he would gladly give up the privileges of being an adult if he could shove the responsibilities of being an adult under the sofa—along with all the torn wrapping paper.

"How did you know?" Daemon asked.

"I used to have one," Saetan replied.

Puzzled, he looked up at his father. "One what?"

"Small Eyrien boy. I learned this lesson the hard way, and now, my darling, so have you."

"You could have warned me."

"You wouldn't have believed me."

So what? You still could have warned me.

Since that wouldn't get him any help, he swallowed the comment and tried to look woeful. It wasn't hard to do. "Help?"

Using Craft, Saetan moved a straight-backed chair from one side of the room, placed it close to Daemon, and sat down. "I'll show you a trick. As long as you don't use it too often, you can get away with it. Especially during this season, when males are forgiven their foibles. Mostly."

"The first problem is figuring out who these gifts were intended for," Daemon said.

"That part is easy. I brought these, so I know which box belongs to which person."

"Bt. Dt. Zt." On the second try, he formed actual words. "You brought these? Then why in the name of Hell didn't *you* put shields around them?"

A raised eyebrow was his only answer—and an unspoken reminder that Saetan could leave the room without incurring a woman's wrath.

Sufficiently chastised, Daemon muttered, "Sorry."

Figuring it was best to confess the worst, he nudged the box Daemonar had pounded on the floor—and winced at the merry tinkle of broken glass.

No response. Just the feel of his father's formidable presence.

"Lesson one," Saetan said, sounding too damned amused. "If you shield all the gifts, you also need to shield and Craftlock the room sufficiently to keep small boys out. Otherwise, that boy will transform from a happy, excited child into a cranky, frustrated child. And trust me, a frustrated Eyrien boy during Winsol is twice as bad as what you're imagining right now—especially when his little brain is dazzled by boxes and shiny ribbons."

"Then Lucivar and I can just . . ." What? Put Ebon-gray and Black shields and locks around the room? That would keep Daemonar out, but it would also keep everyone else out of the room—including wives who wouldn't appreciate being locked out.

"All right," Daemon said, trying not to sigh. "Guard the room when it's my turn. Don't shield *all* the gifts." He nudged the broken gift. "If you tell me where you got this, I'll get it replaced in time." *I hope.*

"That? You can dispose of it. It's just a box of chipped teacups and broken figurines. Helene and Mrs. Beale keep a box of that stuff for just this kind of present."

A red haze appeared in front of Daemon's eyes. "What kind of present?"

"The kind that rattles enough to sound interesting. Especially once things inside the box start breaking."

"You did this deliberately?"

"Yes."

He was trying very hard to remember why he had looked forward to Winsol this year—and why he'd been happy to see his father a few minutes ago.

"Lesson two," Saetan said. "Fragile or delicate gifts go in the back where they're less likely to be noticed by inquisitive children. Even so, they are shielded individually and then are grouped together before a shield 'netting' is put over all of them, and that netting is then connected to the floor with Craft. However, there should be one breakable, disposable gift positioned in the front of the tree to catch a boy's eye. That way, you have a chance of stopping him while he's distracted by the fake present, and you're not trying to explain the loss of an expensive gift."

Daemon looked at the mounds of gifts. All this work to keep out *one* boy? What would happen if . . .

"Marian wants another baby," he said.

A stiff moment of silence. Then Saetan said, "In that case, my darling, you'd better learn some of these spells and work on them until you can pull them together in a heartbeat."

Or they could just all celebrate Winsol at the eyrie, and then it would be Lucivar's responsibility to guard the gifts.

He considered the probability of getting out of guard duty no matter where the family gathered for Winsol—and sighed.

"Lesson three." Saetan called in a small hourglass, turned it over, and set it on air. "Stay focused on the task. When I saw Lucivar racing away with Daemonar, I asked Jaenelle and Marian to have a leisurely cup of coffee before returning to this room."

"Aren't they going to suspect there's a problem and that you were stalling them until it's fixed?" Daemon asked.

"Of course they know there's a problem. But this request is as time-honored as Protocol—and as strictly observed. All things considered, since those two *do* understand the males involved, I estimate you have ten minutes left to put everything back the way it was."

Maybe he could tie a ribbon around his neck and curl up with the other fragile, delicate gifts.

"Gather up the pieces of wrapping paper that have the ribbons and name cards," Saetan said.

He crawled around until he was fairly sure he'd gotten them all. Then he picked up the first box.

"That one is yours," Saetan said.

"Mine?"

Warm pleasure flowed through him. A present. From his father.

As he started to coax the top part of the box off, Saetan reached over and clamped one hand on the box, holding it shut. When Saetan released the box . . .

Daemon wiggled the lid, then looked up in disbelief. "You locked the box. You *Craft-locked my present.*"

"On Winsol, when the gifts are being opened, this is your present," Saetan said. "Until then, it's still my box. And it stays locked."

Fine. Ha! Saetan wore the Black. So did he. He wasn't going to let . . .

There was some Red power twisted into the Black, changing a simple lock into a deviously elegant puzzle that would have to be untangled in order to open the box.

"You locked my present," Daemon said, feeling sulky. "I'm an adult, and you locked my present."

"You're a son who was about to open a present before

it was time to open the present," Saetan replied mildly. Then he looked pointedly at the hourglass. "Do you really want to argue about this right now?"

He had to think about that for a moment.

"Find the name tag," Saetan said, taking the box from him.

After handing that over too, he sat back on his heels.

Saetan set the piece of wrapping paper on the box and smoothed out the wrinkles. "You and Lucivar should be the ones handing out the gifts. Each person won't notice one gift wrapped like this, but anyone handling several ..."

As he watched, the wrapping paper grew out of the scrap and formed around the box.

"It's best to work out your own illusion spell for this," Saetan said. "That way, you'll be able to do it quickly, since it usually *needs* to be done quickly."

The illusion spell was good. If he hadn't seen the paper forming around the box, he doubted he would have noticed the difference in texture. He wasn't sure how someone "unwrapped" an illusion, but he'd find out on the day.

All the wrappings had been restored, he'd gathered up the rest of the scraps of paper and vanished the disposable gift, and he still had a few grains of sand left in the hourglass when he stood up and brushed himself off.

Saetan vanished the hourglass and returned the chair to its usual spot in the room.

They were both standing there, guarding the mound of perfectly wrapped presents, when Marian and Jaenelle walked into the room.

Jaenelle studied the two of them. Marian walked over to the tree, pursed her lips, then reached between two gifts and picked something up.

"The Prince and I have something to discuss, so we'll leave you Ladies to finish sorting out the gifts," Saetan said.

We have something to discuss? Daemon asked on a spear thread.

Yes, we do.

Judging by Saetan's tone, he wasn't expecting a pleasant discussion, but anything was better than staying in that room.

He reached the door when Marian said, "Daemon?"

Saetan left the room. Having no other safe choice, Daemon turned and waited for the Eyrien hearth witch.

There was something purely female about her expression as she walked up to him, adding to the impression that she was laughing at him.

He broke out in a cold sweat.

"You missed a piece," she whispered as she held up a scrap of wrapping paper.

He took the paper, vanished it—and fled.

Catching up with Saetan, the two men retreated to the study, where Lucivar met them.

"I promised Kaelas and Jaal I'd get them a steer for Winsol dinner if they don't let Daemonar out of the room where I stashed him," Lucivar said.

"You promised them the equivalent amount of meat or a live animal?" Saetan asked.

"Apparently it doesn't taste as good if it's already cut up," Lucivar muttered. "Or maybe it wasn't as much fun to eat. They were a little vague about that."

"I see." Saetan delicately cleared his throat. "So you will get them to promise that they won't eat *their* dinner within sight of the dining room windows, won't you?"

Lucivar's mouth opened and closed, but no sounds came out.

"Mother Night," Daemon said. If people lost their appetites because a six-hundred-pound tiger and an eight-hundred-pound Arcerian cat were gorging on a fresh kill, Mrs. Beale would . . .

He wasn't going to consider what Mrs. Beale would do to him and Lucivar.

"I'm almost sorry I'm going to miss this," Saetan said with a smile. "Almost."

In a heartbeat, Lucivar went from stumbling man to warrior. He shifted—one easy side step that effectively blocked any escape through the door.

Daemon moved in the other direction, drawing the eye, keeping the prey focused on what was in front of him instead of the danger behind him.

He and Lucivar had played out this game dozens of times. Hundreds of times. Once they had their prey caught between them . . . Concentrate on one of them, and the other one would be the attacker.

Saetan watched him. Being an intelligent man, he would know exactly what his sons were doing—and what role remained in their little three-person drama.

"I won't be joining you for Winsol," Saetan said quietly. "I stopped by today to drop off the gifts—and to tell you I'll be staying at the Keep."

"No," Lucivar said.

"I don't want to discuss this," Saetan said, still watching Daemon. "I don't want to argue about this. I'm asking you to accept this."

"Why?" Daemon asked softly.

"I love you both. I do. But this . . . frenzy . . . is for young men."

"Well, Hell's fire," Lucivar growled. "We're not going to drag you to parties and things you don't want to attend." He looked at Daemon. "Right?"

"It's not just that," Saetan said. Then he raked one hand through his hair and sighed. "I did this. For decades, for centuries, I did this. The large parties. The social functions that I attended because it was expected of me as the Warlord Prince of Dhemlan. Houseguests and noise. You both have those responsibilities now, and that's as it should be. But this year, I want peace during the longest night of the year. I want to walk in solitude through one of the gardens at the Keep. I want this. And I think I've earned this."

Before Lucivar could snarl about it, Daemon said on a spear thread, *Don't argue about it. Let it go.*

A slashing look was Lucivar's only answer.

"That's really what you want?" Daemon asked Saetan.

"It really is." Saetan's smile held a hint of sorrow—not

for the decision, but for the argument he anticipated was still to come. "I don't expect you to understand, but I'm asking you—both of you—to accept. As a gift to me."

Daemon waited a beat, as if he were discussing it privately with Lucivar. Then he said, "All right. We'll accept your decision—as our gift."

"Thank you." Saetan turned and raised an eyebrow at Lucivar, who reluctantly stepped aside.

The moment the study door closed behind their father, Lucivar turned on Daemon. "Are we really letting him do this? We're going to let our father be alone for Winsol?"

"Yes, we are," Daemon replied, moving closer. "He's feeling his age, Prick. Andulvar, Mephis, and Prothvar are gone. Being here without them is hard. You know that was a large part of his decision to retire to the Keep."

"They were gone last year too," Lucivar argued.

"He was taking care of us last year. Me more than you. Jaenelle was so fragile, and I . . ." Wasn't sure she would survive the winter. Wasn't sure he would want to survive if she didn't.

"I know." Lucivar drew in a deep breath and blew it out slowly. "I don't like it. He shouldn't be alone on Winsol. None of them should, when it comes down to it. Geoffrey, Draca. Even Lorn. They shouldn't be alone. Not for this celebration."

"They won't be."

Lucivar frowned. "But you gave him your word."

Daemon nodded. "He asked for a solitary Winsol, and we'll give him that. Or something close to it. But we'll find a way to give him family too. All of them."

"When you figure out how to do that, you've got me for whatever you need."

He smiled. "I love you, Prick."

That lazy, arrogant smile. "Will you still say that if I decide to pour the contraceptive brew down the sink?"

"Yes. But not as often."

Daemon eyed the plate of fudge that had ended up between Marian and Jaenelle and decided trying to take a piece wasn't worth losing a hand. So he chose grapes and cheese to go with his after-dinner coffee.

It had been a fairly quiet dinner since Daemonar had fallen asleep halfway through the meal. Now that he wasn't moving, he looked sweet and cuddly. At some point during the day, he had acquired a string of bells that he was wearing around his neck as his "Jewel."

Daemon smiled at the sleeping boy. Daemonar had been delighted with the jingling sound. He and Lucivar had been even more delighted when they realized how easy it was to locate the little beast. Neither man had much hope of convincing Marian to make the bells a permanent accessory for the boy, but they were sure going to try to talk her into it.

"So," Jaenelle said as she selected a piece of fudge. "I think we're ready for Winsol."

"I think we are," Marian agreed.

"And I think the two of you are handling the High Lord's decision very well," Daemon said, raising his coffee cup in a salute.

"Decision?" Jaenelle asked. "Oh! That reminds me. Papa did say there was something the two of you needed to talk to us about."

Daemon felt the meal he'd just eaten solidify into solid rock and sink his stomach to the floor.

He didn't, Lucivar said on a spear thread.

Oh, I think he did, Daemon replied. He looked at Jaenelle and Marian—and wondered if he could run fast enough to get out of the room before one or both exploded. "He didn't say anything to either of you?"

"About what?" Jaenelle asked.

"About not joining us for Winsol?"

Their answer was a thunderous silence.

Wearing nothing but a long winter robe, Daemon slipped into the bedroom and joined Jaenelle, who was standing at the glass door that overlooked her private courtyard. Wrapping his arms around her, he drew her back against him to keep her warm and rubbed his cheek against her short golden hair.

"Are you upset about Father's decision?" he asked.

"A little," she replied. "But not surprised once I had time to think about it."

Something more. He could see it in her face, reflected in the glass.

"Before I reached the age of majority, there were parties," Jaenelle said. "Lots of them. The coven was still living here most of the time. The boyos too. Saetan attended an exhausting number of formal celebrations as the Warlord Prince of Dhemlan and stood as my escort for almost as many others. Then the coven and the boyos would go home to celebrate Winsol with their families.

"A dazzling whirl of people for six days. But on the eve of Winsol, just before midnight, Saetan would bring two cups of blooded rum to my sitting room. A toast to the living myth. I always found it embarrassing, being toasted like that. And then we would dance. A court dance. Very formal. Very traditional. A pattern that was only performed during this time of year.

"The next evening, the longest night of the year, was for family. No visitors. No outsiders. Just Mephis, Prothvar, Uncle Andulvar, Papa, and me. A simple dinner. Afterward, we would open the gifts from each other."

"I don't remember you and the High Lord having a private celebration," he said.

"We didn't these past two years. He stepped aside. For you."

"I see," Daemon said quietly. And he did. The Steward yielding to the Consort. The father yielding to the lover. The fact that he was the lover must have weighed heavily in Saetan's decision.

He looked at their reflection in the glass. It was like watching Jaenelle delicately unwrap layers of her heart.

"What else?" he asked.

"Those years were a dazzle of people during Winsol," she said. "A kaleidoscope of colors and faces. Even more so after I became the Queen of Ebon Askavi and had my own list of social events to attend as part of my duties as Queen. But the moment I remember clearly, the moment that stands out from each of those years, is that dance with Saetan."

"I'm sorry, sweetheart. I don't understand what you're trying to tell me."

He saw her lips press together in a tight line, could feel her breath shudder in and out. He held her and waited, watching their reflection.

"One day I'm going to wake up and realize I've gotten old." She lifted her left hand. "You knew when you gave me this ring what the difference in our races would mean."

"Some people spend a few years together and then part for one reason or another. Others have a few decades. And other people have a lifetime. I know what the difference in our races means, Lady. I'll take every day that you're willing to give me."

She nodded. "That's the point. You have social duties. *We* have social duties. But I don't want these days to be a blur of events and faces. I want memories, Daemon. Of you. Of us. I want those clear moments that the heart holds on to. With you."

"And with him."

"Yes. With him too. You waited seventeen hundred years for the Queen you wanted to serve. Saetan waited fifty thousand."

"A few days out of this celebration for just the two of us? That's really what you want?"

"Yes, that's really what I want."

Something inside him relaxed. He kissed her temple. "Then that's what we'll do. And we can start with this." He called in a rectangular box and held it out.

Jaenelle shook her head and turned as she took a step away from him. "We open the gifts on Winsol."

Daemon smiled a very special smile—and watched her blush in response to it. "You need to open this one now so you can plan ahead for when you'll use it."

She hesitated, then took the box and opened it.

Watching her, he swallowed the urge to laugh and wondered how long she would stare at that little bit of nothing.

Finally she lifted the triangle of richly embroidered gold fabric out of the box. "What . . . ?"

"The ribbons circle your hips," he said helpfully.

"Oh." She vanished the box and held the triangle in position. *"Oh."*

Seeing that bit of nothing in place, even held over a bulky winter robe, was enough to make his blood simmer.

"I thought we could have a private dinner sometime during Winsol," Daemon said. "You could wear that under the dress you had made for our dance in the spooky house. Nothing but that."

Even the thought of seeing her in that wisp of a dress made his cock hard.

Blushing and still looking baffled, she said, "This is my present?"

He wrapped his arms around her and pulled her close, leaving her in no doubt about the kind of memories he wanted to make tonight.

"No, lover," he purred. "This is *my* present."

SEVEN

On the third day of Winsol, Daemon walked into Lucivar's eyrie and caught the boy who half leaped, half flew at him.

"Unka Daemon!"

He gave Daemonar a smacking kiss on the cheek. "Hello, boyo. Are you being good?"

He and the boy both ignored the snarl that came from the kitchen in response to that question.

"You read me a story?" Daemonar asked.

"I guess we could read a story after—"

"You read me a story now?"

"Let me ask your papa."

"We gotta tree. I show you!"

The boy was damn hard to hold on to once he started wiggling. Daemon put him down and watched him run to the other end of the room where another Craft-made tree sparkled.

"Look, Unka Daemon!"

Before Daemon could growl "No," Daemonar kicked at the wrapped presents.

Nothing happened.

Then the front door opened, Marian and Jaenelle walked in, and Daemonar raced to meet them. Since it didn't look like he was going to go around his uncle, Daemon prudently got out of the way.

"Auntie J.! Auntie J.! We gotta tree!"

"I see that," Jaenelle said, crouching to receive her hugs and kisses. "Do you like the tree I made for the eyrie?"

"Yes! I read you a story! I read you a story now!"

"Could we read a story after we eat?" Jaenelle asked. "I'm very hungry."

"Okay!"

Marian smiled and held out a hand. Knowing better than to suggest that he could hang up his own coat, Daemon shucked off his overcoat and handed it to her before going into the kitchen.

"You put illusion spells of gifts around your tree?" Daemon asked Lucivar.

"The real gifts are at the Hall," Lucivar said as he pulled a large casserole out of the oven and set it on the table.

"Why couldn't we have the illusion-spell gifts?" Daemon grumbled.

"You can keep the real gifts until we open them on Winsol Night or you can keep the boy."

"I'll keep the gifts," Daemon said too quickly.

"Smart choice." Lucivar tipped his neck from side to side to ease the muscles. "Hell's fire, he's a handful this year."

"I guess Marian won't let you build a cage."

"Not a chance. And whenever I growl about the boy, his grandfather laughs at me."

"Seems petty of Father to do that."

Lucivar used Craft to slice a loaf of bread and put it and the butter on the table. "You know what's really scary? The times when Father looks at me and says, 'You were worse.' Makes me wonder if I'm getting off easy or if I should start preparing." He finished setting the table. "Marian and I usually have ale with this meal since it goes well with the casserole, but I can open a bottle of wine for you."

"Ale is fine."

As Lucivar filled glasses, he said, "How is Yuli? That's where you were this morning, wasn't it? At that school?"

Yuli was an orphan boy he and Jaenelle met while rescuing Surreal and Rainier from Jarvis Jenkell's spooky house.

"He's doing well. Still too afraid of making a mistake and being severely punished for it to relax most of the time—at least, according to the teachers—but Socks isn't afraid of voicing an opinion about anything, so the Sceltie pup balances out the boy." Daemon looked around. "Speaking of pups, where are the wolves?"

"Off doing wolf things, thank the Darkness." Lucivar raised his voice. "Food's on the table."

Jaenelle and Marian sat on one side of the table, the boy between them. Daemon and Lucivar sat on the other. As the adults talked about small things, Daemon became more and more aware that the boy was too excited by the company and all the festivities, and his misbehavior was going to clash with Lucivar's temper soon.

Then Jaenelle spoke one quiet sentence in Eyrien, and Daemon saw the proof that Daemonar had made the transition from toddler to boy in the past few weeks. Because Daemonar's reaction to that voice wasn't a nephew responding to an aunt; it was a Warlord Prince responding to his Queen.

Daemonar quieted and began eating properly, glancing often at his father for approval and confirmation that he was behaving as he should.

The boy was no longer just a small male. He'd been born a Warlord Prince. From now on, the adult males would start treating him like one—and training him like one.

When the meal ended, Jaenelle and Daemonar went into the family room to read a book and Marian disappeared.

Lucivar smiled as he cleared the table. "Some days going to the bathroom by yourself is a luxury."

Daemon stripped off his black jacket and rolled up his shirtsleeves. "I'll wash."

"Deal. Have you thought about what we're going to do about Winsol?"

"I have," Daemon said as he filled one side of the sink with water. "And I have an idea how we can accomplish it."

"The little beast usually naps for a couple of hours after the midday meal, so he'll probably be sound asleep by the time Jaenelle gets to the last page. We can talk after that."

Marian made coffee, Lucivar put Daemonar to bed for his nap, and when the adults gathered in the family parlor, Daemon told them his idea.

"Yes," Jaenelle said, smiling.

"It's wonderful," Marian said.

Lucivar said nothing. He didn't have to because the look in his eyes said it all.

EIGHT

It was late afternoon on the eve of Winsol, and the streets and sidewalks of Amdarh were still crowded. But not with shoppers. These were the merchants who had closed their shops and were now heading home to friends and family.

An hour from now, the streets would still be crowded, Surreal thought as she opened the carriage door and accepted the assistance of a Warlord who was passing by at that moment, in order to step from carriage to sidewalk. Just one of those things she'd learned to accept about living in Kaeleer: It took less time to accept help you didn't want or need than it took to explain to the helpful male why you didn't want or need his help.

The Warlord escorted her to the door of the building where Rainier lived, wished her a happy Winsol, and continued on his way.

She didn't dare look at her driver. Helton had *told* her to take a footman to serve her, but it seemed silly to drag a second man out in order to run a simple errand.

Idiot, she thought as she crossed the lobby to the reception desk, where packages or messages could be left for the residents. *Next time listen to Helton.*

She smiled at the Warlord at the desk, recognizing him from the times when she'd met Rainier there before an outing because it was on the way instead of his taking the extra time to come to the town house.

"Lady Surreal," the Warlord said.

"Happy Winsol," she replied. "I'd like to leave a package for Prince Rainier. Could you make sure he gets it when he gets home?"

A hesitation. "Prince Rainier returned home an hour ago."

"But . . ." *He's supposed to be with his family in Dharo.*

Another hesitation. A deliberate pause of a man deciding whether he should meddle. "Perhaps you would like to deliver the package yourself?"

Surreal studied the man. "He asked you to tell people he wasn't in, didn't he?"

"He said he didn't want to be disturbed."

I'll bet he did. She leaned against the desk. "Have I been sufficiently scary during this conversation?"

"Oh, no, Lady, you've—" He paused. Considered. Smiled as he opened a wall cabinet behind him, removed a key, and handed it to her. "You were quite forceful in your insistence that I give you the spare key so that you could put the Prince's gift in his apartment rather than leaving it here at the desk."

"Since he's been on the receiving end of my insistence often enough, he'll believe the part about my being forceful," she said with a wink.

She climbed the stairs slowly and steadily, but she still heard the rasp in her lungs by the time she reached Rainier's floor. How was he managing the stairs on that leg? Did he have sense enough to float down the stairways?

Probably not.

When she reached his door, she took a moment to catch her breath. No point starting a fight if she couldn't yell at him.

She vanished the present, unlocked the door, and walked into his parlor, only to find Rainier standing there waiting for the intruder, looking pale and furious.

"Surreal . . ."

"You wear Opal; I wear Gray. I outrank you. Shut up."

She could feel his temper taking a sharper edge, but he wasn't a fool. His being a Warlord Prince couldn't make up for the difference in their power.

"You were supposed to be visiting your family," Surreal said.

"I did visit. Now I'm back."

And sounding more bitter than when he'd left.

"Well, that's good, actually, because the family is gathering at the Keep for Winsol. You and I will have a quiet dinner at the town house tonight, and tomorrow afternoon we'll go up to the Keep."

"Surreal, it's a family gathering. I'm not family."

"Oh, that's not a problem." She walked up to him, smiled, and slugged him in the shoulder hard enough to almost knock him off his feet. "Now you're an honorary cousin. If you get pissy about this, I'm going to tell Daemon and Lucivar that you didn't want to be family for Winsol because you didn't want to be related to *them*. Won't that be fun when they show up wanting an explanation?"

"Bitch."

"Boyo, you have no idea." She gave him a minute to appreciate just how cornered he really was. "So, are you still packed or do you need help?"

"I can take care of it tomorrow if you want to go back to the town house now," Rainier said.

She bared her teeth in a smile. "You and your luggage are coming with me to the town house. Where you'll be staying tonight."

"I'm not going to run away."

"Damn right, you're not. I'm not going to face all of them by myself."

He studied her. Then he sighed. "Fine. I'll swap out some clothes. Give me a few minutes."

"Don't take long. The driver is waiting, and Helton will worry if I'm late."

Rainier huffed out a laugh and limped to his bedroom.

Surreal closed her eyes. He didn't need tears or pity or whatever else was being dished out. And he wouldn't get those things. Not at the Keep.

But he would get the warmth of friends who cared about him. And he wouldn't be alone for Winsol.

NINE

"Are you sure she's home?" Lucivar asked as Daemon opened the cottage door. "There aren't any lights on in the sitting room."

"Doesn't mean anything," Daemon replied, touching the hallway candle-light so they could see as they headed for the kitchen. "Allista left this morning to spend a few days with her family, and Manny is celebrating with friends in the village. Tersa told both of them she was staying home tonight."

As they walked into the kitchen, they saw her silhouetted against the open back door, oblivious to the cold air streaming into the cottage.

"Tersa," Daemon called softly.

"It's the boy," she said, sounding puzzled as she looked from him to Lucivar. "Both my boys."

"Yes," Daemon said.

"Why are you here?"

Lucivar nudged her into the kitchen and closed the door. "We've decided to establish some family traditions. Winsol Eve is going to be a time for fathers and daughters to spend together."

"And mothers and sons," Daemon added.

"So we're here to spend the evening with our mother," Lucivar said.

"But . . ." She looked around, as if finally noticing where she was. "There is no food. I should prepare food?"

"We did that," Daemon said, calling in several dishes and settling them gently on the kitchen table. "A couple of things need to be heated, and a few other things need the finishing touches." He took off his overcoat and wrapped it around her, adding a warming spell.

Did she even realize she was shivering?

Lucivar pulled out a chair. "You sit down, and we'll take care of things."

"That does not seem fair," Tersa said. "You are doing all the work."

"Fine," Lucivar said. "You can do the dishes after."

"*That* is not fair!"

Lucivar grinned at her and winked at Daemon.

They talked, they laughed, and they ate. And as Tersa's mind flowed between past and present, they learned more of who they had been when they had been her boys.

"We'd like to ask a favor," Daemon said when he set out the plate of baked goods he'd wheedled out of Mrs. Beale. "A special gift we'd like you to give both of us if you can."

She looked at them—not with the lucidity of madness, but with clear-sighted eyes. "Ask."

So he asked. And after thinking about it for a moment, she said yes.

TEN

Saetan walked through one of the enclosed gardens at the Keep. Stark at this time of year, but not barren. Life slept beneath the snow, beneath the earth, waiting for the light to return.

The Blood came from the Darkness of the abyss—a power inherited from another race whose time as the guardians of the Realms had ended. So they honored the Darkness that separated them from the landens, that shaped their preferences and needs and desires.

Especially their desires.

"I understand now."

Jaenelle's voice came out of the darkness around him.

No, not Jaenelle's voice, he thought as he turned. Too much midnight in that voice, too much of the abyss.

For a moment, when she took the first step toward him, he saw the Self that lived beneath her skin. Saw the living myth, dreams made flesh.

Not all the dreamers had been human—and neither was Witch.

Then the moment was gone, and Jaenelle, lovely and human, kept walking toward him.

"You should be home with your husband," Saetan said.

"No, I shouldn't. Not tonight," Jaenelle replied. "I understand now."

"Understand what, witch-child?"

"The private dance on Winsol Eve."

She took both his hands. Hers were cold, so he put a warming spell on his own to make hers more comfortable.

"We didn't dance these last two years. But you did. Alone. Just as you did for most of your fifty thousand years. You danced for a dream, for a promise. And every year when you performed the steps of that dance, you renewed your own promise to that dream."

He closed his eyes, unwilling to look at her because she would see the truth of her words. She was the sweetest, most painful dance of his life. She was the reason for this unnaturally long life.

"Each year, when we performed that dance, you renewed that promise. But it was no longer to a dream. It was to flesh and blood, to a real Queen."

He had no words for what he felt, so he did something he had done no more than a handful of times during his entire life—he opened all his inner barriers, revealing his heart, his mind, his Self to her without any defenses or shields. As he opened his eyes and stared into her sapphire ones, he realized he wasn't showing her anything she didn't already know about him.

"It's almost midnight," Jaenelle said. "Dance with me, Saetan. Tonight, let's both acknowledge a promise made and kept."

He followed her to one of the sitting rooms. A small bowl of hot blooded rum was on a table, along with two glasses and a crystal music sphere in a brass holder.

He helped her out of her coat, then removed his cape and vanished both.

She wore a black dress made of layers of spidersilk. Widow's weeds. A dress made for a Black Widow Queen— especially one who had once worn Black Jewels.

Jaenelle raised her hand. Music for the traditional Winsol dance filled the room.

He raised his hand and took the first step of the dance. Fingertips touched fingertips. Hands touched hands.

She was no longer a girl indulging her adopted father. She was no longer a Queen accepting her Steward's request for a traditional dance. The woman who moved with him tonight understood the weight of his choices—and the importance of this night that marked each year.

So they danced in honor of a dream—and to renew a promise.

ELEVEN

A warm hand rubbing his bare back coaxed Saetan out of a deep sleep. A loving touch, but not a lover's touch. Sensual without being sexual. Who . . . ?

Then he knew. There was only one person whose psychic scent was so close to his own that it took a moment to pick up the distinctions between them.

"Prince," he said. It was the best he could do. The way Daemon was rubbing his back made him feel boneless—and brainless. A bit odd for a son to be doing.

That thought roused his paternal suspicions, and that woke up his brain.

"Good evening," Daemon said. "Did you sleep well?"

Hell's fire. Every time a son had asked him that, the boy was about to dump a basket of trouble in his lap.

"It's Winsol," Saetan said, turning onto his side and propping himself up on one elbow. "Why aren't you home with your wife?"

"Because my wife is still here," Daemon replied, resting a hand on his father's hip.

A sultry voice. Almost a sexual purr. Daemon excelled at using sensuality to intimidate, and right now the boy was doing an excellent job.

Except he wasn't sure intimidation *was* the response Daemon intended to evoke.

"Did you enjoy your gift?" Daemon asked.

"My gift?"

"You asked for solitude. We stepped back so you could celebrate Winsol Eve in your own way."

With Jaenelle. With Witch.

"Lucivar and I talked it over, and we decided that you had a point—and a lesson we wanted to embrace now instead of later."

"That's good." Maybe. He might sound more enthusiastic if he were more awake—and if Daemon's hand resting on his hip didn't feel more and more like a cat's paw pressing on a mouse's tail.

"We decided to give the first six days of Winsol to our public obligations as rulers of Dhemlan and Ebon Rih. Winsol Day will be for family. And the last six days will be private. Quiet. Jaenelle and I are going to Scelt for a couple of days, and then tuck in at the Hall."

"That's good," Saetan said. And it was.

"Today, being Winsol, is for family," Daemon said. "All of us, together. Here at the Keep."

"All . . . ?"

Sounds just outside the bedroom door. Then Daemonar shouted, "Wake up, Granpapa! Wake up!"

He heard Lucivar's rumble, followed by giggles and squeals that moved away from the door.

"All of us," Daemon said. "Even Tersa."

Honoring the day with his children without the intrusion of the world and its demands. He felt foolishly sentimental—and very happy.

"Just family," he said, his voice husky as he remembered the family members who were no longer with him.

"And Rainier. It seems he was going to be alone tonight, so Surreal declared him an honorary cousin for the occasion."

Too much sentiment, too much feeling. And it wasn't just him. The sensuality was a game, but having the family gathered like this meant a great deal to Daemon too.

Figuring they both needed a moment to step back from deep feelings, he said, "You got through this much of the day without opening any gifts?" If they'd managed that with a boy Daemonar's age in their midst, they had steel balls and no nerves.

Daemon twitched his shoulders. "We let him open his, and the adults each opened one of theirs."

Saetan studied his son—the flushed skin, the sudden avoidance of looking him in the eyes. "So. How long did it take Daemonar to get the bug out of the box?"

Daemon's expression went absolutely blank. Then he muttered, "We found it before Marian did."

He could picture Lucivar and Daemon scrambling around to find the exploding beetle before Marian—or Surreal—found it. Since he didn't think either man was going to find anything amusing about that little adventure—at least for another decade or two—he'd wait until he was safely in the shower before he laughed at them.

"Then it sounds like Daemonar likes his gift. What about you?" He twisted around to plump up the pillows. "Since you were so eager to open it a few days ago, I assume you opened the gift I gave you."

When there was no response, he stopped plumping pillows and looked at Daemon's sulky expression. "Didn't you like your gift?"

"I don't know," Daemon growled. "I haven't been able to unravel the Craft lock you put on the damn box."

Saetan blinked. He'd used that same lock on his sons' gifts when they were young. It used to take Daemon less than five minutes to unravel the thing.

Winsol gifts weren't just found in the boxes. They were the moments, and memories, treasured by the heart. Like this one.

He tried to swallow the butterflies tickling his throat. Seeing the look on Daemon's face, he tried hard.

Then he gave up, plopped back on the pillows—and laughed.

SHADES OF HONOR

This story takes place before the events in The Shadow Queen.

ONE

Prince Falonar stood outside his eyrie, restlessly opening and closing his dark, membranous wings as he stared down at the village of Riada. Within minutes of her arrival, he'd felt Gray-Jeweled power ripple through the village and up the mountains like a challenge—or a warning.

Surreal SaDiablo had returned to Ebon Rih.

He had made two mistakes when he came to Kaeleer two years ago. The first was agreeing to serve Lucivar Yaslana, whom he'd despised from the moment they'd met as boys training in the same hunting camp. He'd thought he could swallow taking Lucivar's orders for five years in exchange for living in Ebon Rih and being in a position to catch the attention of the Queen of Ebon Askavi. He'd been confident that she would see the value of having a true aristo Eyrien Warlord Prince in her First Circle and take over his service contract. Serving in the same court as Yaslana would have rubbed him a bit raw, but he would have accepted having to treat Lucivar as an equal—at least until he could persuade the Queen to find another way for Lucivar to serve her that would keep the man away from Askavi, leaving the Eyriens free to live without the constant embarrassment of acknowledging a half-breed bastard. Whether Yaslana's Hayllian father acknowledged him now or not, Lucivar would always be a bastard with no standing in Eyrien society. And *nothing* would change the fact that Lucivar was a half-breed, and being a half-breed was, in many ways, even worse than being a bastard.

Desperate to find a position in Kaeleer and avoid being sent back to Terreille, Falonar had signed the five-year service contract, gambling that he wouldn't be under Lucivar's control for most of it. But the following spring, Witch had unleashed her power to purge the Realms of Dorothea and Hekatah SaDiablo's taint, and she'd been injured so severely by the backlash of her own power that she was no longer capable of ruling Ebon Askavi. That left Falonar with the choice of bending to Lucivar's will for the full term of the contract or being tossed back to Terreille, where he had no future of any kind.

His second mistake had been responding to Surreal's initial interest in him—and his interest in her—and having sex with her. Oh, she was terrific in bed—strong and experienced and so knowledgeable when it came to playing with a man's body to give him the sharpest release. She was worth every gold mark she'd charged as a whore in Terreille, and he'd had her for the asking. She had also been a sharp, interesting companion outside of bed—when she wasn't trying to acquire skills that should be kept exclusive to warriors.

Except the sex hadn't been as free as he'd thought. At least, not after they came to Ebon Rih and he'd invited her to stay with him in his eyrie. He had been thinking of the relief of having as much sex as he wanted with a woman strong enough to handle being with a Sapphire-Jeweled Warlord Prince. But he hadn't considered that the SaDiablos, by allowing Surreal to use the family name, really would think of her as family. In Terreille, that was something no *true* aristo family would have done, because no matter how skilled she was and how exclusive the Red Moon houses were where she had plied those skills, the fact was that Surreal was still a half-breed whore who had started her career in dark alleys and dirty rooms.

Unfortunately, he had realized too late that even whores could have unrealistic romantic notions. About the time he wanted Surreal to find other accommodations, leaving him free to express his interest in Nurian, the Eyrien Healer, he discovered that Surreal thought they were a step away from a handfast—and that *Lucivar* thought the same thing. As much as he'd enjoyed her, he wasn't about to make any commitment to a woman who wasn't Eyrien, let alone a woman who'd seen so many balls she was now trying to grow a pair of her own.

In the end, Surreal had packed up and left, and Lucivar's civility toward him had developed a sharp edge because of her hurt feelings. No doubt that edge would get sharper now that she was going to be in front of both of them again.

And that other Warlord Prince. The crippled one. Hell's fire. What was the point of bringing *that* one to Ebon Rih to train with Eyrien warriors?

Which only confirmed what he'd suspected all along— Lucivar Yaslana might be Eyrien in looks, and definitely had the skills of an Eyrien warrior when he stepped onto a killing field, but he wasn't, at heart, an Eyrien. As long as Lucivar controlled Ebon Rih, the Eyriens trying to build a life there and retain their heritage and culture were going to suffer.

Unfortunately, for now, there was nothing Falonar could do about that except hide how much he was choking on that bitter truth.

Surreal walked into the room that would be her home for the next few weeks and looked around. The furniture was basic but in good condition, and gleamed from a fresh cleaning. Everything felt a bit rustic, but that was in keeping with the rest of The Tavern. It wouldn't suit an aristo prick who thought his farts didn't smell, but *she* found nothing to complain about.

"We're nothing fancy," Merry said as she hovered just inside the room. "I know we call the place a tavern and inn, but we're really a tavern with a handful of rooms we converted because we had the space. There are two nice boardinghouses here in Riada, and a couple of fancier inns on the aristo side of the village."

Surreal studied the other woman, making note of the nerves. She'd had a passing acquaintance with Merry and Briggs during her previous stay in Ebon Rih, but she hadn't gotten to know the owners of The Tavern because she had been living with Falonar. Merry and Briggs, and their establishment, were too common for a man like Falonar, especially since he thought being Lucivar's second-in-command was a reason to act even more aristo than the aristos in Riada.

Since Merry didn't know her either except in passing, why was the woman so nervous? Maybe the Rihlander had heard about Surreal's former professions and didn't want to rent a room to a whore—or an assassin? If that was the case, she wanted to know before she unpacked her trunks.

"Do you have a problem with me staying here?" Surreal asked.

"Oh, no," Merry replied quickly. "I just wanted you to know there are other options." She hesitated, clearly debating if she should say anything more. Then she sighed. "Look. Lucivar is a good man, and Briggs and I count ourselves fortunate to call him a friend. But he can be single-minded at times. Lucivar likes The Tavern, but it's not to everyone's taste, and I don't think he considered that you might prefer something a bit fancier."

Which confirmed that Merry had more than a passing knowledge of the man who was the second most powerful male in the Realm of Kaeleer. Despite coming from the most aristo family in the Realm, there was nothing aristo about Lucivar's tastes or preferences.

But Lucivar *could* be single-minded about a good many things, and that tickled a suspicion about the real reason for his choice of accommodations.

"He comes in here fairly often?" Surreal asked.

"Every day when he's home," Merry replied. "Sometimes he stops to have a mug of coffee just after we open. Other days he stops in for a bowl of soup or stew. He will have a glass of ale while he talks to the men and waits for me to pack up a steak pie or something else he's bringing home for dinner. But that's not every day."

"Uh-huh." *Hell's fire. You know the man, but you still haven't figured out how a Warlord Prince's mind works, have you, sugar?*

The Tavern was a local gathering place where people could have a drink or a meal, and it did a good business. Dark-haired and dark-eyed, Merry had a pretty face and a nicely curved body that would tweak plenty of men's interest. Her Tiger Eye Jewel, being a lighter Jewel, might dampen the interest of stronger males—or it might heighten the interest of a predator who preferred females who weren't strong enough to fight back. Briggs was a Summer-sky Warlord. Since he wasn't trained to fight, maybe that wasn't enough power to protect his wife and their livelihood.

Unless, of course, that Summer-sky Warlord was quietly backed by an Eyrien Warlord Prince who wore Ebon-gray Jewels, and had a vicious, violent temper and centuries of training as a warrior.

There were predators and there were Predators—and even among the Predators, Lucivar Yaslana was a law unto himself.

Surreal looked at the room again, turning over possibilities of why Lucivar had chosen this place as her home-away-from-home. Then she put those thoughts aside before Merry became too anxious about her being there—or began to wonder *why* she was there.

She opened a door and found the bathroom. Her gold-green eyes narrowed as she considered the bathroom's second door. "I'm sharing?"

"With the Warlord Prince who's also coming in for the training," Merry said.

She nodded. "Rainier. He's a friend, even if he does pee through a pipe. Well, I can try to live with sharing a bathroom with him." She gave Merry a wicked smile. "And if I have reason to complain about his aim, he can just try to live."

Merry blinked, started to say something, then changed her mind—a couple of times. Finally she said, "I can provide you with the midday and evening meals, but we aren't open early in the morning, so I don't usually prepare breakfast."

"That's all right," Surreal said. "We're expected at the eyrie for breakfast."

"Oh."

So much sympathy in one little word. But it was the humor laced in the sympathy that caught Surreal's attention.

"You've met Lucivar's son," Surreal said.

"I have, yes."

Surreal watched Merry weighing and measuring loyalties and obligations.

"There's a coffee shop two blocks from here," Merry said. "And there's a bakery. The two businesses converted the store in between into a dining area used by both. You wouldn't get a full breakfast there—just coffee and baked goods—but it would be a peaceful one. Or you're welcome to warm up whatever soup or stew is left from the previous day."

Giving up your own breakfast? Surreal wondered. "Thanks. We're expected at Lucivar's eyrie tomorrow morning, but I, at least, will take advantage of the coffee shop and bakery most of the time after that."

"Well, then," Merry said. "I'll let you get settled in."

"One other thing," Surreal said before Merry had a chance to escape. Because that was what the other woman clearly had in mind—bolting before this last detail was mentioned. "How do you want me to pay for the food and lodging? By the day or week?"

"That's not necessary," Merry said, her eyes looking bigger and darker in a rapidly paling face.

"Yes, it is," Surreal countered politely.

"No, it isn't."

"Damn him, I *told* him I was going to pick up the tab for my own lodging. So you'll give the bill to me."

"No. Uh-uh. If you want to argue with Prince Yaslana about this, you go right ahead. But he was *very* clear about what he expected from *me*."

Of course he was. The prick. And wasn't it interesting where the line got drawn between Lucivar the friend and Prince Yaslana the ruler of Ebon Rih?

"All right, fine," Surreal grumbled. "I'll deal with him in my own way."

Merry made a sound that might have been a squeak, and the next thing Surreal heard was the woman clattering down the stairs.

"Don't be such a bitch," she scolded herself. "You know what it's like trying to deal with your male relatives. You wear the Gray and they roll right over you. How do you expect Tiger Eye to face down someone like Lucivar?"

No recourse. Daemon would tell her not to be an ass about who paid for what, since the SaDiablo family as a whole was not only the most powerful family in Kaeleer; they were also the wealthiest. Lucivar wasn't going to feel pinched by the tab for her lodgings, but that wasn't the point. Paying for it herself wouldn't pinch her pocket either.

On the other hand, whenever she had accepted a job as an assassin, her client sometimes paid for her expenses as well as her fee.

Which circled back to the question of why she really was staying at The Tavern.

Going to the window, she pulled back the sheer curtain and stared at the mountain Lucivar called home as she lobbed a thought on a Gray psychic thread. *Yaslana.*

Are you going to start whining already?

He sounded amused. He sounded like he'd been waiting for her to contact him.

Damn him. His wife, Marian, either was crazy in love with him or had more patience than was natural.

We need to talk, Surreal said. *Privately. And if you give me any excuses, I'll kick you so hard your balls will end up lodged between your ears.*

If you bring a crossbow to this meeting, I will smack you brainless.

She grinned. Couldn't help it. The last time she'd wanted to discuss something with Lucivar, she'd threatened to shoot him in order to assure she would have his undivided attention. *Fine. No crossbow—unless I have to come looking for you.*

He laughed. They'd come out even in this little pissing contest, so she was pretty pleased too.

This evening, he said. *Once the little beast is tucked in for the night. Do you know the house in Doun where my mother used to live?*

I'll find it.

I'll meet you there.

Are you sure you want to meet there? Apparently Lucivar also wanted to meet without attracting attention. She couldn't think of another reason for him to choose that location.

She unpacked her clothes, then got acquainted with the room. The small desk held a supply of paper, as well as pens, sealing wax, and a couple of decorative seals for guests who might not have a family seal. The bottom of the bedside table had a stack of books—mostly collections of stories, but there were a couple of Lady Fiona's Tracker and Shadow novels, including the newest one, which she hadn't read yet.

No books by Jarvis Jenkell, the writer who had tried to kill her and Rainier. Was that because Merry hadn't liked his work, or had the woman removed anything that would remind her guests of that nightmarish effort to survive?

Any reminder that wasn't still lodged in flesh, Surreal thought as she felt the rasp in her breathing. She would need to take care for the rest of this winter, but her lungs would eventually heal completely. Rainier's leg, on the other hand, would never be the same.

She opened the bathroom door, intending to claim her half of the shelves and storage space, and heard movement in the next room. She rapped on the door.

"It's open," he said.

She opened the door, then leaned on the doorframe to study the Warlord Prince who was one of the few men she thought of as a friend.

When they returned to Amdarh after spending Winsol at the Keep with the rest of the SaDiablo family, he'd retreated during the last half of the holiday, claiming he needed time to get ready for this little "adventure" in Ebon Rih. She hadn't challenged him because she had her own preparations to make for this stay.

Looking at him, she regretted that decision.

He'd lost weight in those few days. All the Blood burned up food faster than landens did, and the darker the Jewel a person wore, the more food was required to keep the body from consuming itself. Rainier obviously hadn't been eating enough to sustain what had been a very fine build. His face looked leaner and harder, those dreamy green eyes were shadowed by more than one kind of pain, and the brown hair that was usually worn stylishly shaggy looked unkempt.

Rainier's leg would never be the same, no matter how skilled the Healer—and he hadn't been helping. What none of them could figure out was *why* he seemed determined to prevent that leg from healing as completely as possible.

"Want some help unpacking?" she asked.

"I can still take care of myself," he snapped as he grabbed several carefully folded shirts and fisted wrinkles into all of them.

"I didn't say otherwise, sugar."

She knew he heard the warning in the word "sugar," because he gave her a long look.

Have you seen Falonar yet?

It was there, on the edge of being said, a deliberately hurtful punch to the heart. But he didn't say it. She saw the decision in his eyes not to throw that emotional fist.

"Have you finished your own unpacking?" he asked.

"Mostly. I was just about to claim my share of the bathroom space when I heard you moving around in here."

He snorted. "Will I have *any* room for my things?"

"As our friend Karla would say, kiss kiss."

He laughed and held out the shirts. "Fine. Just put the

clothes where it will be logical to find them. And I mean male logic, not what passes for female logic."

"My, my. Aren't we feeling pissy today?"

He limped over to the corner of the room that had a stuffed chair and footrest, as well as a reading lamp and side table. Settling in the chair and stretching out his legs, he sighed wearily. "Did Lucivar not consider the stairs when he chose this place, or were the rooms being on the second floor one of the reasons he chose it?"

"I'm not sure that was a consideration at all," she said slowly as she put Rainier's clothes into the drawers and closet. Before she could decide how much to tell him—especially since there wasn't anything definite she *could* tell him—someone knocked on the door.

"It's Jaenelle," Rainier said before she had a chance to send out a psychic tendril and find out who was in the hallway.

"How do you know?" she asked as she walked to the door.

"Her psychic scent was always unique. It's a little different now that she wears Twilight's Dawn, but there's no mistaking it."

Which just proved a Queen was a Queen whether she ruled officially or not. Unless there was a reason to pay attention, psychic scents were ignored in the same way as physical scents. But a male who served in a court would always know when his Queen was nearby.

"Is the fact that you're all still that observant something you don't want to call attention to?" Surreal asked as she opened the door.

"Call attention to what?" Jaenelle asked as she walked into the room.

"An unobservant man makes a poor flirt," Rainier said. His green eyes glittered with a warning to drop the subject.

"If that's the case, you're very observant, Prince," Jaenelle said. "No, stay there," she added when he started to shift in order to get to his feet. "I can check the leg just fine where you're sitting. Surreal, do you want to sit on the side of the bed or go back to your room for privacy?"

"That depends on what we're doing," Surreal replied warily.

"I'm here to assess your current health and report it to the Prince of Ebon Rih, along with my requirements for what can and cannot be included in your training."

"I get tired easily, and my lungs still get raspy if I exert myself too much, especially outdoors," Surreal said. "And I still feel weak, so I won't be able to do much of the training Lucivar has in mind."

Jaenelle waited a beat, then looked at Rainier. "No protest or snarls from the Warlord Prince, which means he was aware of these limitations—and your Healer was not."

Rainier winced when Surreal stared at him. *Sorry. I didn't know you hadn't talked to her yet.*

Yeah. Surreal looked into Jaenelle's sapphire eyes, judged the sharpness of the temper she saw there, and meekly sat on the side of Rainier's bed.

Jaenelle rested her hands on Surreal's chest, her fingers spread wide. Warmth flowed from that touch. Surreal felt it on her skin, then in her muscles. A slow, soothing, pleasant sensation—and as she drifted on and in that sensation, her body told Jaenelle every secret it had.

So, Jaenelle said on a distaff thread, *are you just trying to avoid some of the training or are you exaggerating the severity of the damage you sustained while in the spooky house to misguide Rainier for some reason?*

The chill that flowed along that psychic thread surprised her. She hadn't expected Jaenelle to be so pissed off about what was, after all, a ploy to get out of spending more time with the Eyriens than she absolutely had to. Then she realized she hadn't taken into account that Jaenelle wasn't just a Healer and she wasn't just family. She was also a Queen who had never hesitated to defend a member of her court— and no matter whom he worked for or served in the future, Rainier would always be hers. Lying to him would not be acceptable behavior.

I told Rainier the truth, Surreal said. *But I didn't want everyone to know.*

The chill faded and was replaced by sharp humor. *You don't want Lucivar to know that you haven't recovered fully because he'll fuss over you, but you still want him to release you from a lot of the training?*

When put that way, the logic sounded more than a little fuzzy. *I was hoping that, as a Healer, you could ... Hell's fire, I hate feeling weak.*

All the more reason to do the work that will make you strong again.

Surreal sighed. How could you argue with a woman who, just by standing there, was proof of how doing the work could help a body to heal?

She studied Jaenelle's face, looked into the eyes that saw too much. It wasn't just her body that had been damaged and felt weak. Her heart, too, hadn't healed since she left Falonar's eyrie and Ebon Rih. That was almost a year ago. Wasn't that long enough to let go of something other women could have shrugged off in a few weeks?

"Give me a half an hour to work on Rainier's leg and go over a few things with Lucivar," Jaenelle said. "Then you and I can take a walk around the village. That will give me a better assessment of what your lungs can do in this weather and in this valley."

"Lucivar is downstairs now, waiting for a report?" Had the prick been sitting there a few minutes ago when she had contacted him?

"Of course he is," Jaenelle said.

"Shit." She wasn't ready to deal with Lucivar. Not yet, anyway. Meeting him tonight to discuss The Tavern was one thing; meeting a bossy relative when he had nothing to do except keep an eye on her was quite another matter. "I'll meet you downstairs after your chat with Lucivar."

"Smart plan," Jaenelle said. "Now shoo."

A friendly dismissal was still a dismissal. Surreal scurried to her own room and looked around again. No clock. She called in a one-hour hourglass that she carried with her, turned it, and set it on the dresser. Meeting Jaenelle a few minutes late wouldn't matter. Being a few minutes early and running into Lucivar . . .

As a way to pass the time, she pulled out the stack of books and took a better look at them. Some she put aside, having no interest in them; others she set with the Tracker and Shadow books to read in the evenings. Maybe she would find a story in one of the collections to share with the rest of the family during one of the evenings when they gathered together for a story night.

She looked at a story, read a few paragraphs, then glanced at the hourglass to see how much time was left before she could go downstairs and not run into Lucivar.

And wondered when she had become a coward.

Rainier hobbled around the room, putting the rest of his things away as he tried to ignore the pain in his leg—and the deeper pain in his heart.

As a Healer, Jaenelle wasn't pleased with him. As a friend, she was furious with him. And he didn't want to think about how she would have responded if she'd still formally been his Queen.

He didn't want to talk about this. Not with Jaenelle, not with Daemon Sadi, and certainly not with Lucivar. He didn't want pity. He'd had a bellyful of pity when he went to Dharo to visit his family. Worse than the pity was the unspoken hope he'd seen in too many of their eyes that a crippled leg would somehow diminish the nature of a Warlord Prince so they wouldn't feel as uncomfortable being around him. He was less now. He had no future now. A dancer who couldn't dance? He'd need to depend on his family and take whatever pity-work they could find for him to help pay his way, since, of course, he would have to return to Dharo and live with one of them.

They didn't understand the depth of their cruelty. He'd seen that too when he'd talked to them. They did love him in their own way, but they saw his being born into the caste of aggressive, violent, dominant males as a failing of the bloodlines instead of seeing him as strength. He wasn't like them. Had never been like them. Had never fit into the family. Different tastes, different temperament—and a difference in caste that had made him an outsider even as a child.

He didn't know what to do. He was too damaged to go back to the life he'd known, but he wasn't damaged enough for his family to feel safe in his presence. He'd never done anything to harm any of them, but they couldn't quite hide their regret that his power hadn't ended up as crippled as his leg.

He loved them. He truly did.

And he never wanted to see them again.

Which left him wondering what a maimed Warlord Prince was supposed to do with the rest of his life.

A hard rap on the door. Before he could respond, Lucivar walked into the room.

How was he supposed to explain to an Eyrien warrior like Lucivar what his leg couldn't do? He'd seen Lucivar on a practice field, and he'd seen him in a real fight. The Prince of Ebon Rih was another kind of dancer, and he was brilliant on a killing field.

Right now, that fact scared the shit out of Rainier because, for the next few weeks, Lucivar controlled his life.

"You need to understand a couple of things about your stay in Ebon Rih," Lucivar said as he walked up to Rainier.

Rainier saw Lucivar's mouth curve into a lazy, arrogant smile. He never saw the fist that smashed into him so hard that the blow knocked him off his feet and tossed him on the bed. While he lay there, struggling to breathe, Lucivar leaned over him and pressed a hand against his pain-filled ribs, pinning him to the bed.

"Listen up, boyo, because I will only say this once," Lucivar said. "I don't know what's riding you, and I don't care. From now on, you work it out some other way than damaging that leg. I know exactly the condition you're in right now. I know exactly what you need to do to heal and bring that leg back to the best it can be. And that's what you're going to do. But if you need to be a cripple, I will help you be a cripple. I will shatter your other leg into so many pieces, even Jaenelle won't be able to give you back more than the ability to hobble around with a pair of canes and spend most of your life in a chair. Do you understand me?"

"Yes," Rainier gasped.

"Do you have any doubt that I will do what I say?"

"No."

Lucivar eased back. "There are places an easy walk from The Tavern where you can get breakfast. Think of not dealing with the little beast first thing in the morning as a reward for sincere effort in the training. You start getting sloppy . . ."

Lucivar using breakfast with his boy as a threat made Rainier curious about what really went on in the Yaslana household in the morning.

Then again, Lucivar didn't bother to bluff, so it probably was a real threat.

"I'll see you on the practice field tomorrow," Lucivar said as he walked to the door. "Don't be late."

A bitter anger filled Rainier. "You don't know what it's like."

Lucivar stopped. He turned and gave Rainier a hard stare. Then he was gone.

Rainier waited another minute before he struggled to sit up. Hell's fire, he hurt. He pulled his shirt up and gathered his courage before he looked down.

A fist-sized bruise was already rising dark along his ribs, but there was nothing broken. Nothing even cracked, if his timid probing could be believed. A punishing blow, but Lucivar must have done something to temper that blow to avoid breaking bone.

Still hurt like a wicked bitch.

Rainier lowered his shirt and carefully stood up to finish his unpacking.

But if you need to be a cripple, I will help you be a cripple.

Lucivar Yaslana didn't bluff, and he rarely gave second chances.

How was he supposed to explain to such an active, physical man that there were things he could no longer do?

"I'm trying to decide how hard I should kick your ass," Jaenelle said pleasantly as she and Surreal strolled down Riada's streets.

Mother Night, it was *cold* in the valley. Surreal felt the burn in her lungs, and she couldn't hide the raspy sound of each breath. She began to dread the time she'd have to spend higher up in the mountains, not just because she'd be around the Eyriens, but because of how hard it would be on her lungs.

"Doesn't bother me much when I'm inside," she said. Unless the fire was smoky. Which wasn't a concern at the family's town house. Helton dealt with anything that might delay her healing by the tiniest bit, whether it was a smoky fire or a potential draft. "I'm drinking the healing brew you made up for me, three times a day. I'm resting. I'm keeping my chest protected and warm. I'm doing everything you told me to do in order to heal. Do you think I want to feel like this for the rest of my life?"

"No, you're smart enough to take care of yourself, if for no other reason than to keep Lucivar and Daemon from breathing down your neck every day and challenging everything you want to do."

"Damn right."

Jaenelle smiled. "That's enough fresh air for today— and enough information about your physical health to give Lucivar firm boundaries for what you can and can't do for this training he's inflicting on you."

"Thank the Darkness."

Laughing, Jaenelle raised a hand to catch the attention of the driver of a horse-drawn cab coming down the street. The driver nodded and pulled up next to them. A Warlord got out and smiled as he helped them into the cab and asked their destination. After conveying the information to the driver, he closed the door and stepped back.

"He's going to walk the rest of the way to wherever he was going or catch another cab, isn't he?" Surreal asked.

"Yes, he is," Jaenelle replied.

"Was that for my benefit or yours?"

"Mine. I think." Jaenelle sighed. "When I was still healing, you did me a favor—you convinced Lucivar to stop coddling me and help me get stronger. I'm going to return the favor. I needed to work; you need to be able to step back, especially now when we're still in the sharp edge of winter."

"Meaning?"

"More private instruction rather than the public training that could expose you to a chill."

The look in Jaenelle's sapphire eyes told her she wasn't talking about just the weather.

"Thank you."

Jaenelle hesitated. "Lucivar is worried about you. Take care with his heart, Surreal. You're not the only one here who can get hurt."

She nodded and looked out the cab window.

Backwinging, Lucivar landed on the road near a large, three-story stone house on the outskirts of Doun, the Blood village at the southern end of Ebon Rih. He hesitated. Then, swearing at himself for that hesitation, he went through the gate in the low stone wall that separated two acres of tended land from the wildflowers and grasses now buried under knee-deep snow. No vegetable garden had been planted last summer. Marian had cleaned up the herb garden, flower gardens, and rock garden, letting the plants reseed themselves. Making use of the labor portion of the tithes owed him, he'd had some of Doun's residents keep the beds weeded and the grass trimmed. A few of the women came twice a month to give the house a light cleaning.

Empty rooms, cleansed of psychic scents and memories.

It had been Luthvian's house for a lot of years, a place Saetan had built for her as a courtesy to the woman who had borne him a son. A Black Widow and a Healer, she had earned her living teaching Craft to the girls in Doun, as well as being one of the village's Healers.

Never content, she hadn't appreciated the house or the man who had built it for her, had never appreciated the son who would have loved her if she'd shown him any affection instead of hating him for the very things her own bloodline had given him—the wings and the arrogance inherent in an Eyrien male.

She had died in this house, killed by Hekatah SaDiablo shortly before Jaenelle unleashed her full power and cleansed the Realms of the tainted Blood.

A young Warlord named Palanar had also died there at Hekatah's hand. He'd been at the service fair, along with many other Eyriens, hoping for a better life. He'd barely had a taste of that future before it had been taken away from him.

The only consolation was that Hekatah and Dorothea SaDiablo had finally been destroyed and couldn't take any-one's future away again.

Lucivar released his breath in a white-plumed sigh.

Land and house no longer held any memories of those deaths, or the violence that came after, but he did—and always would.

He didn't bother to circle the house. If something needed fixing, he wouldn't see it in the dark. So he tramped through knee-deep snow to the corner of the property where a stand of trees whispered *forest*. Dark, bare limbs entwined with the night sky until it looked like stars were caught in the branches.

His house now, one of the properties his father had as-signed to his care after Saetan stepped back from the living Realms and retired to the Keep. He could sell it. Hell's fire, he could burn the damn thing to the ground and no one would challenge the choice.

Maybe that was why he could keep it.

He sensed Surreal's presence the moment she took the first step onto this land, but he decided not to notice until she told him she was there.

"Do you have any happy memories connected to this place?" Surreal's voice came out of the dark a few heart-beats later, enhanced by Craft to reach him.

"None, actually," he replied, also using Craft. "Luthvian and I rarely remained civil to each other through a whole visit."

"Then why keep it?"

"The house belongs to the family. I'm responsible for it."

"Doesn't have any sentimental value to me. I could lob a ball of witchfire through a window and give it enough power to burn this place from attic to cellar."

He laughed softly as he turned toward her. "Thanks for the offer, but I'm going to keep the place intact for the time being." He tramped back to the house, where she waited.

"Why?" She sounded genuinely curious.

"It's a good, solid structure that was built as a Healer's House. Plenty of land with it for gardens. Doun could use another Healer."

"So you're thinking of renting it to a Healer?" Surreal asked.

He shrugged, then said quietly, "Or maybe find a teacher with backbone and heart and turn it into a residence for children who need a safe place."

He shifted, not comfortable talking about an idea he hadn't voiced to anyone else, not even Marian.

"So," Surreal said. "You want to tell me why I'm staying at The Tavern?"

"Because I'm saving the guest room at the eyrie as punishment if you start whining about the training you need," he replied.

He studied her face, then opened his inner barriers enough to get a taste of her psychic scent.

Hunter. Predator. Assassin. That surprised him—and intrigued him.

"If you don't like it, you're free to choose another place," he said, watching her carefully.

"Those stairs aren't going to be easy on Rainier's leg," she said.

"He can float up and down them the same as he's been doing at his residence in Amdarh."

"All right, Yaslana. Let's stop dancing. Is there some reason you want a knife under Merry's roof?"

He blinked. Took a step back. "How in the name of Hell did you come up with an idea like that?"

"Tiger Eye and Summer-sky running a very public business. You wandering in at least once a day. Makes me wonder if Merry and Briggs need that kind of protection. Makes me wonder if you wanted protection there that wouldn't be so obvious."

It was tempting to agree, tempting to let her run with that idea. But if he did that, sooner or later the truth would bite him in the ass.

"It's not like that. Lady Shayne doesn't eat at The Tavern, but if there was trouble there, her court would know about it and take care of it." He huffed out a breath. "Look. I'm scorned by some because I don't rub elbows with the aristos in Riada—or anywhere else for that matter. But the truth is, when I'm among those people, I am the Warlord Prince of Ebon Rih. Aristos never forget that, so I can never forget that. But when I walk into The Tavern, I'm Lucivar. I get teased; I get scolded; I get sent on errands. I sit at a table with a bowl of stew and the bread *I've* picked up from the bakery for Merry and hear the village's gossip—who needs help, who needs watching. I hear about families in the other villages in Ebon Rih. I hear all the things an aristo wouldn't and the Queens' courts probably don't. And if I hear something I think Shayne needs to know, I will tell her.

"More than that, Merry and Briggs are friends. And lighter Jewels notwithstanding, they would fit in with Jaenelle's First Circle. Because of that, I thought you and Rainier would be comfortable there. If that's not the case . . ." He shrugged. Marian had voiced the concern that Surreal and Rainier both ran in Amdarh's aristo society and might not like The Tavern. Maybe his darling hearth witch had been right about that.

"So you drop by every day that you're home to keep an eye on the village and listen to the talk that might alert you and Riada's Queen to a problem?" Surreal asked.

"Sure."

"What a boot full of shit."

He stiffened. "I beg your pardon?"

She let out a hoot of laughter. "You're like a damn Sceltie who's handpicked his own flock, and Merry is one of the sheep. Sure, you run errands and put up with being scolded, but I bet you know when her moontime is supposed to start each cycle, and you get bossy when you think she's working too hard. I bet you've even stood behind the bar and served drinks with Briggs after pushing her upstairs to take the nap you decided she needed."

Caught. "What's your point?" Not that he was going to admit to any of this.

"Just making an observation that there is a dual purpose to your visits to The Tavern. And it's good to know there's no trouble for Merry or—" She started coughing. It sounded like her chest was being ripped up.

Swearing, he pulled her close, wrapped his wings to form a cocoon, and created a warming spell around them.

"Damn it, Surreal. Why didn't you tell me you were this sick? We could have had this discussion inside."

She leaned her forehead against his chest. "Don't like being weak. And I'm not that sick."

"Are you coughing blood? And don't try to lie to me or this will get very unpleasant."

"No blood. Jaenelle would have told you if I was coughing up blood."

"Unless you didn't mention it to her."

She laughed a little. It sounded liquid and rough. "I'm not stupid, Lucivar. I'm not going to tangle with Witch over the condition of my lungs."

"All right." He rubbed her back and waited for his heart to settle back into its normal rhythm. "Look. Maybe . . ."

She punched him. Wasn't much of a punch since she was snugged up against him, but it was still a punch.

"This is what you have to work with," she growled. "Deal with it."

"Remember you said that in the days ahead."

"Ah, shit."

He eased back. "Come on, witchling. It's time to get you back to your room. The days start early here."

Rainier waited in his room, as ordered. Apparently Lucivar had a few more things to say to him before he officially started this required training.

But when Lucivar rapped on the door and came in, Rainier felt a jolt of uneasiness because Saetan came in with him.

"High Lord," Rainier said, struggling to get to his feet. Where had he put that damn cane?

"Prince Rainier," Saetan replied. Then he looked at Lucivar and raised one eyebrow as a question.

Lucivar stared at Rainier before turning to his father. "Do you remember what I looked like when I first came to Kaeleer?"

"I'm not likely to forget," Saetan said softly.

Lucivar tipped his head toward Rainier. "Show him." He walked out of the room.

A light brush of another mind against Rainier's first inner barrier. A familiar, dark, powerful mind. He hesitated, then opened his inner barriers, leaving his mind vulnerable to the High Lord of Hell.

He saw the main room of a cabin, as if he were looking through Saetan's eyes. He saw the memory, but the emotions weren't part of it. There was no indication of what Saetan felt when he'd walked into the cabin.

Comfortable place. Not someplace he'd care to stay for an extended period of time, but it would be fine for a country weekend. He'd never been inside, but he guessed this was Jaenelle's cabin in Ebon Rih.

The memory continued as Saetan walked into the bedroom and froze a few steps from the bed.

Lucivar.

Even the High Lord of Hell couldn't cleanse the memory of emotion well enough to hide the shock, the anguish of seeing the man lying on the bed.

Broken bones, shoulder and ribs. Guts pushing out of the ripped belly. A leg ripped open from hip to knee. A foot hanging awkwardly from what was left of an ankle.

Why had someone placed strands of greasy rags on the bed next to a man who was so terribly wounded?

Not rags, Rainier realized with a shock. Wings. He was looking at what was left of Lucivar's wings.

Saetan withdrew from Rainier's mind. Rainier closed his inner barriers and just stared at the other man for a minute before finding his voice.

"How did he survive?"

Saetan sighed. "He made a choice. He didn't want to die. He'd been in the salt mines of Pruul for five years. The slime mold had destroyed his wings, and the years of slavery in the salt mines had taken their toll, to say nothing of the torture he'd endured. He escaped and made his way to the Khaldharon Run. He wasn't in any shape to make the Run, and he knew it, but he was going to die on his terms. Fortunately, Prothvar was standing guard at the Sleeping Dragons that day and brought Lucivar to Jaenelle's cabin. He wasn't conscious, so I'm sure he didn't make the decision knowingly, but I think he felt Jaenelle and gave her everything he had because she asked him for it. And he healed because of that choice."

Saetan walked to the door and opened it. "Lucivar is downstairs if there is anything you want to say to him. If not, he'll finish his drink and go home."

Rainier waited until Saetan left before he scanned the room. Spotting the cane on the floor by his bed, he used Craft to float it over to him. Then he made his careful way downstairs.

Lucivar was sitting at a table, alone, drinking a glass of ale.

Since no one had noticed him yet, Rainier stood at the bottom of the stairs and observed the people. Mostly men, but a few women were there too, enjoying a drink and some gossip. Frequent glances at Lucivar, and more than one person shifting as if about to join him. But a word from

Briggs or a light touch from Merry deflected that person, letting people know the Prince wanted solitude.

You don't know what it's like. That was what he'd said. Like the rest of the boyos and the coven, he'd met Lucivar after the Eyrien had come to SaDiablo Hall with Jaenelle. A strong, powerful Warlord Prince in his prime, Yaslana dominated a room just by walking into it. Yaslana dominated a killing field just by walking onto it. How could he reconcile the predator who moved with such lethal grace and the torn, broken body that had healed against all odds?

Rainier limped across the room. Merry moved to intercept him. After a quick glance at Lucivar, she let him pass and brought a glass of white wine to the table.

Lucivar studied him, then said quietly, "My right ankle hurts like a wicked bitch when I work it too hard, and I've got a few weather bones, as the old men call them. Small price to pay for having so much of me remade."

Rainier sipped his wine, not sure what to say or ask.

"The ankle does just fine with everyday living, even chasing after the little beast," Lucivar said. "But I've learned how to put a shield around the bone when I'm sparring or in a real fight. Since I'm shielded anyway when I'm on a field, it can't be detected."

"It's a weakness an adversary could exploit," Rainier said.

Lucivar gave him that lazy, arrogant smile. "If the adversary lived long enough." The smile faded. "When I came out of that healing sleep, Jaenelle told me there would be no second chances. She'd used up everything I could give her—and everything she could give me—to rebuild my wings and heal the rest of me. If I did what she told me to do, my body would be whole and sound. If I pushed muscles that were still rebuilding themselves and damaged them, the damage would be permanent." He drained his glass of ale. "You've had more than one second chance, Rainier, and now you've run out of chances. If you'd followed her instructions in the beginning, you would have had a weather bone and muscles that would ache when you worked them too hard. But that leg would have held up for you, even dancing. Now you've lost some of that, maybe a lot of that, because you damaged bone and muscles that were trying to heal."

So by trying to prove I wasn't a cripple and didn't need anyone's pity, I turned myself into a cripple. The bitterness of that truth burned his belly.

"You're a man with a damaged leg," Lucivar said. "That doesn't make you less of a Warlord Prince—unless you choose to cripple that too."

Lucivar pushed his chair back and stood. He raised a hand in farewell. Briggs, who was behind the bar, nodded and mirrored the gesture.

"I'll see you and Surreal tomorrow morning at full light," Lucivar said.

"What time is that?" Rainier asked.

"Your leg's injured, not your head. Figure it out."

Rainier watched Lucivar walk out of The Tavern.

Merry came up to the table. "Want something to eat? I've got some stew left and a hearty soup."

He started to refuse, then realized he was hungry. "A bowl of soup would be welcome."

She brought the soup, along with a small loaf of sweet-and-spice bread and soft cheese. He ate slowly, savoring the flavors. While he ate, he watched the people, especially Merry and Briggs.

He wasn't whole. Might never be whole. Other men had faced that same truth and rebuilt their lives around the strengths they still had and the work they could do.

People had died in Jenkell's damn spooky house. *Children* had died in that house because he hadn't been skilled enough or strong enough to protect them. Was damaging his leg under the guise of helping it get stronger some kind of self-punishment for that failure to protect and defend?

No one else blamed him for the ones he couldn't save. Maybe it was time to stop blaming himself.

TWO

Lucivar landed at the communal eyrie and swore as his right ankle sang with pain. He loved his son. He really did. But this morning he didn't love the little beast quite so much.

He didn't think about the aches and pains that came from broken bones or other wounds. No Eyrien did. They were a part of life, a part of being a warrior. And considering the life he'd led during the seventeen hundred years he'd survived in Terreille, he had fewer aches and pains than most men his age. But having that ankle hurt today pissed him off.

He didn't shield the bone in his own eyrie. It needed to work without that brace made of power, especially since the bones didn't actually *need* that brace. Shielding at all was mostly caution on his part. He'd seen enough men go down in a fight because an enemy knew about previous injuries and aimed blows at the weak spots. No one outside his family had known the extent of his injuries—until last night when he'd allowed Rainier to be shown the truth. No one knew his weak spots. In truth, he didn't have any. Jaenelle was an excellent Healer, and the bones and muscles she'd repaired ten years ago might ache a bit quicker than they had a century ago, but they were whole and healthy.

Regardless of being whole and healthy, having a pot slammed into his ankle still hurt like a wicked bitch. Which he would have avoided if Marian hadn't suddenly gotten sick and begun eliminating food from both ends. So he'd been focused on her and not on the boy.

Just a stomach upset that was going around the village, Nurian had said when she checked Marian and gave him bottles of the tonic she and the Healers in Riada had been making nonstop since yesterday. Marian would be fine by tomorrow. Which meant Daemonar would probably be puking all over the bed tonight.

He could do with fewer thrills in his life. Especially today. But for the next couple of hours, his father was looking after his wife and boy, and he could focus his attention on Surreal and Rainier. Jaenelle had given him the boundaries—and some very specific things each of them shouldn't do—but deciding how to work those bodies to best advantage was up to him. So he needed to be here today to take them through careful moves, assessing muscles to help Surreal and Rainier become as healthy as they could be.

In a couple of days, he could turn the workouts over to Hallevar. But he couldn't give anyone else command today because there was something else he needed to assess.

He stopped for a moment and put a protective shield around the bones of both ankles. Then he walked into the communal eyrie.

The front room was big enough for weapons practice and was also used for occasional social events. This morning the eighteen adult Eyrien males who lived around Riada were waiting for him, including Falonar, his second-in-command; Hallevar, the arms master and fighting instructor who had been one of his own teachers; Kohlvar, who was a weapons maker; Zaranar and Rothvar, who were trained guards and good fighters; Endar, who served as a guard but wasn't really suited to be one; and Tamnar, a youth Hallevar had brought with him to the service fairs to get the young Warlord out of Terreille.

Not a lot of men to guard close to half of Ebon Rih, but when two of those men were Warlord Princes—and one of those Warlord Princes wore Ebon-gray Jewels—nineteen men were quite sufficient to take care of any problems around Riada and Doun that couldn't be handled by the courts of Lady Shayne and Lady Alyss.

Of course, when there were only nineteen men, there wasn't much of a buffer when two of them scraped against each other's tempers. It was no secret that he and Falonar had never liked each other, but they had worked well together these past two years—until recently, anyway. Something had changed in Falonar over the past few weeks—or maybe the excitement of settling in a new place had worn off, and Lucivar was now getting a more accurate look at the man Falonar had become.

He spotted Surreal and Rainier standing off to the side just as Falonar turned to see who had come in.

"The weather is fine," Falonar said. "We should be working outside."

Publicly criticizing or challenging every order he gave was one of the things that had changed in Falonar's behavior in the past few weeks. Nothing wrong with the second-in-command challenging an order in private, but these pissing contests in front of the other men had to stop.

"Well, today we're working inside," Lucivar replied mildly, knowing the mildness would sting Falonar's pride in a way responding with temper couldn't, because, in a situation like this, temper was given only to an equal.

"Only the weak need to work inside on a day like this," Falonar said, putting more bite in his voice even as his face flushed at being spoken to as if he were a boy.

Lucivar studied the other Warlord Prince. The tone of that last remark almost sounded like a challenge. Almost. Falonar had aristo arrogance on top of Eyrien arrogance, but he wasn't stupid. He knew Sapphire couldn't survive a fight with Ebon-gray.

"Fine," Lucivar said dismissively. "Hallevar, Tamnar, you're in here with me. Falonar, you can take the others out to play in the snow if that's what you need to do."

Falonar's gold eyes blazed with anger. He shifted his weight into a fighting stance.

The door opened, and Jillian rushed in.

Both men turned toward the girl who had shifted a little more toward being a woman in the past few months.

"You're supposed to be in school," Lucivar said at the same time Falonar said, "You're supposed to be home doing chores."

Jillian lifted her chin. "I want to be here. I can learn to fight, same as Tamnar."

"I forbid it," Falonar said.

"You *what*?" Surreal said, taking a step toward Falonar.

All the Warlords flinched at the cutting edge in her voice and took a step back, indicating they wanted no part of this fight.

Lucivar swore silently. Great. Fine. Wonderful. Just what he needed—Surreal being pissed off at Falonar. Or more pissed off than usual. On the other hand, if they took a couple of swings at each other, maybe that would clear the air a bit.

Falonar rounded on Surreal and said viciously, "Just because you want to grow a pair of balls doesn't mean I should permit an Eyrien girl to do the same."

"Growing a pair of balls is easy," Surreal snarled. "Growing a heart, that's a lot more difficult."

"This is none of your business," Falonar shouted.

"And none of yours," she shouted back. "Just because you're humping her sister—"

"*Surreal!*" Rainier snapped.

"—doesn't give you the right to control Jillian's life!"

"Damn right!" Lucivar roared loudly enough to make everyone flinch. Even Surreal, although *she* was the one who looked ready to ram a knife between his ribs, which was a sharp reminder that dealing with a Dea al Mon witch wasn't the same as dealing with an Eyrien witch. "If anyone gets to control someone's life around here, *it's me*." He pointed at Jillian, then pointed to a corner of the room that was away from the men. "You. Over there." He pointed at Surreal, then pointed at the other far corner. "You. Over there."

Surreal bared her teeth. Her right hand curled.

He wasn't sure if that was a habitual reaction when she was angry or if she was now holding a sight-shielded stiletto.

"Witchling, if you want to kiss dirt, I will let you have the first punch."

He waited, watching her.

She stormed over to the corner he'd indicated. Thank the Darkness for that.

Lucivar turned to Falonar and kept his voice low. "What in the name of Hell is wrong with you? Did you wake up this morning and decide to piss off everyone with tits?"

"She doesn't belong here," Falonar said, keeping his voice just as low. "If we lived as Eyriens should live, she wouldn't have tried to be here. And we wouldn't have to tolerate outsiders among us."

"Surreal is not an outsider. She's a member of my family."

He saw the disgust in Falonar's eyes, the contempt, and almost heard the word Falonar didn't quite dare say. At least, not yet. *Half-breed.* For most Eyriens, family had to do with having the proper bloodlines. Lucivar didn't give a damn about bloodlines. For him, family was about heart.

"If she was good enough to sleep with, she's good enough for everything else," he said too softly.

"Tell that to all the men who paid her to spread her legs."

He didn't play by anyone else's rules, and since Falonar seemed to want him to start a fight over the way Surreal used to earn a living, he wasn't going to oblige.

"Well," Lucivar said with a savage smile, "if that's how you feel about her, I'll have her tally up your bill."

As he walked away from Falonar, he glanced at Surreal, decided she wouldn't explode in the next few minutes—at least, not at anyone but him—and went to the corner where Jillian waited, looking scared and defiant.

Resting one hand on the wall, he spread his wings to give them some privacy. It occurred to him that he could have created a sight shield and aural shield around them—

and he knew that he would seriously hurt any man who cut off a young girl in that way from the watchful eyes of other adults.

"Why aren't you in school?" he asked quietly.

"Because I want to be here." Her voice trembled, but she looked him in the eyes.

Girl has balls, he thought. Of course, running tame in his home might have something to do with it, since she watched Daemonar and was used to being around him. But this was different, and they both knew it.

"School is important," he said.

"So is this."

All kinds of messages in those three words. And he hadn't forgotten what he'd been told about the attack on the Eyriens here two years ago. Hallevar had made light of it at the time to spare the girl's feelings, but Jillian had killed her first man that day, putting an arrow in the bastard's heart. That had been the main reason he'd let her continue an informal kind of training after it became clear that the other women wanted no part of that training.

"Has anyone tried to hurt you, Jillian?"

She hesitated. "Not here."

Not here could explain why Nurian had made the decision to take her younger sister and emigrate to Kaeleer.

"Practice and training are done in the morning," Jillian said.

True enough, but this morning just proved that being around the men wasn't the right time for Jillian's training, not if Falonar was going to snap and snarl the whole time the girl was with them.

He closed his wings and lowered his hand. "You go on to school now. You tell the teacher you're late because I kept you. If she has a problem with that, she can talk to me."

"But ..."

"If you don't give me any sass about this, I will figure out how to work in some regular, formal training for you." Especially now, when the girl might be a good working partner for both Surreal and Rainier.

Jillian's shoulders relaxed. She smiled shyly. "Yes, sir."

He stepped aside and watched her run out of the eyrie, her steps light. Then he walked over to his next problem, who looked ready to tear out his throat with her teeth.

With her black hair and sun-kissed brown skin, Surreal looked like a beautiful woman from Dhemlan or Hayll—until a man noticed the delicately pointed ears. They were an indication, and warning, of her other bloodline. Just as he had a dual heritage of Hayllian and Eyrien but was Eyrien in every way that counted, Surreal was Dea al Mon, one of the Children of the Wood. They were a fiercely private and feral race who lived closer to the land than any other humans. And because they seemed to be born knowing what to do with a knife, they were deadly.

He wasn't afraid of Surreal—he was a Warlord Prince and his Jewels outranked hers—but he never forgot the Dea al Mon side of her nature when he dealt with her temper.

That didn't mean he wouldn't give her a kick in the ass if she needed one.

He braced one hand near Surreal's head and, again, opened his wings and curved them to provide some privacy.

"You dismissed her because she doesn't have balls," Surreal said.

"That's insulting," Lucivar said. "You should know me better than that."

She stared at him.

He blew out a breath. "I sent her to school, which is where a girl her age belongs."

"And the training she wants?"

"I'll work that out somehow, although you might not be as happy with your training schedule because of it."

The angry heat faded from her gold-green eyes, replaced by reluctant amusement.

"Now, I've got a wife at home who started the day by puking and shitting herself. I expect my son will start puking and shitting any minute, which I'm sure will delight my father to no end. So we can do your training assessment here or in the front room of my eyrie, where you'll most likely get to participate in today's adventures."

"Those are my choices?"

"Yeah. Those are your choices."

"In that case, sugar—"

"Go easy, now!" Hallevar said sharply.

Lucivar's head whipped around toward the other men. He'd heard the *clack* of sparring sticks, but he hadn't paid attention to a usual sound when he had a Gray-Jeweled witch in front of him brimming with anger.

Too late, he thought, seeing Falonar connect with the sparring stick Rainier held and knowing how a man would step in response to that move. He reached out with Craft as Rainier's leg gave out, intending to catch the man and stop the fall that would cause more damage to already damaged muscle and bone. But his power tangled with Sapphire power, fouling his and Falonar's attempts to stop the fall.

Rainier cried out in pain as he hit the stone floor—and they all heard bone snap.

"*No!*" Surreal screamed. She rushed over and dropped to her knees beside Rainier at the same moment Lucivar reached Falonar and shoved the Eyrien back a step—and wondered why the man had a Sapphire shield around himself for what should have been a slow warm-up.

"I tried to catch him," Falonar said, sounding regretful.

Except that particular tone of regret made Lucivar think of the hunting camp and the boys who had been hurt during training exercises. It was an aristo tone that meant the boy who had done the harm wasn't sorry at all.

"What's wrong with you?" Lucivar shouted.

"Nothing is wrong with *me*," Falonar snapped. "I just proved what you should have known—a *cripple* doesn't have any place among Eyrien warriors."

Surreal threw herself at Falonar, her scream of rage startling Lucivar enough that he put a skintight Red shield around himself. He grabbed the back of her shirt before she reached Falonar, and began a spin that would lift her away from the other Eyrien.

She lashed out with her right hand as she was lifted and tossed away from the men.

Lucivar felt Falonar's Sapphire shield break under a punch of Surreal's Gray power as she lashed out. Saw the blood on the Eyrien's left arm. Felt the big knife that slid on his Red shield instead of slicing him along the waist as Falonar responded with a counterattack. Tossing Surreal aside, Lucivar continued the spin, calling in his own fighting knife.

By the time he faced Falonar, he was armed, he was balanced, and he was ready.

The fury in Falonar's eyes was aimed right at him, but the man stepped back and lowered his knife.

Lucivar glanced at Falonar's left arm. A deep slice through muscle, freely bleeding.

"Surreal," he said, never taking his eyes off the other Warlord Prince, "go to the Keep. Now."

"I'll go back to The Tavern after—"

"Unless you want a knife dance with me, you will do as you're told," he snapped.

As he felt her stare at his back, he'd never been more aware of how much of her temper and inclinations came from her Dea al Mon heritage.

There were good reasons why the Children of the Wood were feared by the other races in Kaeleer.

She moved slowly, circling around him and Falonar.

"*Prince* Falonar may have proved that a cripple has no place among Eyriens, but I just proved he wouldn't have survived that demon-dead bastard any better than Rainier did."

Mother Night, she's riding the killing edge. The wild look in her eyes wasn't quite sane. That, more than anything else, was why males didn't want witches involved in physical fighting. Females were a lot harder to control once they rose to the killing edge.

"Go to the Keep," he said firmly. "I will deal with this." *And I'll hurt you if I have to.*

The moment she walked out of the communal eyrie and it was safe to move without provoking an attack, Zaranar and Rothvar rushed over to Rainier.

Rothvar's hand hovered over Rainier's leg. "Hell's fire, there are healing spells already holding those muscles and bone together."

Lucivar backed away from Falonar, who stood straight and proud despite the bleeding arm.

"Get that arm tended," he said. "I'll talk to you later."

Falonar looked at the wound that had come from the sight-shielded blade held by a furious woman. "What is there to say?"

Plenty, Lucivar thought. "Get it tended."

He waited until Falonar left before sending out a call on an Ebon-gray spear thread. *Daemon!*

Lucivar?

I need Jaenelle here as a Healer. Now.

Who?

Rainier.

We'll be there.

The link between them snapped as Daemon shut him out. He didn't take offense. He'd just dumped a basket of problems in his brother's lap, the most dangerous being the Queen they both loved and still served—the Queen who was also a Black Widow and a Healer. There wasn't going to be anything pleasant about being in a Coach with Jaenelle while riding the Winds to Ebon Rih, not after telling her that Rainier was the reason for the urgent call.

Vanishing his knife, Lucivar looked at Rainier, who lay on the floor, his eyes closed, his face tight with pain. Then he looked at the two Warlords. "Can you get him to the Keep?"

They nodded. Using Craft, they lifted Rainier and gently floated him out of the eyrie.

Hallevar looked at the rest of the Warlords, then jerked a thumb toward the door.

The men bolted, no doubt glad to be clear of the anger and whatever problems were coming.

"Falonar is a Sapphire-Jeweled Warlord Prince and your second-in-command," Hallevar said. "I trained you both when you were youngsters in the hunting camps, and that gives me some leave to speak my mind, but a Warlord Prince only tolerates so much of that."

Lucivar just waited.

"It started with Falonar saying something about assessing Rainier's skills, and Rainier saying he thought it was best to wait for you. Guess that didn't sit well with Falonar because the next thing I knew, he tossed a sparring stick to Rainier and started the moves. Once you're that far, the choice is counter the moves or get whacked. I began watching close. You'd said the Dharo Warlord Prince had been wounded in a fight and you had him here to heal and improve his skills. I don't think you said how bad the leg was. That's not an excuse, but I don't think you actually said."

"A war blade sliced through the muscles of Rainier's leg and halfway through the bone. He was fighting a demon-dead Eyrien Warlord who had worn Jewels stronger than Opal," Lucivar said.

"Then Rainier never had a chance."

"No. He wasn't supposed to have a chance. He wasn't supposed to survive. No one who had been trapped in that spooky house was supposed to survive."

Hallevar sighed. "I don't know what's wrong with Falonar lately, but I do know it's something to do with you."

Lucivar echoed the sigh. "Not surprising."

"Not surprising," Hallevar agreed. "But I think you'd best find out why."

ThRee

Lucivar and Daemon waited in one of the Keep's sitting rooms while Jaenelle did what she could for Rainier.

Daemon had blocked him from talking to Jaenelle when they arrived at the Keep. She'd gone to the room where Rainier had been taken; Lucivar had ended up prowling a sitting room with a brother whose effort to control an icy temper was much too obvious.

"How angry is she over this?" Lucivar finally asked.

"Old son, you don't want to ask that question," Daemon replied softly.

"It wasn't Rainier's fault. Something's been pushing at him and he's been stupid about the leg because of it, but this wasn't his fault."

"He's not the only one who has something pushing at him," Daemon said. "I've been informed, discreetly, that Surreal isn't sleeping well, is up reading or just pacing in the town house's sitting room through the wee hours of the morning. She locked down so tightly after getting out of the spooky house, I don't think she's allowed herself to feel. Sooner or later that control will break."

"And things will get messy."

He circled the room a couple of times before Daemon said, "What's chewing on you?"

"A lot of things, but the one bothering me the most is *how* she went after Falonar. Sight-shielded knife. Man sees a pissed-off woman throwing herself at him with nothing

visible in her hands, he thinks of fists and flailing and angry
words and boohooing. She knew that. She didn't challenge
him, didn't square off for a fight."

"She's not Eyrien, and she's not male. Surreal doesn't
play by those rules."

"Sometimes she does," Lucivar said. "Sometimes she'll
draw the line, and there's no mistake she's looking for a
punch-and-roll brawl. But she wasn't interested in giving a
warning this time. She went for him, Daemon. If I hadn't
been there, she would have killed him before he'd realized
that was her intent."

"Are you sure that was the intent?"

He nodded. "If I hadn't been swinging her away, she
would have been in position to drive that knife right
through his heart. Even if he realized the intent at the last
moment, Sapphire shields wouldn't have stopped a blade
backed by Gray power. *Didn't* stop a blade backed by the
Gray."

"Do you want to know what I'm wondering?" Daemon
asked. "Surreal has a tendency to kill a man in a way that
balances the harm he did to his prey. She hid a physical
knife. What kind of blade was Falonar hiding—and who
was it aimed at?"

Before he could think of an answer, Jaenelle walked
into the room.

"Kindly inform Prince Falonar that if he gets near
Prince Rainier again, I will strip his legs, muscle by muscle,
until there is nothing left but skin and bone."

Hell's fire, Mother Night, and may the Darkness be
merciful. The look in her eyes made Lucivar shiver, made
his knees weak. This was no idle warning, no embellished
expression of anger. Jaenelle meant exactly what she said,
and though she no longer wore Black or Ebony Jewels,
there was more than enough power in Twilight's Dawn to
deal with a Sapphire-Jeweled Warlord Prince.

Daemon rose, a deliberate move to draw her attention,
for which Lucivar was grateful.

"How is Rainier?" Daemon asked.

"He tore muscles that were already held together with healing spells and spider silk, and the bone is broken all the way through," she snapped. "How do you think he is?"

They said nothing.

Jaenelle closed her eyes and took several deep breaths. When she looked at them again, sharp temper was still there but so was the usual control. "My apologies, Prince Sadi. You don't deserve my anger."

"No, I don't," Daemon replied, "but I'm not feeling polite right now either, so I understand."

"Rainier wants to see you. I suggest you go now. He won't be awake much longer."

Lucivar waited until Daemon left the room before asking, "Will Rainier be able to walk on that leg?"

Jaenelle rubbed her hands over her face. When she let her hands fall, he saw the frustration and regret in her eyes. "He'll walk. I'm not sure he'll be able to do more than that at this point, but he should be able to walk."

Sorrow burned in his chest. "I'll work with him. Whatever it takes, I'll work with him."

Jaenelle sank into a chair. "I meant what I said about Falonar."

He looked at her—and remembered that some of who and what *she* was had also come from the Dea al Mon. "I know."

Rainier drifted, fighting the sleep he needed, fighting the healing spells and the healing brew for a little while longer.

He heard no sound, but he felt the dark power when Daemon walked into the room and sat beside the bed.

"I feel like something that had been hidden and festering got lanced," he said. "I know if my leg wasn't wrapped in numbing spells, it would hurt like a wicked bitch, but I feel better. Does that make sense?"

"It makes sense to you," Daemon said. "Maybe it's easier to accept when there is no longer a possibility of taking up the life you had."

"Maybe." Was Sadi weaving a soothing spell in his voice,

Rainier wondered, or was it the healing spells that made him feel like he could float on the sound?

"Would you like me to read to you?" Daemon asked.

Rainier laughed. It sounded like heavy syrup. "I'd be asleep before you read the second sentence. I don't want to waste the offer."

"All right. Another time, then."

His arm was so heavy. He wasn't sure he'd actually moved it until Daemon took his hand.

"I want to stay in Ebon Rih. Have a reason to stay now. Jaenelle won't like me staying, so I need you to stand for me."

"Why do you want to stay?"

Something he'd seen in Falonar's eyes, something he'd felt when Falonar's Sapphire and Lucivar's Red powers had crashed into his own effort to keep himself upright, leaving him vulnerable in too many ways. "I'm not sure. . . ."

"Whatever you tell me now will stay between us," Daemon soothed.

As I was falling, I felt Falonar ram against my inner barriers, and with all the power slamming around me, I couldn't keep my mind shut tight, couldn't keep everything private. Might not have been intentional. He could have been flung against me by the Red, but intentional or not, Falonar grabbed at the chance to find something, anything, I might know that he could use against Lucivar. Some secret, some weakness. The pain in my leg . . . I was afraid I wouldn't be able to protect a confidence, so I floated a lie near the surface where it would be easy to find that Lucivar's left ankle was badly damaged when Yaslana first came to Kaeleer, and even now it's weak and wouldn't support him if it received a couple of hard blows in a fight.

Did he say the words? Did he voice the suspicion of what Falonar had hoped to achieve by causing him to fall?

"Shh," Daemon said. "Rest now. I won't act on what you've told me unless I have proof that it's true. And I'll talk to Jaenelle so that you can stay in Ebon Rih for a while."

Having those assurances from the Prince he served, he drifted off to sleep.

Lucivar found Falonar at Nurian's eyrie. Not unexpected since they were lovers and she was the Healer the Eyriens around Riada and Doun came to when they were injured or ill. The Eyriens who lived in camps in the northern end of the valley complained about having to see one of the Rihlander Healers in Agio because there wasn't another Eyrien Healer in Ebon Rih, but there wasn't anything he could do about that. He would have accepted another Healer if one had been willing to sign a contract with him and had the disposition needed to settle comfortably in Kaeleer, but Nurian had been the only one who had been willing to settle in Ebon Rih and live under the rule of a man most Eyriens still thought of as a half-breed bastard despite his bloodlines.

She looked tired. That wasn't unexpected either, considering the number of people who had become ill recently, but he didn't think the strain he saw in her face was due to fatigue.

Falonar was settled in her parlor, his left arm shielded and wrapped to protect the fragile, newly healed muscle and skin. He looked comfortable, but his eyes were yellow stones filled with anger.

"Will the Dharo man prance again?" Falonar asked.

"No," Lucivar replied. "But we're hopeful he'll walk on that leg again. You should be hoping that too, because if he can't walk, neither will you."

"Is that a threat, Yaslana?"

No title, no courtesy in the voice. More and more, Falonar seemed to be forgetting who ruled and who served.

"That, *Prince* Falonar, is the message from an enraged Queen drawing a line and stating what the blood debt will be for damage done to one of her court."

Falonar paled. "There is no court. Hasn't been one for almost two years."

Lucivar huffed out a laugh. "You be sure to explain that

to Witch while she's stripping all the muscle out of your legs."

Falonar paled even more.

"Stay away from Rainier. You won't get another warning. And if the Queen has a reason to go after you, you won't find anyone strong enough to stand in her way who *will* stand in her way. Is that clear?"

"As clear as what passes for Eyrien honor here."

Ah. Lucivar gave Falonar a lazy, arrogant smile. "So let's hear what passed for Eyrien honor in Terreille."

Falonar exploded out of the chair.

Lucivar waited, watching the other man's eyes.

"We're Eyriens who aren't allowed to *be* Eyriens," Falonar snarled. "We should *rule* this valley instead of having to pretend that the Rihlanders are our equals. These mountains should be filled with our kind, but there are less than two hundred Eyriens in Ebon Rih."

"The others who came through the service fair had no interest in living in Ebon Rih," Lucivar said.

"No, they had no interest in living under *you*. Instead of having a new life, they chose to go back to misery rather than serve *you*. The only thing you honor about our race is our fighting skills and what we can do on a killing field. You've cast aside everything else and expect us to accept that, swallow that."

Well, that's interesting. Lucivar shifted his expression into puzzlement. "What else is there beyond what was learned in the hunting camps?"

"Our traditions, our customs, our heritage! You send Jillian to school to learn what? Nothing Eyrien."

"Last time I looked, Eyriens can read the same words and tally the same numbers as Rihlanders or Dhemlans."

"What about our history?"

Now, that *was* a sore spot, since Eyrien history was something he wanted Daemonar to learn. "There aren't any storytellers who can teach the youngsters the old stories," Lucivar said with genuine regret.

"There were some who came to Kaeleer, but none who would come here," Falonar said bitterly.

"That was their decision."

"So you'll condemn the rest of us instead of making an honorable choice?"

"Meaning what?"

"No matter what you say, there is no longer a Queen ruling Ebon Askavi, which means you're no longer bound by any contract to that Queen. Give up Ebon Rih. Let it go to another leader Eyriens *will* follow. Let us build a life here, an *Eyrien* life. And if you won't think of the rest of us, think of your own son. Is he going to grow up as an Eyrien or as a Rihlander with wings?"

"And I suppose you, as the leader the other Eyriens will follow, would make sure he was treated as a young man from an aristo family and not the son of a half-breed bastard?"

He saw the truth in Falonar's eyes.

"Your *family* is wealthy." Falonar spit out the words. "You can live anywhere. Do something for your people. Go live elsewhere and let us have Askavi."

Lucivar smiled. "Funny how all of a sudden you become my people when you want something that would be convenient for you and give me nothing in return. No, Falonar. I am where I choose to live. As for the other Eyriens living in Ebon Rih? I was here first. And the Eyriens who were in this valley before me? They were my uncle and my cousin and the men who served them."

Falonar stared at him for a long time, then said bitterly, "The only Eyrien thing about you is your wings."

As Lucivar walked to the door, he tossed back, "My mother would have been pleased to hear you say that."

FOUR

When a man's ability to move was severely limited, being in a room with Surreal all day was unnerving, especially when her mood kept swinging from being oversolicitous to looking like she'd explode if she didn't rip apart everything in the room. Since he was one of the things in the room, Rainier felt giddy relief when Jaenelle ordered Surreal to take her own walk and rest period.

Then Jaenelle worked on his leg, weaving her healing spells around and through the broken bone and severed muscle. Satisfied that, this time, he had done exactly what he'd been told to do, she had given him permission to sit downstairs this evening and have the passive company of Merry and Briggs's customers.

Wasn't much of a trade in some ways, since Merry was keeping as sharp an eye on him as Surreal had done, but the difference in personalities made him feel easier. Besides, Merry had plenty of other people to look after—and *didn't* look like she wanted to rip out everyone's throat.

Rainier sat at a table with his left leg resting on cushions that floated on air and enough shields around that part of the table to barricade a whole house—and *none* of those shields were his. Still, he was happy to be around other people for a while and concerned that Surreal was taking *another* walk to work off more temper—and he wondered if there was some way for him to find out if there was a problem in Ebon Rih or if Lucivar had a problem with just one man.

Lucivar prowled the sitting room at the Keep. He'd spent the day trying to figure out whom he could talk to who would just let him talk. Marian would have listened, but he didn't want to share this with her. Not yet. Not when it might change how she felt or acted around some of the other Eyriens.

So he'd come to the Keep, wishing he could have talked to his uncle Andulvar, or even Prothvar, but finally choosing the man he hoped could understand.

"I'm not leaving Ebon Rih for any prick-ass's benefit," he said, "but Falonar *was* right about some things." He braced when his father rose from the chair where Saetan had sat silently and passively while Lucivar recounted his discussion with the other Eyrien Warlord Prince. But the High Lord just settled on the wide arm of the big stuffed chair and crossed his arms over his chest.

"Was he?" Saetan asked blandly.

Hell's fire. He'd asked—no, demanded—to be allowed to talk without having to deal with someone else's anger, but this blandness in face and voice hid too much, giving him no clue to Saetan's thoughts or temper.

"What, exactly, was he right about?" Saetan asked.

Lucivar bristled. Couldn't stop himself. "Look, I didn't want to deal with anger, but I didn't say you couldn't express an opinion."

"As long as it's expressed politely?"

He swore savagely. "I was hoping you would understand."

"I do," Saetan said, his voice still viciously bland. "Better, I think, than you do at this moment."

Lucivar snapped to a stop and looked into Saetan's eyes. Something there, something that warned him that he could hear nothing or he could hear it all.

"Stop that." If he had to submit to a scolding, he was *not*

going to listen to it delivered in that bland, no-balls voice—
not from *this* man.

Saetan's gold eyes filled with sharp amusement. "Would
you prefer a whack upside the head? It's what you would
have gotten from your uncle."

"Why?"

The bland expression vanished, which wasn't a relief because now Saetan's face held the look of a family patriarch
annoyed with one of his offspring. Not angry, not threatening, just annoyed enough that if Lucivar had been younger,
Saetan would have grabbed him by the scruff of the neck as
a warning to pay attention and *think*.

"Point by point, then," Saetan said. "There are about
two hundred Eyriens in Ebon Rih. How many of them are
you supporting?"

"I can afford it," he mumbled, not sure how much
trouble he was in, but certain he was in trouble. "Besides,
they work for me."

"Do they? It's been two years since the last service fair,
two years since the last contracts were signed that were
part of the emigration requirements to live in Kaeleer."

"No," Lucivar said quickly, "there were a handful this
past summer."

"Eyrien women who have young children and were desperate enough and determined enough to leave what they
had known. They didn't come through the service fairs,
since those fairs no longer exist. They came to the Keep in
Terreille, asking for help. And Draca asked you to consider
adding them to the women living in the mountains near
Doun. Which you did. How many other Eyriens who signed
contracts with you are still under contract?"

Not sure he liked where this was going, he shrugged.
"They're still serving."

"Are they? Being a dark-Jeweled Warlord Prince, Falonar
has to serve for five years in order to remain in Kaeleer after
the contract is completed. The others, not being of that caste
and not wearing dark Jewels, have fulfilled that obligation
and are free to live elsewhere now."

"If a Queen will permit them to live in her territory."

Saetan tipped his head in agreement. "I think some of those men have already talked to Eyriens who accepted service contracts with Rihlander Queens and have discovered that those Queens are not intimidated by Eyriens or impressed by aggression and arrogance, that those Queens are not going to pay them to sit on a mountain scratching each other's asses while complaining about the ruler they are supposed to serve."

Lucivar took a step back. It still shocked him when his father expressed an opinion so crudely. It would have sounded natural if Andulvar had said it, but Saetan? No. And that crudeness focused his attention as nothing else could have.

"How many are still under contract to you, Lucivar?"

"I'm not sure."

A flash of anger, like a flash of lightning, filled the room.

He waited to hear the thunder, waited for the gauge that would tell him how close the storm was—and how violent.

The silence that followed scared him because it indicated an anger too deep to gauge.

"Andulvar didn't like paperwork any more than you do, but he knew every man who served him directly. Contracts were a formality. He didn't need those pieces of paper to know who served and who didn't, who was loyal and who wasn't, who lived by the Blood's code of honor and who didn't. He *knew*—and so do you."

Lucivar swallowed hard. "Except for the women I took in last summer, Falonar is the only one who hasn't fulfilled the full contract."

"Then he and those women are the only ones who should be receiving anything from your share of Ebon Rih's tithes—*if* they're fulfilling the tasks you've assigned them as their part of the bargain. The others should be informed that they have fulfilled their agreement and are free to live elsewhere. If they want to remain in Ebon Rih, and you're still willing to let them live here, they will have to find work to support themselves. If they want to work for you, and receive wages from you, and have a skill that you want for the Eyrien community in your keeping, they will stand before you and witnesses and make a formal, *binding* pledge of loyalty for whatever amount of time you specify. They will do this according to Eyrien tradition, understanding that the penalties of breaking that loyalty also will follow Eyrien tradition. And yes, Prince, that does mean execution. And yes, there were times when Andulvar had to hold up that part of Eyrien honor."

Lucivar wanted to pace, but that storm of temper could still come down on him, so he didn't move. "I can't cut them loose like that. They're just starting to build a life." He wasn't thinking of the men. Not most of them, anyway. But the women? And what about men like Hallevar and Tamnar? What would they do to support themselves sufficiently?

"Eyriens prefer plain speaking, so I'll speak plainly," Saetan said quietly. "The reason most of the Eyriens who are now settled in Askavi Kaeleer came here was to escape the control of Prythian and all the corrupted Queens who followed her lead. Well, Prythian and those Queens and everyone who was tainted by them are gone. Dead. Destroyed. Purged from all the Realms. If the Eyriens living in Ebon Rih don't like the boundaries that are set by the Queens in Kaeleer, they can return to Askavi Terreille and take up their old lives."

"Would there be anything left of their old lives?"

"I don't know. The point is, they could go back to Askavi Terreille and build the life they seem to think would be so much better than what they have here. I'll open the Gate myself to accommodate them. But if they're going to stay here, it's time for them to start *living in Kaeleer* instead of expecting the Shadow Realm to change into the same, but more advantageous, place they left."

Lucivar started pacing. He needed to argue and push because it was helping him see some things he hadn't considered, but he was nervous about what might swing back at him if he argued and pushed.

When has knowing there was a price ever stopped you?
"Two hundred Eyriens living in the mountains around a valley this size isn't a lot."

"How many Eyriens do you think usually lived in the land owned by the Keep?" Saetan asked, his voice laced with amused curiosity.

Lucivar stopped pacing. Wherever this discussion was going, it was going to bite him in the ass. He just knew it. "Falonar indicated two hundred are a lot less Eyriens than there should be. If I wasn't the one ruling here, more would settle in the valley. In Terreille there were courts and hunting camps and communities of Eyriens in the mountains. Hell's fire. Marian used to live in the Black Valley before she came to Kaeleer. So I know Falonar is right about that—there were hundreds, even thousands of Eyriens living in the mountains around this valley."

"Yes, there were. *In Terreille*," Saetan said, his voice now filled with an amusement that could, in a heartbeat, turn cuttingly sharp. "My darling, you and Falonar have both missed a step in your education."

Shit.

"Eyriens are not native to Kaeleer. The Rihlanders are Askavi's native race in the Shadow Realm. The only reason there have ever been Eyriens living in these mountains, the only reason you are now living in an eyrie Andulvar had built for himself, was that during the time when Andulvar served Cassandra, a winged race was attacking Rihlander villages in the northern parts of Askavi. He was assigned to take care of the problem, and he and the Eyrien warriors who served under him went out and fought the Jhinka and established the line between what was considered Jhinka territory and what belonged to the Rihlanders. In thanks, the Rihlander Queens in Ebon Rih invited him and his men to establish homes in the mountains around the Keep. Which Andulvar did because, even though he ended up being the Warlord Prince of Askavi in both Realms, he liked what he found in Askavi Kaeleer a lot more than what he'd left behind as a youth in Askavi Terreille. So no matter what Falonar may think, there has never been more than two or three communities of Eyriens living in Ebon Rih. Ever."

Lucivar shifted his weight from one foot to the other. It made sense. A hunting camp was usually paired with a court or a community. When he'd first made the decision to accept Eyriens into service, he'd scouted the mountains for other suitable eyries and found them in the mountains near the Rihlander villages. But now that he thought about those places being occupied, he realized there weren't many of those old eyries that were still empty, and the ones that were tended to be isolated, more like overnight camps instead of homes.

"The valley below us belongs to the Keep in all three Realms," Saetan said. "It always has; it always will. You were given Ebon Rih to rule on behalf of the Queen of Ebon Askavi. You were given the responsibility to watch over the land and the people who live here, whether they were landens or Rihlanders or Eyriens. When you made the pledge to defend and protect, you not only made it to the living Queen you served; you made it to the Keep and those who serve the Keep. Which is why you still rule here even though Jaenelle is no longer a ruling Queen." He pushed up from the chair and ran his fingers through his hair, the first sign of exasperation he'd shown. "What is actually going on here, Lucivar? Do you trust Falonar so much that you've missed something obvious?"

Right now he didn't trust Falonar at all, but that wouldn't be a wise thing to say to his father—or his brother, for that matter. "Like what?"

"A challenge?"

Lucivar huffed out a laugh. "He's arrogant, not stupid. He couldn't survive me on a killing field."

"But he is an aristo Warlord Prince who served in a less-than-honorable court. Was he free to leave, or would he have been considered a rogue when he left Prythian's court and slipped in with the other Eyriens to try his luck at the service fair?"

"He said he couldn't stomach what he was ordered to do," Lucivar said. "I assumed he was rogue, but I didn't care."

"A man who lived by traditional Eyrien honor would have cared," Saetan said. "Or at least cared about why a man broke an oath of loyalty."

Snarling at the truth of that, Lucivar resumed pacing.

"So Falonar appeals to your sense of honor and tries to get you to give up your claim to Ebon Rih for 'the good of the other Eyriens.' What do you think would happen if you did step down?"

"Falonar would step in and become the next Warlord Prince of Ebon Rih and rule the valley in traditional Eyrien fashion." And blood would be shed up and down the valley. The Rihlanders here, Blood and landen, wouldn't tolerate the presence of another race who expected them to be accommodating, especially when accommodating meant becoming little better than slaves.

"If you step down, there will be no Warlord Prince of Ebon Rih," Saetan said. "If you leave Ebon Rih, no one at the Keep will deny Falonar's claim to being the leader of the Eyriens living in the valley, but the Rihlander villages here will have no duty to him. There will be no tithes to support him or his followers, because he will have no right to that income. He may be considered an equal to the Queens who rule the Blood villages, but not their superior. He would not be permitted to glut this land with Eyriens who can't support themselves, and he certainly wouldn't be permitted to bring in more warriors, because the number of warriors already here is sufficient to help the Rihlanders defend this land and its people."

"And if he did try to bring in more?"

Saetan gave him a long stare before saying softly, "Don't underestimate what guards the Keep, Lucivar."

He heard the warning. Oh, yes, he heard the warning.

"I will give Falonar two points," Saetan said. "First, you *aren't* thinking like an Eyrien when it comes to the Eyriens in Ebon Rih. Who would you want with you on a battleground, Prince Yaslana? Who would you want supporting those men? Whose skills are useful? Who should be dismissed because they're only extra weight? No one has reminded you of those completed contracts because they would have had to earn their living instead of expecting you to provide them with everything they want simply because you agreed to give them a chance to live in the territory you rule. They aren't your children. Since you have sense enough not to spoil your own son, don't spoil them. Give them a choice to stay or go, because the ones who can't give you loyalty are no use to you in a fight—or in a healthy community."

"Could I release Falonar from his contract?" Lucivar asked.

"If he wants to return to Terreille, you could forgive the rest of his contract. If he wants to stay in Kaeleer but no longer can serve you honorably, his contract could be transferred to a Queen of sufficient rank—meaning one who wears a Red Jewel or darker—who is willing to have an Eyrien Warlord Prince in her court."

"I won't let him serve Karla," Lucivar said. She wasn't the only Queen who wore Jewels darker than Sapphire, but after what Falonar did to Rainier, he wasn't going to let the man near the Queen of Glacia and her weakened legs. "What's the second thing?"

"People didn't stop dying two years ago. Those who made the transition to demon-dead didn't stop coming to Hell, didn't stop wanting a last chance to take care of unfinished business."

"So?"

"Come with me."

He followed Saetan to the private part of the Keep's huge library. On the blackwood table was a wooden box with a dozen audio crystals nestled in heavy silk.

Saetan put one of the crystals in the brass stand and used Craft to engage the sounds held in the crystal.

Andulvar's voice. Lucivar's chest ached. Hell's fire, he missed his uncle. Saetan's love and discipline and code of honor had shaped the core of who he was, but Andulvar, by being Andulvar, had shaped his sense of what it meant to be Eyrien.

How could he have forgotten that?

Then he focused on the words and gasped. "Stories?"

"Some stories," Saetan replied. "Some legends as he was taught them. Some accounts of battles he was in. Prothvar has some stories and accounts of battles on a couple of those crystals too. And then there are these." Returning that audio crystal to its place in the box, he called in another crystal and put it in the stand.

Lucivar didn't recognize the voice, but he knew what he was hearing. "How? Where?"

"A historian storyteller from Askavi Terreille. He made the transition to demon-dead a couple of weeks ago. When he came to the Dark Realm, his main regret was that he had no apprentice while he walked among the living, had no one to learn the stories, and he worried that no one would remember what Askavi had been like before the purging, that the most recent history would be lost. So I showed him what Andulvar and I had done over the course of several winters."

"He's doing the same thing now?" Lucivar asked. "Recording the stories of Eyrien history so they won't be forgotten?"

"Yes. If someone was interested in becoming the historian storyteller in your community, meetings could be arranged and held at the Keep."

Maybe the storyteller could have an apprentice after all before he returned to the Darkness.

Saetan called in a thick sheaf of papers, carefully bound. He handed it to Lucivar. "Eyriens don't have a lot of use for books, but I had all of Andulvar's stories transcribed. I made two copies. One copy and the audio crystals will remain here in the Keep's library, available to scholars and our family. The copy you're holding is a gift from your uncle, and you may do with it as you please."

"Thank you." His throat was so tight it was hard to swallow. "I've let some things slide for the past couple of years. There were reasons for it, but now that needs to change."

"Yes, it does. And there will be some who won't like that change."

Lucivar put a shield around the bound pages to keep them protected, then vanished them. "I'd better go. I promised Jaenelle I would tuck in Surreal and Rainier tonight, since they'll both be resuming their training tomorrow."

"You're going to put a weapon in Surreal's hands?" Saetan looked mildly alarmed. "Are you going to shield your balls?"

He laughed. "Damn right, I am."

He headed for the library's door. Saetan stayed at the table.

"Lucivar?"

He looked back.

"The next time someone tries to manipulate your heart by saying you don't know Eyrien tradition, you remind that person that you follow Eyrien traditions that are far older than anything he could possibly know. Because, my darling, that is true. Andulvar was proud of you, as a man and as an Eyrien warrior. Does anyone else's opinion really matter?"

Glancing up from the solitary card game he'd been playing, Rainier saw one of the younger Eyrien Warlords standing in The Tavern's doorway, scanning the room.

Endar. Had a wife and two children—and lived with them, which, he'd gathered, was atypical in Eyrien society.

Despite what Lucivar sometimes said about his little beast, Rainier couldn't imagine Yaslana living apart from his family, coming to the family eyrie for only an hour to see his children or have sex with his wife. Couldn't imagine Yaslana tolerating that separation.

As Endar approached his table, he saw Merry start to veer from the table she'd been heading toward.

It's all right, Rainier told her. *I'd like to know why he's come.*

She turned again so smoothly, he doubted anyone else would have realized anything had happened.

"Prince Rainier," Endar said when he reached the table.

"Lord Endar."

Endar pointed at another chair. "May I?"

"Please do."

An awkward silence. Then Merry appeared and said, "I know what Prince Rainier is allowed to drink. What would you like?"

Hasn't been in The Tavern before, Rainier thought as he watched Endar stumble over a simple request for ale.

"I guess your training is done now," Endar said.

Rainier shook his head. "We report to Prince Yaslana tomorrow morning to resume training."

"I mean no disrespect, but what can you do right now?"

"I think my part of the training tomorrow consists of standing, walking a few steps, and bending my knee a few times to help stretch the muscles Lady Angelline is rebuilding. Yaslana's part of the training is pounding on me if I do anything stupid."

"He wouldn't hurt an injured man," Endar protested.

Yes, he would. "I'd rather feel Lucivar's fist than my Healer's fury."

"Ah." Endar took a couple of swallows of ale, then set the mug aside and called in four books. He looked embarrassed. Almost ashamed. "Since you need to rest that leg so much while it's healing, I thought you might find these useful."

Setting the cards down, Rainier checked the title of each book. He'd read all of them, but he wasn't going to say that, since it was clear it hadn't been easy for Endar to bring them or admit to owning them. "Thank you. These will help pass the time."

Surreal walked through the door and the chatter in the room stumbled before picking up the rhythm again. As she approached their table, he noticed how much Endar tensed, how ready the man was to take up a defensive position. Couldn't blame him. Not after her attack on Falonar.

"Surreal, darling, Endar kindly loaned me some books. Could you take them up to my room so they'll be safe?"

By the time she'd unbuttoned her heavy coat, he knew she'd assessed his visitor, and his ease with the Eyrien, and understood what the loan of those books meant.

"Sure," she said, taking the books. "You want anything from your room while I'm up there?"

"No, thanks."

When she walked away, Endar gulped in a breath, then gulped some ale. Rainier picked up his cards and resumed his game.

Endar watched for a bit.

"I've played every card game I know more times than I care to consider," Rainier said. "Do you know any?"

"Betting games, you mean?"

He shook his head. "The healing brews I have to drink are strong enough to give me a muzzy head."

"Well, there is hawks and hares. But it's a children's card game."

Rainier smiled. "I could handle that. I think."

Endar called in a different deck of cards. "I keep them with me," he mumbled as he shuffled the cards. "To distract the little ones when Dorian needs some peace."

Rainier said nothing, just absorbed all the messages under and around the words.

Lucivar walked into The Tavern, glanced at the table ringed by Eyriens, and reached the bar just as Surreal lifted the tray of drinks and went off to tend a couple of tables.

"The way she kept staring at everyone, folks were afraid to come up and order a drink," Briggs said, standing on the other side of the bar. "Merry suggested that she look after a few tables while she was keeping an eye on things, and she agreed—and promised not to poison anyone's drink. She was joking about that, wasn't she?"

"If Surreal promised not to poison anyone tonight, she won't."

Briggs stared at him. "You want ale?"

"I'd rather have a very large whiskey, but I'll take coffee if you have it. It's my night to give the little beast his bath, so I'll need my reflexes sharp beforehand and the whiskey after."

Laughing, Briggs went to fetch him a large mug of coffee.

Leaning against the bar, he idly watched Rainier and Endar playing some kind of game, encouraged by Hallevar, Kohlvar, Zaranar, and Rothvar.

"Endar showed up first," Surreal said, setting a tray of dirty glasses on the bar. "Loaned Rainier four books. I gathered reading isn't a shameful activity if a warrior is so badly injured that there isn't much else he can do."

Lucivar winced at the sharp edge in her voice.

"The others showed up a little while ago."

"I'm surprised they aren't entertaining Falonar," he said.

She huffed out a breath. "Nothing has been said—at least nothing I heard while moving around the tables—but I have the impression they're all feeling uneasy about what Falonar did. They haven't criticized him openly. . . ."

"But they're here tonight, giving Rainier company," he finished. Showing support and indicating they saw Rainier as one of their own instead of being with the leader who hadn't taken care of an injured man.

"I haven't heard Rainier laugh this much since before we walked into that damn spooky house."

Lucivar narrowed his eyes. He hated feeling suspicious about men he liked, but the Eyriens hadn't made much effort to get to know the people of Riada. "How much has Rainier lost? And how much has he had to drink?"

"It's not a betting game," Surreal replied. "Some game called hawks and hares."

Children's card game. Daemonar was just learning to play it.

"And his so-called muzzy head, which might be somewhat genuine, is a result of Jaenelle's healing brews. They've also sneaked him sips of ale. Not much, and within the limits Jaenelle told Merry he was allowed to have."

He let the play continue while he drank his coffee and

ate the sandwich Merry put in front of him. Then he waited until Hallevar looked his way. He made a twirling motion with one finger.

"Last hand, boys," Hallevar said loudly enough to carry back to the bar. "We all need to get some rest."

The only man who didn't glance his way was Rainier, who studied the cards in his hand with heightened intensity. It was so like Daemonar's response to the first "bedtime" call, Lucivar almost laughed out loud.

He wasn't sure if Endar deliberately lost that round to finish up quickly, or if Surreal was right and Rainier was nowhere near as muzzy-headed as he was allowing people to think, but the game ended fairly soon after and the Eyriens departed, making a point of thanking Merry and Briggs for the hospitality.

"Do I have to go upstairs now?" Rainier asked woefully.

"It's bath night."

"I don't need help taking a bath."

"No, but my boy does."

"Ah."

Rainier shifted his left leg. Merry and Surreal rushed toward the table. Lucivar gave them both a look that had them pulling up short.

"Give the man some room," he said firmly.

Two pairs of female eyes narrowed at him.

Ah, shit. "Do not give me any sass."

The eyes narrowed a little more.

Can we get out of this room, please? Rainier asked, studying the women.

Yes, if you make some effort.

He got Rainier upright and felt those eyes watch him until they reached the stairs that led up to the rooms.

Since Rainier cooperated, it didn't take long to get him settled for the night. Sitting beside the bed, Lucivar called in a jar of ointment.

"What's that?" Rainier asked.

"Healing salve." After putting a tight shield around his hands, Lucivar scooped out a generous amount of salve and began smoothing it over Rainier's left leg from hip to knee.

"I can do that."

"Not tonight, you can't. Right now, Jaenelle wants someone else getting a careful feel of those muscles, and that someone is me."

Rainier said nothing for a few minutes, letting him focus on the leg. The ointment was laced with spells—warming spell, numbing spell, he didn't know how many others. His fingers carefully followed the lines of muscles, feeling a ridge at the spot where they were originally severed and then repaired so many times.

"Lucivar?"

"Hmm?"

"Is there any honorable work a young Eyrien male can do except fighting? Or does he have to be permanently wounded badly enough to be a liability in a fight before he can do something else without shame?"

Lifting his hand from Rainier's leg, Lucivar gave the other man a long look. "Why do you ask?"

"Nothing certain. Just impressions."

"You were Second Circle in the Dark Court at Ebon Askavi, and you're an observant man."

Rainier took a deep breath and let it out slowly. "I had the impression that Endar was trying to find out how serious this leg injury is. What I could no longer do. He doesn't like being a guard. He doesn't like the bloodshed that comes in a fight. I gathered that's a shameful thing for an Eyrien male to feel. Would he fight to defend his family? Without hesitation or question. But he doesn't like it as his work, and he's afraid to say anything because he likes living here and his wife likes living here. If someone can't offer him a way to keep his standing with other Eyriens, I think the day might come when he drops his guard during one of the workouts, quite by accident, and receives a blow that will make him a cripple who has to do some other kind of work."

Lucivar resumed smoothing the salve over Rainier's leg.

"Did you get any impression about what kind of work he might want to do?"

"No. The other Eyriens came in at that point, and he shied away from the subject."

"I'm going to be looking for a teacher. Someone for the Eyrien youngsters. Someone who can teach them reading and writing and their sums, as well as Eyrien history and basic Protocol."

"Basically the same initial education as any child in Kaeleer, with the history and traditions specific to a race."

"Yes."

"Fighting?"

"Hallevar is arms master. He'll take care of that part of the education." *If he stays.* "Haven't worked out how it will be done, but it's going to be done."

He could almost feel Rainier putting the information together.

"This isn't common knowledge yet?" Rainier asked.

Lucivar shook his head. "Not for a few more days."

"But if a particular person were to ask my opinion about a possible alternative to being a guard?"

"You could mention that you'd heard I was looking for a teacher."

He left Rainier a few minutes later and went into the bathroom. He washed the salve off his shielded hands and then, dropping the shield, washed his hands again. Then he tapped on the other door.

"It's open," Surreal said.

He walked into her room and stopped, feeling his heart kick once.

Short blades, long blades, slim blades and double-edged. Even an Eyrien hunting knife she'd probably had Kohlvar make for her the last time she'd stayed in Ebon Rih.

Her gold-green eyes were focused on him as her hands unerringly stroked a blade over the whetstone. There was something terrifyingly erotic about watching Surreal hone her blades.

"You won't need those tomorrow," he said.

She just smiled.

Because of what he saw in her eyes, he didn't get near her. That was simply caution. He could meet her in a fight and win. They both knew it. He also knew he needed to talk to Daemon very soon.

He could meet her in a fight and win. But outside of a fight, he wasn't sure what to do with a Gray-Jeweled witch who might be drifting too close to the borders of the Twisted Kingdom.

FIVE

Surreal set two plates on the table, then poured two cups of coffee and took a seat.

Rainier studied the chunks of chicken and ham on top of a generous portion of casserole. "Didn't Merry serve this casserole for dinner last night?"

"It has eggs, so today it's a breakfast casserole. Toast?" Her sharp smile told him what he could do with his next comment about the casserole.

He took a piece of toast and dug in to his meal.

They'd gone down to the coffee shop and bakery every morning, so having breakfast in The Tavern's main room felt strange. Then again, a lot of things had felt strange lately. When Endar and the other Eyriens came to see Rainier, she'd been ready to fight, almost *needed* to fight.

But there was no reason to fight, because Endar, Hallevar, and the other men had been making an effort to help Rainier, working with him, even being protective of him as he began exercising the damaged leg.

Feeling easier about Rainier after that first workout, she thought she'd gotten over whatever was riding her temper. Then Jillian showed up yesterday morning. The teacher was sick. School was canceled. Lucivar let the girl stay to be her partner with the sparring sticks, having Endar stand as their instructor.

Nothing wrong with Endar. He was a gentle man with an abundance of patience. But she saw him raise a sparring

stick and step toward Jillian—which was what he was supposed to do because he'd been demonstrating a move—
and she almost attacked him, almost gutted him.

She'd have to talk to Jaenelle before she did something
that couldn't be undone. It was possible there was some
unexpected residue from the poisoning. Maybe the poison,
and the illness that followed, had stirred up memories that
plagued her dreams but disappeared by morning, leaving
her feeling tired and vulnerable.

But today there were simpler problems to face.

"I think we should run The Tavern," she said. "Merry is
down with that stomach upset, and Briggs bolted upstairs
at the first whiff of food."

"You're going to cook?" Rainier asked. "Not that you
can't, but Merry usually makes a significant amount of
food for a day."

"And we won't. I'll see what's left over from yesterday.
We can make sandwiches, maybe a soup. And serve drinks
and coffee. Anyone who wants more can go somewhere
else. You could settle yourself on that stool Briggs keeps
behind the bar for the slow times. I'll wait on the tables."

"We should check with Lucivar." Rainier glanced up as
the door opened.

"Go away. We're not open yet," Surreal snapped without looking around to see who had come in.

"You're not open *yet*?" Lucivar asked as he walked up
to their table and looked at Rainier. "And what do you
need to check with me?"

Shit shit shit. "Merry and Briggs are down with that
disgusting stomach illness," she said. "Instead of them losing a day's business as well as feeling miserable, I thought
Rainier and I could run the place for them."

"Well, having the two of you running things would either scare away all the customers or bring in a crowd to
watch the show," Lucivar said.

Choosing to ignore him because he was right, she ate a
neat bite of her breakfast.

"We could open late, after the day's training," Rainier said.

"No training today," Lucivar said. "That's what I came to tell you."

"Is there a reason for that?" Surreal asked.

"Yes, there is."

She glanced at Rainier. *Something going on here, and Rainier knows what it is. Or at least knows some of it.*

"Marian's making a couple of soups this morning," Lucivar said. "If you bring a pot and the supplies up to the eyrie, I think she'd be willing to make a pot for you to serve here."

"All right."

Rainier called in a leather case similar to the ones Daemon and Lord Marcus, his man of business, used when conveying documents.

"I reviewed them and sorted them as you asked," Rainier said. "And confirmed what you already knew."

"Thanks." Lucivar vanished the leather case and gave Rainier a sharp look. "Daemon should be at the Keep by now. He and I have something to discuss. Then he'll be coming here to talk to you."

"Why? I haven't done anything to annoy him."

"I know you haven't," Lucivar said.

"I haven't done anything either," Surreal said primly.

"Don't push your luck. You, I'm not sure of."

She laughed, more to encourage him to leave than because she was amused.

The moment he did leave, she leaned toward Rainier. "What's going on? He's been flying all over the valley and hasn't been focused on any of the workouts except yours."

"And yours," Rainier said. "He flies around the valley all the time, keeping tabs on the Rihlander villages and the Eyrien camps."

She shrugged that off. "This is different. Obviously he asked you to do some paperwork for him, quietly. And now Sadi has arrived for an early-morning meeting—and Marian is making a lot of soup, which means she wants something easy that she can offer to a lot of guests."

They studied each other. She didn't want him to break

a confidence, but she'd seen the same thing that he had during the workouts over the past couple of days: The Eyrien males around Riada seemed to be dividing between two leaders instead of understanding that there was one leader and his second-in-command.

"Let's just say, for now, that it's a good thing we'll be running The Tavern for Merry and Briggs," Rainier said.

"So we're all going to find out today?"

"Yes."

Well, won't that be interesting?

Lucivar watched Daemon tap the thick stack of contracts back into a neat pile. "When it was just me and the Rih-landers, I knew what I was supposed to be. I stood for Blood law and honor. I drew the line and defended it. But this?" He blew out a breath. "I'm not sure about this."

Daemon poured himself a cup of coffee from the pot Draca had provided. "You're making this difficult, Prick, when it's really quite simple. You're the Warlord Prince of Ebon Rih. You rule this territory. And now you're going to fulfill one of your obligations to the Eyriens who live in your territory by completing the last step in the service contracts they signed with you. And Lucivar? You still stand for Blood law and honor—and you're still drawing the line and defending it."

"Even today?"

"Especially today. Once you make your announcement, you'll have a good idea of who is staying, who is going, who you can trust, and who should never see your back. The ones who think you're a good leader and want the kind of life and community you're offering will be pissed off when you toss these papers at them. They'll be the first to want to talk, and they won't be polite."

"Eyriens rarely are," Lucivar said with a grim smile.

"That's the first group, the equivalent of your First Circle. The second group is going to be shocked by the possibility that they'll be cut loose and might have to serve someone who isn't Eyrien or go back to Terreille. They'll realize they do like it here and want to stay, and they'll make some effort to prove it to you. There also will be the ones who aren't ballsy enough to come to you personally but will seek advice from someone you trust.

"The women will be different," Daemon continued. "They'll come to your home when they're fairly sure that Marian will be around. Easier to talk to you there. Again, the ones who want to stay will make an effort to talk to you quickly. Even the ones who don't want to work for you but want to stay in Ebon Rih will come and talk soon."

"If they want to live here, why not work for me?"

Daemon looked amused and exasperated. "Some of them might prefer to pay you a tithe and run their own businesses—and possibly make a better income than what you can provide. Do you resent Merry for running her own business and paying a tithe instead of working for you?"

"No. But she doesn't pay a tithe to me. She pays it to Lady Shayne's court."

"The point," Daemon said pointedly, "is that Merry and Briggs don't serve in anyone's court; they work for themselves, because that's what they want to do."

When it was put that way, he wondered how many of the Eyrien women had been waiting to be safely cut loose in order to try out their own ambitions.

"After my chat with Rainier, I'll come back to the Keep and be available if you need any help."

"Thanks." Lucivar blew out a breath. "Guess I'd best get on with it."

"Good luck, Prick."

Leaving the Keep, Lucivar flew to the communal eyrie. He'd spent the past couple of days looking at the Eyrien camps or, in the case of the women, the settlement tucked low in the mountains near Doun. He'd looked every man in the eye as he would if he were deciding if a man was an ally or an adversary. The women were harder, because most weren't easy around men, but he'd gotten a sense of them too. There were some men he hoped would stay—

and some he would encourage to leave Ebon Rih and go all the way back to Terreille.

Rainier studied the Warlord Prince of Dhemlan and wished he had some idea what Daemon wanted to discuss.

Not much use to him, am I?

Daemon had been paying for his living expenses since the night he'd been injured. But he couldn't expect Sadi to carry him forever. Didn't *want* to be supported forever. He just didn't know yet what he could do to earn a living.

"Lucivar says the leg is healing," Daemon said. "That's good."

"I guess it took me a while to understand some things." *That pity can be as crippling as a physical wound, for one thing. And after being shown what he had survived, I understand why no one gets pity from Lucivar.*

"And now that you understand those things, you're ready to work on healing?"

"Yes."

"What about other kinds of work?"

"I haven't been useful lately," he admitted.

Daemon raised one eyebrow. "Oh? Lucivar found your assistance very useful. There is more than one kind of dancing, Rainier. You learned some of those other steps while working with the coven and the High Lord. Now I'd like you to consider using those skills for me."

"Meaning?"

"I need a secretary, someone I can trust with private matters."

Anger flashed through Rainier. "You're offering me pity work?"

"In that Lord Marcus asked me to take pity on him and hire a secretary, yes. You're an Opal-Jeweled Warlord Prince. That alone gives you weight when dealing with much of the Blood—enough weight to act as my representative at the SaDiablo estates or the minor Dhemlan courts in much the same way that Mephis represented my father. It would be helpful to have you staying at the Hall or in Halaway a couple of days a week to help with the paperwork there, but otherwise you could reside in Amdarh, either at the family town house or in your own apartment—although I would prefer that you work out of the study in the town house."

"May I think about it?"

"Yes, but I'd like an answer soon. I am going to oblige Marcus and get a secretary. If not you, then someone else."

Rainier studied Daemon, who looked as sleek and elegant as usual, but also a little uncomfortable.

"So you're doing this because Marcus asked you?"

A hesitation that was too long for Sadi. "I owe him. He took a Sceltie puppy home for Winsol."

"Mother Night. Couldn't he sidestep taking the pup?"

"Not after I tied a pretty ribbon around the puppy's neck and gave her to Marcus's daughter to play with while he and I took care of some last-minute business."

When Rainier finally stopped laughing, he agreed to take the job. He wasn't sure what he was agreeing to do, but he was damn sure his days would be interesting.

Lucivar watched the Eyriens as they entered the big front room of the communal eyrie. Hallevar and Kohlvar entered first, followed by Rothvar, Zaranar, Tamnar, and Endar. He'd excused Endar's wife from this meeting, asking her to help Jillian look after the children who had been left at Nurian's eyrie. After all, she'd hear about this from her husband soon enough.

He picked up a sense of puzzlement in Hallevar and his companions, especially after Eyriens from the northern camps walked in, but there was no wariness in the men he worked with the most, no worry that he'd found out about some less-than-honorable activity.

Falonar came in with Nurian. He was full of hot impatience and likely pissed off because he knew no more than the others about why this meeting had been called, despite being Lucivar's second-in-command.

Nurian hurried up to the table Lucivar had set up at the back of the room.

"Prince, am I really needed for this meeting?" she asked. "There are still a lot of people who have that stomach illness, and I promised the Riada Healers that I would help them by making more of the tonic."

"This won't take long," he said—and wondered if the tonic would be made after she heard what he had to say.

The last group to arrive were the women from the settlement near Doun. They hugged the wall, watching the men from the northern camps with an uneasiness that made Lucivar wonder if there had been "visits" he should have known about or if this was just the fear that had come with them from Terreille. He also noticed the way one of them gave Kohlvar a timid smile of greeting—and the solemn, respectful way the weapons master tipped his head in acknowledgment.

When the last man had stepped into the room, Lucivar called in the leather case and took out the papers. A few papers were placed on the right-hand side of the table; the rest went on the left.

"It's come to my attention that many of you are no longer content to live in Ebon Rih," he said, using Craft to make sure his voice carried to everyone in the room. "And I've been reminded lately that I've neglected one duty as the Warlord Prince who rules here."

"More than one," someone muttered near the back of the room.

He ignored the remark, but he caught Falonar's quickly suppressed smile of satisfaction.

That smile made him choose words that would act as a fast, clean break. "Besides the Eyriens who came to Ebon Rih last summer, there are a couple of you who still have time to serve on the contracts you signed with me. The rest of you have fulfilled the emigration requirement of service and no longer have to serve me in order to remain in Kaeleer. You are free to seek service in a Queen's court or find another kind of work. If you stay in Ebon Rih, you will be required to pay the tithe in both labor and coin the same as anyone else who lives here. If that is not acceptable to you, you're free to leave. You have seventy-two hours to tell me if you're staying in the valley I rule."

"What about wages?" one of the men from the northern camps asked.

"You'll receive what is due to you up to today," Lucivar replied. "After that, my financial duty to you is done. From now on, I only pay the people who work for me. That's all. You're dismissed."

Stunned silence.

"What in the name of Hell are you doing?" Falonar finally asked with lethal control.

"What every other ruler in Kaeleer has already done," Lucivar replied. "What I didn't do and should have—released everyone who has fulfilled their emigration contract."

"You kept us on to have cheap labor," one of the men shouted.

"I kept you on because I'd mistakenly thought you were content to live here," Lucivar snapped. "Since that's not the case, there is no reason for you to stay—and there is no reason for me to continue to support you. And since you all did damn little to earn your keep, I wouldn't call you cheap labor."

"You should have paid us more," the man argued. "We're Eyriens, not some Rihlander drudges."

"Ebon Rih belongs to the Keep, and it tithes to the Keep. As the ruler of Ebon Rih, I receive part of that tithe, which I distributed to all of you equally. What you got is the same as what I kept for myself. Are we clear on that? I shared with you what came to me from this valley. Since what I can give you isn't enough, you need to look elsewhere."

"Look where?" Falonar asked hotly. "Do you know how many Eyriens are struggling to survive because the Queens severed those contracts?"

"Probably every Eyrien who had refused to see that the

Shadow Realm is *not* Terreille, who refused to see that the Queens are not going to bend for a race that is coming in from another Realm. If you want to live here, you adapt to the way the Queens rule Kaeleer—or you end up dead. The bitches you all ran from are gone, purged from the Realms. If you don't like it here, go back to Terreille. If you don't like the way I rule Ebon Rih, then leave."

Lucivar paused, tightened the leash on his temper. "I've said all I have to say. Now you all need to decide what you're going to do."

"I'm not going to pay a tithe to that half-breed bastard," a rough voice said.

Lucivar focused on the sound. The man thought he was hidden well enough by the crowd? Fool.

"Pay him to live *here*?" the man continued, laughing harshly. "He should have been grateful that any of us were willing to take a shit in his little valley."

"That's enough!" Hallevar shouted.

No room to maneuver for a one-on-one fight, and there were women in the room who could get hurt. Not that there weren't other ways to kill a man. One blast of Ebon-gray power would burn out the bastard's mind. But that wasn't the Eyrien way of meeting a challenger.

Lucivar whistled sharply. "Yes, that's enough." He pointed at the man. "You. Get out of my territory. And take everyone who feels the same way with you."

The man looked around at his comrades. "You think you can take all of us?"

Lucivar laughed and noticed that the men who had seen him fight turned pale. Falonar, on the other hand, looked thoughtful, which was something he wouldn't forget.

His gold eyes swept from one end of the room to the other, and he nodded as he saw what some of those men no longer bothered to hide.

"I've marked you," he said softly. "You're no longer welcome here. If you try to stay in Ebon Rih, then you're nothing but walking carrion—and you won't be walking long. Now. All of you. *You're dismissed.*"

The women from the settlement fled. So did the men from the northern camps. Hallevar and some of the other men who lived around Riada lingered until a sharp look from Falonar made them retreat, taking Nurian with them.

"Don't you care at all for the Eyrien people?" Falonar asked as soon as they were alone.

"I care as much for them as they care for me," Lucivar replied.

"I don't want to stomach being your second-in-command if you're going to rape Eyrien traditions and then ignore what Eyriens need on top of it."

"Fine. You're no longer my second-in-command."

He saw the shock in Falonar's eyes. Why the surprise? Falonar should know him well enough not to call his bluff. He'd let the other Warlord Prince assume the role of second-in-command because it was a duty worthy of Falonar's power and caste. And while it had often been useful, he hadn't *needed* someone to help him rule the valley.

But if you accept the other duties Andulvar left on your shoulders when he returned to the Darkness, you do need someone you can trust to look after things here when you have to be elsewhere—when you have to stand as the Warlord Prince of Askavi.

Not something he would say to Falonar. Not something he wanted to think about right now. And nothing he wanted said out loud. Not yet. The day he acknowledged that he *was* the Warlord Prince of Askavi, that Andulvar had made it clear to the Queens in Askavi that the Demon Prince had a successor, that the Ebon-gray would continue to defend not just the Keep's territory but all of Askavi . . . The day he acknowledged that, there would be nowhere in Askavi for the Eyriens who didn't like him to go.

"Well?" Falonar said. "Will you release me from my contract?"

"If you want to return to Terreille, I can release you from the contract," Lucivar said. "If you want to remain in Kaeleer, you have three more years to serve."

"With you."

"A Queen who wears darker Jewels than you could take the rest of the contract. There is one Rihlander Queen who wears the Red. She's the only other choice if you want to stay in Askavi." She had always been gracious to him when he'd visited, but the Eyriens she had allowed to serve in her court to fulfill emigration requirements had tested her tolerance and her authority once too often.

And judging by the look on his face, Falonar already knew enough about that Queen to know she wasn't going to offer another contract to *any* Eyrien.

"You're going to destroy us," Falonar said.

"I didn't ask you to come here. I just offered you a place that was as close to the land you left behind as you'll find in Kaeleer. I told you two years ago that if serving me was going to be a bone in your throat, you should take one of the other offers you'd received. Sounds like you're choking on that bone, Falonar, but at this point you don't have many choices besides me. Not if you want to stay in Kaeleer."

Giving Lucivar a look filled with bitter anger, Falonar turned and walked away.

Lucivar waited a minute to make sure he was alone and would be alone for a little while. Then he rubbed his hands over his face. *Bastard?*

Prick? Are you okay?

Everything he needed was in his brother's voice—love, acceptance, and a willingness to kick him in the ass when he needed a kick.

Yeah, I'm okay. It went as well as you'd expect. And there are a few Eyriens who may be seeing Hell soon if they don't get out of Ebon Rih.

If it comes to that, I'll go with you to deal with them, Daemon said. *I'd suggest taking Surreal to watch your back, but I think she's a little too eager to use a knife right now.*

You felt that too?

Yes. I'm just not sure why. I'll ask Rainier. He might know.

Unless she attacks someone, let it go for a day or two. I've already stirred up enough people.

All right. I'll be at the Keep if you need me.

Lucivar broke the link between them. He'd stay at the communal eyrie for another hour so he would be easy to find—if there was an Eyrien anywhere in Ebon Rih who wanted to find him.

Falonar found Nurian in her workroom. The ingredients and tools were set out on the large table in preparation for making more of that damn tonic, but she just stared at them.

"Do you see now?" Falonar snarled. "Do you see what he's really like? He doesn't care about the Eyrien people. He doesn't care about our traditions. He doesn't care about anything but himself!"

"He cares about the people in Ebon Rih," Nurian said. "All of them. He doesn't divide people between those who have wings and those who don't, like most of you do."

Falonar took a step back. "Like *most of us* do? You're Eyrien too."

She looked him in the eyes. "But not like you, Falonar. I don't think I'm the same kind of Eyrien as you or those men who spoke out today."

"They said a few things that needed to be said," he snapped.

"If you ruled this valley, would you divide the tithe evenly among every adult Eyrien?" she asked.

Of course he wouldn't. *Couldn't.* But Yaslana's family had more wealth than even an aristo like he could imagine. Lucivar could afford to be generous. Could have afforded to give them all a bit more, even if it had meant tapping into the SaDiablo family's pockets.

"There's no proof he shared as much as he got," Falonar argued.

"He said it. No other proof is required."

"You're being a fool, Nurian. We could be the dominating presence in this valley, the same as we were in Terreille, but Yaslana keeps hamstringing us with every decision he makes."

"The Rihlanders were here before us," Nurian said. "You're talking about doing the same things we hated in Terreille, about becoming the same kind of monster as Prythian and the Queens who fawned over her."

"How dare you?" Remembering what it was like in Prythian's court, he swung. He tried to pull it back, and that took some of the force out of the blow, but the flat of his hand cracked across Nurian's face.

They stared at each other.

"Nurian . . ."

"Get out of my home," she said quietly, "and don't ever come back. You're not welcome here. Not in my home, and not in my bed."

"Nurian . . ."

"Stay away from me and my sister. You stay away from us, Falonar."

"Is that what this is really about? That I strapped a little sense into your sister for her own good?"

Nurian looked sick.

Hell's fire. It had been only a couple of light blows. Just a warning. He'd told the little bitch to keep silent. Looked like she had.

"*Stay away from us!*" Nurian screamed.

"Nurian?" Jillian hovered in the doorway, with Dorian behind her.

He left. Wasn't anything he could do until Nurian calmed down enough to listen.

Lucivar had hoped Hallevar would return, but the first person to storm back into the communal eyrie was Nurian.

He felt her anger and distress as she strode toward him, and figured he was the cause of both. Then he saw the mark on her face, and the heat of fury burned over his skin. He swung around the table and headed for the door to explain a couple of things to Falonar. Maybe the bastard wouldn't feel so much contempt for the Rihlanders when he had to ask one of their Healers to set the broken bones in his hand.

"No!" Nurian made a grab for him as he passed her, then skipped back a step.

Stung by that instinctive move of fear, he stopped and waited.

"You're not going to do anything about this," she said, waving her hand at her face.

"That will be true when the sun shines in Hell," he replied, trying not to snarl. A woman who had been hit by a man didn't need another one snarling at her.

"I didn't come here for that. Let it go, Prince."

He'd hit women, and he'd killed women. But he'd never raised a hand to one unless she'd hurt someone else first.

"Was this the only time?" he asked.

She nodded. "And it will be the last."

He studied her. Something there in her eyes. She might have forgiven Falonar for one slap, especially today, but not more than one. And not . . .

"Jillian?" he asked.

There it was, that flash of anger that told him what had pushed this woman to draw the line.

"Strapped for her own good," Nurian said bitterly.

Maybe it's the first time here, he thought, *but you've both felt the kiss of leather at some point, haven't you?*

"You say what you want to say, Nurian. Then I want Jillian to report to me here. Is that understood?"

He saw her anger crumbling. Not surprising. Healers didn't look for a fight unless they were fighting for someone they were healing.

"I knew my service contract expired, and I should have said something." Nurian's voice sped up so the words tumbled over one another. "But I thought, since you didn't say anything, that you were satisfied with my work and the contract could just continue. All right, I know contracts don't just continue, but I wanted it to. I want to live here, Prince. I want to work here. I can be the Healer for the Eyriens in Ebon Rih and help the Riada Healers so that I do enough work to earn my keep. And I want Jillian to live here. She can fly around these mountains or go down to the village on her own *and be safe*. You don't know how much that means to me. How much that means to her. And *I know* it's because of the way you rule this valley. I don't much care about Eyrien traditions. I want what is here for my sister. I want it for me. And I want Jillian to have the weapons training. She's always been intrigued by weapons; she's always tried to imitate the moves she saw the men performing—"

And gotten strapped for it? Lucivar wondered.

"—and now she has a chance to learn." Nurian raised her chin and almost looked him in the eyes. "And I want to learn too."

Surprised, he rocked back on his heels. "Why?"

She blushed and no longer even tried to meet his eyes. "Your wife is graceful," she mumbled.

"I think so. What's that got to do with weapons?"

"It's the way she moves, the way the training . . ."

Hallevar would shit rocks if he heard that a woman wanted to learn to use the sparring sticks in order to be more graceful. On the other hand, Eyrien warriors *were* graceful, more so than most of the Eyrien women. He'd initially insisted that the women learn to use weapons so that they could defend themselves sufficiently until help could arrive. He'd eventually stopped insisting after so many of them whined about handling weapons that shouldn't be used by anyone but an Eyrien warrior.

Personally, he didn't care why they wanted to learn as long as it helped the women acquire skills to protect themselves. Convincing the other men to accept this renewed female interest in weapons might be a bit more difficult.

"You want to work for me?" he asked.

"Yes."

No hesitation from her, but *he* felt a slight hesitation that compelled him to say, "Your working for me won't sit well with Falonar. Not after today."

She looked sad, confused, sorry. "I love him. I do. But he

comes from an aristo family, and I don't—and that seems to matter to him more and more. I don't know what he wants from his life, but I'm sure he and I don't want the same things anymore."

"All right," he said gently. "Once I know who's staying, we'll figure things out. Until then, get some rest."

She sniffled once, then squared her shoulders. "I have some tonics to make."

He waited until she reached the door. "Send Jillian to me." Seeing the momentary slump of her shoulders before she hurried out, he smiled grimly and thought, *Hoped I would forget, didn't you, witchling?*

Then Hallevar, Kohlvar, Rothvar, and Zaranar walked in, and it was time for the next dance.

A shadow. A flutter of air. The sound of boots behind him.

Startled, Rainier stopped his careful walk down the street so that he wouldn't take a misstep.

"Prince Rainier?"

Leaning on his cane, he looked over his shoulder and smiled. "Lord Endar."

"Could I talk to you?"

"I need to walk to the end of the street to fulfill the day's exertions. I could meet you back at The Tavern when I'm done or at that coffee shop across the street."

"I don't mind walking."

A few minutes is too long to wait? "All right."

It took a few steps before Endar matched his pace to Rainier's careful walk. Then, "Have you heard what happened? Yaslana cut us all loose. We've got nothing. I have two children, and now we have nothing. I'm not sure if we're still allowed to live in our eyrie, or if we have to leave because all the eyries belong to him."

Wondering whom the young Warlord had been talking to, Rainier said, "The way I understand it, the emigration contracts were finite, a set time to prove that the person coming to Kaeleer could adjust to living in the Shadow Realm. Just like any other contract, each side fulfilled the length of time and the terms. Then the contract ended. You all knew this day was coming. That's not the same as being cut loose, Endar. When a contract ends, a man is free to negotiate another one with the same person or head out and try something new somewhere else. Maybe you're used to staying with one court forever, but I know plenty of young men who take short contracts and then move on to another court or even another Territory. They gain polish and experience and spend a few years looking around while they decide what they want to do."

"But I'm Eyrien, and Dorian and I don't want to live somewhere else. We like it here!"

"Then talk to Prince Yaslana. Tell him you'd like to stay in Ebon Rih. If you're interested in working for him, tell him that too."

"But . . ." Endar said nothing until they reached the end of the street. "Every Eyrien male is trained to fight, but not all of us are good at it."

And those of you who aren't good at it are usually the first to die on the killing field, Rainier thought. *Not an easy truth for a man who loves his wife and children.*

"I'm pretty sure Rothvar and Zaranar want to stay, and if they do, Yaslana won't want to hire someone like me as a guard. Not when he could have them."

"Then offer to do some other kind of work," Rainier said. He stood at the corner, debating with himself if he wanted to cross the street and go up to the coffee shop or just turn around and go back to The Tavern. Coffee and sweet pastries or soup?

I'll have the soup later.

As he shifted his weight to take the first step into the street, Endar said, "Take my arm to steady yourself. Despite what *some* people say, there is no shame in accepting help."

"There's no shame in being something besides a guard," Rainier said quietly.

"What else could I be?"

Does their thinking get stagnant because they're a long-lived race and have so many years ahead of them? "I don't know, but I've heard Yaslana is looking for a teacher for the Eyrien children—someone who has the education to teach them the basics as well as Eyrien history."

"Eyrien history."

The words were barely loud enough for Rainier to hear, but that didn't diminish the excitement in Endar's voice.

"I've also heard that an Eyrien historian storyteller has recently come to the Dark Realm and is willing to teach someone what he knows before he becomes a whisper in the Darkness," Rainier continued.

There was so much *wanting* in Endar's face it was painful to look at him.

"I'm not old enough," Endar said. "And I'm sound, so—"

"I don't recall Yaslana mentioning anything about age as a requirement, only a specific amount of education," Rainier said tartly. "And I don't recall him saying a man had to be lame in order to teach. If anything, I would think you'd need some speed and agility to keep up with the children. Lucivar isn't chained to traditions that don't suit this territory or this Realm. If you want to pass up work you'd enjoy because you're young and sound, that's your choice. But Lucivar is going to get a teacher for the children, and he's going to give someone the opportunity to learn from that historian storyteller. You have to decide if that person is going to be you."

They stopped in front of the coffee shop. Endar stared at him. Then the Eyrien Warlord smiled.

"Will you be all right finishing your walk alone?" Endar asked.

"I'll be fine. What about you? Will you be fine?"

The smile brightened. "I think so. I have to talk to Dorian, but I think we'll all be fine."

A two-fingered salute. Then Endar stepped into the street, spread his dark wings, and flew home.

Rainier watched the Eyrien and began to understand what Daemon meant about a different kind of dance.

Lucivar?

Rainier.

Endar needs a little time to talk things over with his wife, but I think you'll have your teacher.

One more down, Lucivar thought as he leaned against the table and watched Jillian shuffle toward him. He'd ask Daemon to go over Endar's credentials and suggest what the Warlord needed to add to his own education to fulfill the requirements of the new position. If Rainier's impression was correct and Endar had more book learning than most Eyriens, the man would suit the job, at least in terms of temperament. He'd confirmed that when he'd had Endar act as instructor to Surreal and Jillian.

He pointed to a spot in front of him that, to a young girl's eye, would look like she was out of reach. She wouldn't be, not with his speed and reflexes, but he thought she'd feel more comfortable with a little distance between them.

He closed his hands over the edge of the table and waited until she stood in the required spot.

"You got strapped," he said.

"Yes, sir," she mumbled.

"When?"

"Couple days ago."

"How bad?"

She shrugged.

"You didn't let your sister check your back for injuries?"

She shook her head.

"Did you go to another Healer in Riada?"

Another headshake. "Wasn't supposed to tell."

"Then you *don't* know if you're all right."

She squirmed and kept her eyes focused on his boots. "Tamnar looked at my back. He said it wasn't bad, and none of the marks were close to my wings. He said he'd gotten worse."

Something Lucivar would discuss with Hallevar. As far as he knew, the old arms master was still giving out the slaps that were meant to sting pride rather than injure flesh. He'd gotten his fair share of those in his youth, so he had no problem with that bit of discipline. But if someone else had been doing more here, in his valley . . .

"Did you deserve the strapping?" Lucivar asked mildly.

"*He* said I did."

His breath caught. *That* tone of voice should not come from a girl Jillian's age. That level of hatred should not *be* in a girl Jillian's age. She should not have experienced anything that would put a knife-edge in her voice.

Because he knew two women whose voices sometimes took that same edge, and because he knew *why* that edge was there, he had to ask.

"Jillian, are you a virgin?"

Her mouth fell open in shock, and because of her silence, the word *rape* hung in the air between them. She hadn't been broken. He was sure of that. Jaenelle and Surreal hadn't been broken either by the violence of rape, but they both carried emotional scars.

"Jillian?"

She didn't answer. Then she jumped when the wood cracked under his hands.

"I am," she said quickly. "I am!"

He released the table and stood up. "If I ask a Healer to look at you, will she tell me the same thing?"

"Yes, sir."

Thank the Darkness for that.

He'd been rising to the killing edge, and he took a moment to pull back and regain control.

"All right, witchling. Listen up. You are going to school. Maybe with the Rihlander children, maybe not, but you are going to school. Weapons training will be considered an extra. As long as you keep up with your studies, I will see that you get training in bow, sticks, and knives. You shrug off one, you lose the privilege of the other. We clear on that?"

"Yes, sir!"

"Next, you do not get strapped by anyone but me. Ever.

If someone thinks you've misbehaved to the point of deserving it, the charge will be brought to me. If I decide you do deserve that punishment, I will wield the leather. We clear on that too?"

"Yes, sir."

"If someone else tries to strap you or hurt you in any way, what are you going to do?"

"Kick him in the balls."

Lucivar blinked. Swallowed a tickle in his throat. Damn tickle. Felt like a laugh. "After that."

Jillian pondered for a moment. "Come to you?"

"That's right. Although you might consider just getting away and coming to me first. If he deserves it, I will hold him while you kick him in the balls."

She gave him a bright smile. Probably thought he was teasing her. Probably just as well to let her think that.

"Anything else I should know?" he asked.

She shook her head. "Does this mean Nurian and I can stay in Ebon Rih?"

"That's what it means. She's going to work for me as a Healer, and—"

"And I can work for you by helping Marian take care of Daemonar."

He laughed. "Fair enough. Now get home before your sister frets about this chat."

"Yes, sir."

A bright smile. Clear eyes. Didn't take much to set Jillian's world right and give her a sweet wind under her wings.

He would do his best to make sure things stayed that way.

Surreal cleared the table and stacked the dishes on a tray. The Tavern didn't open until late morning, but apparently these two men came in once a week at this time to have a quiet breakfast of whatever was available while they talked business for an hour. They'd been startled to find her instead of Merry, but they were quite happy with the casserole, chicken, and coffee she put on the table. And even though they kept a running tab here, they'd left a generous tip. She wasn't sure whether that was to thank her for letting them have the breakfast or for not tossing them out in the snow.

Smiling, she set the tray on the bar, took a step back, and extended her arms.

Her body flowed, slow and easy, in a series of moves she'd seen Jaenelle make with practice sticks no longer than her arm. This wasn't training for an Eyrien weapon. These moves belonged to the Dea al Mon.

As she completed the last turn, she saw Falonar watching her from the doorway.

What was he doing at The Tavern? He knew she was staying here, so unless he was looking for a ripping fight, why in the name of Hell would he come to see her?

"Every time you pick up an Eyrien weapon, you mock my race," he said.

My skill with weapons was one of the things that used to intrigue you. At least until we got better acquainted. "And here I thought I was just honing my skill with a knife. Besides, those moves weren't created for an Eyrien weapon." She swung herself over the bar. "We're not officially open yet, but I can give you a cup of coffee."

He walked up to the bar. "I suppose you're pleased with what happened today."

She filled two mugs with coffee. "The gossip hasn't reached me yet, so I don't know if I'm pleased or not."

"Lucivar is pushing the Eyriens out of Ebon Rih."

"All of them, or just the ones who think having a cock entitles them to food, shelter, and sex whenever they want it?"

Anger flashed in his eyes.

She sipped her coffee and watched him. She had been attracted to the arrogant Eyrien Warlord Prince who had shown some respect for her skills—attracted enough to let her heart as well as her body get tangled up with him. But the Falonar she'd first known wasn't the same man as the one staring at her now. She wouldn't have slept with *this* man unless she was planning to drive a knife between his ribs while he came.

She assessed him as a client. As prey. A man could hide his true nature—and true feelings—for only so long, and she was finally seeing what desperation and ambition had hidden for almost two years.

Falonar hadn't changed because living in the Shadow Realm had soured him somehow; he'd just gotten comfortable enough to slip back into being what he had been *before* coming to Kaeleer.

"I'm trying to remember that you're not tainted," she said quietly.

"What?"

"You survived the purge two years ago, so whatever corruption is in you didn't come from your association with Prythian or Dorothea or Hekatah. Maybe it's simply what you are because you're an Eyrien aristo."

"I don't know what you're talking about."

"Don't you?" She set her coffee aside and leaned on the bar, looking friendly and vulnerable. She was neither. "It must have pissed you off when you came strutting into the hunting camp as a boy and realized there was a half-breed bastard there who was stronger and better than anything you could ever be. He should have groveled in front of you, grateful to lick your boots. Instead he looked you in the eyes and not only told you he was better than all of you; he *showed* you he was better. Must have choked you to have to compete with him and never win—at least not fairly."

"I never cheated in a competition," Falonar snarled.

"No, you probably didn't. But that doesn't mean you weren't pleased when someone else did something that pushed the odds in your favor." She leaned a little more, showing more cleavage—and watched the way his eyes lingered a moment too long.

"You finished your training and were no longer in Yaslana's shadow because he defied Prythian and ended up a slave being controlled by a Ring of Obedience, while you ended up an aristo male moving in court circles, serving a bitch you hated, but you were always careful not to step too close to a line that might be seen as a challenge. And there was Lucivar, who, despite being a slave, was always crossing those lines and growing into the most lethal and feared warrior in the Realm of Terreille."

She felt pressure on her first inner barrier. Not an actual attempt to force open the first level of her mind, more like someone leaning against a door to push it open just a crack and find out what was on the other side while claiming that he didn't *do* anything.

A man could find out a lot of useful information while not doing anything. And maybe—*maybe*—because it was a passive move, it wouldn't be considered a breach of the Blood's code of honor.

She usually wore her Birthright Green Jewels, just like today, but she no longer hid the fact that the Gray was her Jewel of rank. Had he forgotten that? Was he actually hoping that she'd be lax about maintaining the barriers that protected her mind from the rest of the Blood? Was he that much of a fool?

"Skipping a few centuries, the Realm of Terreille becomes a *very* bad place, and people are scrambling to get away from the bitches who rule there," she continued. "Among those people is an Eyrien Warlord Prince who comes from an aristo family and has significant social standing. And wearing Sapphire Jewels means he is a powerful, dominant male—a leader other men obey without question. No reason to think that will change. Aristo is aristo; power is power."

She drifted down into the abyss until she reached the level of the Gray, then drifted back up until she was under him. She reached up with one delicate psychic tendril to get the honest flavor of his emotions.

She didn't like the taste of those emotions. She didn't like them at all. Apparently the story she was weaving around the little she knew and the lot she guessed based on knowing the two men was close to the truth.

"And what happens?" she said. "You come to Kaeleer

with your credentials polished, expecting the Queens to fight over who gets the privilege of having you in her court, and there's your old friend Lucivar, already here before you. And he's not only serving the Queen the rest of you would give your balls to serve; he's the ruler of the most prized bit of land in Askavi. Not only that, he's no longer a half-breed bastard the rest of you can ignore. He comes from *the* most aristo family in the whole damn Realm. His father and uncle are *the* most powerful men in the whole damn Realm, not to mention being Witch's Steward and Master of the Guard, which gives them even more status."

"Just because they acknowledged him doesn't mean he actually carries the bloodlines," Falonar snapped.

"Blood sings to blood—and blood doesn't lie. Sure, there are generations between Lucivar and Andulvar, but he is the High Lord's son, and his mother did come from Andulvar's line. An aristo among aristos. And he still doesn't give a damn about any of that, does he? He's just who he's always been—a warrior, a leader, a strong man. Except now all the Eyriens who would have spit on him before have to walk softly because one word from him—*one word*—and that person gets tossed all the way back to Terreille. If the fool isn't killed first."

"What does any of this have to do with him gutting Eyrien culture and tradition?" Falonar shouted.

"What goes on in Ebon Rih is his version of Eyrien culture and tradition," she replied sweetly.

"His *version*?" Falonar paced away from the bar and back. "You can't have different versions and have the same people!"

"Maybe that's the point. Maybe there needs to be a different version for the people who would otherwise be excluded from Eyrien culture."

"Like who?"

"Besides Lucivar? How about Endar and Dorian's little girl? A Queen. But her hair has curl. Not only is she not pure Eyrien; that curl proves she has a bit of a bloodline that isn't from any of the long-lived races. What about

Tamnar? He wouldn't have had much of a future among your people, which is probably why he risked the service fair in the first place. Eyrien culture and tradition were already rooted here, Falonar. It's just not the same as what you left."

Falonar's mug shattered. "Back in Askavi, if a bitch like you spoke to me like that, I'd have you whipped."

Surreal called in a towel and tossed it on the bar to sop up the coffee. "Bitch like me. Yes, let's address that final topic before you go. Well, two topics really, and that's the second one. You know what none of you big strong Eyriens have admitted? Except Lucivar. The man may be a pain in the ass, but he does have brains. You all came to the Shadow Realm expecting the other races to be cowed by a warrior race. Because that's what the Eyriens are, aren't they? Warriors, bred and trained. But no one was cowed by Eyriens because, in Kaeleer, you are not the race that is feared."

Surreal slowly reached up and hooked her long black hair behind one delicately pointed ear. "They are called the Dea al Mon. The Children of the Wood. They know as much about fighting as you do. Maybe more, since they have always followed the Old Ways of the Blood. Which brings us to the last topic—my bloodlines."

"You have no bloodlines." Falonar's voice was harsh, and his hands were clenched.

"On my sire's side, you're probably right."

"You have no connection to the SaDiablos beyond what they give you."

"That's true too. I don't have one drop of blood in common with Lucivar or Daemon or the High Lord. I only used that name when I came to Kaeleer as a way to spit in Dorothea SaDiablo's face. But the High Lord decided to let that claim stand and accepted me as family. So you're correct that calling myself a SaDiablo doesn't give me the right to call myself aristo. My mother, on the other hand . . ." She brushed her finger over the curve of her ear. "My mother was a Dea al Mon Queen and Black Widow. If she hadn't been broken by Dorothea's son and then murdered by one of the bitch's assassins, she could have been the Queen of the Dea al Mon's Territory. As it was, when she made the transition to demon-dead, she became the Queen of the Harpies. So no matter how you turn it, my mother's bloodline is more than aristo enough to make up for any lack by the cock and balls who sired me."

She straightened up and stared at him across a slab of wood that either of them could destroy in a heartbeat.

She vanished her Green Jewel and called in her Gray. Then gave him a moment to remember just whom he'd been trying to play with.

"My mother and I skinned my father and hung him up as meat for the Hell Hounds while he was still alive. We soaked in a hot spring and listened to him scream while they fed. So I think I come by my interest in, and skill with, a knife honestly. Don't you?"

He backed away from her. Backed all the way to the door.

She waited until he flew away before she used Craft to turn the physical lock. Then she added a Green lock on the door.

She cleaned up the coffee and broken mug, relieved that Briggs must have some kind of shield on the wood to keep it from being damaged by spills.

Then, having made her decision, she sent a Gray psychic thread to a Black mind.

Sadi?

Surreal?

Are you busy?

That depends on what you want.

She heard the amusement in his voice and rolled her eyes. Maybe it was better if he felt amused. *I'd like you to find out what you can about Falonar's bloodlines.*

Cold now shivered along that psychic thread.

Why? he asked too softly.

I have a suspicion that one of the things that bothers him the most about Lucivar—and now me—is the realization that we come from families that are far more aristo than his, and I'm curious why that matters so much.

If you want this to stay between the two of us, it will take a couple of days. You know what Lucivar is like when he has to deal with paperwork, and I think this particular deluge is going to test his self-control. Besides, Father and I promised to work up a rough draft of a contract for serving the Warlord Prince of Ebon Rih.

Yes, she knew what Lucivar was like. A tiger with a sore paw was more agreeable than Yaslana confronted with a stack of paperwork. *It can wait.*

She broke the link and went back to preparing The Tavern for business. A few minutes later, Rainier tapped on the door. He had two loaves of sweet-and-spice bread to serve with the soup, along with some pastries just for her.

Pushing Falonar to the back of her mind, she spent the rest of the day listening to gossip and working with a man whose company she enjoyed.

SIX

It was late afternoon on the following day when Falonar walked into Kohlvar's workshop to have a private meeting with the men he considered the core group of Eyrien males living around Riada. They nodded a greeting, but no one shifted to attention, ready to take an assignment from him.

Had they already heard he'd been stripped of his position as second-in-command?

"We need to talk about what we want for ourselves and the Eyrien people before Yaslana makes any other decisions for us," Falonar said.

"Already know what I want," Hallevar replied. "That's why I gave him my hand yesterday."

"We all did," Rothvar said, tipping his head to indicate the men present.

"You signed a contract with him?" Falonar said, made too off balance by that news to hide his anger.

"Don't have the paper yet, but we will," Hallevar said. "We can change our minds if we don't like the final terms, but from what he said, we'll still have the eyries we've made our homes and a quarterly wage drawn from Lucivar's share of the tithes, and work that suits us."

"The way Yaslana rules this valley," Zaranar said, studying Falonar. "Why does it chew your ass?"

"Because we weren't born to be tame!" Falonar shouted. "He expects us to be content with training exercises instead of meeting an enemy. By the time he's through gutting the heart out of what we are, we'll be nothing but Dhemlans with wings. Look what he's doing to Endar. A *teacher*?"

Kohlvar wiped the knife he'd been sharpening on the whetstone and picked up the next one. "Why not? It's the work Endar wants to do, and here there's no shame in being a teacher at his age. You're aristo, and aristos get more schooling than the rest of us. If Lucivar is willing to let all Eyrien youngsters have more schooling than we got, let them have it—especially if it's something all the other children in this Realm are getting."

But it belongs to the aristos, Falonar thought. *It's the difference between a good leader on a battlefield and a ruler.*

Rothvar fanned his wings, then closed them. "I've spilled my share of blood on plenty of killing fields. I've been in fights where I've killed friends who were on the other side of a line just because some bitch Queen needed the sight of slaughter in order to come. There was no honor in that bloodshed. I'm not against fighting or killing. I was trained to do both, and I've done both. But I won't feel cheated if most days I hone my skills against another man for the fun of it and don't have to spill blood for someone else's pleasure."

Falonar stared at the Warlord guard. Rothvar *couldn't* mean that. "You're willing to accept that?"

Rothvar shrugged. "I guess it's different for you, not having any court intrigues to deal with. But for us, this life isn't so different from what we left."

"Except it's better," Zaranar said.

Hallevar nodded in agreement. "I'd like to have a few more youngsters to train. Hell's fire, I'd even give another try at training a few of the women."

"I don't have to wonder if following Lucivar's orders will soil my honor, and I sleep easier knowing that," Zaranar said.

"And with Lucivar, you don't have to wonder whether the person giving you an order will deny it later—especially if there was something dirty about the job—and leave you to be the one to take the punishment." Rothvar's expression made it clear that he'd known men who weren't whole afterward, even if they survived the punishment.

"Lucivar says what he means and means what he says," Hallevar said. "Straight words, straight work."

"Guarding Rihlanders," Falonar sneered.

Zaranar made a crude, angry sound. "Some of us are willing to do the work we agreed to do, and that includes protecting the Rihlander villages, Blood and landen. I heard there was a Jhinka raid on a landen village a few weeks ago, and it was the *Rihlander* guards from Agio who stepped in and drove the bastards off. The Eyriens in the northern camps should have been patrolling that part of the valley and should have spotted the Jhinka *before* they reached that village. But they couldn't stir themselves to raise a bow let alone shoot a single arrow. I won't blame Lucivar a bit if he tosses every one of those lazy sons of whoring bitches out of the valley."

"The Rihlanders aren't used to dealing with Eyriens," Falonar argued. "If they showed the proper respect, they'd get the help they need."

"Oh, they're used to dealing with Eyriens," Rothvar said. "Just not in daylight. Prothvar Yaslana and a hand-picked troop of men used to patrol the northern part of Ebon Rih as well as the Sleeping Dragons at the end of the Khaldharon Run. The Queen's court might have had more contact with Prothvar himself, but the Eyriens who served him were known to the Blood in Agio, at least to some degree. First time I walked into a tavern there, it was late afternoon and the owner looked confused to see me. Then he offered me a glass of yarbarah. Apparently Lord Yaslana and his men stopped by there on occasion, so the man kept bottles of the blood wine on hand."

Falonar swallowed his growing disgust. Rothvar and Zaranar were the best fighters among the Warlords Lucivar had brought to Ebon Rih. They should be troop leaders controlling their own portion of the valley, with men under their command.

He ignored the memories of how many men were killed or maimed in fights that started because a troop leader needed to expand his territory—and increase his income—in order to pay his gambling debts.

Then he focused on the knives Kohlvar was sharpening and no longer tried to swallow his disgust. "Hell's fire, Kohlvar. You made some of the finest weapons in Askavi, and now you're sharpening *kitchen knives*?"

"These blades get dull like any other," Kohlvar replied as he studied the edge of the knife. "Doesn't hurt my pride to give the women some help, and who would know better than me how to put an edge on a blade?"

"What about your reputation?" Falonar demanded. "You're a *weapons maker*. This is menial work. Who did Lucivar have doing it before you?"

"No one. He did it himself."

And that lack of understanding, of distance, was the reason Lucivar had no business ruling anything, let alone a prime territory like Ebon Rih.

"You've been up to the women's settlement at Doun?" Zaranar asked.

Lucivar had made it clear that no man who wanted to keep his balls went to the settlement without his permission.

Kohlvar shrugged. "Lucivar came by not long ago and asked if I wanted to go with him. I wasn't busy, so why not? And I was curious." He looked a little uncomfortable, but he also looked amused. "The man walked in, took a look around, and started scolding the women for hauling things that were too big for them to handle instead of waiting for him to help. And a couple of the women started scrapping right back, saying they had brains and Craft and plenty of hands and didn't need a penis in order to get things done."

An uneasy silence. Then Rothvar asked, "What did he do to them?"

Kohlvar laughed. "He grinned and went to check the woodpiles and other things he wanted to check. Later he told me one of the women who'd been scrapping with him had come to Kaeleer this past summer, and she'd been so afraid of men she would puke from fear when he walked into the room. He said it was good to see her growing her backbone and heart.

"Anyway, we ended up in the kitchen, drinking coffee. Then he called in his whetstone and started sharpening the knives. I wasn't going to sit there like a fool, was I? So I gave him a hand. Most of the females were keeping to the far end of the room, but the boys were hugging the table, watching him while they answered his questions and asked plenty of their own. He slapped down a boy with nothing but a look when that boy tried to bully the one girl who got brave enough to approach the table. When he was done with the last knife, Lucivar took all the children outside for a flying lesson."

Kohlvar vanished his own whetstone and the kitchen knives. Then he looked at Hallevar. "There isn't a youngster in that settlement who would be old enough for a hunting camp, but there are some there who are old enough to start learning what you can teach. You should talk to Lucivar about going with him the next time he visits."

"I think I will," Hallevar replied.

Falonar listened to them a few minutes more, then made an excuse to leave. They didn't see the truth about their future, didn't understand how a leader who was so common he didn't see anything wrong with taking care of menial tasks would diminish the standing of all Eyriens in Kaeleer.

These men belonged to Lucivar, and for the time being, there was nothing he could do about that. So he was going to have to look to the men in the northern camps for the help he needed to save all of them.

Surreal dropped from the Green Wind and landed lightly in the courtyard of Lucivar's eyrie. If she'd been polite, she would have used the landing web and climbed the stairs to the courtyard, but she wasn't feeling polite since she was the messenger who had to hand over this basket.

Merry woke up this morning feeling hungry and well and had been cooking and baking since sunrise. The goodies in the basket were her thanks for the pot of soup Marian had made yesterday.

"This is payment and more for a pot of soup," Surreal grumbled as she banged on the door. "And I deserve these goodies as much as anyone." Especially after the dream that had ripped through her sleep last night—the boy Trist, torn and bloody as he'd been in the spooky house, smiling at her and saying over and over, "The worst is still to come."

Maybe it was just lack of sleep, or maybe it was something more that made the floor and walls of her room seem to rise and fall this morning—and made her chest hurt in a different way. Maybe she should stop and see one of Riada's Healers before going back to The Tavern. Maybe . . .

The door swung open. Lucivar looked edgy, heading toward pissed off, and he was wearing the heavy wool cape he used as a winter coat. Wishing she'd just left the basket, she started to step back when he reached out, grabbed her coat, and hauled her inside.

"Some of this has to go in the cold box until you're ready to eat," Surreal said, trying to hand him the basket.

"Fine." He hustled her into the kitchen and put the basket on the table. Then his hands clamped down on her shoulders, holding her in place. "Marian is in the village running errands. Falonar needs to talk to me. He says it's urgent. I need you to stay here and watch Daemonar."

"No."

"Thirty minutes. An hour at the most. Tassle and Graysfang are on their way back here, so you won't be alone with the boy for long."

Her heart banged against her chest so hard she could barely hear him. "Lucivar, I can't do this."

"Yes, you can. Just sit and read him stories. He loves that. And he's housebroken, so you don't have to worry about changing diapers."

He couldn't pay her enough to change a diaper. "I have to go."

Lucivar gave her a smacking kiss on the forehead and was moving toward the door, saying, "Daemonar! I'll be back soon."

Little feet running. The sound of small boots smacking on a stone floor as Daemonar raced into the large front room. "Papa! I want to go with you!"

"Not today, boyo. Play nice with your auntie Surreal." Lucivar looked at her. "One hour."

He was outside and flying off before she reached the door.

"Lucivar!"

Sick shivers. Feverish heat. Too damn hard to breathe.

She closed the door and turned around. Daemonar gave her the sweetest smile.

She hadn't been alone with a child since that night in the spooky house. Had made sure she was never alone with a child. But maybe this wouldn't be too bad. After all, this was Lucivar's home, not a place that had been designed as a trap to kill members of the family. And he'd promised he'd be back in an hour.

She slipped out of her coat and hung it on the coat tree near the door.

"You want to play a game, Auntie Srell?" Daemonar asked, following her into the kitchen.

"All right." Her heart gave her chest another kick. "Let me put this food away first, and then we can play a game."

Steak pie. Vegetable casserole. A small jar of chopped fruit to be served over sweet biscuits. She put everything but the biscuits in the cold box. Leaving those on the table, she set the basket on the counter and looked around.

"Daemonar?"

A little-boy giggle. "Come find me, Auntie Srell. Come find me."

No.

She crept toward the archway that led to the large front room. "Daemonar?"

The patter of small boots on stone.

She moved fast, following the sound. The eyrie was a

warren of rooms, but the boy should be easy enough to find. It wasn't like he was being *quiet*.

Then there was no sound. None at all.

"Daemonar?"

She headed for the bedrooms, then heard, from behind her, "Come find me," and the sound of feet running back toward the kitchen.

She dashed back to the kitchen and took a quick look under the table. It would be easy enough for a boy his size to dart between the chairs and hide.

No little boy under the table.

So damn hard to breathe. Had she drunk her healing brew this afternoon? Couldn't remember.

She moved through the rooms, searching. Sometimes she heard a giggle, sometimes the scrape of boot on stone.

The worst is still to come.

The bad things hadn't happened yet. She had time to find the boy. Lucivar's little boy. Couldn't let him get hurt by twisted bitches or lethally honed blades. Couldn't let the bad things happen to him. Not to Lucivar's boy.

The worst is still to come.

She opened a cupboard and saw serving bowls, platters, and other kinds of dishes—and heard a boy screaming and screaming and screaming. Then the screaming stopped, and she knew what that meant.

"Come find me." Was that Daemonar saying that, or Trist?

The worst is still to come.

Her breath hitched, rasped in her chest, hurting her as she tried to draw in enough air to think, to move, to *act*. This time she wouldn't fail. She would find the boy and get him out of this damn house, and she would find a way to get Marjane out of that tree before the crows took the girl's eyes, and . . .

She dashed into the front room and glanced at the door. "Kester, no!"

A flashed image, as if a sight shield had dropped for a heartbeat. Just enough time for her to see the wings and the blood spraying everywhere as the Eyrien bastard ripped into the boy. Then gone.

Kester. Not Daemonar. Like Trist, Kester had died in the spooky house. She still had a chance to save Daemonar.

She tore through the bedrooms, opening every door and drawer she could find. She tore through the weapons room and Marian's workroom and the laundry room, circling back to the kitchen, where she yanked out drawers and opened more doors.

She opened the cold box, then the door to the freeze box inside it—and stared at the little brown hand so freshly severed the fingers were still curling up against the cold.

She bolted across the kitchen, just reaching the sink before she vomited.

Then she stumbled out of the kitchen, stumbled around the eyrie, hearing Daemonar's voice, sounding scared now, saying, "Auntie Srell?"

Couldn't save him. Couldn't save any of them. Not Trist, not Kester, not even Rainier. Not Jaenelle. Hadn't been good enough, strong enough, fast enough to save them.

"Auntie Srell?"

And now the boy. Lucivar shouldn't have trusted her with his precious boy.

She stumbled, hit a carpeted floor on her hands and knees, and went all the way down.

Tears and pain and poison. This time the poison would take her all the way down.

This time she wouldn't fight it.

"Would you like some coffee?" Falonar asked.

Lucivar undid the buttons and belt on his winter cape but didn't take it off. "No, thanks. I left Surreal alone with Daemonar, and I promised I would be back as soon as I could." *And I don't want to drink whatever you're offering.*

A month ago he wouldn't have thought twice about accepting food or drink at Falonar's eyrie. When had that changed? And why? They'd always respected each other's fighting ability and not liked each other much for anything else. That hadn't changed. And while some of Falonar's ideas about the Eyriens here had pissed him off, he wasn't concerned, because he made the final decisions in Ebon Rih.

"We need more aristos living here to balance out the Eyriens who have common skills, to balance out our society," Falonar said. "We should have another Healer. We should have a Priestess. If some of the Eyriens will be leaving Ebon Rih, bringing in others wouldn't swell the numbers beyond what you're willing to allow here. And aristo families would bring their own wealth, so they wouldn't be a burden on your purse."

Lucivar studied the other Warlord Prince and wished he felt easy enough to accept that cup of coffee. "I would be willing to consider Eyriens who have other skills to offer the community, whether they come from aristo families or not."

Falonar looked puzzled. "Skills?"

"Healer. Priestess. Craftsman. Tailor. Seamstress. Although a couple of the women in the Doun settlement might be taking care of that last one."

"I don't think you understand," Falonar said. "I meant *aristos*. They don't need to work."

"They do if they want to live in Ebon Rih," Lucivar replied. "There isn't an adult living in this valley who doesn't have some kind of work, and anyone who isn't willing to agree to that doesn't belong here. The Queens in the rest of Askavi might feel differently, but I don't see any reason for anyone to sit around idle, no matter who they are or what bloodlines they can claim."

"You can't expect an aristo to stoop to menial labor," Falonar protested.

"I didn't say they would have to clean the horse shit off the streets; I just said that if they want to come to Kaeleer and live in Ebon Rih, they have to be willing to do some kind of work that will benefit the Eyrien community at the very least." Lucivar continued to study Falonar. "Is there someone in particular you want living here? A friend? Family? Is that what this is about?"

"No. It's not about someone in particular; it's about a whole level of Eyrien society that is missing. Can't you feel that?" Falonar's voice rang with frustration.

Lucivar huffed out a sigh. "No, I can't feel that. I never saw that part of Eyrien life, and the little time I spent around Eyrien courts before I was sent away from Askavi didn't impress me—and neither did the aristos in those courts. Whatever you think is missing . . . I never experienced it, so I don't feel the loss."

"That's the point, Lucivar! You *don't* know what the rest of us are missing."

He heard the passion in Falonar's voice and the conviction, but Hallevar, Kohlvar, and the other men willing to voice an opinion hadn't given him any indication that something was lacking.

Maybe Daemon or Father can tell me why this is so important to him. "Write up a report that explains what you think we need. Maybe we can find a way to bring some of that into the community." Did Falonar understand how much of a concession he was making by offering to read a damn report?

Apparently not. Judging by the resignation he saw in Falonar's eyes, what he was offering was nowhere near what the other man wanted.

"Maybe you should go back to Askavi Terreille," he said quietly. "There must be some Eyrien aristos who survived the purge. Maybe you'll find life there more to your liking now. I think it's clear to both of us that whatever you were hoping to find by emigrating doesn't exist in the Shadow Realm. At least not the way you hoped."

"Are you forcing me back to Terreille?" Falonar asked.

"I didn't say that."

"We rub against each other. Perhaps I should take command of the northern camps. That would give us both some breathing room."

Something floated in the air between them. Something subtle, almost hidden. When he'd been a slave and couldn't trust anything about the Queen who controlled him or anyone in her court, he survived because he never ignored what instincts couldn't shape into words.

He wasn't going to ignore his instincts now.

"I didn't renew any of the contracts of the men from the northern camps," Lucivar said. "I'm giving them a few extra days to pack their gear, but after that, they are barred from Ebon Rih."

Falonar looked shocked. "*You let all of them go?* Who's going to patrol that end of the valley?"

"Rothvar, Zaranar, and the other Riada Eyriens will have to stretch out a bit and work with the Agio Master of the Guard."

"Rihlanders aren't the same caliber of fighter as an Eyrien and you know it!"

"Yes, I do. But the Eyriens in those camps didn't do a damn thing when they were needed—and proved to Agio's Queen, her Master of the Guard, and me that they aren't needed here. Or wanted here."

They stared at each other.

"There's nothing more to say," Falonar said.

"No, I don't think there is."

Lucivar turned and walked out of the eyrie. Unless he had Ebon-gray shields already in place, it was the last time Falonar would see his back.

Falonar poured the coffee down the sink and carefully rinsed the pot. The spelled liquid he'd added to the coffee wasn't a *true* violation of the Blood's code of honor. It was too mild to be considered a compulsion spell, but adding it to food or drink helped make a person more open to suggestions.

He'd taken a lot of risks in order to buy those vials of liquid from a Black Widow. In the decade since then, he'd used the liquid carefully, slipping a few drops into a glass of wine or ale when there was a real chance that his words would make a difference, when that added *something* would help him influence people into making the right decisions. He'd used that influence to temper a punishment when a man didn't deserve to be punished at all. He'd used the liquid to stop perversions that would have harmed common Eyriens as well as aristos. That had to count for something.

But he'd used too much of the liquid when, at his father's demand, he tried to save his older brother from a punishment the fool had deserved. The change in the Master of the Guard's chosen method of discipline had been too pronounced. No one had suspected Falonar of causing that change, but the discovery that *someone* had tried to manipulate the Queen's Master had thrown the Lady into a rage.

The new punishment had gone beyond cruel. Falonar, his father, and their other male relatives had been required not only to witness the punishment but to participate in order to retain the family's social standing and their own status in the courts where they served. When it was done, the Queen let what was left of his brother live and sent him back to the family. And that had been the cruelest punishment of all.

His father couldn't publicly blame him without bringing attention to himself, but neither of his parents forgave him for what had happened to the favored son, and his mother deliberately began closing social doors, leaving him vulnerable to the whims of Prythian and the most elite members of the High Priestess's court.

The service fair had offered him a way to escape his family and Terreille, but it hadn't given him a way to regain his standing in Eyrien society because *there was no Eyrien society*. He accepted invitations for social events held by Riada's aristos, but it wasn't the same. He wasn't *someone* among the people who mattered.

There was nothing left for him in Askavi Terreille. What he needed he would have to build here. Since his effort to influence Lucivar had failed, he had no other choice except to eliminate the obstacle that stood in his way.

Lucivar opened the front door of his eyrie and smelled vomit.

Shit, he thought as he used Craft to remove the winter cape. Had Surreal come down with that stomach illness?

He didn't have time to wonder, didn't even have time to turn and hang up the cape. The wolf pups rushed him, so panicked their attempts to communicate were completely incoherent. Then Tassle appeared and . . .

"Papa! I'm sorry, Papa! *I'm sorry!*"

He heard Daemonar's voice, heard the slap of boots on stone, felt the change in air as something launched at him.

As he dropped the cape and reached out, he formed a skintight Ebon-gray shield around himself. His hand filled with fabric, and in the heartbeat he had to decide whether to shove something away or pull it close, he realized he'd grabbed Daemonar and pulled his boy close.

Little arms wrapped around his neck in a choke hold. "I'm sorry!"

Mother Night. When had Daemonar learned to create a sight shield? He was *much* too young for that level of Craft.

Sorry sorry sorry! the wolf pups wailed.

That probably explained *how* the boy had learned it.

"Okay, boyo," he said soothingly. "What are you sorry about?" From the smell of him, the boy had wet his pants, proving he wasn't as housebroken as Lucivar had thought.

"I broke Auntie Srell!"

Lucivar's legs went out from under him. He sank to his knees, clutching his son, trying to make sense of the words. He looked at Tassle.

Graysfang is with her. She will not hear us, Yas. She cries like she is being torn up in a trap, but we cannot smell a wound.

Sweet Darkness, have mercy.

He pried Daemonar off him. "Listen to me, boyo. You have to drop the sight shield."

"I don't know how!" Daemonar wailed.

"All right. Tassle will help you. You stay with him. I have to help Auntie Surreal. *Stay here*, Daemonar."

He whistled sharply as he headed toward the family's rooms. Graysfang howled in reply.

He found Surreal in the parlor on the floor, crying in a way that went beyond simple pain. He dropped to his knees and gathered her in his arms.

"Surreal? Surreal! It's Lucivar. You're all right now. You're all right!"

"He's just a little boy!" she screamed, feebly beating on his chest. "How could you leave me with a little boy?"

"I'm sorry. I didn't realize . . ." What? That she wasn't easy around children? That she'd been fine playing with Daemonar at Winsol as long as Marian or Jaenelle was also there, but she'd joined the adults the moment she was the only one with the boy? He just hadn't considered *why* she'd responded that way.

Her breathing wasn't good. It sounded like she'd torn something in her chest.

"I couldn't save them," she whimpered.

He cuddled her because it was the only thing he could do at that moment. "Surreal."

Words poured out of her. Names that made him sick just to hear them. Marjane. Rebecca and Myrol. Dannie. Rose. He knew those names. How could he not? He'd heard them whenever Jaenelle had nightmares about a place called Briarwood.

Trist. Kester. Ginger. The children who had died in the spooky house.

He held on to her, not sure she knew she wasn't alone.

When Marian suddenly appeared in the parlor doorway, he said, "Get Nurian. And Father." Late enough in the day for Saetan to be awake, and he wanted the strongest Black Widow available to examine Surreal.

Words poured out with a pain he couldn't imagine. How had she kept this inside her for so long?

She stopped speaking in midword, and he hoped that she was finally aware that he was there, that he would help.

She sagged in his arms, and there was a sudden, and terrible, silence.

SEVEN

Lucivar paced the length of the eyrie's large front room, back and forth, back and forth. The parlor would have been warmer but not more comfortable—not while he could taste Surreal's pain in the air and imagined he still heard the echoes of her crying.

Needing the movement, he continued pacing and kept an eye on Daemon, who had taken a position at the glass doors and done nothing but stare at the snow that had been trampled by Daemonar and the wolf pups over the past few days. Too silent and too still. Lucivar found this side of Daemon's temper the most frightening because there was no way to gauge the ferocity hiding under passivity—or how that temper would show itself when the passive surface broke.

"It wasn't Daemonar's fault," Lucivar said. "Or the wolf pups'. They were playing a game. They didn't know—"

Hell's fire. Who could have known Surreal would react by tearing the eyrie apart and scaring the youngsters so badly the wolf pups forgot how to drop the sight shield?

Daemon turned away from the glass doors, his gold eyes changing from blank to annoyed. "Of course it wasn't their fault. They're just children."

"If you're going to blame someone, blame me."

Daemon's annoyance held a sharper edge. "For what?"

Lucivar stopped pacing and faced his brother. "She didn't want to stay with the boy. Not by herself. But,

Daemon, I swear by the Jewels and all that I am, I didn't realize she was *afraid* to stay with the boy."

"None of us realized that. She wasn't troubled being around him when we were all at the Keep for Winsol."

"Because *we* were there. She wasn't responsible for keeping him safe. For keeping him alive." Lucivar started pacing again. "Before she collapsed, she kept talking about the dead children, how she couldn't save them."

"That answers the question of what's been eating at her these past few weeks," Daemon said, his voice bleak and angry.

"I can understand her feeling raw about the children who died in the spooky house, but she's been shouldering the weight of children who were dead before she knew they existed."

Saetan walked into the room.

Lucivar pivoted and Daemon moved with him. When they stopped, they stood shoulder to shoulder as they faced the High Lord.

"Nurian says there is nothing physically wrong with Surreal," Saetan said.

"Wasn't she listening to Surreal breathe?" Lucivar snapped. "If she's that incompetent, I'll kick her ass out of Ebon Rih."

"There is nothing wrong with Nurian's skill as a Healer," Saetan snapped back. "But if you need to kick someone's ass, kick your own for not considering the condition of Surreal's lungs when you insisted that she spend several weeks in the mountains during deep winter."

Lucivar rocked back, hurt by the verbal slap.

Saetan huffed out a sigh and held up a hand. "If Jaenelle had thought being here now would harm Surreal's health, Surreal would not be here. Right now, her breathing is raspy and she probably will have a wicked bitch of a sore throat from the crying and . . . screaming. And she has scrapes and bruises. But those things are understandable. Hell's fire, she went through every drawer, cupboard, and closet searching for the boy. The Darkness only knows what she thought she saw in the kitchen that led to the collapse. And *that* is the point. There is no physical reason for the way she collapsed after Lucivar found her."

"Bleeding in the brain?" Daemon asked.

"No."

"Nurian found nothing," Daemon said. "What about you?"

Saetan shook his head. "She's not in the Twisted Kingdom. Of that I am certain. But she's gone somewhere inside herself, and I don't know where to begin to look. Which is why Jaenelle is on her way. I think Witch is the only one who can help Surreal now."

And if Witch can't help her? Lucivar thought.

"I'll stay with Surreal until Jaenelle arrives," Saetan continued. "Nurian is checking Daemonar. Marian is going to keep him in his room until things are calmer. Tassle and Graysfang have taken the pups back to the wolf den and their mother." He looked at Daemon. "What about you?"

"Surreal asked me to look for some information in the Keep's library," Daemon replied. "I'll take care of it so she'll have it when she wakes up."

If she wakes up, Lucivar thought. They were all thinking it—and not one of them would say it.

"Is there anything concerning the Eyriens that needs to be dealt with right now?" Daemon asked.

Lucivar shook his head. "There is nothing that can't wait." Including making the decision about whether he could allow Falonar to remain in Ebon Rih.

He waited until Daemon left the eyrie and Saetan returned to the guest room where Surreal drifted in that unnatural sleep. Then he put on his winter cape and went outside, needing the sharp, cold air.

Wasn't anyone's fault—not the boy's, not the wolf pups', not even his. But if Surreal didn't recover, her loss would leave scars on all of them.

Daemon glided through the stone corridors of the Keep until he reached the room that held the Dark Altar—one of the thirteen Gates between the Realms.

He picked up a kindling stick, then used Craft to create a tongue of witchfire. Once the kindling stick was burning, he extinguished the witchfire and began lighting the four black candles that would open the Gate and take him from the Keep in Kaeleer to the Keep in Terreille, which was where he needed to go in order to find the information about Falonar that Surreal wanted.

An empty shell. That was what he'd seen before Saetan pushed him out of the guest room and told him to wait with Lucivar. Nothing but an empty shell.

He'd held an empty shell once before. He'd lain beside Jaenelle's bloody husk while the Sadist tricked Witch into leaving the Misty Place and rising high enough in the abyss so that he could force her to heal the young body that had been violently raped. Now it was Surreal that Saetan was trying to coax back into the body she had abandoned.

The first time he saw Surreal, she had been ten years old. Big eyes and long legs. Ready to bolt because she'd already learned that men were the enemy, but she'd had enough steel in her spine to stay beside her mother, Titian, while he listened to Tersa's request to help the woman and her daughter.

Pretty girl all those years ago. Beautiful woman now. And she still had steel in her spine.

Would it be enough this time? And what would it do to the boy if his auntie Surreal never recovered from what should have been an innocent game?

"Sweet Darkness, for Daemonar's sake and for her own, let Surreal come back to us," he whispered as he lit the last candle in the four-branched candelabra and blew out the kindling stick.

The wall behind the Dark Altar changed to mist, and Daemon walked through the Gate.

Four steps. That was all it took to move from one Realm to another. Four steps.

The moment he took that last step and walked into the other Dark Altar's room, he knew something wasn't right.

He'd been in the Terreille Keep's Altar room, and it didn't look like *this*. This room was rougher, smaller, *colder*.

Leaving the room, Daemon called in his heavy winter coat and put it on while he glided through the corridors to the doorway that should lead him to one of the courtyards.

Too dark. Too cold. Not enough candle-lights in the wall braces—not for this part of the Keep.

And the air smelled different.

He found the door and went out to the courtyard that would give him a view of Ebon Rih—or the Black Valley, as it was called in Terreille.

Twilight. That wasn't right. There had still been daylight when he'd returned to the Keep from Lucivar's eyrie.

There were lights in the valley, indicating a gathering of people, but he wasn't sensing enough people down there to populate a village. Of course, the witch storm two years ago had devastated the Blood's population in Terreille, so maybe it wasn't surprising to sense so few minds. But that explanation, while valid, didn't *feel* right.

It was winter here, as it should be, but there was an underlying cold that had nothing to do with the season, as if this place never felt the sun.

When he finally focused on the plants growing around the courtyard walls, he realized he'd never seen anything like them before.

There were three Realms, and the black candles were lit in a specific order to open the Gate to a specific Realm.

He'd been thinking about Surreal, distracted by the fear that she might not recover, and he'd opened the Gate without paying attention to the order in which he'd lit the black candles.

"Mother Night," he whispered, looking out over the valley. "This is Hell."

Rainier laid out the cards for a solitary game and watched a middle-aged Warlord approach the bar. Briggs kept his eyes on the stranger, giving the man no reason to look at anyone else in the room. Rainier nodded, silent permission for Briggs to notice him and bring him to the Warlord's attention.

A few moments later, the Warlord approached the table. "I'm Lord Randahl, Lady Erika's Master of the Guard. Could I have a few minutes of your time, Prince?"

Rainier tipped his head to indicate another chair at the table. "What brings Agio's Master to Riada?" he asked as Randahl took a seat.

"Wanted to talk to Prince Yaslana, but when I reached the landing web for his eyrie . . . Well, when shields go up around a home in *that* way, you know there's some trouble there—accident, illness, death."

An unspoken question. Because Rainier sensed concern rather than curiosity, he said, "Accident."

"Something a Healer can fix?" Randahl asked.

"We hope so."

A nod. "If there is any assistance Agio's court can give, just send word."

That told Rainier all he needed to know about how Randahl felt about Lucivar.

"So I felt those shields and came down here, mostly looking for a drink and a bite to eat," Randahl said. "Followed an impulse and asked the man at the bar where I could find a person Lucivar might trust with delicate matters. He pointed me to you."

"Why didn't you approach Lady Shayne or her Master?"

"Like I said, it's a delicate matter."

"Wouldn't you normally ask for the second-in-command?"

Randahl looked Rainier in the eyes and said nothing—and that told him everything.

Hell's fire.

"Yaslana rules the Eyriens," Randahl said.

"Yaslana rules the whole valley and everyone in it," Rainier countered.

"But specifically, he rules the Eyriens. None of them serve in a Rihlander court. They serve him."

Rainier tipped his head to acknowledge the distinction.

"That said, Lady Erika respectfully requests that the

Eyriens now residing in the northern camps be relocated if Yaslana intends to let them stay in the valley."

Rainier played a couple of cards to give himself time. "Has there been trouble?"

"Not yet, but it's coming." Randahl clasped his hands, rested his arms on the table, and leaned forward. "There's a storm growing in those mountains, and we're not sure why."

"You think it's because the emigration contracts are done?"

Randahl shook his head. "If anything, I'd think that would be more reason to walk softly. This has been building for a while now, but the Eyriens keep it hidden most of the time—especially when Lucivar is around."

"But not when Falonar visits the camps?"

Randahl let out a huff of air tinged with anger. "The words weren't said, you understand me? The last time Falonar was in the northern part of the valley, the Eyriens in the camps seemed pleased and stirred up, and I got the impression . . ." He hesitated.

"Just say it, Randahl."

"Is Lucivar going somewhere else? Is he planning to leave Ebon Rih?"

"No. Why?"

"From what we've observed lately, Falonar doesn't act like a second-in-command. At least, not with the Eyriens in the northern camps. And they don't *think* of him as the second-in-command, you understand me? So it's made some of us wonder if the valley is going to get split between the two Warlord Princes. And frankly, if that happens, Lady Erika doesn't want her people in Falonar's part of the valley."

"Lucivar isn't giving up any piece of Ebon Rih to anyone," Rainier said. "And a fight is out of the question."

"Because only one side walks away from a killing field. I know," Randahl said, nodding. "I know. But we don't feel easy about having Eyriens living so close to us when they aren't being held on a tight leash. Not *those* Eyriens, anyway. We'd really like to get those bastards out of the mountains around Agio. Just wanted Lucivar to know that."

"I'll see that he gets the message." *All the messages.*

Randahl sat back. "Thank you. I'll be heading back, then."

"Stay and have a bite to eat," Rainier said, raising a hand to catch Briggs's eye. *Food?*

He'd barely finished the thought when Merry swung out of the kitchen with a tray. She set plates on the table, said, "It's time for your healing brew," and headed back to the kitchen.

Randahl stared at slices of roasted beef and the mound of fresh vegetables. "Did we decide what to eat?"

"Apparently we did." Smiling, Rainier picked up a fork and dug in.

A thick-vined plant tried to eat him, which snapped Daemon out of his complacent wandering of the Keep's outer courtyards. In Hell, the Realm of forever twilight, most of the native flora and fauna welcomed the opportunity to dine on fresh blood, and any man who stumbled into this Realm was meat for the taking.

Even if that man was a Black-Jeweled Warlord Prince.

He turned toward the door and mentally stumbled when he saw Draca standing there, clearly waiting for him.

She said nothing. Just the same, he felt chastised for staying in the Dark Realm so that he could look round a bit— and for his boyish excitement at seeing a place that was usually forbidden to anyone who still walked among the living.

"Draca," he said pleasantly, as if the past hour or so had been nothing out of the ordinary. Hell's fire. How long had she been keeping track of him?

"Prince Ssadi," she replied. "Come with me."

She led him back to the Dark Altar and opened the Gate. Moments later, he felt the difference and knew they were in Terreille. Which was where he should have been in the first place.

"You're probably wondering why I was wandering around the other Keep."

"You are your father'ss sson," Draca said. "The firsst time he ssaw Hell, Ssaetan alsso became disstracted and forgot to return to the Gate."

The look she gave him muzzled curiosity. Doing his best to appear meek, since he had a feeling that anything else would get him tossed out of the Keep, he followed her to one of the sitting rooms that had a large blackwood work-table.

"It iss a cold day," Draca said. "You should eat ssome-thing hot."

"I just wanted to talk to Geoffrey about . . ." Daemon studied the Seneschal. "Thank you. That would be wel-come." And he was going to eat it whether he wanted it or not.

He also understood that he was supposed to stay where he had been put. Too bad this particular room was singu-larly uninteresting. Maybe that was the reason she had put him here.

Slipping his hands in his trouser pockets, Daemon wan-dered over to a window. Another courtyard. Here the plants slept under a cover of snow.

He knew this was Terreille, but he felt more uneasy, more vulnerable, than when he'd been foolishly wandering around the Keep in Hell.

He turned when the door opened and watched a ser-vant set a tray at one end of the blackwood table and re-treat, pausing in the doorway to let Geoffrey enter.

The Keep's historian/librarian looked around the room, then looked at him with black eyes that glittered with sharp humor. "What did you do to end up here?"

"Wandered where I wasn't supposed to."

The black eyes still glittered, but the humor was gone. "A dangerous thing to do."

"Yes," Daemon replied quietly. "And not something I'll do again without permission." It suddenly occurred to him that most people who stumbled into the Dark Realm never returned to the living—and he had too much to live for to be so careless.

"In that case, is there something I can do for you?"

"Surreal wants whatever family information you can find about Falonar."

"That might take a little while, but I should be able to tell you something from the registers," Geoffrey said. "Eat your meal while it's hot." When he reached the door, he stopped and turned back. "Pondering this should keep you out of trouble for a while."

As soon as Geoffrey left the room, a large piece of parchment appeared above the blackwood table, then drifted down to cover half the surface.

Not exactly a map, Daemon decided, feeling an excited chill. Two webs, one drawn in black ink, the other in red. The center point was labeled "Ebon Askavi" in his father's handwriting.

He picked up the bowl of soup and ate while he walked back and forth, studying the markers. The Keep. SaDiablo Hall. The Khaldharon Run and the Blood Run. The *cildru dyathe*'s island. The Harpies' territory. The thirteen Gates. Not a map showing terrain or boundaries. Not a map useful to anyone who couldn't ride the Black Winds, but he learned a great deal about Hell in the hour he spent perusing that piece of parchment, including the locations of the most benign and most dangerous sections of the Dark Realm.

Then the parchment vanished, the door opened, and Geoffrey returned.

"I found some information that might be of interest to you," Geoffrey said. "You can review the material in the private section of the library. Then you will go home."

Daemon let out a huff of laughter. "I guess I overstepped a few boundaries. Are you going to mention this to my father?"

"That you're looking into Falonar's bloodlines? Why should I?"

Messages received and understood, Daemon thought as he and Geoffrey went to the private section of the library.

Geoffrey hadn't shown him that parchment because he was the High Lord's son. Geoffrey had shown him that parchment because he was the High Lord's heir.

EIGHT

Her chest hurt like a wicked bitch, it was damn hard to breathe, and whatever she was lying on was too cold and too hard for any comfort.

Surreal moved her hands slowly, testing the surface beneath her. When her left hand found an edge and then air, she carefully rolled to her side so she wouldn't fall off whatever she was on. As she pushed herself upright, she felt an odd, painful pressure in her chest, and when she touched the spot . . .

She ripped her shirt open and stared at the rough, swollen, black lump between her breasts. Her muscles clenched, and the thing seemed to swell.

"What in the name of Hell . . . ?"

"Not Hell," said a lilting, lyrical voice full of caverns and midnight skies. "This is the Misty Place."

Apt name, Surreal decided as she looked around. Mist and stone, and nothing else except the altar she was sitting on.

"Where, exactly, is the Misty Place?" she asked.

"In the abyss."

"I've never seen it before."

"Very few can survive this place, and none without invitation."

What walked out of the mist was female but not human. Medium height, slender, and fair-skinned. An erotically beautiful face framed by a gold mane that was somewhere between fur and hair. Delicately pointed ears and a small spiral horn. Human torso and limbs, but also a fawn's tail and dainty horse's hooves. Human hands that had cat's claws instead of fingernails.

Surreal didn't recognize the body, but she recognized those sapphire eyes.

Living myth. Dreams made flesh. Witch. This was the Self who lived within Jaenelle's human skin.

"You brought me here?" Surreal asked. "Why?"

"Because of that." Witch pointed to the black lump.

"Poison?" She gingerly pressed the skin around the lump. Hell's fire, it hurt.

"Not a physical poison, but a poison all the same. A poison of the heart. You can't see it in the physical world, but it will cripple you, Surreal—has been crippling you for months now. So it's time to cleanse the heart."

Oh, that didn't sound good. "Should I lay down so you can cut it out?"

Witch shook her head. "This is up to you now."

"You expect *me* to cut it out of myself?"

"Not cut. Push. A kind of birthing, if you prefer."

"I don't prefer," she muttered. "What if I don't do this?"

"You were in so much emotional pain, you broke the connection between your Self and your body in order to escape. If you don't heal this now, you won't be able to mend that separation, and your empty body eventually will wither and die." Witch bared her teeth and snarled. "Show some balls and do this!"

Surreal bared her teeth and matched Witch's snarl. Then her chest muscles clenched. The skin at the top of the lump split, and a thick, black pus pushed out of the opening. When she forced her muscles to relax, the pus retreated.

Shit shit shit.

"You have to clean it out, all the way to the core," Witch said urgently. "If you don't, your dreams will never find fertile ground."

"What dreams?"

"The ones you're not ready to know. The ones I've seen in a tangled web."

The pressure in her chest was becoming unbearable, and she wanted to back down, wanted to say she didn't care what happened to her body. Then she imagined Lucivar trying to explain to Daemonar why Auntie Surreal never woke up after playing with him. "What do I need to do?"

"Push them out. Let them go. Forgive yourself for what you couldn't do."

Surreal shook her head, not understanding. Her chest muscles clenched again. Pus rose, but not far enough.

"Tell me their names," Witch said as she pointed to the black lump.

"Whose names?"

"The ones you couldn't save."

Suddenly she knew what the lump and pus had formed around—the feelings of blame, regret, sorrow. "I can't."

"Yes, you can," Witch insisted. "Tell me their names!"

A boy defying an order. Wings. Blood spraying the walls and floor. "Kester."

Her muscles clenched. Black pus burst out of the lump and soiled her shirt.

She relaxed her muscles and took a breath. Hell's fire, that stuff smelled putrid.

A boy screaming and screaming. A plucked eye rolling off the shelf.

"Trist," she cried, bearing down to push out more of the pus. "Ginger."

"Not your fault," Witch said.

"I should have been stronger, faster, *something*."

"You were injured and then poisoned. You did far more to defend and protect than the enemy had believed possible." A beat of silence. Then, "Who else didn't you save?"

The pressure in her chest kept building and building. Now that the wound was open, the older, harder pus was pushing up. "Marjane, who was my friend Deje's girl. You remember Marjane."

"Yes, I remember Marjane. I remember Rebecca and

Myrol, Dannie and Rose. They were just some of the girls who died in Briarwood."

More pus burst from the lump as Witch spoke each name.

"They were dead before you knew they existed," Witch said. "Yet you carry their names. Who else didn't you save?"

"You." Panting and sobbing, Surreal looked at the dream whose existence had changed so many lives. "I didn't get to Briarwood in time to save you."

"You weren't in time to save me from the rape, but you got me away from that place, and that saved my life."

Black pus continued pushing out of her chest, fouling her clothes and the altar. As an assassin, she had killed a lot of men as payment for girls whose names she never knew. She didn't carry the weight of those girls because she had settled the debt that was owed for their pain, for their loss.

More pressure, but this pus was so old, had been in her for so long, it was rough and hard, scraping the skin around the open sore.

"You're down to the core," Witch said. "The last name. Tell me the name of the first girl you didn't save, the name that has hurt your heart for so many years."

She clenched her muscles and *pushed*. Had to get the core out of her or it would all come back.

"Tell me."

"I don't know!"

"Then I'll tell you." Witch reached out and rested one claw above what was left of the black lump. "Her name was Surreal."

Pain. Agony. Twelve years old and hiding from whoever had killed her mother. Trying to survive in dirty alleyways. Raped but not broken. She hadn't been able to protect her body, but she'd been able to protect her Green Birthright power and her inner web. Twelve years old and beginning both careers—whore and assassin.

The hard black core pushed out, pushed out, pushed out

until Witch hooked it with a claw and pulled it out the rest of the way.

Surreal lay back. Her chest hurt, and it felt hollow—and it felt clean. For the first time in too many years, she felt clean.

She closed her eyes. The altar felt much warmer and softer now. Comfortable.

"Rest now, Surreal," Jaenelle said. "Rest."

She snuggled farther under the spell-warmed covers, breathed an easy sigh, and slept.

NINE

"Daemonar!"

Surreal jerked awake and struggled against the hand pressing on her shoulder, holding her down. Then a tenor voice said, "Be easy, cousin. Be easy. The boy is well."

She flopped back, boneless with relief as the voice and words were absorbed. Then she looked at the man who released her shoulder and took her hand, hiding none of the Gray-Jeweled strength behind his gentle touch. Long silver hair and slightly oversized forest blue eyes. Delicately pointed ears and a slender, sinewy build that was much stronger than it looked. "Chaosti?"

The Warlord Prince of the Dea al Mon smiled. "Welcome back."

Hell's fire. How long had she been gone?

"Two days," Chaosti said as if she'd actually asked the question. "It's been two days since you collapsed."

Snips of memory. Lucivar leaving her to watch the boy. A hunt for the missing child. Fear that turned into unbearable pain. And . . .

"How much of the eyrie did I wreck before I went down?" she asked.

A sharp, amused smile. "All of it. Every closet, cupboard, and hidey-hole. You were impressively efficient."

Shit shit shit. "Didn't find the boy." A small ache in her chest where the black lump had been.

"He and his furry brothers used the wolf pups' newly

learned skill of sight shielding to give themselves an advantage in the game of hide-and-seek. If you'd been aware of that, he would have remained hidden only for as long as you chose to let him have the advantage. As it was, Daemonar is very sorry he scared his auntie Surreal. Whenever he's slipped away from us, we've found him outside this door, hugging an armful of his books, waiting for you to wake up so he can read you a story."

"He can't read yet."

"I know. But it's the only thing he can do to take care of you."

Tears stung her eyes. She blinked them away. "Is there any reason I can't get up?"

"None." Chaosti squeezed her hand gently. "But there is something I'd like you to think about before you see the others."

She studied his face, but she couldn't read him as well as she could read Lucivar. "Think about what?" she asked warily.

"Coming to Dea al Mon for a visit with your mother's clan. Grandmammy Teele would like to have some time with you." He hesitated. "While we waited for your return, Lucivar and I discussed the training he wanted you to have and why he wanted you to have it. I agree with the why—"

Of course he did. He'd been just as upset with her for not shielding before going into the spooky house as Lucivar had been—and just as adamant that she polish her defensive skills.

"—but I think a different how and where would suit you better."

She blinked at him. "Say that again?"

"You're not Eyrien. While learning the Eyrien way of fighting is physically beneficial, it's not natural to who and what you are."

"Because I'm Dea al Mon."

"Yes."

Hadn't she thought along similar lines the day she'd clashed with Falonar in The Tavern?

"I'd like to make that visit, and I'd like some training with you, if you're willing. But not just yet." Weighing loyalties and confidences, she decided Chaosti was as much family to Lucivar as she was. "Something is going on here."

"Lucivar's decision to have some of the Eyriens leave Ebon Rih is not your concern, cousin."

"No, it's not, but he needs someone watching his back until they're gone."

"Isn't that what his second-in-command is supposed to do?"

"That's what a second-in-command is *supposed* to do," she agreed. "But there's more than one way to stab a man in the back."

"Like striking at his family?" Chaosti tipped his head to indicate the other people in the eyrie.

She nodded. "Or good friends like Merry and Briggs."

"Not wounds Lucivar would recover from easily," Chaosti said.

"If at all."

"Do you want me to stay?"

"No. But it wouldn't hurt to have the Eyriens in Riada get a look at another side of the SaDiablo family."

"Lucivar is with the other men now. I'll go over there and personally give him the news that you've recovered."

"Yeah. About that." He helped her sit up, then pulled the covers away so she could swing her legs over the side of the bed. "Was Marian upset about me tearing up the place?"

"She said it has given her an opportunity to look at what's been stored and pass along what is no longer needed."

Meaning the hearth witch must have been shocked when she'd returned to her home. "Shit."

He laughed as he helped her to her feet and bundled her into a robe. She didn't need that much help. She was sure of it. But she wasn't feeling steady enough to argue with a Warlord Prince *and* take care of herself.

He helped her to the bathroom, then helped her to the kitchen, where Jaenelle and Marian were talking.

"You're looking wobbly, sugar," Jaenelle said. "But you'll do." She sounded amused, but Surreal heard approval beneath the amusement.

"*Jaenelle!*" Marian scolded. "Be nice."

"Instead of honest?" Jaenelle asked innocently.

Marian narrowed her eyes at Jaenelle, then gave Surreal a brilliant smile. "We're glad you're feeling better. Are you hungry?"

Surreal's stomach growled. They all laughed.

"Auntie Srell!"

One moment she was standing on her own feet. The next, Daemonar flung himself at her and would have knocked her down if Chaosti hadn't caught her. He positioned a chair behind her and laughed in her ear as he said, "We really do need to work on your defensive skills, cousin."

She would have said something sharp and concise, but she was being hugged breathless by the boy in her lap.

"I'm sorry, Auntie Srell!"

"I know you are, boyo." She gingerly put her arms around him. "I know."

"Let Auntie Surreal sit by herself now and have something to eat," Jaenelle said.

Daemonar scrambled off Surreal's lap and into the chair next to hers. "Mama made good soup. You eat some. You eat too, Auntie J.!"

Hell's fire, Surreal said on a Gray psychic thread aimed at Jaenelle. *He's already got the bossy attitude.*

Uh-huh. Jaenelle set the table. *A Warlord Prince is born a Warlord Prince. Doesn't take long for the personality traits of that caste to show up.*

Any chance of me taking a bath by myself?

Only if you wait until nap time. Jaenelle brought the bread and butter to the table while Marian ladled the soup.

They ate quietly. Surreal saw the fatigue in Jaenelle's

and Marian's eyes, felt the fatigue in her own body. The past two days had been hard on all of them.

One more step, Surreal, Jaenelle said quietly. *You've cleansed your heart. In a day or two, when you're feeling stronger, let Lucivar give you a chance to cleanse the past from your body.*

I don't understand.

You will.

The door of the communal eyrie opened.

Since he was sparring with Zaranar, Lucivar didn't look toward the door, but he noticed the refreshing scent of crisp, clean air—and he noticed the psychic scent of the male who entered.

Chaosti's presence didn't break his concentration, but it broke everyone else's, including Zaranar's. By rights, Lucivar should have thumped the man for getting distracted when an adversary stood in front of him, but he understood why Zaranar instinctively turned toward the door, so he deliberately stepped away, ending the sparring match.

Even when Chaosti was relaxed and wearing his Birthright Green Jewel, as he was now, there was something wild about his physical and psychic scents that made other men wary. That had been true of the young man Lucivar had met years ago, and it was more true of the mature leader who protected the people and land of the Dea al Mon. Hell's fire, even Daemon recognized Chaosti as a serious adversary, despite the difference in the strength of Black against Gray.

It was fortunate for the Realm of Kaeleer that one man was married to Jaenelle and the other was related to Jaenelle. That connection was the only reason they were easy being in a room with each other—at least after the first minute, when they both struggled to leash their predatory natures.

So Lucivar didn't take advantage of Zaranar's distraction. Instead, he vanished his sparring stick and waited for Chaosti to cross the large room and join him.

No anger. No distress. But Lucivar didn't feel the tight muscles in his shoulders relax until Chaosti smiled.

"Surreal is awake," Chaosti said. "And since your boy has to divide his attention among his three favorite women, she'll have some chance to eat in peace."

Lucivar grinned. Surreal was back. Thank the Darkness for that.

"I've heard the Dea al Mon are skilled fighters," Falonar said with a tight smile. "The most feared warriors in the Realm. Would you be willing to give us a demonstration?"

Chaosti turned toward Falonar. "The Dea al Mon and Eyriens don't fight in the same way. I don't think you would find our weapons impressive compared to your own."

Having seen Dea al Mon weapons, Lucivar didn't agree with that, but he recognized the diplomacy of a warrior who didn't want to offend his hosts.

"Lucivar is quite free with teaching others how to use Eyrien weapons," Falonar said. "I assumed he'd shown you."

Why does that bother you? Lucivar wondered as he absorbed the odd note in Falonar's voice.

"He did," Chaosti replied. Then he shrugged. "If you'll find it of interest."

"It isn't necessary," Lucivar said, not liking the undercurrent of emotions that put an unsettling bite in the air.

He didn't object to the suggestion itself. After all, *he'd* enjoyed sparring with centaurs and satyrs as well as the Dea al Mon, not to mention playing stalk and pounce with Kaelas and Jaal. Pitting his skills against someone who had received a different kind of training had added zest to familiar workouts. But there was something about Falonar's suggestion that felt off.

Chaosti shrugged again. "I don't mind. In fact, I would welcome a chance to warm up muscles that have grown tight during the bedside vigil."

Lucivar couldn't argue with that, since it was the same reason he was here this morning—that and Jaenelle's firm suggestion that he leave the eyrie for a few hours because, according to her, he'd become too edgy to live with.

"Fine." He called in two sparring sticks and handed one to Chaosti. "We can start with the warm-up and move into a ten-minute spar. Hallevar? You'll keep the time?"

"I will," Hallevar replied.

Falonar stepped into the sparring circle. "I'll spar with Prince Chaosti. That will give your weather bones a chance to rest."

Lucivar rocked back on his heels. What the ... ?

Does he have a brain illness? Chaosti asked on a Gray psychic thread.

Not that I'm aware of, Lucivar replied.

In that case, I'll follow his lead, and we'll see where the path ends.

Chaosti's tone told Lucivar he wasn't the only one who thought there was something wrong, but the Dea al Mon stepped into the circle, holding the sparring stick with easy familiarity.

Lucivar moved away from the other men to have an unobstructed view of the match—and so that there was no one in his way if he needed to move fast. He'd never liked that Warlord Princes emigrating to Kaeleer had to serve five years to prove themselves when everyone else served two years or less. Now, watching Falonar, he appreciated the wisdom of demanding that extra time from males who came from such an aggressive caste. A man could hide for only so long before his true nature cracked the mask.

If the past two years had been a mask, who was the man behind it?

Falonar's moves were a little too quick, a little too sharp, to allow his opponent a safe warm-up. And judging by the puzzled, or disapproving, looks of the other Eyriens, Lucivar wasn't the only one who thought so.

Under other circumstances, he would have demanded a return to the proper speed and rhythm of the warm-up moves—or ended the match before it began. Except Chaosti had told him, more or less, to stay out of it in order to find out what Falonar *really* wanted.

And Chaosti had already warmed up his muscles before coming to the eyrie. That was clear by how fluidly he responded to the increase in speed. Clear to Lucivar, anyway. The fact that a supposedly stiff Dea al Mon was matching moves and speed with an Eyrien seemed to be pissing off Falonar.

They were in the last combination of warm-up moves. Falonar was now a half beat behind, which meant Chaosti committed to the move first. The last moves were partial turns to stretch side muscles. Fine for the grace of the warm-up, but a move that left the ribs vulnerable in an actual fight.

Chaosti twisted at the waist, lifting his arms, his weight slightly off balance.

That was when Falonar broke from the warm-up completely and struck. Since most Eyriens shielded between the warm-up and the actual sparring match, the blow would have bruised, if not broken, a few ribs.

Chaosti whipped through a one-footed spin and blocked the blow with his own stick—a move that had several Eyriens sucking in a breath at the speed and balance required.

"That's—" *Enough.* Lucivar didn't have time to finish the command before the sparring match escalated, and he didn't dare interfere, since it might break Chaosti's concentration. Besides, the Dea al Mon now had a tight Gray shield around himself and wouldn't sustain an injury more serious than a bruise while fighting against a man who wore Sapphire.

Chaosti was working hard, but Falonar was working harder to maintain the pace he'd set. As the match continued, it became apparent that Falonar was an excellent fighter—and Chaosti was so much more than an excellent fighter.

Lucivar glanced at the hourglass floating on air next to Hallevar. Only a minute left. Then he could drag Falonar away from the others and find out what in the name of Hell was wrong with the man.

The sparring match would end in a draw. He didn't think any man in the room would feel a bite to his pride that an Eyrien couldn't defeat this particular opponent.

Except, apparently, Falonar.

One moment there was the clash of sparring sticks. The next moment, there was a flash of sunlight on metal and Falonar was holding his bladed stick.

Chaosti raised his sparring stick to block a chest-high blow. The blade on Falonar's stick sliced cleanly through the wood—and the next move should have sliced through Chaosti's waist.

Eyriens fought in the air or on open fields—places that suited a race with wings who needed room to maneuver. But the Children of the Wood were a more intimate kind of fighter.

Lucivar expected it, but even he didn't see the transition from a broken sparring stick to Dea al Mon fighting knives. Moments after Falonar made that first aggressive move, he was lying on the floor, bleeding from a handful of wounds while Chaosti stood over him, one knife ready to slice his throat while the other knife was in position to rip through the Eyrien's belly.

Every Eyrien in that room now understood why the Dea al Mon were feared.

"Chaosti," Lucivar said quietly. "It's done. Step back."

"Is it done?" Chaosti asked just as quietly.

"Yes." *If he makes a move against you now, I will string him up with his own intestines and leave him for the carrion eaters.*

Chaosti stepped back, but he didn't vanish those long, elegant knives until he was out of the circle.

The Eyriens stared at him. Finally Hallevar said, "Thank you for the demonstration, Prince. It was . . . educational."

Chaosti tipped his head. "Yaslana is family. It was a pleasure to oblige him."

No one mentioned that it hadn't been his idea, but Lucivar figured the warriors knew the obliging had nothing to do with the match and everything to do with not killing Falonar.

The Dea al Mon walked out of the communal eyrie.

No longer concerned about provoking Chaosti into more of a fight, Lucivar felt his temper slip the leash, turning hot and jagged as he walked up to Falonar. "That's the second time you've used a sparring match to strike at a man. I guarantee you won't survive if you try it a third time."

He motioned to Zaranar and Rothvar. "Get *Prince* Falonar back to his eyrie and summon the Healer. The rest of you are dismissed—except you, Hallevar."

The two men hauled Falonar upright, ignoring his snarled protest, and carried him out. The other men departed as quickly as they could.

When he was alone with the arms master, Lucivar said, "Do you know what's wrong with him?"

Hallevar shook his head. "But I'm guessing he's finding it harder than the others to accept that when it comes to fighting, we might be second best in this Realm. Not you, of course." He hesitated, then added, "We're an arrogant race, Lucivar. You know that as well as I do."

"We are, and I do. But we're not stupid, and when a man wears the Sapphire, attacking a Gray-Jeweled Warlord Prince during a friendly sparring match is plain stupid, no matter what race the Gray comes from."

"Something has been chewing at him lately, that's for sure, but I can't tell you what I don't know. I *can* tell you that, even as boys, you and Falonar lived by different shades of honor."

"Honor is honor," Lucivar snapped. "It doesn't come in shades."

"Yeah." Hallevar smiled. "As boy or man, that line was always clear to you. I don't think it was ever that clear for Falonar, which is probably why the two of you can't get along any better now than you did back then. And there's the other thing." He frowned, then shook his head.

"Say it."

"You've fought your battles, and you've got nothing to prove. So you're content to rule a territory that isn't churned up all the time with power struggles and fights."

"In that, I'm no different than any other ruler in Kaeleer."

"Maybe that's the point. Hard for a man to make a name for himself if there aren't any battles to win." Hallevar sighed. "You made your name, Lucivar, whether you intended to or not. You spent most of your life away from Askavi, but you gained a reputation on the killing fields, and hearing your name was enough to put fear in strong men's eyes. No one is going to feel that way about Falonar."

No, no one would fear Prince Falonar. Not in Kaeleer, anyway.

"Now can I ask you a question?" Hallevar said.

"Sure. Ask."

"Why have you been so soft with the Eyriens in Ebon Rih? Those lazy bastards in the northern camps don't want to hold their own cocks when they take a piss, let alone do anything useful. Why didn't you kick their asses off these mountains sooner?"

"To go where?" Lucivar asked quietly.

"What difference does it make where—" Hallevar stopped. Stared.

"Yeah." Lucivar smiled grimly. "Everything has a price."

"You kept them close so they wouldn't become someone else's problem."

"And because I had hoped that I could build an Eyrien community here. The community didn't happen, but keeping them close to avoid trouble had worked for a few years. Now it doesn't, so it's time for them to go."

"Between the women's settlement in Doun and those of us who are staying in Riada, that's the start of a community, isn't it?"

Lucivar smiled. "Yes, it is."

"You think the other Eyriens will survive once they leave Ebon Rih?"

"Not for long. Not in Kaeleer." He blew out a breath. "If anyone needs me, I'll be down at The Tavern for an hour or so. I want to check on Rainier." *And Merry and Briggs.*

"You have any objections to the girl working with Tamnar this afternoon? Boy didn't get any practice in this morning, and the girl is always eager for a chance."

"I told Jillian she could have the training if she kept up with her schoolwork," Lucivar said as he headed for the door. "So I have no objections."

"Tamnar isn't a child, but he's not an adult yet."

Lucivar stopped, hearing discomfort in Hallevar's voice. "So?" If there was any question of the boy behaving inappropriately around Jillian, the arms master wouldn't have asked for permission to have them train together.

"Being a bastard and all, boy hasn't had much schooling with books and such. Wouldn't want to shame him by putting him with the little ones, but . . ."

Understanding the point of the conversation, Lucivar smiled. "I'll talk to Endar. I think we can work something out."

Hallevar didn't smile back. "That answer right there is the reason the people in this valley will never feel about Falonar the way they feel about you."

Yaslana is family. It was a pleasure to oblige him.

And that, Falonar thought as he sat alone and embraced the pain from his wounds, was more proof that Lucivar Yaslana wasn't one of them beneath the skin and shouldn't be ruling over real Eyriens. To acknowledge something like Chaosti as *family?* No man respectful of his race would admit to such a thing—even if it were true.

The Children of the Wood. They weren't natural, weren't *human*, despite their shape. Nothing human could have blocked an Eyrien—blocked *him*—that way or moved fast enough to inflict several wounds before he even saw the blade.

This place was making the Eyriens weak, making them less. Diminishing them a little more each day.

He had to save his people. It was fortunate Surreal had that unexplained breakdown. It had kept Lucivar occupied, and had bought more time for the rest of them. But Surreal had recovered, and Lucivar would once again focus on driving out the people who should have first claim to this land.

Falonar pushed himself out of the chair. It wouldn't do his wounds any good to be riding the Winds to the northern camps, but it had to be done.

If he was going to save his people, he'd better do it soon.

Lucivar walked into his eyrie and hung his winter cape on the coat tree near the door. All he wanted right now was a quiet, peaceful evening and an hour to soak in the eyrie's heated pool.

"Papa!"

But if he couldn't have peace, he'd settle for a happier kind of uproar.

He caught Daemonar and swung him around, making the boy laugh. "Hello, boyo."

"I read stories with Auntie J., and Mama made soup, and I didn't scare Auntie Srell!"

"Sounds like you had an excellent day."

"Yeah!"

"Meet me in the bathroom, and we'll wash up together for dinner."

"Okay!"

He put Daemonar down and watched his happy bundle of boy run. Shaking his head, he went into the kitchen, where Marian was adding her finishing touches to a beef roast and fixings.

"Hard day?" she asked, wiping her hands as he moved toward her.

"I've had harder days." He wrapped his arms around her and breathed in the scent of her, the warmth of her. "Where is Surreal?"

"She went back to The Tavern. She said if she had to have a male watch her take a bath, it was going to be

Rainier. Daemonar asking if her udders made milk probably weighed in on that decision."

He laughed. "Mother Night."

"Papa!" It sounded like the boy was near the bathroom, and if he wanted the boy to stay near the bathroom, he had to move his ass.

He sighed, then kissed Marian's forehead. "Your men better get washed up for dinner."

"And after dinner, will we talk, Lucivar?"

The choices and decisions he was making would change her life too. He nodded. "Once we've got the boy tucked in, we'll talk."

They ate dinner, took care of evening chores, and got their son settled in bed. Then they went to the heated pool in the eyrie, stripped down, and relaxed.

He told her about Falonar inviting Chaosti to a sparring match and then breaking honor by changing it to a real fight at the end when he realized he wasn't going to win.

He closed his eyes and tipped his head back to rest against the edge of the pool. Opening his wings, he fanned them just enough to have the water clean them.

"What did I miss, Marian?" he asked. "Until recently, I considered Falonar a good second-in-command."

"Maybe being second isn't enough for him," Marian said.

Second-in-command—and always second best to the half-breed bastard? That had mattered to Falonar a lot when they were boys. Maybe it still did.

"Three more years to fulfill his contract might feel like too long a time before he can fulfill his own ambitions," Marian continued.

Lucivar opened his eyes. "He's not being tortured or beaten every day. He's not chained or caged. That being the case, three years isn't a long time for someone from the long-lived races."

"Depends on whether you feel that you're being kept from something you want."

"What is it he wants?" Frustrated, Lucivar sat up. "I provided a place to live, basic furnishings, and a wage to cover personal expenses. If Falonar dreams of being wealthy, there are investments he can make and people he can talk to about those investments—my father being one of them."

"Maybe he misses aristo society," Marian said.

"He rubs elbows with the aristo families in Riada—and in Doun and Agio, for all I know. So he can't say he's got nothing but rough-and-tumble common folk for company."

"But the aristos are Rihlanders, not Eyriens."

"And that's my fault?"

"Of course it's not your fault."

Lucivar heard the bite in her voice. His hearth witch was getting riled on his behalf. It tickled him that she was defending him against himself, but since he didn't want to end up sleeping alone tonight, he figured it was best not to mention that.

"We could end up being the only Eyriens in Ebon Rih," he said. That wasn't really true, but in a few days, there would be so many less than there were now.

"When I came to this valley, the only other Eyriens I knew about were you and Luthvian. If our family ends up being the only Eyriens in Ebon Rih, or Askavi, or the whole Realm of Kaeleer, so be it. If they can't figure out how fortunate they are to have you as their ruler, then they don't deserve you."

She rose from the waist-high water with enough angry energy that he ducked his head to keep from being splashed in the eyes.

"Marian? Are you pissed off at *me*?"

Stepping out of the pool, she wrapped a towel around herself and stomped to the doorway. "I'm pissed off at Eyriens, and you're the only one handy. You figure it out."

Lucivar stared at the doorway for a full minute after she left, then sank back in the water.

"Well . . . damn." He might be sleeping alone tonight after all.

TEN

"Stop hovering," Surreal said as she and Rainier walked into the communal eyrie.

"I'm not hovering. I have my own workout to do. Frankly, I want to go home, and I can't until I've completed all the steps Lucivar and Jaenelle have decided are required." Rainier shivered. "Mother Night. I never thought about it being so *cold* here in winter."

Winter in Amdarh was much milder, not to mention all the shops, dining houses, and theaters that could be enjoyed during an idle, wintry afternoon. And the lovely sitting room in the town house where she could curl up and read for hours at a time if she felt like it.

What was winter like in Dea al Mon? She hadn't thought to ask Chaosti before he returned home to prepare the clan for her visit.

How much preparation did they need to do to accommodate one person? Maybe she should ask Jaenelle about that. She didn't want to cause problems for her kinsman.

"When do you think you'll go back to Amdarh?"

"Hopefully soon." Rainier hesitated. "I wish my leg hadn't been injured, and more than that, I wish I hadn't acted like a fool about it. But the work Daemon offered me will be challenging, and I'm ready to get started."

"And ready to tell your family that you don't need pity work and they can take a piss in the wind?" she asked.

He sighed. "That too. Although I *will* be more polite in how I phrase it."

Surreal grinned. "That's because you're not a cold bitch."

He huffed out a laugh. "Come on. We're here to sweat, so let's sweat."

She stripped off her coat, called in her sparring stick, and began going through the warm-up moves.

She felt good, better than she had in weeks. Still a touch raspy when her lungs were working hard or when she'd been out in cold air too long, but she felt lighter now, freer.

Except for one piece of unfinished business that kept scratching at her—the piece Jaenelle said Lucivar would help her finish.

Thank the Darkness this practice was in the afternoon, when few Eyriens would be present. She didn't want an audience for whatever Lucivar had in mind.

She'd completed her warm-up and was going through the moves a second time when Lucivar walked in, followed by Hallevar, Tamnar, and Jillian. The girl ran to the selection of sparring sticks that were kept on one wall and returned with two. Handing one to Tamnar, she settled into her own warm-up routine.

Surreal watched Lucivar watch Jillian. Any male who thought the girl didn't have a father to protect her was in for a rude, and rather terrifying, surprise.

After a nod of approval to Jillian and Tamnar, Lucivar called in his sparring stick and went through the warm-up. Then he stepped into the sparring circle, looked Surreal in the eyes, and smiled his lazy, arrogant smile. "Come on, darling. Let's see if you learned anything."

She stepped into the circle. "I've learned more than you think, *darling*."

"Shield," he said as he created a Red shield around himself.

She created a Green shield around herself.

He shook his head. "No. For this, witchling, you'll need the Gray."

"To spar?" she asked, surprised.

"To cleanse," he replied quietly.

She understood then what he was offering—to be a target for her anger against all the enemies she hadn't fought but who had crowded her dreams, including the Eyrien bastard who had killed Kester and hurt Rainier. In order to do that, Lucivar wasn't going to hold back, so that she *couldn't* hold back.

She glanced at Jillian, Tamnar, and Hallevar. "Maybe they should leave." She didn't care if Rainier stayed, but she didn't want Lucivar to have trouble with the Eyriens over this kindness to her.

"No," he said. "There are lessons that need to be learned. Let them learn."

With that, he began the sparring match, his strikes against her stick so light and controlled it was almost an insult. But she didn't push harder, didn't escalate. Not yet.

Light. Easy. Wouldn't stay that way. She could feel the anger rising, that last piece of unfinished business. But nothing was pushing her temper enough to snap the leash, and the sparring they were doing would exercise the body but it wouldn't finish cleansing the heart.

Then Jillian took a step closer to the circle, and Lucivar turned on the girl and struck out. She squealed, but raised her stick and blocked the blow.

A deliberate move, but not against Jillian. The move was intended to provoke *her*. And it worked. Surreal felt her temper snap the leash, and she went after Lucivar hard and fast, using everything he'd taught her about fighting with the sticks.

He met her, matched her, a powerful adversary. She didn't know how long they'd been fighting, wasn't going to care if some fool called time. But Hell's fire, she was feeling the rasp and burn in her lungs, so she wasn't going to be able to go on much longer.

She used Craft to enhance the sound of her raspy breathing to make sure her adversary heard it and thought she was fading. She fumbled a move, deliberately—and saw him hesitate for a heartbeat before he responded.

"That's enough, Surreal," he said.

"No, it's not." Not until she won.

She feinted, clumsily—and saw another hesitation. Then she planted her feet in a way that looked unbalanced, and he made a move that would take a lesser opponent out of a fight. But it left his ribs exposed for just a moment.

And she struck, putting Gray power into the blow.

He couldn't counter the move in time. Her Gray shattered his Red shield. He got his stick up enough to deflect some of the blow, but her stick still met his ribs with savage force.

Pain flashed across his face before he regained control and danced away from her.

She didn't follow because that look of pain cleared her mind and snuffed out her anger. He was no longer the adversary; he was Lucivar. She stared at him, seeing him again on the killing field in the spooky house. Grace and deadly power. Lucivar had walked into that place to save her and Rainier. And he'd walked out again without the smallest scratch. How could he get hurt now?

"You son of a whoring bitch," she said. "You did that on purpose." Because there were lessons that needed to be learned.

"I made a mistake, chose the wrong move," he replied.

"And the sun shines in Hell. *You did that on purpose.*"

"I fell for a trick and miscalculated the strength of my adversary's blow. I made a mistake."

Made a mistake. Like she'd done in the spooky house. She had miscalculated there, underestimated there. Wasn't the first time she'd made a mistake and probably wouldn't be her last. But making mistakes didn't make her weak.

She stared at Lucivar and understood what he'd wanted to give her before she left Ebon Rih. Maybe in a few weeks she would feel grateful. Right now she hated him for the price he'd just paid to give her this last lesson.

She dropped the stick and walked out of the eyrie.

Lucivar waited until Surreal left before he set one end of the sparring stick on the floor and leaned on it. He'd taken a risk giving her that opening, especially since she was channeling her Gray strength and he had stayed with the Red so that she would be the dominant power.

He really hoped what he'd seen in her eyes before she walked away wouldn't be there every time she looked at him from now on.

Everything has a price, old son. You gave her what she needed to finish healing.

"How bad?" Rainier asked.

"Ribs hurt like a wicked bitch, but I don't think any of them are broken," he replied.

"That was a damn fool thing to do," Hallevar said. "I'd better summon Nurian to look at you."

"Do that." That move had been a lot more foolish than he'd anticipated.

Rainier studied him a little too long. "Was it worth it?"

Fortunately, Nurian burst into the eyrie at that moment and he didn't have to answer.

But he did wonder if he would ever have the answer.

"Are you certain you can do this?" Falonar asked the Warlords who were the dominant males in the northern hunting camps.

"Are you certain about the information you got about that weak left ankle?" one asked.

"I'm certain," he replied.

"If we destroy his weak spot, he'll go down like any other man."

"I always thought his reputation was more farted air than truth," the second Warlord said.

"It's not like he made that reputation in Askavi among real warriors," the third Warlord said.

"He's also nursing bruised ribs that he got in a sparring match with a half-breed witch," Falonar said.

"Well, Hell's fire, this won't be any kind of challenge," the first Warlord said, laughing nastily. "It sounds like tomorrow will be a good time to put what is left of Lucivar Yaslana in a grave. You just make sure the only men left to come with him are committed to fighting on the right side of the line."

"I'll make sure of it," Falonar said. "By tomorrow evening, I'll be the Warlord Prince of Ebon Rih, and we'll be able to live the way Eyriens should."

ELEVEN

The following morning, Lucivar walked into The Tavern five minutes after it opened. He should have stayed home and given the ribs a day to rest, but his getting hurt for "foolish reasons" had scraped the wrong side of Marian's temper. By the time he'd swallowed breakfast, he'd also swallowed enough of her angry sympathy.

He'd gone to the communal eyrie only to discover that Falonar had taken half of Riada's Eyrien Warlords to do a flyover of Doun and the landen villages in that part of Ebon Rih. The remaining men had signed a new contract with him grudgingly but preferred working with Falonar—which made him wonder why Falonar hadn't taken *those* men with him on the flyover.

He couldn't stay home, and he didn't want to stay at the communal eyrie. So he ended up at The Tavern, being given a narrow-eyed stare by another woman.

"You pissed at me too?" he asked as he carefully settled himself on a stool at the bar.

Merry considered the question much too long before crossing her arms and nodding. "Yes. Yes, I am."

"Since I outrank you, can I get a cup of coffee anyway?"

Too many feelings in those dark eyes, and most of them translated to a "whack him upside the head" mood.

"I won't bring you coffee because you outrank me, but I will bring you some out of pity, since you are looking pretty pitiful right now."

"Fine, then. Bring me a large mug of pity." If he was getting this much temper and sass from lighter-Jeweled witches, thank the Darkness Jaenelle hadn't come here to check his ribs. She'd probably yank one out and beat him with it. Of course, she would put the rib back and heal it when she was done, but still . . .

Merry returned with a large mug of black coffee and a warmed piece of berry pie.

"Did you get any breakfast?" she asked.

"Some."

"I could make you a sandwich or heat up some soup."

She wasn't through being pissed at him, but unlike Marian, she hadn't gotten a look at his ribs, so she had less reason to hold on to her anger.

"Thanks, but this is plenty." He dug into the pie.

Merry looked like she was getting the place set up for business, but she wasn't actually accomplishing anything except keeping an eye on him. Finally she came up beside him.

"You did it on purpose, didn't you? Surreal was *raging* about you yesterday, and what she said made sense."

Well, that wasn't good. Of course, it was never good when a raging female made sense to other females, because that usually got a man into a whole lot of trouble.

"It doesn't matter what you said; you didn't make a mistake," Merry said. "You knew exactly what you were doing when you left yourself open for that last blow."

He sipped his coffee and studied her. Then he sighed. "She needed to beat an enemy into the ground. I figured I was the only one who could take the pounding she needed to inflict."

"Well, why didn't you ask Jaenelle to make one of those fancy shadows and fix it so Surreal could beat it into a mushy pulp?"

He shook his head. "Jaenelle has made some of those shadows for me to beat down to a mushy pulp, so I can tell you it doesn't feel the same. It's safe because you know it isn't real. There are no consequences for what you do or serious risks for yourself. Most of the time that's a good way to purge temper and bad feelings. But when something has festered for a lot of years like it has with Surreal, sometimes you need to work off that temper by fighting against a flesh-and-blood opponent, knowing there are consequences and risks."

"You let yourself get hurt."

He heard the undercurrent of anger building in her voice again. She just wasn't going to let go of that detail. "Okay, that part *was* a mistake. Your gender gets *mean* when you fight, and while I took into account that Surreal is stronger than she looks, I forgot that she can be a sneaky bitch. She used her own illness as the bait for the trap, and I fell for it." And damn if he didn't admire her for it. Hearing that raspy breathing and seeing her falter, he'd hesitated instead of pushing harder to put her on the floor and end the match.

The coffee had cooled enough, so he drained his mug with long swallows before setting it on the bar.

Merry fetched the coffeepot and refilled his mug. "You're the Warlord Prince of Ebon Rih. You're not supposed to fall for a trap."

"If she'd been anyone but family, I wouldn't have."

She offered no other comment, but his answer must have satisfied some unspoken concern, because she finally started doing her own work while he finished the piece of pie.

When he and Merry reached their usual easy silence, Lucivar figured it was time to leave if he wanted to avoid running into Surreal. He wasn't ready to deal with her yet.

As he eased off the stool, he said, "Thanks for the pie and coffee."

"If Marian is still annoyed with you come midday, I'll have a spicy stew cooking," she said. "And if you can avoid riling up the women you know for a few hours, I can leave out the big dose of pity."

Lucivar gave her a sharp grin. "Darling, whatever you're dishing out is too tart to be pity."

She didn't laugh, but she couldn't keep a straight face either. "Go away."

"I'm going. Even if Marian works off her mad, save me a bowl of that stew."

As he reached the door, a young Eyrien Warlord from the northern camps burst into The Tavern, followed by the Eyriens who had been at the communal eyrie.

"The landen villages at the north end of the valley are under attack!" the Warlord said.

"Who's attacking?" Lucivar demanded.

"Don't know. I was heading back to camp when I was ordered to come here and find you. Not just Jhinka. Whoever is fighting the Eyriens is also Blood. Our men have pushed the fight away from the villages, but we need help. We need it now."

"Did you contact the Master of the Guard in Agio?" Lucivar asked.

A moment's hesitation. "I didn't, no. I was told to fetch you. Someone else must have gone for Lord Randahl."

Most of the Eyriens in the northern camps wore Jewels with sufficient power to send a psychic call for help to the Blood in Agio. Hell's fire, there were plenty of them who could reach him here. If they needed help so badly against this unknown enemy, why waste time having a Rose-Jeweled Warlord ride the Winds to Riada to fetch him?

There was one reason he could think of.

Lucivar eyed the Eyriens Falonar had left behind this morning. "You coming with me?"

"We are," one of them answered.

"Then head out. I'll meet you there." He turned and walked toward the short hallway in the back of the building that held the water closets available to customers.

"We'll wait for you," one of the Warlords said.

Lucivar stopped. Turned. "I'm not driving a Coach to a killing field, and I'm not shielding all of you on the Red Winds and then dropping down onto a killing field. So you catch the Winds and go. I'll still arrive close behind you. But first I'm going to take a piss."

"The Red Winds?" one of the men asked. "Not the Ebon-gray?"

Lucivar shifted his weight—and deliberately winced. "Not today."

Two flashes of emotion filled the room, equal in intensity, at his inability to hide how much an imprudent move hurt his ribs—alarm from Merry and relieved anticipation from the Eyriens who watched him.

"Go on," he said.

Waiting until the Eyriens left The Tavern, he raised a hand and used Craft to put a Red lock on the front door. Then he went into one of the water closets. He'd opened his fly when Merry burst into the small room.

"Hell's fire, woman," he growled.

"Something is wrong," she said. "This all sounds wrong."

Of course it did. It *was* all wrong. "Get out of here."

"Lucivar."

"Merry, he's young and excitable. If things in the north were as bad as he said, he would have been there fighting with the other Eyriens, and I would have been summoned on a psychic thread by Lady Erika's Master of the Guard. So stop fussing. I'll take care of this." He gently pushed her out of the room and closed the door in her face.

He had no doubt in his mind that he could—and would—take care of this. He just hoped he could convince Merry of that sufficiently to delay her sounding the alarm. He didn't want anyone standing with him. Not today. Today he wanted to know with absolute certainty the faces of his enemies.

That much decided, he quickly prepared for the coming fight.

First he created the Ebon-gray shields he usually put around his anklebones to give them extra support. Next, he shaped an Ebon-gray shield over his ribs. Then he called in the Ring of Honor that Jaenelle had given every male in her First Circle. She no longer wore Ebony Jewels, but the Ebony power she had put into those Rings to fuel the shields in them was still as potent as ever.

He slipped the gold Ring over his cock and used Craft to adjust the size to a comfortably snug fit. Engaging the

Ring, he created a skintight Ebony shield around himself, then layered an Ebon-gray shield over that, and finally a double Red shield.

Would any of the men he was about to meet look beyond that second Red shield for what lay underneath? Especially when the Eyriens who, supposedly, were going to fight alongside him told their comrades that Lucivar Yaslana was already too injured to wear the Ebon-gray?

He vanished the pendant that held his Birthright Red Jewel, called in the pendant that held the Ebon-gray, then put a sight shield over it. He held out his right hand and carefully triggered the spell in his Red ring—a spell he'd never shared with anyone except his uncle Andulvar and cousin Prothvar. Seven thin psychic "wires" spun out from the Red Jewel in the ring, stopping when they were a handspan in length. When fully extended, those wires could slice through lighter-Jeweled shields as easily as flesh, and he could slaughter dozens of men with a single sweep of his arm. Drawing the wires back into the ring, he ended the spell.

After fastening his trousers, he took another minute to call in and check all his weapons.

He walked out of the water closet and found Merry blocking the end of the hallway. He didn't have time to negotiate, so he locked his hands around her upper arms, lifted her, and set her back down out of his way.

The shields around his ribs were working just fine. He'd hurt tomorrow, but the sore ribs and bruises weren't going to interfere with anything he had to do today.

"Lucivar! This isn't right. It has to be a trap!"

Which just proved she was a smart, observant woman.

"I know," he said.

"Then you need help."

"No, I don't. Merry . . ."

"Don't you 'Merry' me," she snapped. "There could be *thousands* of them out there waiting for you!"

"There aren't thousands of Eyriens in the whole of Askavi Kaeleer, let alone in Ebon Rih."

"Well, there are still lots of them and one of you."

"Merry . . ." Did any of them understand what his wearing Ebon-gray Jewels meant? Did the Eyriens really know what kind of power was about to meet them on a killing field?

He kissed her forehead. "If I get hurt, you can yell at me all you want. I'll be back in time for that bowl of stew. Until then, rest easy."

Releasing the Red lock on the front door, Lucivar walked out of The Tavern, caught the Ebon-gray Winds, and headed north.

The moment Rainier returned from his walk, Briggs gave him a "need you" tip of the head.

"Merry is in the kitchen," Briggs said. "Something happened this morning while I was out getting supplies. She says she's not supposed to say anything yet, but maybe she'll talk to you, since you work for Prince Sadi."

"Why would that make a difference?" Rainier asked as he took off his coat and vanished it.

"Because I think it has something to do with Lucivar."

He'd worked his damaged leg right up to its limit today, so he moved with care to the kitchen. He paused in the doorway, watched Merry pull a baking sheet of biscuits out of the oven, and wondered if the woman realized they were burned past edible.

"Merry?" he asked quietly, taking a step into the kitchen. "Is there something you need to tell me about Lucivar?"

She piled the biscuits on the cooling racks into cloth-lined baskets, then slid the ones on the baking sheet to the cooling racks.

"I don't know. He said not to worry, but how am I not supposed to worry? It felt *wrong*. It all felt wrong. But I don't think I'm supposed to say anything yet, and that feels wrong too."

Rainier wrapped a soothing spell around his voice. He didn't want to diminish her feelings; he just wanted her to calm down enough to give him information instead of jumbled words. "What happened this morning?"

A torrent of words spilled from her. Then she finished with, "I don't like any of this because *I* think this is a trap, but Lucivar was being too stubborn to listen. Here. Take this basket out."

Rainier almost dropped the basket she thrust into his hand, unprepared for the weight. He looked at the biscuits, thought about how much he valued his teeth, and limped out to the bar. Setting the basket on the counter, he told Briggs, "Don't let anyone eat these—and don't drop any on your feet."

"Is she right?" Briggs asked. "Is there trouble?"

"Yes, I think she's right, and there is trouble." Since he knew who was in Ebon Rih this morning, may the Darkness have mercy on whoever was causing that trouble—especially if anything happened to Lucivar because of it.

Surreal set the papers down and looked at the two Black-Jeweled men standing on the other side of the table. "That's it?"

"That's it," Daemon replied. "Both of Falonar's parents can claim aristo bloodlines, but they aren't on a level with your mother's bloodline—or with Lucivar's bloodlines. Falonar has an elder brother, who doesn't wear Jewels as dark as his, and he has a few cousins but . . ." He shrugged.

"Darling, there are no dark secrets to explain Falonar's behavior," Saetan said. "Eyriens feel animosity toward anyone whose parentage can be questioned or whose parentage isn't pure Eyrien. That has been true for as long as I've known the race—and it's more true of the aristos than the other levels of their society. A man who wants a leader who can keep him alive on a battlefield is going to be more interested in the man's ability to fight and lead and be much less picky about bloodlines than an aristo looking to marry and mate—and to use both to advance his own ambitions."

"I see," Surreal said. And, finally, she did. The romance and the emotions had been on her side, never on his. Falonar had used her professions of whore and assassin as the excuse to walk away because it wasn't in him to see her as an equal. "I guess that's why some of the Eyriens, like Rothvar and Zaranar, are comfortable working for Lucivar, and others will never see him as anything but a tool to be used."

"Yes, that's why," Saetan replied with an edge in his voice. "And that's why it's time for the Eyriens who won't acknowledge him to leave Ebon Rih. They're nothing but salt in an old wound."

She heard something else in that deep voice, something that made her shiver. *Do you think Uncle Saetan remembers that he retired from the living Realms and isn't supposed to interfere?* she asked Daemon on a Gray psychic thread.

Do you think he cares about such details right now? Daemon replied mildly.

Shit shit shit. How long had Saetan been watching those fools thumb their noses at his son, waiting for Lucivar to reach his own conclusions about Eyrien society? And how much longer would the High Lord of Hell wait before taking care of the troublesome little problems himself?

Surreal?

Rainier?

We might be in for some trouble here. Could you come back to The Tavern?

Hell's fire. *On my way.*

Could you ask Prince Sadi to find a reason to stay with Marian until this is sorted out? Rainier hesitated. *It might be prudent to have Jillian stay at Lucivar's eyrie too.*

Mother Night. She turned to Daemon and Saetan. "Rainier says Daemon should stay with Marian—and Jillian should be under his protection too."

"Where is Lucivar?" Daemon asked too softly. A minute later, he answered his own question. "He's in the northern end of the valley, and he doesn't want company." He exchanged a look with Saetan.

"Who is with him?" Surreal asked. "Who's watching his back?"

"No one is with him because that's the way he wants it,"

Daemon replied. A pause, but his expression indicated a quick conversation with someone beyond this room. Then he focused on her again. "And we're watching his back. You go to The Tavern. Rainier is going to escort Nurian and Jillian to Lucivar's eyrie. He'll also bring Lord Endar's family there."

She heard what was being said under the words—*they were going to lock down and defend everyone who could be used as a weapon against Lucivar.* "Where in the name of Hell are the other Eyriens?"

"That is the question, isn't it?" Saetan said. "And until Lucivar returns and provides the answer, I don't think you should count on them for help of any kind."

Or trust them, Surreal thought. She stepped away from the table and made a formal bow. "High Lord."

"Lady Surreal."

She walked out of the sitting room with Daemon on her right. She called in her heavy winter coat and put it on as they headed for an outside door. He didn't bother.

"Do you have any sense of where Falonar is?" she asked.

"Not in Riada, and not with Lucivar," he replied.

"A second-in-command should be there to watch his back."

"He doesn't need a second-in-command," Daemon crooned. "Lucivar has family."

TWELVE

Lucivar put a sight shield around himself the instant he dropped from the Ebon-gray Wind and glided toward Agio. His psychic probes revealed nothing out of the ordinary, and his view of the countryside below showed him a village with streets cleared of snow, smoke rising from chimneys, and people going about their business.

Lord Randahl? Lucivar called on a psychic thread.

Prince Yaslana? May I be of service?

No, I was just flying over the northern end of the valley. Anything I should know about?

We haven't seen the Eyriens these past couple of days. I guess they're packing up. So it's been quiet around here and in the landen village too. We took a look around there this morning. Randahl paused. *Didn't check out the other landen villages in the north, though. I was planning to send some men out tomorrow. Should I send them out now?*

No need. I'll fly over. If I see anything that needs your attention, I'll let you know. Otherwise, a visit tomorrow will be fine.

Lucivar broke contact and flew toward the mountains and the other landen villages. No sign of trouble, fighting, or any kind of attack. No sign of Jhinkas. Pumping his wings to fly higher, Lucivar caught an air current and rode it back to where the Eyriens had gathered. He studied the men—and the killing field—below him.

No fighting. No sign of dead or wounded. A handful of Eyriens with bows were hidden among a tumble of boulders that were distant enough that a person approaching on the ground wouldn't consider those boulders part of the killing field.

But he did now, and as he rode the currents, he considered the shape and the boundaries of the killing field—and the honor of the men who were waiting for him.

He descended into the abyss to the level of his Ebongray Jewels and waited for the Eyriens to arrive from Riada. When he spotted them leisurely gliding toward the other men, he caught the Red Wind, headed south for a few minutes, then turned and headed back. Removing the sight shield, he dropped from the Winds and glided down to the same spot they had.

They saw him coming and began moving into position. If he hadn't seen the archers, it would look like the men were simply shifting to give him room to backwing and land. Since he *had* seen the men hidden among the boulders, he knew the spot they had chosen was the only place that gave all the archers a clean line of attack.

Lucivar landed. The other Eyriens closed around him in a half circle, leaving the archers' side open.

He took a careful look at men who were now the enemy. Hallevar wasn't among them. Neither was Kohlvar, Rothvar, Zaranar, or Endar. Neither was the youngster Tamnar or the handful of other Eyrien Warlords from Riada who had wanted to work for him.

"I gave you a chance to build a new life, and this is your choice?" Lucivar asked quietly.

"When Falonar rules this valley, we'll have more," one of them said.

"You're not going to follow the Blood's code of honor and invite me to step onto the killing field?"

"Honor doesn't apply to a half-breed bastard."

Old heart wounds, old painful memories, and old anger rose with him to the killing edge. "Then there is nothing left to say." Lucivar smiled a lazy, arrogant smile. "Go ahead. Since I'll be taking the last one, you can have the first blow."

Five arrows hit the shields on his left leg between knee and ankle.

Lucivar spun before the other Eyriens thought to move. As he spun, he called in his bow, already nocked. A ball of Ebon-gray-fueled witchfire formed around the arrowhead as he drew the bowstring back and released it the moment his spin aligned him with the boulders. As he finished the spin, he vanished the bow and called in his war blade.

His arrow hit the boulders, and the witchfire exploded with a furious heat that cracked the boulders and charred the marrow in the bastards' bones before they had time to fall.

A heartbeat of stunned silence. Then the rest of the Eyrien warriors threw themselves at him, and the fight began.

Surreal walked into The Tavern and looked around. No more than a dozen people sitting at tables, grabbing an early midday meal.

"Gentlemen," she said, using Craft to enhance her voice. "If you have children, you will fetch them from school and take them home. If your wives are out doing the marketing or working, you will tell them to meet you at home. Whoever in your family wears the darkest Jewels will put a shield around your residence. Go home and stay there. Do it quietly, and do it now."

She opened the door and stared at them.

"What did the Queen of Riada say?" one of the men asked.

"About me delivering Prince Yaslana's orders? Not a thing. Lady Shayne's court is taking care of their part in locking down this village."

They left their meals half-eaten and hurried out to gather up their families and get home.

Surreal closed the door, shrugged out of her coat, and put a Gray shield around The Tavern.

Merry took a step toward her. "What has happened?"

"Nothing yet—and we want to keep it that way." She had a feeling there was plenty happening. But not in Riada.

A minute later, Rainier gave her a psychic tap. She dropped the Gray lock on the door long enough for him to slip inside, then locked it again.

Rainier said, "Until someone makes a move, we've done what we can do."

Surreal nodded—and hoped what they had done was enough.

Eyriens called it red rain. The gritty mist made from the flesh, blood, and bones of bodies exploded by unleashed power sometimes hung over killing fields for days, suspended by the very power that had destroyed the bodies.

The young Warlord who waited at the edge of the killing field couldn't see much, not with the rain hanging so thick around the center of the field, but he could still hear the fighting—the snarls of enraged men, the clash of war blades.

He hadn't expected Yaslana to last this long, not with so many superior fighters working to bring him down. Not when a half-breed was fighting against *real* Eyriens.

An explosion of power ripped past him. Thunder drowned the field and shook the ground. Red rain hit him, even here at the edge of the field, and something struck his face. He pulled a small shard of bone out of his cheek and stared at it until he realized there were no sounds. None at all.

But *something* still moved on the field. He was certain of that.

The young Warlord backed away. He thought about calling to the other men, but he wasn't sure who—or what—would answer him. If some of the Eyriens made the transition to demon-dead during the fight, they would be looking for fresh blood to consume. It would be better if he didn't confront his comrades when he was alone.

He backed away from the field until he was able to catch the Rose Wind and race back to Riada with the terrible news that Lucivar Yaslana was dead.

THIRTEEN

"What are we still doing out here, Falonar?" Rothvar asked. "We've done a flyover of Doun and the landen villages that answer to the Queen there. We've checked the settlement—"

Kohlvar growled an opinion about so many men going there without Yaslana—especially since *he* was the one who had been required to offer assurances about the men who were with him.

"—and the women are tucked in just fine. Plenty of food, plenty of wood," Rothvar continued.

Tucked in, Falonar thought as he turned to face Rothvar. Some of those women should have been providing domestic service for the northern camps instead of keeping their skills—and their bodies—to themselves. Not one of them wore dark Jewels or came from a female caste that carried any prestige and required being handled with care. He'd allow the children to remain in the Doun eyries and work out a rotation for the women. A few would remain to care for the children while the others provided the service they should. If their performance was satisfactory, they would be allowed to visit their children and rest during their moontime days before returning to the camps.

Some might think that was harsh treatment, since these women hadn't been required to cuddle anyone but themselves, but the new arrangement would benefit the warriors, and in the end, what benefited the warriors benefited all Eyriens—including the aristo Ladies who would soon have a reason to settle in Ebon Rih.

"Do you have a problem with following orders?" Falonar asked coldly.

"Nope," Hallevar said. "But we could have spread out and taken a good long look at this part of the valley from the Keep to the southernmost edge in half the time."

"If we're spread out, then each man is a single target," Falonar said.

"We weren't flying in a fighting formation," Zaranar said. "Routine check of this part of the valley, you said. Nothing different from what we do every week."

"Except only a handful of men usually go out for these flyovers," Rothvar said. "And we're more than a handful of men."

"Funny how all the men assigned to this flyover are the ones who signed on to work for Lucivar," Hallevar said. "Wasn't any reason for me to be out here today. Or Tamnar, Endar, or Kohlvar."

Zaranar and Rothvar had already descended to their full strength, and they were already protected by at least one shield. Within moments, the other men would do the same. No dark Jewels among them, but if a fight started, they would focus on bringing him down, not on surviving—would focus on buying enough time for whoever was sent from the fight to warn the Queens and the Keep.

He couldn't afford that fight. Backing down left a sour taste in his mouth, but this morning proved one thing: He wasn't going to be able to trust any of these men once he became the Warlord Prince of Ebon Rih. That was a hard disappointment, especially the loss of a weapons maker of Kohlvar's skill.

But he would deal with that another day.

"I followed my instructions, and that included who was assigned to this flyover," Falonar said. "If you have a problem with those instructions, take it up with Yaslana."

"We'll do that," Rothvar said.

They moved out in two fighting formations, flying hard

and fast until each group caught the Wind that could accommodate all of them.

Falonar stayed on the mountain overlooking Doun. He'd catch up to them easily enough, and be back in his eyrie when the news came from the north.

There were only four people in The Tavern, but it felt much too crowded, and the air felt too stuffy to breathe. Slipping into her coat, Surreal released the Gray lock on the door, stepped outside, and studied Riada's main street.

Nothing moved. Not a horse, not a cart, not a person. Not even a dog. The village was locked down. Lady Shayne hadn't hesitated when Surreal had given that order—and hadn't asked why *she* was giving the order on Yaslana's behalf instead of Falonar. And wasn't that interesting?

Sadi? she called on a psychic thread.

Something wrong? he asked.

No, it's quiet— Wait. She saw the Eyriens arrowing toward Riada. Fighting formations. That couldn't be good.

Holding the psychic link open between them, she wrapped herself in a Gray shield and stepped to the edge of the sidewalk. Being the only person in sight, she wouldn't be hard to spot.

They came in fast, then backwinged and landed half a block from where she stood. Rothvar and Zaranar led the formations. They were the ones who approached her, along with Hallevar and Kohlvar. The others called in crossbows or war blades and watched the buildings and the sky.

"The village is locked down?" Rothvar asked. "Why?"

"Where is the Healer and her sister? Endar's family?" Zaranar asked.

She spotted Falonar gliding toward them, backwinging with too little concern considering how tense the other men were. She waited until he joined the four men who seemed to be the unofficial leaders of the group.

"There is trouble in the north," Surreal said. "There's a chance it's going to spill over onto Riada. So we've prepared the village and alerted the Queen and her Master of the Guard. Nurian, Jillian, and Endar's family are with Marian."

"Yaslana?" Hallevar asked.

She looked straight at Falonar. "He's gone north to deal with the problem." *You hadn't figured the Queen would lock down the village, putting everyone on alert, did you, sugar? And as sure as the sun doesn't shine in Hell, you weren't expecting anyone from Lucivar's family to be anticipating a fight here.*

"When did he leave?" "We were just farting over Doun with that flyover. Why didn't he call us?" "Who did he have with him?" "Who's guarding his eyrie?"

A jumble of voices since all four men were asking the same questions, throwing the words at her.

Thunder rolled down the mountain, a warning of temper that silenced all of them.

"Prince Sadi is guarding the eyrie," Surreal said. "Yaslana will have to answer the rest of your questions when he returns."

The door behind her opened. Rainier stepped out, followed by Merry and Briggs. Not bothering to swear at them for leaving the shielded building, she put a Gray shield around the three of them and said, *Stay put.*

"Have they heard from Lucivar?" Merry asked.

"No," Surreal said, watching the Eyriens. All the Warlords were angry. If there *was* trouble in the north, they shouldn't have been pissing around with a flyover. Maybe they wouldn't have followed Lucivar north, but they would have formed a guard to watch over Doun and Riada.

Nothing that was done today made sense if there was *real* trouble.

She'd barely finished that thought when an Eyrien came winging in from the opposite direction—from the north.

He stumbled as he landed. Bloody face, bloody clothes.

He's the same one who came this morning to fetch Lucivar, Merry told her.

Surreal felt the cold rage twining down the link she still had with Sadi. Shit shit shit. She should have broken the link when she had a chance. If she cut him off now, he'd be down here among the Eyriens looking for answers, and he wouldn't be concerned about who, if anyone, survived that little chat.

"He's dead!" the young Warlord cried as he stumbled toward them. "Yaslana is dead!"

"No!" Hallevar roared. "There's nothing in this valley strong enough to bring down the Ebon-gray!"

Except his brother, Surreal sent. The snarl that came back to her was full of hot anger, not cold rage. Thank the Darkness for that.

"Where?" Rothvar shouted as Zaranar said, "Are you sure?"

"That bastard was expecting this," Rainier whispered in her ear.

She looked at Falonar and swore.

Rainier was right. The other Eyriens were angry, upset, outraged. But Falonar stood there, looking stiff and accepting.

"I don't believe it," Rothvar said. "I've seen Yaslana fight. You look me in the eyes and say it again."

"I saw it!" the young Warlord shouted. "Lucivar Yaslana is—"

Surreal threw her arms over her head as the Warlord's body exploded with such force the pebbles of bone against her shield sounded like hail against a window. Behind her, Merry screamed, and Rainier and Briggs both cried out in shock.

A moment later, she felt that Ebon-gray presence and looked down the street.

He was covered in blood that ran from his half-opened wings and dripped from the war blade. She'd seen that glazed look when he'd fought in the spooky house. She eased back enough to shelter Merry.

"I *told* you nothing could bring him down!" Hallevar yelled.

Shouts and cheers as Lucivar walked toward the Eyriens, although how they could see him through the red rain clouding the street was beyond her. It settled faster than it should have, given the amount of power that had been punched into that fool, as if a hand were pressing it down.

Surreal? Daemon asked.

*He's alive, I think—and *very* pissed off.*

You think?

He's covered in so much blood it's hard to tell. Shit. Shouldn't have told Daemon that.

Lucivar stared at Falonar, who seemed frozen.

Rothvar, however, took a step forward. "How may we be of service, Prince?" he asked Lucivar. "Is there any cleanup that needs to be done in the north?"

Lucivar continued to stare at Falonar. "No cleanup. This prick was the last enemy on the killing field."

"What about the Eyriens who fought with you?" Zaranar asked. "Do any of them need help?"

"There weren't any."

Stunned silence.

"*None?*" Hallevar finally said.

"None," Lucivar said.

Surreal didn't like the flat sound of Lucivar's voice. It wasn't *Lucivar*.

He turned his head and looked at her. "Are you well?"

That's the question I'd like to ask you. "Yes, I'm well. What can I do for you, Yaslana?"

"Inform the Queen that the trouble has been dealt with. She can release the village from lockdown. Where is my brother?"

Don't you know? "At your eyrie."

Lucivar focused on Rothvar and Zaranar. "Take your formations and do a sweep over Riada and its landen villages."

They nodded, but Hallevar said, "I've been out doing flyovers around Doun all morning. I'd appreciate a chance to thaw out these old bones."

Old bones, my ass, Surreal thought, watching Hallevar, Kohlvar, Tamnar, and Endar leave the formations and come up beside her. If the Gray was going out to report to

Riada's Queen, there would be sufficient warriors to take her place guarding The Tavern.

"Falonar," Lucivar said too softly. "With me. Now." Spreading his wings, he launched himself skyward and headed for Falonar's eyrie.

Falonar didn't look at any of them, said nothing to any of them. He hesitated a moment, then followed Lucivar.

Sadi? Surreal called.

No answer. Sometime during the past few moments he had quietly broken the link between them. She had a sick, shivery feeling it was because he didn't want anyone to know what he was thinking.

Lucivar waited in the front room of Falonar's eyrie. He just stared at the other Warlord Prince, saying nothing.

"They're all dead?" Falonar finally asked, keeping his mind blank of all thoughts—and disappointment.

"While I was going over that field, making sure I finished the kill on every one of those bastards, I kept thinking about how you used to benefit from schemes you had no part of— at least on the surface," Lucivar said.

"You finished the kill on all of them? Why? Were you afraid they would make the transition to demon-dead and remain a threat?"

"You fool. I was afraid of what would happen to the rest of the Eyriens if one of those bastards made the transition and ended up having a chat with my father," Lucivar snapped. "I'm not interested in any explanation or justification for why they were on that field, standing against me. They told me the Blood's code of honor doesn't apply to a half-breed bastard, and that's all I needed to know. But my father might see things differently, and I don't want him to have a reason to start thinking about a purge."

For a moment, Falonar couldn't breathe. "He would do that?"

"You stupid son of a whoring bitch," Lucivar roared. "What did you think you'd gain by this maneuver? A title? Think again. The *Keep* decides who rules in this valley. You would have been allowed to stand as the ruler of the Eyriens, but you wouldn't have been given control of Ebon Rih. You and the people you ruled would have to make a living out of what you could grow and hunt on the mountains."

"No," Falonar said. "That's not the way it is."

"That *is* the way it is! Your little scheme killed off most of the Eyriens in Ebon Rih today. Every man who would have served you is gone. But do you know what would have happened if they had succeeded in killing me? You wouldn't have become the leader of the Eyriens, because *there would be no Eyriens*. When I was taken from him, my father told Prythian that when I died, the Eyrien race would die with me. The *whole damn race*, Falonar. Here and in Terreille. Everyone."

"It can't be done!" Falonar said. "He couldn't do it."

"It can—and he has."

Falonar staggered back until he could brace a hand against a wall.

"The people from the Zuulaman Islands killed one of his sons," Lucivar said. "An infant."

"There's no such place as Zuulaman," Falonar whispered.

"Which is why Prythian knew it wasn't a bluff—because there were a handful of the demon-dead who did remember Zuulaman and knew Saetan could—and would—do exactly what he said."

"But now . . ."

Lucivar shook his head. "That death spell is still in place. He won't revoke it—and after today, he'll have more reason to reinforce it."

He didn't tell Falonar about the spell he'd asked Jaenelle to add to Saetan's. She had obliged him, up to a point.

If Lucivar Yaslana died on a killing field, or by anyone's hand, Saetan's death spell would take the Eyrien race, sparing no one but Lucivar's wife and children. But if Lucivar died of natural causes in the fullness of his years,

Saetan's spell would be absorbed by Jaenelle's, and the Eyrien race would survive.

"If you die, we all die? Then what were you doing on that killing field?" Falonar cried. "On *any* field?"

"I'm not going to live in a cage for the benefit of a people who want nothing to do with me," Lucivar said. "I'll take my chances, and you'll have to take them right along with me. But not in Ebon Rih. You're confined to your eyrie until I can find a court that will take you."

"If you believe I was behind the attempt to kill you, why don't you execute me?"

The Warlord Prince of Ebon Rih studied him, then smiled a lazy, arrogant smile. "You're not worth the effort."

Lucivar walked out—and an Ebon-gray shield locked around Falonar's eyrie.

Lucivar landed lightly on the edge of the courtyard in front of his eyrie. It was his home, and his family was inside, but until Daemon released the Black shield around the eyrie and eased back from the killing edge, he didn't dare come any closer.

The door opened, and Daemon stepped out. Those gold eyes, glazed and murderously sleepy, examined him from head to toe.

"Hell's fire, Prick," Daemon said, moving closer. "You *reek*." His gold eyes warmed and his expression changed to puzzlement as he watched blood and gore drip into the snow. "How did so much red rain penetrate your shields?"

"I let it."

"Why?"

Lucivar opened his wings quickly. The air around him turned a misty red as the rain was pushed through all the small holes he'd left in the Red shields. "Looking at me, do you have any doubt about where I've been or what I did?"

Daemon stared at him a moment longer. Then he sighed. "You can't come in the eyrie until you get cleaned up. You'll terrify the children."

He couldn't deny the truth of that. "I know. I'm going to

the Keep. It has a special area for this kind of cleanup. But I wanted to make sure everyone here was safe."

The door opened again and Marian rushed out. Daemon reached for her, but she dodged around him and threw her arms around Lucivar's neck, pressing herself fully against him.

"Are you all right? Are you hurt?" Marian cried. "Oh, Lucivar! I was so worried about you."

"Marian . . ." Lucivar put his hands on her waist and tried to ease her away from him, certain that she hadn't *looked* at him. When she tightened her hold and came close to strangling him, he gave up and put his arms round her. "Sweetheart, I'm all right. Sore muscles and bruises. Nothing more. I swear by the Jewels, those are the worst of it."

She started crying. "I'm sorry I was so bitchy about your ribs. You did it to help Surreal, and I shouldn't have been angry with you."

"You were right to be bitchy about the ribs," he said. "It was a dumb thing to do, and I deserved getting jabbed for it."

"Oh. Well, maybe a little." Sniffling, she eased back and he let her go. She wrinkled her nose. "Lucivar . . ." *Then* she looked down at her own clothes and swayed.

"Marian!"

Lucivar made a grab for her, but Daemon caught her as she stumbled back, her eyes glassy with shock.

"He's all right, darling," Daemon crooned. "Lucivar is all right. A man gets messy in that kind of fight."

You don't, Lucivar thought. Which was actually more terrifying? To see a man walk off a killing field covered in the carnage made by his own hand, or to see the man who had created that carnage walk off the field pristine?

A different image, a different message. He knew which one *he* found more frightening.

"I'll go with him to the Keep," Daemon crooned. "Help him get cleaned up. Why don't you go back inside through the side door? You'll be able to change clothes and wash up. I'll take care of Lucivar."

Marian lifted a hand but didn't touch the dark, wet stains on the front of her tunic. "Yes. These clothes need to soak." She focused on Lucivar again.

"I'll take care of him," Daemon said firmly. He led her to the gate that opened on her garden, which had access to the side door closest to the laundry room.

Lucivar waited until Marian was inside and Daemon returned. "Soothing spell?"

Daemon nodded. "I thought it best if she didn't think too much about what was on those clothes—and why."

He agreed with that. "Come on. I'd rather give this report only once—but I'm going to say *this* here and now. This isn't your territory, Bastard, and while I appreciate you being here to protect my family, whatever happens to the people in this valley is my decision, not yours."

"Of course," Daemon said. "I never thought otherwise."

He knew his brother too well to trust the words.

"Shall we go?" Daemon asked.

They rode the Ebon-gray Wind to the Keep, dropping to the landing web closest to the courtyard with the shower. Lucivar wrapped another shield around himself to avoid dripping gore through the corridors. He suspected that what lived within the walls and shadows would welcome the blood and bits of meat, but he didn't want to excite their hunting instincts, so he took the shortest route.

He pushed open a door and stepped into the courtyard.

"Hell's fire," Daemon said. "You're going to shower outside? In the *winter*?"

"Show some balls. It's not so bad." A few minutes ago, he wouldn't have noticed. Now he was starting to feel the cold and wanted to get cleaned up enough to go home and soak in the heated pool for an hour or two.

"If you show your balls in this weather, you'll freeze them off," Daemon growled as he studied what looked like a jumble of pipes over a round area with drains that flowed directly down the mountain. "Is there any reason why I can't put a warming spell around this area?"

His body ached. His teeth began to chatter. "None."

If he hadn't been so tired—and, more to the point, feeling hollowed out—he would have thought of that himself.

"Mother Night."

Turning at the sound of his father's voice, Lucivar saw the shock in Saetan's eyes before the High Lord locked away all feelings.

Do I really look that bad? he asked Daemon.

Prick, you have no idea how bad you look, Daemon said grimly.

Damn. He should have warned Saetan, should have told him he wasn't hurt before arriving at the Keep. It hadn't occurred to him that Andulvar and Prothvar must have looked like this the day they became demon-dead. Having won that battle, they had walked off the killing field, but they no longer walked among the living.

"There's nothing wrong with him that a good scrubbing and a hot meal won't fix," Daemon said with enough bite to make Lucivar snarl in response.

But the bite and snarl were exactly what Saetan needed to relax. He called in a porcelain dish and used Craft to float it over to Lucivar. "I'll cleanse your Jewels for you."

"I can—"

Let him do it, Daemon said. *Just in case we find anything under all that blood that you don't want him to see.*

Lucivar removed the Ebon-gray pendant and the Red ring, put them in the dish, and floated it back to his father. Then he stripped out of his clothes, wondering if it was worth the effort to clean them.

Saetan must have wondered the same thing, because he shook his head and vanished the clothes, including the boots, belt, and knife sheath. He turned and walked inside, saying nothing.

"Seeing you like this hit a nerve, and I don't think he's feeling as steady as he's pretending to be," Daemon said. "The sooner we get you cleaned up, the better."

Shivering, Lucivar stepped under the pipes, twisted the lever that controlled the water, and let out a breathless scream as the frigid water hit him, turning to steam as it battled against Daemon's warming spell.

When hands grabbed him and spun him around, his own hands balled into fists, but he managed to stop himself from hitting Daemon. He hadn't realized Sadi had intended to strip down and actually help him wash up.

"What's wrong with you?" Daemon's hands tightened on Lucivar's arms, the nails just pricking the skin.

Coming to the Keep and shocking Saetan with his appearance. Stepping under an ice-cold spray of water instead of waiting for the hot water to get through the pipes. Daemon had good reason to ask the question.

"Nothing physical," Lucivar said.

Those long-nailed fingers clamped on either side of his head as Daemon stared into his eyes. He felt the Black brushing over his inner barriers, looking for damage, for some kind of wound.

"Nothing wrong with my mind either."

"Then what?" Daemon's question sounded more like a demand.

"Shades of honor. All the Eyriens on that field chose to turn on me because, in their eyes, I was still just the half-breed bastard and always would be. I'm done with that. Anyone who wants to live in my territory can accept me for what I am or they can leave."

Water poured over both of them. Daemon's hands slid down Lucivar's face to rest on his shoulders.

"Every one of them is dead?" Daemon asked softly.

"Every one."

"Will any of them become demon-dead?"

"No."

Daemon studied him. "You could have killed them all with one blast of the Ebon-gray. Why did you give them a chance to fight and take the risk of getting hurt?"

"Their fate was decided from the moment they stepped on that field, so it wasn't about giving them a chance." Lucivar's smile wobbled, and for a moment his eyes were tear-bright. "I just needed to work off some temper."

Daemon studied him a moment longer, then nodded. Calling in two sponges and a small bowl of soft soap, he handed one sponge to Lucivar. "You take the front; I'll take the back."

They worked in silence. Even with the strength of the shields he'd had wrapped around himself, there were some bruises, some aches. But not one single slice or cut.

He mentioned that to Daemon, figuring it would be a good thing to point out to their father.

"I wouldn't lie to him if I were you," Daemon said dryly as he crouched down.

"What?" Lucivar winced and swore as Daemon's sponge rubbed over his left leg.

"You've got a slice just above your ankle," Daemon said. "It's not deep—won't need more than the cleansing ointment and basic healing Craft—but it's there."

"Shit," Lucivar muttered.

"How did any of those bastards get through your Ebon-gray shield, let alone the shield in Jaenelle's Ring of Honor?" Daemon sponged the cut again. "You *were* wearing the Ring with the Ebony shield, weren't you?"

"Yes, I was. At least until I walked off the killing field."

"So how did you get injured?"

"I was still feeling pissy, and when I rammed the knife through my shields and back into the boot sheath, I must have sliced through the leather and cut my leg."

"Ah, Prick." Daemon huffed out a laugh.

"Don't tell Merry, all right?"

"Why not?"

"Because I said she could yell at me if I got hurt, and I don't want my ass chewed because I cut myself with my own knife."

Daemon resoaped the sponge and began scrubbing Lucivar's right leg. "I'm surprised there is so much gore on your lower legs. Were you higher than the men you were fighting?"

"Nope." Lucivar lathered soap into his hair. "But a number of them were focused on striking my left ankle, which made them easy targets. Damned if I know why. If you know of a weak spot, you might concentrate your blows there to bring down an enemy, but there was no reason for any of them to think my ankles would be any more vulnerable than theirs. Especially the left ankle, which was never damaged in the first place."

Frigid air washed up the backs of his legs, there and gone.

Daemon rose up behind him. "Open your wings. I want to make sure I cleaned all the shit off them."

Something wrong here. Something off. Feeling vulnerable, but knowing what might happen if he refused, Lucivar spread his wings. Daemon's touch was light and careful as he moved the sponge over the wings, but Lucivar knew when he was being touched by the Sadist.

What had he said to bring out this side of Daemon's temper?

"There. Done." Daemon took a step back.

Lucivar rinsed the soap out of his hair, then turned to face his brother. Water poured over them, steamed around them. "Daemon . . ."

Daemon pressed a finger against Lucivar's lips.

That light touch—and what he saw in Daemon's eyes—told him he couldn't stop whatever was coming.

"Whatever happens to the people in this valley is your decision, not mine," Daemon said too softly. "I agree with that—and I'll respect it. I expect you to do the same."

"Meaning?"

"Don't interfere with me taking care of my own." Daemon turned and walked through the steam. "You should talk to Father before you go home. And be sure to put a healing salve on that cut."

Lucivar turned off the water and hurried into the Keep. Once inside, he rubbed himself dry with the warm towels that had been left floating just inside the door.

The cold that made him shiver had nothing to do with the weather.

*   *   *

Dressed and polished, Daemon waited for Geoffrey in the private section of the Keep's library.

. . . There was no reason for any of them to think my ankles would be any more vulnerable than theirs. Especially the left ankle . . .

"But there was a reason, brother," Daemon whispered. "There was a reason."

"Prince Sadi?"

Daemon turned at the sound of Geoffrey's voice, then took a moment to consider the degree of wariness in the historian/librarian's black eyes. He smiled—and saw Geoffrey's inability to completely hide the shiver caused by that smile.

"I need your assistance," he said, still smiling.

"In what way?" Geoffrey asked.

"The map you showed me the other day? I'd like to see it again."

FOURTEEN

Surreal stared at Daemon and tried to decide how badly she would get hurt if she hit him.

Badly enough, since he didn't look like he was in an indulgent mood.

"That's it?" she snarled. "Falonar just gets sent away like some little prick who played a nasty joke? He set Lucivar up to die on that killing field. You know that!"

"Of course I know that," Daemon snarled back. "The whole damn valley knows that. Or suspects it. Why do you think the remaining Eyriens have made such a pointed effort to let the Queens in Ebon Rih know they serve Lucivar, they support Lucivar, they want to live in this valley because it *is* ruled by Lucivar?"

Her room at The Tavern was a comfortable size, but now she needed to move, pace, do *something*, and Sadi was clogging up too damn much space.

"Lucivar has decided not to execute Falonar, and there is nothing we can do about that," Daemon said.

"When the sun shines in Hell." She paced in what little space was available without getting too close to Daemon. "Falonar is always going to be a knife aimed at Lucivar's back. You know that."

"I know a great many things," Daemon replied. "And one of the things I know is that there is nothing we can do about Falonar while he is still in Lucivar's territory."

Surreal stopped pacing. What she saw in his eyes was

the reason she feared him, cared about him, and trusted him to help her protect whatever she held dear.

"According to Lucivar, there is no real proof that Falonar was behind the attack," she said, watching Daemon.

"That is correct. Or at least there is no proof that Lucivar is willing to share."

"Does someone else have proof that Falonar was involved in the attack on Lucivar?"

"Yes."

"What do you want me to do?"

"Nothing. Chaosti is coming to the Keep tomorrow to escort you to Dea al Mon. Go with him. Spend time with your mother's people."

"Is that what you're going to do? Nothing?"

The Sadist smiled. "Prince Falonar and I have some personal business to settle—after he leaves Ebon Rih."

Something about his smile dared her to ask—and something about that smile warned her against asking.

"I guess I should pack," she said. "Get ready for tomorrow."

Daemon hesitated, then asked, "Do you want to see Lucivar before you leave?"

She thought about Yaslana in the sparring circle, pushing her so that she could release the last bit of anger and emotional venom—leaving himself open to a blow that must have hurt like a wicked bitch because *she* needed to strike that blow. And then she thought of Lucivar stepping on that killing field—one man against so many warriors who'd had just as much training, if not half the natural talent or power—with his ribs already banged up and hurting, probably taking hits he could have avoided if he hadn't already been hurt.

Her temper flashed like heat lightning.

The dresser exploded. She couldn't tell whether Daemon had expected her to lash out or if his reflexes were that fast, but the Black shield that snapped up between them and the dresser prevented injuries—and minimized the damage to the rest of the room.

"He's an arrogant prick who thinks he's invulnerable!" she shouted. "The only reason I'd want to see him right now is to rip off his balls and stuff them up his nose!"

Daemon blinked.

She looked at the chunks of dresser now scattered on the floor and shrieked. "And look what he did! *My clothes were still in that dresser!*"

"It's not his fault you killed the dresser," Daemon said mildly.

"Oh, don't you get ballsy with me. Don't you dare."

Daemon blinked again—and took a step toward the door. "Fine. I'll tell Lucivar you'll talk to him in a few weeks."

"You do that. And you can tell him that as soon as I figure out what was destroyed, I'm going to buy two of everything and send him the bill!"

Daemon didn't waste time leaving, but she still heard it before he completely closed the door—that choked effort not to laugh.

"Rip off my balls and stuff them up my nose?" Resigned to giving his body another day of rest, Lucivar wandered over to a window. Jillian was out there, playing some kind of game with Daemonar and Alanar, Endar's son.

"The expression sounds juvenile, but the intention was sincere," Daemon replied.

"Fine. I'll let Chaosti deal with her."

"She'll get over being angry with you."

"Will she?"

"Eventually." Daemon joined him at the window. "What game are they playing?"

"No idea. But they're doing enough running that they'll all be happy to sit for a while once they come inside. And since Marian is visiting the Eyrien women in Doun, I'll be glad to have the children stay quiet for a bit."

"How much longer is Falonar going to remain confined to his eyrie here?"

"He leaves tomorrow to serve in a Red-Jeweled Queen's court."

"I was under the impression the only Red-Jeweled Queen in Askavi wouldn't take any Eyrien at this point."

"Actually, there are two Rihlander Queens who wear the Red. I hadn't considered Perzha at first because . . . well, she's Perzha."

Daemon raised an eyebrow. "And that means . . . ?"

"She rules one of Askavi's coastal Provinces. There's not a mountain in her territory."

"Meaning no eyries."

Lucivar nodded. "She's a bit eccentric, dresses oddly, and doesn't much care for the formalities of being a Queen. But that's Perzha as Perzha. Perzha the Queen is quite formidable and ruthless when required."

"She sounds a bit like Jaenelle."

"Nothing in the theater can match the entertainment of listening to the two of them at a dinner party. Just don't eat anything until you get their assurance that there aren't any surprises in the food."

"Such as?"

"Being served a seafood soup and having a tentacle rise up out of the bowl and grab your spoon. No one was sure if the squids were real or illusions, but the surprise did prevent everyone from realizing that the cook had ruined the soup."

Daemon burst out laughing.

"On top of that, Perzha lives in a village called Little Weeble."

"You're joking."

"No, I'm not."

"Is there a Big Weeble?"

Lucivar shook his head. "If you ask anyone in the village about the name, they give you a wink and say if you understand where the name came from, then you'll understand the name."

"But they don't tell outsiders."

"Nope."

"And this is where you're sending Falonar?"

"Perzha offered to take him, as a favor to me."

"Why are you letting him remain in Kaeleer?"

Lucivar turned away from the window. "Because he won't be in my face every day, but he won't be that far away if I need to deal with him. And because I've learned a few things from you and Father about the just payment of debts."

"Meaning?"

Lucivar smiled. "Despite her eccentricities, Perzha is a Queen with the kind of bloodlines that puts her above most other aristo families. Which means she doesn't give a damn about being aristo. Rather like Father in that way."

"Ah. So for someone like Falonar, who defines everything by whether it's aristo . . ."

"I figure serving Perzha for the next three years will be punishment enough."

FIFTEEN

Hearing a burst of male laughter in the corridor outside his room, Falonar choked on bitterness. He'd been in Little Weeble only two days. He would go mad if he had to spend the next three years among these people, serving this Queen. And not even in her First Circle, which was where he *should* be, given his caste, rank, and aristo bloodlines. No, he was a *Third Circle escort* who was always kept under the watchful eye of the Master of the Guard or confined to his bedroom or the common rooms when he wasn't on duty.

He was isolated, alone, the only Eyrien in the whole damn Province. And this land! Water on one side, farmland on the other. And what these people considered hills was laughable.

What was the point of living in Askavi if he couldn't live in the mountains?

Not his choice. Nothing was his choice. He couldn't ride the Winds without permission. He couldn't contact other Eyriens without permission. He could barely take a piss without permission.

Lucivar had survived centuries of this treatment when he was a slave.

Further proof that Yaslana wasn't a real Eyrien. But Lucivar did understand Eyrien pride. Being exiled from Ebon Rih when he'd hoped to rule the valley was shaming, but being forced to serve a Queen like Perzha and admit to living in a place called Little Weeble was the real punishment.

He deserved something better, something more!

The room dimmed. He felt an odd pressure inside his skull. No, that pressure was in the abyss, near the level of his Sapphire strength, surrounding his Self and pulling it down slowly, gently, past his Sapphire web.

Something better? a deep voice crooned. *Something more? A place you truly deserve? I know exactly where you should be.*

Claws hooked into his Self, pulling him down down down into the abyss, far too deep for his mind to withstand. He fought, trying to escape, but he could no longer sense his body, could feel nothing but crushing pressure.

And then he felt nothing at all.

Falonar opened his eyes and stared at the night sky. How did he get outside? The unbearable pressure was gone, but his head felt stuffy, his body ached, and he couldn't seem to reach the power that always flowed within him.

He tried drawing from the reservoir of Sapphire strength stored in his Jewel—and found nothing. He reached for the reservoir in his Birthright Opal.

Nothing. *Nothing!* Terror filled him as he realized he hadn't been drained; he'd been broken back to the limited power needed for basic Craft. How? Why? He remembered fighting against something that had caught him and tried to pull him too deep into the abyss, but . . .

"You're awake," a deep voice said. "How delightful."

Falonar turned his head and stared at the man watching him. "Sadi?"

Daemon smiled a cold, cruel smile. "Everything has a price, Falonar. It's time for you to pay the debt."

Falonar struggled to roll over and get to his feet. Something was wrong with his left wing, something bad, but it was too dark for him to see the extent of the damage. "What did you do to me?" he snarled.

"Nothing you didn't deserve."

"You can't blame me for Lucivar being challenged by those Warlords."

"Yes, I can," Daemon said pleasantly. "But this isn't about Lucivar. This is about Rainier."

"Rainier?" He took a step back, then jumped forward when something tried to curl around his calf. "What about Rainier?"

"Let's start with you using a warm-up as an excuse to push an injured man so that his damaged leg would go out from under him, ripping the muscles that were just beginning to heal. Let's continue with using that man's pain and his vulnerability in that moment to force open his inner barriers and see if he knew anything you could use against Lucivar—or, more to the point, if there was any information you could give someone else to use against Lucivar. And Rainier did know something about Lucivar. He knew about a weak left ankle, a spot that would be more vulnerable to a blow that in turn, might be enough to hobble even the best warrior when he was fighting against so many trained adversaries."

"Anyone could have told them about Yaslana's ankle!"

"Why would they?" Daemon sounded surprised. "The information about Lucivar's ankle was a lie Rainier let you find."

Falonar stared at Sadi.

"Rainier was Second Circle in the Dark Court at Ebon Askavi," Daemon purred. "He was well trained."

"That son of a whoring bitch." He'd thought Rainier was in too much pain to sense the intrusion, let alone try to deceive him.

"Rainier serves me, and I do take care of my own," Daemon said. "Which brings us to your new, if temporary, place of residence."

Falonar took a step toward Daemon. He would demand that Sadi take him back to that damn village, would demand that Sadi answer to a tribunal of Queens for breaking another Warlord Prince.

A vine whipped around Falonar's lower left leg, its

curved thorns digging into his skin, chaining him to that spot.

"It doesn't have a quaint name like Little Weeble," Daemon purred, "but I think the place, and its name, suits you better. Welcome to the bowels of Hell, Prince Falonar." He turned and walked away.

"Sadi!" Falonar shouted, as another vine wrapped around his right leg. *"Sadi!"*

Ignoring Falonar's increasingly shrill screams, Daemon glided along a path in this forever-twilight Realm. One moment he was alone; the next a dozen males with glowing red eyes stood in front of him. Since a couple of them had been Eyriens, judging by what was left of their wings, he knew their eyes hadn't started out red. Did these males use an illusion spell to look more terrifying or did some physical change take place because of this particular location?

That was an interesting question for another day. For now, he bared his teeth and snarled, a soft sound that rolled through the land like thunder. And with that sound, he sent a whisper of his power.

"It's *him*," one of them said, shuddering.

"But . . . I thought he would be older," another said.

"Did you?" Daemon asked too softly. He raised his right hand and rubbed a finger against his chin, giving them a good look at the long, black-tinted nails and the Black Jewel in his ring.

They stepped aside, making sure they gave him enough room to avoid accidentally touching him.

As he passed them, Daemon said, "There is fresh meat at the end of the path—if the plants don't consume it all first."

They bowed, and one of them said hesitantly, "Thank you, High Lord." Then they rushed to get their share of the feast.

Daemon walked a few minutes more, observing the flora and fauna that moved toward him, drawn by the scent of the hot, fresh blood running through his veins, and then withdrew when they brushed against the feel of his power and the cold depth of his temper. Satisfied that he'd seen enough for the moment, he caught the Black Wind and rode to the Keep. He slipped in and out, staying only long enough to tuck a folded piece of paper between two of the books his father was sorting. A courtesy, really, to inform the current ruler of Hell about the delivery of meat.

Then Daemon caught the Black Winds again and rode to the Hall, where his wife, and Queen, waited for him.

SIXTEEN

Surreal studied the room that would be her home for the next few weeks. The furniture was basic but in good condition, and gleamed from a fresh cleaning. Everything felt a bit rustic, but this was Dea al Mon. Could *any* furnishing be considered rustic when there was a tree growing through the room?

Chaosti had told her there were a dozen homes within sight of the meadow that served as a play area for the children. She hadn't been able to spot *one* of them—and she wasn't sure she'd be able to find *this* one again on her own.

Nervous butterflies fluttered in her stomach as she put her clothes away. Her mother had lived nearby in a house like this. The people who lived in the houses around this meadow came from the same clan, were kin. Even now in the heart of winter there was a sharp beauty to this place. She could picture her mother playing beneath these trees, watching the stars. Such a long way from the slums in Terreille where Titian had tried to raise a daughter and survive.

She was looking over the selection of books she'd bought during a two-day shopping spree in Amdarh, and pondering which to read first, when Chaosti knocked on her door.

"You're settled in?" he asked. "Is there anything you need?"

"Yes, I'm settled in, and no, there is nothing I need." *But you're not settled*, she added silently. "Something wrong?"

"You're safe here, Surreal," he said. "Nothing will enter our land and harm you. I give you my word."

Mother Night. "All right. Although I will point out that I'm pretty good with a knife."

His lips curved in a hint of a smile. "How could you not be? You're Titian's daughter." Then he sighed. "Falonar has disappeared, just vanished from the court of the Rihlander Queen he was serving. It's thought by some that he's gone into hiding in the Askavi mountains."

"If that is what people think, then it must be true," Surreal said.

Chaosti studied her. "And what do you think, cousin?"

"I think that just as I am Titian's daughter, Daemon Sadi is his father's son."

Chaosti's eyes filled with understanding. "I see. Something understood among the family but unspoken?"

"Yes." Although if she ever felt ballsy enough, someday she might ask Daemon if Falonar was still a threat to anyone. Problem was, anyone who asked the question would most likely receive the answer from the Sadist—and regret it.

But maybe someday.

"So whatever business you brought from Ebon Rih is finished now?" he asked.

"It's finished."

Chaosti held out a hand. "In that case, cousin, Grandmammy Teele is waiting to meet you."

Family

Ten years later . . .

ONE

Pulling the collar up around her ears, Sylvia added more power to the warming spell in her coat as she followed another path through her hosts' gardens. She needed the crisp night air and the silence. More, she needed to be away from her hosts. Was her uneasiness due to staying at an estate that bordered the Territory called Little Terreille, or was there a tangible reason she wanted to grab her sons and Tildee, catch the Winds, and flee?

Remembering the cloying, desperate civility that had surrounded her at the dinner table, she used Craft to put a shield around herself under her clothes—a subtle precaution that made her feel better. And because having that much protection did make her feel better, she stopped trying to rationalize her feelings.

There was something wrong with this place, with this family, maybe with the whole damn village.

Her son Beron had reached the age where he was allowed to attend house parties in order to become acquainted with youngsters beyond his home village. At one of those parties he had struck up a friendship with Haeze, a Warlord his own age, and had asked if his new friend could spend a few days with them at the end of Winsol. Her father had chaperoned Beron to that particular party and had voiced no objection to Haeze, so she agreed.

Haeze had been staggered by the proximity of Beron's home to SaDiablo Hall—and even more staggered when the boys passed the Warlord Prince of Dhemlan on the street and Daemon stopped to talk to them, making it clear he took a personal interest in young Lord Beron. Add to that a couple of weapons lessons from Prince Yaslana and Haeze's first encounter with a kindred Sceltie, and she'd seen the impact that a few days with them had on the boy. By the end of the visit, Haeze had sounded more confident and carried himself with an assurance that had been hidden by his initial shyness.

A few weeks later, Haeze extended an invitation to Beron to visit his family's estate. Sylvia would have asked a Warlord from her Second or Third Circle to stand escort for the short visit, but the invitation had included her other son, Mikal, claiming that Haeze's younger brother was eager to become acquainted. Making connections was an intrinsic part of the Blood's society, not just for friendships in general, but for the kind of association that could eventually provide a young man with the opportunity to train in a specific court.

This house party hadn't sounded like it would be any different from others Beron had attended, except that the invitation hadn't included her, and it should have if a boy Mikal's age was going to be visiting a family who was unknown to her. That had scratched her sense of propriety enough that she had declined the invitation on her sons' behalf.

The next invitation from Haeze's family arrived shortly after that, crammed with apologies and gorged with assurances that they had meant no insult. They did not have the means to entertain a Queen, since that would mean guesting her escorts as well, and they had thought she wouldn't want to visit their small estate simply as a mother with her sons.

Having been in the position of entertaining to excess because a guest brought several unanticipated companions— and having her children grumble about the other parties they couldn't attend after she paid the bills for that excess— she understood the dilemma Haeze's mother faced: Pay for a visit by a District Queen that might not net enough social value to be worth the cost, or have the means to send Haeze to several parties in other villages.

Her Steward and Master of the Guard had voiced no objections to Sylvia not bringing a human escort because Tildee was coming with her. The Sceltie, who was a Summersky witch, poked her nose into everything that had to do with her family, especially when it came to Mikal, who was her special human.

So Sylvia had accepted the second invitation for a family visit.

She stopped walking. She'd been careful not to wander beyond the formal gardens, but she was still alone in the dark. Thinking about the invitation that brought her family here, she used Craft to create several balls of witchlight and tossed them in the air to float above her as she headed back toward the house.

There would have been room for a couple of escorts because she and her boys were the only guests—and that second invitation had given her the distinct impression the house would be crammed with guests. Haeze's younger brother wasn't eagerly waiting to meet Mikal as she'd been told. The boy wasn't even there, and the excuses being made for his absence rang false.

She should have listened to Tildee when the Sceltie growled about something smelling wrong near the house. The dog had wanted to get away from this place and these people within minutes of arriving.

Thank the Darkness she had a code phrase the Sceltie promised to obey. If used, Mikal would be taken away from the danger, no matter what else might be lost.

When had a sense of something wrong turned into a conviction there was danger?

Mother? Beron called on a psychic thread.

Coming, she replied. If a son had noticed her absence and come looking for her, she had been out in the garden longer than she'd intended.

Sylvia lengthened her stride, the witchlights bobbing along with her. Hearing Beron's voice helped her make her decision. She didn't care if she was being rude. She didn't care if she embarrassed her son and his friend. She was taking her boys home!

The attack came without warning. A bolt of power hit her in the chest, knocking her down, shattering the shield beneath her clothes. As she scrambled to her feet, a male figure, dressed in black, rushed toward her.

"Bitch," he snarled. "This is your brat's fault."

She threw a Purple Dusk shield between them, certain the feel of power clashing would bring the men in the house running to help. The man shattered that shield and kept coming toward her, destroying the next one too as she backed away.

A hint of rotting meat in the air now, and a foulness to his psychic scent that gagged her more than the physical smell. In the moments before he struck again, she knew why Haeze's brother wasn't home. Since she couldn't hold this Warlord off for long and it was clear she wasn't going to get any help from the people in the house, she made her choice.

Everything has a price.

Beron! Run! she shouted on a psychic thread. *Tildee! Run now!*

As the enemy lunged at her, she wrapped shields around herself and ran, hoping to lure him away long enough for her boys to escape. She didn't worry much about Mikal. Asking Tildee to run meant something terrible had happened, and the Sceltie would protect the boy with everything in her while getting him to a safe place. But Beron . . .

"Mother?" Beron shouted, sounding much too close. "Mother?"

Run! she screamed.

A blast of power hit her legs, breaking her shields and exploding her knees. She struck the ground hard and rolled, denying the pain while she twisted around to face the enemy.

"Mother!"

No time to argue with Beron about running toward her instead of running away. She blasted the enemy with everything she had in her Purple Dusk Jewel. It didn't break his shield, but it stopped him for a moment. He was stronger, had a deeper reservoir of power than she did, and that meant he would win this fight.

She'd still make the bastard work for the kill.

Slipping on the blood and shattered bones, he fell on her and began tearing at her clothes. She tore at him with her nails, breaking through his shield long enough to rip her fingers on a protective mesh that covered his face.

He rammed a knife between her ribs. Before her body registered pain, he yanked it out.

"I'm going to give you a smile from ear to ear," he snarled.

A blast of power knocked him off her. Leaping to his feet, he grabbed her torn clothes and used Craft to fling her far out into the garden.

As she flew through the air, in those moments before the physical death, she saw the enemy attack Beron.

Daemon followed Jaenelle into her sitting room, closed the door, then wrapped his arms around her.

"I love listening to you sing," he said as he nuzzled her. "And so did everyone else tonight."

"I was pleased that we had a full house." She tipped her head to give him access to his favorite spot on her neck.

He brushed her hair back before giving that spot a delicate taste. After years of keeping her hair sleek-short or shaggy-short, depending on her mood, she had finally let it grow out. It wasn't as long as it had been when she was twenty-five, but it now hid the spot between neck and shoulder that the Warlord Princes who served her found so intriguing.

"You always have a full house," he said, feeling a swell of pride, among other things. She owned a music shop in Halaway and sang there twice a month, hosting Dhemlan musicians as well as musicians from many other Territories in Kaeleer—and beyond. "Since you included a couple of folk songs from Shalador Nehele, I was surprised you hadn't asked Ranon to come here and play with you."

Jaenelle gave him a wicked grin. "I knew better than to ask Ranon. I asked Cassidy and Shira if he could indulge me. They—and Vae—ganged up on him. He'll be here for the next concert."

Daemon laughed. He felt a keen sympathy for the Shalador Warlord Prince because he knew how it felt to be backed into a corner, but he laughed anyway.

Then Jaenelle kissed him with heat, and the parts of him that had swelled along with his pride responded with enthusiasm. But he eased back a little before he forgot what he'd wanted to discuss.

"You're going to be thirty-seven this year," he said.

"And that is significant because . . . ?"

"You've never been thirty-seven before. I thought we should do something special for your birthday."

"We always do something special for my birthday." She rocked her hips, brushing against him. "And some part of the 'something special' usually involves you being deliciously naked."

The world narrowed to his need to make love with her—to play and seduce and savor until they were both boneless and satisfied. His arms tightened around her, and just as his mouth touched hers . . .

Daemon!

daemondaemondaemondaemondaemon.

He raised his head, snarling. *Go away!* One Sceltie might be cowed by the snarl traveling along the psychic link, especially when he made no effort to hide that he was aroused and wanted to mate. But cowing three of them? Wouldn't happen.

Daemon!

daemondaemondaemondaemondaemon.

"I like Shuveen," Daemon growled as he stepped away from Jaenelle, "but why can't we send Boyd and Floyd back to Scelt for more . . . seasoning?"

"Ladvarian is staying here with us for a while and wanted those two with him for extra training." She looked toward the door and frowned. "They seem upset."

"They probably got in trouble with Mrs. Beale again." And wouldn't sorting that out be a fun way to end the evening?

Daemon! Shuveen called.

Boyd and Floyd began barking outside the door.

Swearing, Daemon strode to the door. He would tolerate them interrupting him when he was in his study working. After all, they were young, and living with him and Jaenelle was part of their training to become a working member of a household. But he wouldn't tolerate their intrusion when he was about to make love to his wife, and that was something they also needed to learn.

Then Ladvarian passed through the wall and said, *Sylvia told Tildee to run.*

Daemon! Shuveen shouted.

daemondaemondaemondaemondaemon, Boyd and Floyd yapped.

Daemon rose to the killing edge in a heartbeat. Telling a Sceltie to run was the code Jaenelle had established between the Scelties living in Dhemlan and their human families. It meant life-threatening danger, and the dog's task was to grab the special human friend—usually the child—and get them both out of harm's way.

Daemon!

daemondaemondaemondaemondaemon.

He used Craft to open the door. Letting the young Scelties in was the only way to shut them up.

"Sylvia isn't in Halaway," Jaenelle said. "Or if she is, she's not able to respond to a psychic call."

She is far, Ladvarian said. *They are visiting. Tildee isn't sure where.*

"Tildee has Mikal?" Jaenelle asked.

Yes.

Far far far, the youngsters yapped.

"How far can Tildee reach on a psychic thread?" Daemon asked Jaenelle.

"Not that far," she replied.

Ladvarian said, ★Tildee called. Other Scelties answered, then called to me.★

Daemon swore softly, straining to keep his temper leashed. Upsetting the youngsters wouldn't get him the information he needed. If that call for help had traveled from Sceltie to Sceltie, Sylvia and her boys could be anywhere in Dhemlan. "Where were the other Scelties? Could you tell?"

All four Scelties spun to face the same direction.

"South," Daemon snarled. He moved swiftly, out of the room and down the corridors. ★Beale, I need a Coach on the landing web, and a driver to come with us.★

"If Tildee is running, someone is going to need a Healer," Jaenelle said when she caught up to him.

★Rainier!★ Daemon called.

★Prince?★

★Contact Sylvia's Master of the Guard. I want to know exactly where she is and who is with her. There's trouble. We need to find her.★

★Can you wait for Surreal?★

★Only if she can get to the Hall by the time you have the information. If not, you'll have to tell her where to meet us.★

★We were on our way home, so I'll stop at the Master's house and she'll come up to the Hall.★

When Daemon and Jaenelle reached the great hall, Beale and Holt were waiting, holding their winter coats.

"The driver will bring the Coach around in another minute or so," Beale said. He helped Daemon into his coat while Holt helped Jaenelle into hers.

Daemon wanted to snap at the delay. There had been time to bring the Coach around to the landing web in front of the Hall. But he held his tongue. Once they caught the Winds, they would be out of touch, so they couldn't leave until Rainier found out where Sylvia went.

"There are blankets and winter boots in the Coach," Beale said. "Mrs. Beale is putting together a basket of food and jugs of water."

We aren't going on a picnic, Daemon thought. On the other hand, Tildee was running, and if whatever was happening around Sylvia was as bad as that indicated and Jaenelle was needed as a Healer, he wouldn't want her eating or drinking anything that didn't come from the Hall in case it had been tainted in some way.

Prince? Rainier called on a spear thread.

Where is she?

His temper turned viciously cold as Rainier gave him the information. As soon as Rainier broke the link, he turned to Jaenelle. "Let's go. Lord Ladvarian, your presence is requested."

The youngsters whined. Daemon pointed a finger at them, then at Holt and Beale. "You three tell them everything you know about this." He looked at Beale. "Do whatever you can."

Beale nodded.

Holt rushed to open the door. Daemon, Jaenelle, and Ladvarian walked out of the Hall.

Within moments of the driver setting the Coach on the landing web, a horse-drawn cab raced up to the Hall's front doors. Surreal sprang from the cab and ran to the Coach. She didn't say anything until they were inside and Daemon was settling into the other chair in the driver's compartment.

Jaenelle is going in as a Healer? she asked on a Gray thread.

Yes, he replied.

Then I'll protect Jaenelle, and you and Ladvarian take care of the rest.

Agreed.

Letting Jaenelle and Ladvarian explain the situation, Daemon lifted the Coach off the landing web, caught the Black Winds, and raced toward a village on the border of Little Terreille.

Sylvia fought her way up from a sludgy kind of sleep. Her legs were filled with a dull, draining ache, and her eyes wouldn't open. She couldn't remember where she was or why she felt so strange, but she knew her boys were in danger and needed her. She knew that much.

Then she remembered all of it—the attack, the pain, telling Tildee to run, and Beron coming to help her instead of running away.

Tildee would get Mikal to a safe hiding place. But Beron . . .

She couldn't see, couldn't hear. Her body didn't work.

She'd died in those moments when her attacker flung her far into the garden. But that had been the body's death. The Blood had the ability to survive beyond the physical death and become demon-dead.

How long did it usually take to make the transition? Minutes? Hours? How much time had passed?

Her vision was cloudy. Her hearing returned halfway. Was this normal?

That bastard who attacked her was demon-dead. That was why he smelled like rotting meat. Had she managed to damage him at all?

Her fingers twitched. A few moments later, she was able to fist both hands.

Blood was the living river, and through it flowed the power that made the Blood who and what they were—and it was that power that sustained the flesh after the transformation to demon-dead. Dead flesh wasn't capable of renewing the power, which was why the demon-dead drank the blood of the living.

She had died before completely draining her Purple Dusk Jewel, but there wasn't much power left, so her Birthright Summer-sky was sustaining her body right now. Once the power completely drained from both Jewels, the final death would occur, and her Self would become a whisper in the Darkness—and she wouldn't be able to do anything to protect her family from a faceless enemy.

Beron? she whispered, not sure if the lack of response meant he was too far away to hear her or meant that he too was dead.

She felt too exposed to send out a psychic call for help that might alert the people in the house to her location. If they weren't looking for her yet, they would be, for no other reason than to make sure she couldn't tell anyone about what happened.

Sylvia pushed herself to a sitting position. She wasn't sure how much power was needed to sustain dead flesh, but she didn't think she had a lot of time.

If all she wanted to do was gasp out a last message, Halaway would be the prudent destination. But her boys had been lured to this estate in order to be that monster's prey, so she needed the help of someone who knew the demon-dead and could help her survive long enough to destroy that nameless, faceless enemy.

She needed Saetan.

Using Craft, she floated through the gardens, keeping low to the ground, moving away from garbled sounds that might have been people shouting or dogs barking. When she found a tether line for the White Wind, she caught it and headed north, carefully shifting to a darker Wind whenever she could until she was riding the Purple Dusk Wind to the Keep.

Dropping from the Black Winds, Daemon aimed the Coach at the estate that was a couple of miles from a village on the border of Little Terreille. He didn't intend to announce his presence until he was right on top of the problem, but since the District Queen who ruled this village didn't live here, he reached for the males in her home village and let his voice thunder a message through a psychic spear thread: *Get here. Now.*

Once he landed the Coach and let his Black power roll over the land, they would know where to find him—and they would do everything they could to accommodate him, because they, and their Queen, wouldn't want him looking in their direction. Not when his temper had turned cold and he was riding the killing edge.

The door to the driver's compartment slid open. Jaenelle

said, "We need to find Beron and Sylvia. Mikal should be safe with Tildee."

I will find Beron, Ladvarian said. *I can run faster, and I can smell him, even if he is hiding.*

Daemon didn't argue, since the dog was right. He wrapped the Coach in a Black sight shield as they approached the estate.

"Front door?" he asked, glancing back as Surreal moved up to join them. Both women now wore trousers, boots, and body-hugging tops that wouldn't get in the way of fighting or healing.

"Front door," Jaenelle agreed.

"I'm not sensing anyone in the front lower rooms," Surreal said. "There are clusters of people in the upper rooms. We should go in fast and quiet."

"Agreed," Jaenelle said. "These people haven't lived around kindred. They have no reason to think Tildee sent a message that could have reached us so fast. If Sylvia and Beron are being held, no one will be expecting us. Not this soon."

Daemon landed on the drive, using Craft to create a blanket of air so that the Coach silently came to rest just above the gravel.

As soon as the Coach settled, Ladvarian passed through the door and disappeared.

Sylvia, Daemon called on a psychic thread. *Sylvia!*

No response of any kind, not even a weak effort of someone sick or injured. *Beron?*

Barely a flicker, but he thought there was some response.

Daemon stepped out of the Coach, then waited for Jaenelle and Surreal. The three of them moved up to the front door together, then passed through it one by one. Daemon took the lead while Surreal guarded their backs. As he headed up the stairs, probing and searching, Ladvarian shouted, *Jaenelle!*

Daemon leaped up the remaining stairs, moving fast to

stay ahead of Jaenelle, following the sounds of barking and shouting. He burst into the room, a Black shield fanned out in front of him to protect the women behind him.

A huddle of people—several adults and the boy, Haeze. A Healer cringed near a narrow bed, her eyes on Ladvarian. The Sceltie floated on air above the bed, snapping and snarling to keep the woman away from Beron, who lay in the bed, bloody and too still.

Jaenelle rushed over to the bed. Surreal remained by the door, a knife in her hand. Ladvarian continued snarling at the Healer. And Daemon, riding the killing edge, watched everyone in the room as he assessed the stink of the adults' psychic scents. Fear, desperation, and a petty satisfaction that it wasn't their boy lying wounded in the bed. And something more that he couldn't identify—yet.

"You whoring bitch."

Planting one knee on air, Jaenelle threw herself across the bed, grabbed the Healer's Jewel, and channeled a blast of power through cold rage.

Surreal yelped in surprise. Other people screamed, and the Healer shrieked as Jaenelle shattered the woman's Jewels, both ranking Jewel and Birthright, breaking her back to basic Craft. Windows shattered. The walls of the room cracked in patterns that made Daemon think a violent lightning storm had been etched on the plaster.

He felt as if the Winds had turned into a funnel of speed and power that would sweep away anything in its path, and he was standing at the edge of that fury.

Then the power and fury were gone, reclaimed by the witch who had unleashed it.

Jaenelle opened her hand. The shattered pieces of the Healer's Jewel fell to the floor, completely empty of power. Pushing against air, Jaenelle returned to the other side of the bed.

"Lady?" Daemon asked sharply.

"She was destroying Beron's vocal cords under the guise of healing his throat," Jaenelle snarled.

He didn't ask how she knew or if she was certain the harm was deliberate. Jaenelle wouldn't have broken a Healer that way unless she was certain.

Daemon looked at the adults, then at Haeze, who was curled up on the floor.

Everyone in the room had known the bitch was doing it—including the boy who was supposed to be Beron's friend.

That was the something more he had picked up in their psychic scents—their worry that someone would find out they had stood by and allowed Beron to be harmed.

Well, someone had, and he wasn't about to overlook or forgive *anything*.

While Witch's fury shook the room, Ladvarian had pressed himself against the bed over Beron's legs. Now he stood up, shook himself vigorously, and looked at Jaenelle. *This room has bad smells, and it is getting cold. You should take Beron to the Coach so you can heal him properly. Surreal will guard you while the Prince and I look for Lady Sylvia.*

Why aren't you being that bossy? Surreal asked Daemon on a Gray thread.

I wouldn't have dared. Not yet, anyway, he replied dryly.

Jaenelle looked at Beron. "Agreed." She pulled the top sheet loose. Ladvarian jumped off the bed as she floated the boy on air and wrapped the sheet around him.

Can you handle this? Daemon asked Surreal.

Do you have a problem with me burying anyone who upsets her?

No problem at all.

Then I can handle this.

Ladvarian went with the women as they hurried to get Beron to the Coach. Daemon remained, his hands in his coat pockets, doing nothing but staring at the people huddled together. Now that Witch was out of the room, he was, once more, the dominant predator.

"Prince?"

The male voice was unfamiliar and cautious. Not surprising, since the man was coming up behind him and wouldn't want to be mistaken for an enemy.

Looking over his shoulder, Daemon studied the Warlord wearing the badge of a Master of the Guard. "Come in."

The Master entered the room, flanked by several other Warlords. "Someone has been hurt?"

"The Queen of Halaway's son," Daemon replied. "And Lady Sylvia is missing."

"How may we be of service?" The Master's voice turned grim.

"Lord Ladvarian and I are going to search the grounds for Lady Sylvia. Have some of your men search the house." Daemon pointed at the Healer, then at the adults he assumed were Sylvia's hosts. "Keep them under guard, separately, until I'm ready to have a little chat. Take the boy to his room, under protection."

"Done," the Master said.

Daemon walked out of the room as the Warlords swarmed around the people being detained. The Master followed him out.

"Something else?" Daemon asked, pausing at the top of the stairs.

"Does this have anything to do with the missing children?"

Cold rage swept through him, but he kept it chained. "What do you know about missing children?" *And why hadn't you shown some balls and come up to the Hall to tell me about them?*

The Master licked his lips, a nervous movement. "Sometimes borders are just lines on a map. The folks living in the towns and villages on the other side of the border in Little Terreille? They're good people. We have no quarrel with them. When children started going missing, they asked us to keep a lookout for them. Not hard to do. A child from Little Terreille isn't going to have the looks that would blend in with Dhemlan children, so he's easy enough to spot. Most of the time, when a youngster runs away, he's angry or unhappy, but no one has done him real harm, if you understand me."

"I do. And if you do suspect real harm?"

"The youngster is brought before the Queen and isn't returned to his family unless she's satisfied that the reason he left home wasn't more than growing pains."

"Do you think the missing children are runaways?"

The Master hesitated, then shook his head. "No, I don't think so. We've checked the runaway houses within our Queen's territory."

Most small villages had at least one runaway house—a safe place an unhappy child could go to receive a hug, nut-cakes, and a sympathetic ear, or be given some space to brood over some trouble at home.

"I want to know if there are any children missing from Dhemlan villages."

"I'll check with the village guards, but I haven't heard of any children going missing," the Master said. Then he finished grimly, "Which doesn't mean there haven't been some that have gone missing."

"I want daily reports until this is settled," Daemon said as he started down the stairs.

"You'll have them."

"And get in touch with the Province Queen's Master and make him aware—"

Daemon!

The urgency in Ladvarian's voice made him rush down the rest of the stairs and out of the house. Dim balls of witchlight hung over a spot in the garden, so it wasn't hard to find the dog.

And it wasn't hard to see what the Sceltie had found.

Ladvarian circled the lower halves of two severed legs. The legs were bare; the feet were still covered by ankle boots.

These smell like Sylvia, Ladvarian growled as he daintily walked on air to avoid leaving paw prints in the blood. *And I smell dead flesh.*

Daemon caught himself before pointing out that the

severed legs *were* dead flesh. The dog had grown up at the Hall and had been given the same training in Protocol as any other young male who had resided there. Ladvarian wouldn't use a disrespectful description simply because a person was demon-dead, so calling someone "dead flesh" was an indication of the dog's contempt for the person—an indication that the scent belonged to an enemy.

"Track the dead flesh, but don't go farther than these gardens," Daemon said. "I'll search for Sylvia. And stay shielded."

I will. Ladvarian headed down a path that led away from the house.

Daemon put a Black shield around the legs to prevent anyone from taking them. Then he searched the ground for a blood trail. Nothing clean about the severing, so there should be plenty of blood for him to follow.

Unless the attacker had used Craft and vanished Sylvia. Those personal storage cupboards the Blood created with Craft and power couldn't support anything that was alive. But you could move a body that way—or kill someone who was wounded.

He found blood splashed over the tops of plants, following a line where there was no trail. Stepping up on air to stand level with the tops of the plants, Daemon created a brighter ball of witchlight and followed the spray until he found a spot in the garden that looked crushed by a body—and he found pools of blood. Not as much as he'd expected, not if Sylvia had still been alive when she'd landed there, but enough to tell him where he needed to look for Halaway's Queen.

Ladvarian trotted up to him, also balanced on air. *The dead flesh is gone, but its smells are strong in some parts of the garden.*

"Hunting here?" Daemon looked around. Sylvia had landed close to one of the garden paths. If she did make the transition . . . He sighed. "She's not here."

Tildee and Mikal are not here either, Ladvarian said. *I have called Tildee. She doesn't answer.*

"All right. Let's take care of the living, and then we'll see what we can do about the dead."

They retraced their steps back to the house. As they passed the point of attack, Daemon wrapped a tight shield around the legs and vanished them.

Seeing Surreal standing near the front door, talking to the Master, Ladvarian trotted over to the Coach, then had to wait for Jaenelle to create an opening in the shields and let him in. Reassured when he saw the precautions his Lady had taken, Daemon joined Surreal and the Master.

"They didn't find Mikal or Tildee—or Sylvia," Surreal said.

"And no one seems to know where the younger son of the house has gone," the Master said.

"Oh, sugar, I think they know," Surreal replied.

Which meant there was at least one child whose disappearance had gone unreported. Either Sylvia stumbled onto something evil here or she'd been lured here to be sacrificed. Either way, none of the people he needed to talk to the most were here.

"Surreal, go get the boy," Daemon said. "Pack up anything you can as fast as you can. We're taking him with us." No matter what part Haeze had played in setting this trap, Daemon wasn't going to leave a child in this place.

"Give me ten minutes." She opened the front door and went inside.

"Do you want us to stay?" the Master asked.

"No. You need to keep a tight watch on your own village. I'll contact the Province Queen and have her send in some guards."

"This village has guards," the Master said. "Do you want me to talk to them before I go?"

"Do you think it will make any difference?" Daemon's voice was dry, biting.

The Master stared at him, then swore. "They're blind to what's going on in their own village, and it may be deliberate. That's what you're saying?"

"That's what I'm saying. This village is under your

Queen's hand. As her Master, these guards are under your command same as the men in her home village. Would you vouch for them?"

"A couple of months ago, I would have. Now?" The Master shook his head. "They knew about the children that had gone missing across the border. If there was any hint of something being wrong here, my Queen should have been told."

And the Queen of Halaway should have been informed so that she wouldn't have come to such a place without an escort, Daemon thought. *If she came at all.*

Unless he was totally wrong about the man standing in front of him, that mistake wouldn't be repeated. He suspected that, by tomorrow, the Master would contact every other Master of the Guard in Dhemlan, encouraging them to insist that their Queens have an escort for any kind of visit outside the home village.

But if the other Masters weren't informed, that would tell him something about this man too.

The front door opened. Surreal came out, one hand loosely gripping Haeze's arm. She said nothing to the men, just escorted the boy to the Coach.

"What do you want done with the Healer and this family?" the Master asked.

He wanted to rip them all apart to find out what they knew about Sylvia's attacker. But the prudent thing to do—the *right* thing—was to let the District Queen deal with the people in her territory.

And if he wasn't satisfied with how the District Queen dealt with these people, he would take care of them. Quietly.

"Take them to your Lady," Daemon said. "I'm sure she'll have some questions about what happened here tonight."

"I'm sure she will," the Master said.

Telling himself to be satisfied with that—for now— Daemon walked over to the Coach and went in. The driver was warming some milk and talking softly to Haeze, who huddled in one corner of a short bench. The man tipped his head toward the driver's compartment and made a face Daemon took to mean, *There's trouble in there.*

More than trouble, he decided when he opened the compartment door and Surreal swiveled her chair to face him.

"Jaenelle wants to leave as soon as you're ready," she said. "She has Beron in the bedroom at the back of the Coach."

He stayed in the door, assessing her temper. "Tell me." *Bad place for a fight*, he thought, *especially with Jaenelle doing a healing.*

"There is some damage to Beron's vision and hearing." Surreal's voice was low and savage. "That Healer wasn't just destroying his ability to speak. She was destroying his ability to see and hear."

Because she was so close to snapping, he kept his voice quiet and calm—and kept his own temper viciously leashed. "Could the loss of vision and hearing be conditions that had developed prior to—"

She shot out of the chair and stood in front of him. "There was nothing wrong with him before that bitch put her filthy hands on him. And I'm telling you now, Sadi, one way or another, she is *not* going to be among the living much longer."

"We have other things to deal with first."

He waited to see if she had any control left and was relieved when she nodded and blew out a breath.

"Yeah," she said. "Yeah, we do." She returned to her seat.

Daemon took off his winter coat and vanished it before closing the compartment door and taking the other seat.

They didn't speak again until he lifted the Coach and used Craft to glide it through the air. Once they reached one of the village's landing webs, he caught the Black Winds and headed for Halaway.

"Did you find any sign of Sylvia?" Surreal asked.

"Yes."

She stared at him, then looked away. "Shit."

"We take care of Beron, find out what Haeze knows about what happened and why, and figure out where Tildee took Mikal," Daemon said.

"And Sylvia?"

He sighed. "I think the High Lord is more likely to find her before we do."

TWO

Saetan lit the black candles on the Keep's Dark Altar and opened the Gate between Hell and Kaeleer.

Sometimes it was damn hard not to interfere with the living, especially when children were involved.

Especially when some of them lately were arriving so mentally and emotionally damaged they couldn't be allowed to stay on the *cildru dyathe*'s island, let alone be with the children now residing at the Hall in the Dark Realm. He'd given mercy to the ones who were too damaged, draining their remaining power to finish the kill, giving them what peace he could in the process.

It wasn't his place to interfere or step in. He had held that line for thousands of years—at least most of the time. But that last mutilated child had come from Dhemlan, and he didn't consider it interfering to inform the Warlord Prince of Dhemlan about that boy—not when the Prince was his own son.

Saetan?

A whisper of thought on a psychic thread, barely strong enough to reach him. But no matter how weak, he knew that voice, had loved that woman. *Sylvia? Where are you?*

Landing web. Keep. Not sure which one.

He left the Dark Altar and moved swiftly, straining the muscles in his bad leg as he moved through the corridors in the Keep.

Draca, Saetan called. *Sylvia is here. Something is wrong. We need to find her quickly.*

I will inform Geoffrey, Draca said. *We will look.*

It wouldn't be just the Keep's Seneschal and historian/librarian who would look. What guarded the Keep would be aware of Sylvia and would inform Draca. Meanwhile, he headed for the landing web most often used by people who didn't live in Ebon Rih.

Saetan? Sylvia called again, her voice fading.

He found her sprawled on the landing web, trying to push herself to an upright position and too weak to do it.

He rushed over to her and dropped to his knees, lifting her enough to hold her against him. "Sylvia, what . . . ?"

Demon-dead. He knew the scent, knew the feel. How could he not know after ruling Hell for so many years? She was demon-dead and fading. Both of her Jewels, the Purple Dusk and her Birthright Summer-sky, hung around her neck and she wore both her rings. Only a drop or two of power left in each of them.

"Saetan." Her voice was barely audible, but she still found enough strength to grab a fistful of his jacket. "I know how you feel about interfering with the living, but I'm begging you. Help me save my boys."

He didn't ask questions. He simply called in a small vial, flipped off the top, and closed his hand around it to give the contents a moment's warmth. Then he pressed the vial against her lips and said, "Drink."

She swallowed once, then tried to get away from him. He held her tight, and held the vial away from her to prevent her from knocking it out of his hand.

"Hell's fire," she gasped. "What *is* that?"

"A vial of Jaenelle's undiluted blood," he replied dryly. "If you think it's bad now, you should have tried it when she wore Ebony. A couple drops of *that* used to feel like you swallowed lightning."

"You're a mean bastard."

"And you want my help, so stop being a whiny girl. Just hold your nose and take your medicine."

"I am *not* whining, you—"

He poured the rest of the blood down her throat. Since he and Geoffrey usually split one of those vials, he knew exactly what he'd done to the woman he loved—which was why he let her swear at him until she wound down enough to sound sane again.

He vanished the vial. "Let's get you cleaned up. Then we can . . ."

That was when he realized what was wrong with her legs.

Using Craft to take part of her weight, he picked her up and headed for a guest room located near his own suite of rooms.

Lucivar! he called on a spear thread.

Father?

Jolting Lucivar awake would hone the sharp edge of an always-sharp temper, but he'd deal with that when he had to. *I need your Healer at the Keep. It's urgent.*

We'll be there. Lucivar broke the link.

Draca waited for him at the doorway of the guest room. When she saw Sylvia, she looked into the room. A marble slab appeared, heavily padded and floating on air.

It is more practical, Draca said.

Nodding, he went into the room and laid Sylvia on the padding.

"All right," he said, winding a soothing spell through his voice. "Let's take a look at you."

"No," Sylvia said.

He ignored her, pulled aside the torn coat and shirt, and stared at the knife wound that had killed her. He vanished the coat and shirt, then hesitated over the brassiere. It shouldn't matter now, but it would, so he didn't remove it. Instead, he called in a blanket and wrapped it around her so she wouldn't feel embarrassed when Lucivar thundered into the room.

Which Lucivar did a minute later, followed by Nurian.

"Mother Night," Nurian said as she rushed over to the slab. She reached out, her hands hovering over Sylvia's ruined legs. "What happened?"

Saetan put his arms around Sylvia, pressing her face against his shoulder. "You need to make a clean amputation, then force the healing to create a closed stump."

"But she's . . ." Nurian swallowed hard, but she met Saetan's eyes. "I don't think it can be done when the flesh is no longer living."

"When it's done within a few hours of dying, the body still remembers what it feels like to be alive and will respond."

Nurian looked at Sylvia's Jewels and shook her head. "It would drain her beyond surviving."

"She's just had fresh blood. That will sustain her and provide you with what you need to draw for the healing," Saetan said.

"Whose blood did you give her?" Lucivar asked.

"Jaenelle's."

"Half a vial?"

"A whole vial."

Lucivar looked at Nurian. "Do it. You've got more than enough power to work with, so tap everything you need because you only get one chance at this kind of healing. If more blood is needed, I'll supply it."

Holding Sylvia close, covering her face with one hand, Saetan watched Lucivar call in a small knife and efficiently cut away the trousers while Nurian began making the cleansing brews she would need.

Lucivar studied the jagged bones and torn flesh, saying nothing, but Saetan had the impression those bones told his Eyrien son a great deal.

There wouldn't be pain, because the numbing spells would take care of that. Some discomfort, yes, because flesh so newly dead still remembered, and the potency of the blood he could provide for her would keep her close to the line that separated the dead from the living. At least for a little while.

When Nurian was ready, Lucivar shifted Sylvia's hips, straightening the legs. He pressed his hands on her thighs, holding her in place.

She cried, and it ripped at Saetan's heart. Lucivar's body blocked most of her line of sight, but Saetan still covered her eyes so she wouldn't get even a glimpse of Nurian's work. And while he held her, he sent out a call to his other son.

*Daemon. *Daemon!**

No answer.

Jaenelle!

No answer.

Surreal!

No answer. Which meant they weren't at SaDiablo Hall or in Halaway. Or anywhere in that part of Kaeleer, for that matter. Of course, if they were riding the Winds, they couldn't hear him.

Swallowing a snarl of impatience, Saetan continued to wrap soothing spells around Sylvia until he felt her go limp. Laying her down, he smoothed the hair away from her face.

Lucivar gave him a sharp look.

"I did that," Saetan said. "Her mind needs to rest. Lady Nurian, can you do without us for a few minutes?"

"I'll be fine," Nurian said.

He and Lucivar stepped out of the room and moved a few paces down the corridor.

"A blast of power hit her knees, blowing them out and taking the lower part of her legs with them," Lucivar said, keeping his voice low. "If she was shielded, whoever did this wore an Opal, a Green Jewel at the most."

"How can you tell?"

Lucivar gave him an odd look. "Because I know how her legs would look if I had hit her with my Red strength."

Of course. "Her boys are in trouble."

Lucivar nodded. "There must have been a fight somewhere. Did she bleed out from the legs?"

Saetan shook his head. "She probably would have bled out if none of her guards survived to help her, but a knife between the ribs is what killed her."

"What did Daemon say?"

"He's not answering."

"All right. You look after Nurian, and I'll go to the Hall and find out what's happening." Lucivar hesitated. "Do you think her boys are going to become *cildru dyathe*?"

"I hope not, but I do need to talk to Daemon about some children who have become *cildru dyathe* in the past few weeks."

"I'll let him know."

Saetan watched Lucivar walk away. His sons were strong leaders and powerful men. He would trust them to take care of the living while he took care of the dead.

THREE

Alert for anything or anyone who didn't belong around his home, Daemon watched Jaenelle and Surreal hustle Beron and Haeze into the Hall, followed by Ladvarian. Just as he was about to go inside, he heard hooves and carriage wheels coming up the drive. He stopped and nodded to Beale, who closed the Hall's front doors. Then he turned and waited for his visitor. Considering the hour, it didn't surprise him when Rainier stepped out of the horse-drawn cab. What did surprise him was Lucivar's sudden appearance on the landing web. He'd expected to see his brother, just not this soon.

Give me a minute, Prick, he said.

Lucivar stepped off the landing web but didn't come closer.

"Report," Daemon said quietly to Rainier.

"Sylvia's court is furious," Rainier replied. "Her Master and Steward had no reason to think any harm would come to their Queen. They had the impression that the guest rooms were already stuffed with people, which was why Lord Haeze's family fumbled over having even one escort staying with Sylvia."

"There were no other guests," Daemon said.

"This was a trap set for Sylvia?" Rainier shook his head, as if answering his own question. "No. I was told the first invitation didn't include her."

"Unless she's visiting close friends, a Queen usually travels with at least one escort," Daemon said, "so Sylvia's presence could have been inconvenient if she'd arrived with one or two of her First Circle in attendance."

"According to the Steward, the second invitation was extended to Sylvia's family *as a family*, not to a Queen and her sons. They gambled she would sympathize with another woman's desire to reciprocate invitations without beggaring her own family."

"Unfortunately, they gambled correctly."

"Prince?"

He heard the alarm in Rainier's voice, but chose to ignore the question under the word. "I brought Haeze back with us. The boy needs protection from whatever is wrong in that place. I'd like you to talk to him and find out everything you can about what's been going on around his house and the village. You may have to circle around this, but I want to know why his younger brother wasn't at home."

"Done." Rainier looked at the Hall, then at Lucivar, who was still waiting near the landing web. "Did Sylvia come back with you?"

"No," Daemon said softly.

Rainier took a couple of slow, steady breaths. Then he approached the Hall's doors, which opened before he could reach for the knocker. When the doors closed again, Lucivar walked up to Daemon.

"How bad?" Lucivar asked.

"Beron's hurt, and at least half of his injuries were caused deliberately by the bitch Healer that family hired to take care of him. Jaenelle's working on him, has been since we found him. She says he'll be all right—and may the Darkness have mercy on that family if she can't bring him all the way back to full health."

"Mikal?"

"Sylvia told Tildee to run. We haven't found her or Mikal yet." Daemon blew out a breath and watched the white plume it made. "You've seen Sylvia?"

"Yes."

"Has Father?"

Lucivar looked sad and grim. "Yes. She made the transition to demon-dead and reached the Keep before draining her Jewels completely. He poured a vial of Jaenelle's blood down her throat."

Daemon huffed out a pained laugh. "Well, that should give her temper plenty of scratch and kick." The moment he said the word *kick*, he felt grief clog his throat. "I brought her legs. I wasn't going to leave any part of her there. Now I'm not sure what to do with them."

"Saetan wants to see you. He's troubled by some *cildru dyathe* who have appeared in the Dark Realm recently. You can ask him what should be done." Lucivar shifted his weight, rubbed his hands together.

"Do you want to go in?" Daemon asked.

"I figure you have a reason for standing out here in the cold."

That simple. It usually was between him and Lucivar.

He blew out another breath just to watch it plume in the cold night air. "If you were Tildee, where would you run?"

"You already know the answer, old son."

"I'd like confirmation that I'm thinking like a Sceltie."

"All right. If she or Mikal are wounded, she would go to the closest Sceltie for help protecting the boy. If they got out before things turned ugly, there are four places I would look: here, their home, Manny's cottage, and Tersa's cottage. I would go to Tersa's first. Mikal considers it his second home, and he's her 'Mikal boy.' He's family."

"And Tersa is dangerous when it comes to family."

"Yeah. Which is why I would go there to hide if I were a Sceltie running from danger with one of Tersa's boys." Lucivar remained silent for a minute. Then he huffed out a breath. "So are we going to go down and knock on her door, or wait until morning, or just stand here and freeze our balls?"

The Hall's doors opened. Beale said, "Prince? The carriage will be around front in a minute." He closed the doors.

Lucivar looked at Daemon. "Did you ask for a carriage to be brought around?"

"Apparently."

"Did you think to ask for hot coffee and something to eat?"

Daemon said blandly, "We'll have to find out."

Surreal paced the corridor, guarding the guest rooms that held Beron and Haeze. At the midway point, she passed Ladvarian, who trotted in the opposite direction. At the end of the corridor, they both turned and resumed their patrol.

The restless pacing wasn't necessary. She could have sat in one place and used a psychic probe to remain aware of everything and everyone in and around those rooms, but she needed to move.

All right, the truth was she wanted to go after the son of a whoring bitch who had hurt at least one boy she liked and a woman she considered a friend. She wanted to rip and tear and stab until the enemy was nothing more than a bloody pile of shit. Or find her prey and make the kill quietly, using one of those elegant death spells Sadi had taught her so many years ago.

So damn hard to pace and wait. Since he hadn't been with them, Rainier would have better luck coaxing information out of Haeze, and her presence in the room would interfere with that. She was more than useless in Beron's room while Jaenelle was working on the delicate healing needed to restore the boy's vision, hearing, and voice.

Then Ladvarian froze. Surreal called in her favorite stiletto and stood still, listening.

It's Tildee, Ladvarian said. *She is tired. Mikal is upset. They are with Tersa.*

Sadi! Surreal called. *Tildee and Mikal are with Tersa.*

We're almost at the cottage, he replied.

Any news about Sylvia?

A hesitation. *She's with the High Lord.*

He didn't need to say more.

"The Mikal boy is upset," Tersa said, blocking the stairs that led to the bedrooms. "The Sceltie is upset and says they must hide."

Daemon wasn't sure if she was asking for clarification or warning him not to push. He took her hands because sometimes physical contact helped her mind stay focused on the mundane world instead of wandering down a path in the Twisted Kingdom.

"Beron is injured, and Sylvia is dead," he said gently. "I need to see Mikal to make sure he wasn't harmed before Tildee got him away from that place."

"Oh," Tersa said softly. "He's so young to lose his mother."

I was younger when I was taken from you, Daemon thought as he drew her away from the stairs.

"Perhaps some warm milk?" Tersa looked at him, then at Lucivar.

"Do you need help making it?" Lucivar asked.

"No, I can warm milk."

She walked down the hallway to the kitchen, leaving them to climb the stairs.

Mikal was in the "Mikal boy's" bedroom, since he was Tersa's most frequent guest. The covers were pulled out and rumpled, which Daemon found alarming, since it looked like a struggle had taken place. Then he saw part of Tildee's head poking out from the covers at the bottom of the bed. *She* had done the rumpling to have a hiding place from which she could easily attack. And since Mikal was pressed against the headboard on the side of the bed farthest from the door and would draw a person's eye first, an intruder moving toward the boy would put himself in a position to receive intimate damage from a pissed-off Sceltie with sharp teeth. Even if the intruder's shield held against her Summer-sky, the clash of power would alert everyone nearby that there was trouble.

"Lady Tildee, please attend," Lucivar said. "Prince Sadi needs to speak to Lord Mikal."

Using the formal titles turned the request into a command.

Tildee wiggled out from under the covers and followed Lucivar downstairs.

Daemon sat on the edge of the bed near Mikal. "Are you hurt?" he asked quietly.

Mikal shook his head. Then he frowned and pushed up one sleeve. "Well, my arm hurts a little, but Tildee didn't mean it. She grabbed me and said we had to run and hide. Mother said so. I wanted to find out why, but Tildee wouldn't let go of my arm, so we left, and she wouldn't stop, and it took a long time to ride the Winds, and then we were here, and Tildee told Tersa that something bad had happened, but she didn't know what the bad thing was, only that we were supposed to hide."

Daemon lightly brushed his fingertips over Mikal's arm. The Sceltie hadn't broken the skin, but she'd clamped down hard enough to leave bruises.

"Prince? Before Tildee caught the Winds and took us away from that house, I heard Beron yell. It sounded bad. Is he hurt?"

Daemon swallowed the lump in his throat. "Yes, he's hurt. But Lady Angelline is doing the healing, and she's taking good care of him."

"Then who's taking care of Mother? She wouldn't have told Tildee to run unless something bad happened."

He brushed back Mikal's hair. The boy needed to have it cut soon. Who would remember the small things like that now? "I'm sorry, boyo. I am so sorry, but your mother is dead."

Mikal was silent for so long, Daemon wondered if the words had been understood.

"Can't the High Lord fix her so she can come back and live with us?" Mikal asked in a small voice. "She would have to sleep in the daytime, but that would be all right. I'd get my chores and schoolwork done before she woke up. I would."

"It's not that easy for someone who is demon-dead to be among the living." Who was he to say such a thing to this child? Most of his family had been demon-dead and had lived at the Hall for years in order to be with Jaenelle.

Saetan had not only been Sylvia's lover; he'd been Mikal's surrogate father.

"The High Lord could fix it," Mikal insisted. There was hope and conviction in those words—and fear that it wouldn't be true. "Can't you ask him to fix it?"

Daemon's eyes filled with tears. He pulled the boy close and hugged him, rocking them both for comfort. "I don't know if he can fix this, Mikal. I don't know if he can. But I'll ask him. I promise that I'll ask him."

An hour later, Mikal and Tildee were snoring in a freshly made bed, and Daemon and Lucivar were in the carriage heading back to the Hall.

"You couldn't have said anything else," Lucivar told him. "Not to a boy who has rubbed elbows with our family as much as he has."

"Sylvia is a Queen," Daemon said wearily. "Letting a demon-dead Queen continue to rule would set a dangerous precedent, and it would be hard for her to remain anywhere near Halaway and watch another Queen rule her people—especially if she didn't like some of the choices the new Queen made. Families and villages and Territories need to let go of the dead and move on—and the demon-dead need to let go of the living."

"The boy doesn't give a damn about Sylvia the Queen. Right now, he just wants the assurance that his mother will still be there to read him a story and tuck him in at night," Lucivar said.

"I know that, Prick. I know." Daemon pressed his fingertips against his temples and tried to ease some of the tension.

"Do you think Sylvia's father will want the boys to live with him?" Lucivar asked.

"Maybe. What the boys want will have more weight than any adult." A trickle of anger pushed aside the weariness. "But I'll tell you who isn't going to have the boys. Their sires."

"I didn't think either of them had been granted paternal rights—or wanted them."

"They didn't. But Mikal's sire has come sniffing around a couple of times in recent months, expressing interest in his son and wanting to become acquainted."

"Why?"

"From what I found out after the first time he came around, his service as a Consort has earned him notoriety rather than the lucrative and illustrious positions he'd envisioned would be his when he walked away from Sylvia and her little village."

"And I thought Father was the only one who disliked her former Consorts," Lucivar said dryly.

Daemon lowered his hands and rested his head on the back of the seat. "You will never repeat this to Jaenelle, but after that son of a whoring bitch came around a second time, I told Kaelas and Jaal that if he trespassed on any property that belonged to the family—and that included the land around Manny's and Tersa's cottages—they had my permission to eat him. I said it within the bastard's hearing. I haven't seen him since."

Lucivar stared at him for a moment before laughing. "Hell's fire, Bastard. You do like to dance on the knife's edge."

"Maybe." Or maybe he felt fairly sure that Jaenelle wouldn't object too strenuously if she did find out.

Prince?

Rainier, Daemon replied. *Anything to report?*

I know why Sylvia's family was lured down to that place, but I didn't find out anything that will help you hunt down the bastard. If you and Prince Yaslana are coming back to the Hall, Surreal wants to go back to our house in Halaway and get some sleep. She knows she has a suite at the Hall and I have a suite too, and there's no point in you reminding her because Beale already has—twice—but she wants to be in the village, closer to Tersa and Manny. Just in case.

All right. I'll stop by in the morning before I go to the Keep. He broke the link and closed his eyes. "Can you stay until morning?" he asked Lucivar. "I'll be heading to the Keep after I talk to Rainier."

"I can stay. I'll check on Tersa and Mikal while you get Rainier's report. Maybe between us we can give Sylvia a little peace."

And maybe by tomorrow he would have a better idea of how to find the bastard who had ended a good Queen's life.

FOUR

Sylvia jerked awake and tried to pull herself out of a memory-dream about Mikal and Tildee. It was during the first year Tildee had lived with them. Mikal had snitched some goody from the kitchen earlier that day and hidden it under his bed for the two of them to have as a treat late that night, not realizing that the treat would spoil if left outside the cold box on a summer day. Tildee had thought it smelled bad, but the boy assured her it was wonderful, so boy and Sceltie had gobbled up the treat.

She still remembered Mikal's panicked yells, and running into his bedroom to discover that Tildee had vomited all over his lap. In the seconds it took her to realize the dog was extremely ill and needed healing help from someone who knew kindred, Mikal began throwing up. So there she was, very late at night, pounding on the Hall's front door, holding a blanket-wrapped Sceltie who was covered in Mikal's puke, while her court Healer was taking care of Mikal, and Beron was running to fetch Manny and Tersa.

Jaenelle had taken one look at Tildee, asked what she and Mikal had eaten, and then poured a tonic down the dog's throat. An hour later, Sylvia was back home with an embarrassed, freshly bathed Sceltie, who was greeted by an equally embarrassed, freshly bathed boy. For a few years after that incident, on the days when Mikal attended the village school, Tildee went up to the Hall for her own kind of lessons.

The two of them had gotten into their share of trouble since then, but when Tildee told Mikal something was bad, the boy didn't argue.

Why would I dream about that now? she wondered. Then she remembered she'd told Tildee to run. *The boys!*

Rolling over on her side, Sylvia tried to fling the covers back and push her legs over the edge of the bed, but an arm tightened around her waist.

"Easy," Saetan said. "From now on, you have to think before you get out of bed."

"The boys!"

"Are safe. Beron was injured, but he's at the Hall in Jaenelle's care. We'll find out more when Daemon and Lucivar arrive here in a couple of hours."

Sylvia shivered. "And Mikal?"

Saetan's arm didn't move from her waist, but the covers settled in place around her. "Tildee grabbed Mikal and didn't stop running until she got them to Tersa's cottage. They're upset, but otherwise they're fine."

"Thank the Darkness." All her strength seemed to drain away once she knew her sons were safe. She rolled onto her back—and remembered the rest.

The candle-light in the bedside lamp began to glow softly, providing just enough light for her to see the man who raised himself up on one elbow to look at her.

"You're not under the covers," she said. "Is it because of how my legs look?"

"My darling Sylvia, I am the High Lord of Hell. I have seen much worse than truncated legs. No, I'm above the covers because I didn't want you to wake up alone, but you weren't in any condition to extend an invitation to sleep with you."

She let out a pained laugh. "You're still going to insist on propriety?"

"Your body is dead; you are not. That being the case, I see no reason to dispense with propriety or any other courtesy," he said with just enough bite to make her feel chastised.

No, he wouldn't dispense with propriety or courtesy or the Blood's Protocol or their code of honor, and she doubted the demon-dead were allowed to dispense with those things either. Not if they wanted to extend their existence a while longer after the physical death.

"Saetan . . ." She wasn't sure what she was asking of him, wasn't even sure if she *was* asking anything. But he bent his head and gave her one of those slow, thorough kisses that used to make her knees weak. When his mind surrounded hers, she felt the wave of sensuality that used to bring her an orgasm before his hands touched her.

Now it felt comforting, but it was her heart and not her body that felt that comfort.

He ended the kiss and eased back enough to look at her. "Everything has a price."

Being demon-dead wasn't the same as being among the living. Her Self was now encased in dead flesh. Sylvia the woman could still feel love, but her body no longer felt the pleasures of sex.

She tried to shift away from him, but he rolled just enough to pin her.

"I think you would like some answers to some questions you don't want to ask," Saetan said. "Can I love you when sex is no longer part of that love? Yes, I can and do. Do I still want to spend time with you and sleep with you? Yes, I do. I couldn't remain with you when you were among the living, but there is no reason why we can't be together now—if that's something you want too."

"For how long?" she asked.

"For as long as you want," he replied. "You'll know when it's time to go, and I won't ask you to stay a day longer."

"My legs."

"An illusion spell and some Craft to air walk can hide the loss from the eye."

"That would be a constant drain of power."

"Yes, it would—and not a necessary drain on most days, in my opinion." He looked at the two pendants resting on her chest. "It looks like the dose of Jaenelle's blood had enough power in it to fuel the healing and fill both of your Jewels' reservoirs partway. That's a good start."

Good start? Oh, no. "Hell's fire. You're not going to make me drink more of that stuff, are you?"

"Not immediately," he said dryly. "But it's a simple fact that the darker the power, the less blood that's required to sustain someone who is demon-dead."

"Plain speaking, High Lord."

"Once your power is restored, yarbarah will be sufficient most days. Twice a month, you'll have a small amount of fresh human blood."

She narrowed her eyes. "Whose blood?"

He gave her a smile that had her pressing into the bed. "That depends on whether a certain Lady thinks you look peaky. I strongly recommend not draining yourself to the point of looking peaky."

"Mother Night."

"And may the Darkness be merciful." Saetan shifted so he no longer pinned her. "But as I said earlier, you should be grateful you never had Ebony-strength blood poured down your throat." He rolled out of bed. "All right, witchling. Nurian will be back before sunup to take a look at your legs, but she already confirmed that her shields will keep everything protected so you can have a bath beforehand. I expect Daemon and Lucivar to arrive before sunup as well, since they both know you'll need to sleep during the daylight hours. Karla's wheeled chair was left outside the room. You can use that until we can arrange to have one built for you."

"But you said I could air walk!" She didn't want to be seen in a chair like that, didn't want her sons thinking about the parts of her legs that weren't there.

Saetan gave her a dry look. "It's like anything else, Sylvia. There needs to be a balance between using Craft to move around and using your body. The wheeled chair is practical." He snarled softly as he came around to her side of the bed. "You were not a vain woman when you were alive. You are *not* going to become vain now that you're dead."

Her mouth was still hanging open and her brain was still trying to think of a reply when he flung back the covers, picked her up, and took her into the bathroom.

Ignoring the breakfast breads, ham, and fruit that had been set out for him and Lucivar, Daemon poured himself a second cup of coffee and sat back.

"Let's begin with the simple and work up to the nasty," he said.

"Why is Sylvia glaring at me?" Lucivar asked Saetan. "It was only a few drops of Red added to the yarbarah. It's not like I opened a vein and poured Ebon-gray down her throat. I added a few drops to your glass too, and *you* aren't acting bitchy about it."

"I'm going to overlook that poor choice of words," Saetan replied, giving Lucivar a look that said, *Say another word and I'll kick your ass.* "Prince Sadi, please report."

"As I told you last night, Mikal is upset, but he's fine except for the bruises Tildee's teeth made on his arm. He and Tildee are staying with Tersa for the time being."

"I thought my father might want to take him," Sylvia said, her voice troubled.

Are you hoping he'll take them, or are you hoping someone will step in and prevent that arrangement? Daemon wondered. Something wasn't right between grandfather and grandsons, but he wasn't going to wade into *that* family quarrel unless Jaenelle wanted him to. "Right now, Mikal has Tildee, Ladvarian, and Jaal protecting him. Your father might be willing to argue with two Scelties, but I don't think he'll want to deal with a tiger. So Mikal stays with Tersa, since her response to finding Jaal in her parlor was to send Ladvarian out to buy more milk."

"And Beron?" Sylvia asked.

Lucivar gave her that lazy, arrogant smile. "He remembered more of his training than you did. But I guess I'll overlook that, since you're all weak and helpless now."

The Prick sure does know how to rile up women, Daemon told Saetan as they watched Sylvia change from wounded, vulnerable woman into a pissed-off Queen. *Think she'll go for his balls?*

I locked the wheels on her chair after I tasted the yarbarah, Saetan replied.

"Beron is wounded," Daemon said. "He'll need several days of rest and care to fully heal, but he will heal. He'll stay at the Hall with us until this is settled. He'll be well protected there. Nothing will get past Kaelas—or me."

Sylvia looked at each of the men. "Why so much protection? The trouble is in the southern part of Dhemlan, not in Halaway."

They had reached the nasty part of this report. "We brought Haeze back to the Hall last night. After talking with Rainier this morning, I'm glad I made that choice." Daemon took a deep breath and let it out slowly. "A Warlord in Little Terreille has been preying on young boys for the past few years. There is even a story whispered in schools near Goth about No Face, a Warlord who tortures and kills boys who slip out at night instead of staying home as they should." No Face indulged in physical, sexual, and emotional torture, but Daemon saw no reason to tell Sylvia what had been intended for her younger son.

"No Face." Sylvia turned her hand palm up and stared at her fingers. "He had some kind of mesh covering his face. I thought my fingers were ripped up by it when I was fighting him."

Saetan cleared his throat. "Nurian was able to heal your fingers before the flesh could no longer respond like it was still living."

He broke his own rules in order to repair her body this much, Daemon thought. *He won't regret that decision, but he isn't comfortable with having made that choice.* "Some of No Face's victims might have made the transition to *cildru dyathe,* but more likely, he used them up and made the final kill so there wouldn't be anyone to bear witness against him."

"Until now," Saetan said too softly. "The *cildru dyathe* who have reached Hell in the past few weeks . . ." He didn't glance at Sylvia, but Daemon understood why his father chose not to continue. "The last one was a boy from Dhemlan. Something I wanted to discuss with you, Daemon."

Was he mutilated? Daemon asked on a Black thread.

Yes.

"No Face has either grown careless or too confident," Daemon began.

"Or bored," Lucivar said, breaking in.

Daemon nodded. "Or bored. The bastard shifted his hunting ground to villages near the Dhemlan border. All of a sudden, village guards in Little Terreille were paying attention and responding faster when a child disappeared. More of a challenge for him, and far more exciting."

"Then he made the mistake of straying over the border into Dhemlan." Lucivar helped himself to one of the breakfast breads. "He sees a brown-skinned child and forgets that the Dhemlan people are a long-lived race, and that child probably has lived as many years—or more—than him. That means the child is a little more mature in some ways than other children and may not be as easy to grab. Combine that with an adolescent male who had the luck to become friends with the Queen of Halaway's son, and the bastard has more trouble than he's prepared to meet."

"Haeze soaked in the weapons lessons Lucivar gave the boys, and used his spending money to buy a knife," Daemon said. "When the District Queen makes some pointed inquiries, I suspect she'll discover more than one child has gone missing from that village before Haeze came to visit Beron."

"He wanted to learn to protect himself," Saetan said.

"More likely, to protect his younger brother," Lucivar said. "Like Beron, Haeze is too old to be of interest to No Face."

Daemon glanced at his father. The look in Saetan's eyes

was enough to confirm the age of the children who had reached Hell.

"The invitation," Sylvia whispered. "The house party was a ruse to bring Mikal within reach. Why lure a boy who lives in a distant village instead of hunting one within reach?"

"We think No Face blames your family for his death and the inconvenience that comes with the physical death," Daemon said. "Haeze's younger brother was the intended prey. But when No Face attacked, Haeze rushed in and managed to land a killing blow. Not an instant kill, since the boy was knocked out by a blast of power and his brother was taken, but he changed the battleground. No Face became demon-dead."

"People in the border villages are going to notice if a Warlord from Little Terreille no longer goes out during daylight or sits down for a meal," Lucivar said. "Whatever face the bastard hides behind that mesh is no longer going to go unnoticed—and people will start connecting him with the missing children."

"So his game was spoiled," Daemon continued. "All because Haeze went to Halaway to visit Beron."

"Why didn't Jaenelle's purge get rid of that monster?" Sylvia asked.

"That witch storm was over a decade ago," Saetan said, "and it was unleashed to purge the Realms of Dorothea's and Hekatah's taint, not eliminate every person who is twisted in some way. If No Face comes from Little Terreille, which sounds likely, he's from a short-lived race. He may have been young enough then to have avoided any kind of detection, or maybe his taste for this didn't develop until maturity, when he would have the physical strength to overpower his chosen prey. Maybe he was the one who started the story of No Face to begin with—or maybe something happened to him and he told it as a story at school to hide the truth about a real predator."

"Do we care about why he kills boys?" Lucivar asked.

"I don't," Daemon replied. "I just want to find him and put him in a deep grave."

Saetan might be willing to wonder if a boy became a monster after being brutalized by one, but *he* had the duty to protect the people of Dhemlan. Until No Face was contained, he had no room for pity.

Sylvia set the unfinished glass of yarbarah on a side table. "He's going to come after my sons, isn't he?"

"We think so," Daemon said. "It's another reason the boys are safer where they are. After making the transition to demon-dead, No Face snatched a servant's child. The boy was violated and mutilated, and then sent to Haeze's family with the demand that they convince you to allow Beron and Mikal to visit. Once he had Mikal, he would return Haeze's brother unharmed."

"Revenge on me and mine because Haeze fought back," she said. "Exchanging one child's life for another's."

"Yes. But he didn't count on you and Tildee—that you would fight him and Tildee would be able to take Mikal out of his reach. He didn't count on Beron charging in to attack." Daemon paused. "Beron ripped off the mesh and saw the enemy's face."

He and Lucivar suspected that was why the Healer had been destroying Beron's ability to communicate. From what Jaenelle had told him, the bitch had a little of the Hourglass's skills—enough to strip Beron of even psychic communication by locking him within his own mind, which she would have done if Jaenelle hadn't intervened. A boy like that would be at the mercy of a predator.

How many of the recent *cildru dyathe* had arrived in Hell in the same condition?

"Do you think Haeze's brother is still alive?" Sylvia asked.

"No," Daemon replied. "But having seen the servant's child and believing their own boy was still alive, they decided to sacrifice your child instead, knowing what that bastard intended to do to Mikal."

"They didn't have a choice," Sylvia said.

"Yes, they did." Daemon's voice held a hint of ice.

"What choice?" The fire in Sylvia's voice challenged the ice in his.

"They could have gone to the District Queen for help. Haeze's father could have gone to the Queen's Master of the Guard if he didn't think the village guards would help him. Someone could have gone to the Province Queen or come to me when the first child in that village went missing. They had other choices, Sylvia, and the choice they made resulted in Beron being injured and you being killed." He shoved out of his chair. "Save your pity for someone who deserves it. Now, if you'll excuse me, I have a butcher to hunt."

He walked out of the room, walked out of the Keep, and caught the Black Winds that would take him home.

Sylvia watched Lucivar fill up a plate with breakfast foods before wandering out of the room. He made it look casual, but it wasn't. She didn't think Saetan had caught up with Daemon before Sadi left the Keep, but Yaslana was getting off the battlefield before the High Lord returned.

Moments after Lucivar left, Saetan came back into the room. He walked over to the table beside her wheeled chair, picked up her glass of yarbarah, and warmed it over a tongue of witchfire before handing it to her.

"Finish that," he said.

She bristled at the disapproving chill in his voice. "I'm entitled to an opinion."

"And we're entitled to think you're being a softhearted ass for having that opinion," he snapped.

"You're not a mother!"

"No, but I am a father, and *I am the High Lord of Hell*. I've seen that bastard's victims, Sylvia, and I gave mercy to some of them because they were so damaged that was the only thing I could do."

"Haeze's mother was just trying to save her son!"

"He's dead!" Saetan roared. "No Face was never going to give her back a living boy. He was dead before you arrived for that visit."

Sylvia shrank back in her chair, trembling. "You can't be sure of that."

"Oh, but I *am* sure of that. And before you say Daemon and I don't have a personal stake in your sons, I suggest you consider how our families are connected." He walked out of the room, slamming the door behind him.

She didn't need to consider or think. She knew all about the connections.

When Jaenelle was fifteen and had tried attending school with other children, Beron had been her friend. Even now, when he was still an adolescent and she was a grown woman married for more than a decade, they were still friends, and he told Jaenelle things he wouldn't think to tell anyone else. Mikal spent as much time with Tersa as he did at home, and because of that, Daemon was the adult male he had the most contact with outside of Sylvia's own First Circle.

Many years ago, her father had come to Halaway to find work and a wife. He'd found both, and he'd been enormously proud of his daughter, the Queen. He was a good man, and he loved her as much as she loved him. But their love had been strained by her love of another good man—because that man was the High Lord of Hell and the patriarch of the SaDiablo family. Her father saw things one way; Saetan saw things another. Neither was wrong, and both cared deeply for family, but it had scraped against her father's pride that her sons had found the SaDiablo way of thinking more appealing, even though its rules and code of honor were more demanding.

Having a man so old and powerful and lethal as her lover and her sons' surrogate father had not sat well with the man who had raised her. Of course, he had thought the two Consorts who had sired her sons were great fellows because they fit into the social circles that minor aristos like her father found comfortable, and she suspected he'd been behind the interest Mikal's sire had been showing in his offspring recently.

Daemon and Jaenelle would make room for her father and brother because they were her family, but whether her blood relatives liked it or not, her sons had become absorbed into the SaDiablo family, and the SaDiablos took care of their own.

She drained the glass of yarbarah and set it aside. Then she pulled up the long skirt and looked at what remained of her legs.

The SaDiablos took care of their own. Would Saetan have given anyone else a vial of Jaenelle's blood so that a Healer could shape shattered bone and ripped flesh into clean stumps? Or heal her fingertips so that she could have full use of her hands? She knew enough about the restrictions he placed on the demon-dead to understand that he'd bent many of his own rules to give her this much.

If another woman had come to the Keep asking for his help, most likely he would have summoned his sons or trusted demon-dead Warlords to save the children, and he would have provided the blood that would have given the woman enough sustenance to keep the Self inside the flesh until she had the reassurance that her children were safe. What would have happened to her after that? Most likely, in a few days or weeks, that woman's power would have faded and she would have become a whisper in the Darkness. Saetan was realistic. He had to be. Hundreds of Blood died every day. He couldn't take care of all of them personally.

But he could, and did, protect the living from the dead. And wasn't that part of Saetan's—and Daemon's—anger? No Face was demon-dead and was still hunting in a living Realm, was hunting now in Dhemlan.

Instead of recognizing the rage growing in two Warlord Princes, she had remained focused on another woman's fear as if it were her own—even though she knew that woman's choice would not have been hers. She *would* have gone to the District Queen or the Province Queen or broken down the door at SaDiablo Hall if that was what it took to get help. She wouldn't have sacrificed another woman's child, even at the cost of her own.

Sylvia lowered the skirt and carefully arranged the folds. She was a spectator now, nothing more. As hard as it was to wait, she had to trust the living to take care of the living.

FIVE

*B*eron walked along Halaway's streets, looking into shop windows and wishing he'd brought along a few coins so he could suggest buying dishes of flavored ice.

"I have money," Jaenelle said.

He looked at her. Long golden hair and sapphire eyes, wearing one of those peculiar outfits that were too big for her. Only fifteen years old, but her eyes were ancient.

Fifteen? "You're older now," he told her.

"I can be," she replied cheerfully as she held up a silver mark. "It's your dream. But at either age, I still have enough money for two bowls of flavored ice."

He laughed. It made his throat hurt enough that he really wanted that ice.

"It's bad out there," he said. "But you know that. You knew that before the rest of us did."

"There are also strong men out there who will defend and protect," she said. "They won't let you come to harm."

"I've seen his face."

"Show me. Let him take shape here."

Beron shook his head. "If I show you, you'll be in danger too."

Something brushed against him, muscle and fur hidden within a sight shield. More movement and soft sounds all around them.

"We won't be the ones in danger," Jaenelle said softly.

The face of the enemy floated in the air before them.

"He's rather pretty, isn't he?" she said. *"You would never guess what was hidden under the skin. No matter. Now he doesn't have any masks to hide behind."*

Beron opened his eyes. The room looked cloudy, and his ears felt plugged. His heart jumped when someone sat on the bed. He struggled to make his eyes work.

Don't push it, Jaenelle said on a psychic thread. *Your vision and hearing will improve daily unless you disobey your Healer, being me, and do something stupid, which will give you swollen balls.*

Why? he asked.

Because I will kick them.

Of course she would. Jaenelle the Healer didn't tolerate any nonsense or sass.

Can you sit up? she asked.

I think so. She helped him sit up, and being closer helped clear his vision enough to know he was looking at Jaenelle as she was now rather than the girl in the dream.

There. She settled herself on the side of the bed and reached for the two bowls of flavored ice floating on air. She handed him one. *Raspberry. Your favorite.*

He grinned. *It's as if you knew I wanted some.*

She grinned in return. *Imagine that.*

A voice full of lightning and caverns and midnight skies floated through the Darkness, winding its way through sleep and dreams.

We know your face, the voice whispered.

For most, whether they were demon-dead or living, there was a kind of comfort in hearing the words, in being known by that voice.

We know your face.

But one man opened his eyes and shivered with fear, knowing his time was running out.

SIX

Daemon tucked his hands in his trouser pockets. Then, remembering the gesture didn't belong to the boy whose face he now wore, he withdrew them and asked, "How do I look?"

Tersa studied him, looking confused in a way that worried him. The mundane world was a fragile thing for his mother, more like an illusion she could interact with than solid ground and living people. For Tersa, the roads of the Twisted Kingdom were far more real.

"You look shorter," she finally said.

Did she see the illusion Jaenelle had made or did she see right past the illusion to a memory of the boy he had been?

Are you sleepy? I am sleepy. It is time for bed now.

Daemon looked at the shadow, the complex illusion that Jaenelle had made using Tildee as the template. "Hush."

The Sceltie looked at him. Then she sneezed.

"Jaenelle talked to you about this," he said to Tersa. "Remember? I'm pretending to be Mikal to catch the man who hurt Beron and Sylvia."

Tersa nodded. "Yes. You have to catch him so that the Mikal boy can stay with me again."

"That's right."

She frowned. "And I am supposed to pretend to be a weak female who is no threat to him."

"Yes." He stepped up to her and took her hands. "Darling,

he is going to come here, to your cottage. When he does, don't get in his way. Let him come up here, to the Mikal boy's room. I'll be here, pretending to be Mikal, and I will deal with him. Do you understand?"

She nodded. "I will let him come up and see the Mikal boy."

Are you sleepy? I am sleepy. It is time for bed now.

"I'll warm up some milk for you," Tersa said. "You shouldn't have a nutcake so late at night, but it's all right if it's a special treat." She walked out of the bedroom.

Are you sleepy? I am sleepy. It is time for bed now.

"Shut up," Daemon growled.

The Sceltie growled back.

Rolling his eyes, he reached for the mind of the woman who meant more to him than anything else in the Realms. *If you had to stick me with a shadow Sceltie, did you have to make it so realistic?*

Her laughter rippled through the psychic thread. *Problem?*

The dog is so damn bossy! If she bites me for not going to bed . . .

More laughter. *I'm making a sacrifice too.*

And that would be?

It's winter. You're not here at night. My feet are cold.

He blinked. *You're sleeping with a fuzzy, eight-hundred-pound cat. Put your feet on him.*

I do, but he whines about it. You don't.

Kaelas came from Arceria, one of the northernmost Territories, and lived in a den made out of snow. Why in the name of Hell would he whine about Jaenelle's feet? He should be happy to have a cool spot since he'd grown his winter coat and was staying in a room that was much too warm for him.

Of course, sometimes Jaenelle's feet were breathtakingly cold during the deep part of winter.

Is everything all right there? he asked.

Yes. Beron is asleep and has Shuveen, Boyd, and Floyd with him.

Shuveen was sensible and would wake Jaenelle if Beron needed a Healer's help. Boyd and Floyd, on the other hand, were younger and pretty brainless most of the time. However, those two could make enough noise to wake the entire Hall if a stranger walked into Beron's room.

Get some sleep, love, he said. *I'll see you in the morning.*

The psychic thread faded.

Are you sleepy? I am sleepy. It is time for bed now.

"Tersa is bringing up warm milk and nutcakes. We'll have our snack, and *then* go to bed."

Snack? The shadow wagged her tail.

Ignoring the illusion that could fool the eye and, sometimes, even fool the sense of touch, Daemon went to the window and studied the ground in Tersa's backyard. The snow was all churned up from the play of boy and dog, but he didn't think there were any fresh tracks.

Lucivar would know.

Jaenelle had taken Beron's memory of his attacker and brought it into a tangled web of illusions. From there, she'd created a basic shadow—an illusion that was a stationary imitation of a person. An artist came from Amdarh and made a sketch of the shadow, and that was taken to a printer. By the end of that first day, every village in the southern part of Dhemlan had a copy of that sketch, and Daemon hadn't asked if some of those copies had found their way across the border to worried men in Little Terreille.

He had sent an official letter and a copy of the sketch to Little Terreille's Queen. She wasn't a personal friend of Jaenelle's, but his Lady didn't consider her an enemy either. So he'd given the Queen the courtesy of sharing the information they had because there were families around Goth who were also grieving the loss of children.

We know your face. Witch's voice had whispered through the Darkness that first night. For the three nights since then, Daemon had spent the hours between sunset and sunrise in Tersa's cottage, waiting, wrapped in a strong illusion that would make even a demon-dead predator's eyes see Mikal, the chosen prey.

Are you sleepy? I am sleepy. It is time for bed now.

Daemon sighed. It could have been worse. If Jaenelle had made a shadow that had Tildee's real personality, he and the dog would be in a relentless argument about bedtime by now—and he'd be on the losing end of that argument, since the shadow wouldn't see past the illusion spell Jaenelle had created for him.

Snack? the shadow asked.

He turned away from the window, frowning. Why was it taking so long to warm up some milk?

Tersa carefully poured the warm milk into a mug and a small bowl. Her boy would make sure the Mikal boy would be allowed to live with her. The tangled web she'd woven after Sylvia left the living Realms had told her that much. The grandfather was a good man, and he had been a good father for the daughter. But he was not the right man for her sons. Lives would be soured, and the love that existed now would die if the grandfather took the sons. So the Mikal boy and Tildee would live with her, and Beron . . . Witch knew best what to do for Beron. She'd seen that too in her web.

She rinsed out the pot and left it in the sink to wash later with the mug and bowl. As she turned to get a plate for the nutcake, she saw the stranger in her kitchen, standing close enough to touch.

She shrank back, a response to the foulness of his psychic scent rather than fear of his physical presence.

He grabbed her wrist, squeezing until she flinched in pain. "Where is the boy?" he snarled.

The boy? Wasn't he supposed to ask her about the Mikal boy? "The boy is upstairs."

"Show me." He dragged her out of the kitchen and down the hallway. Then he released her wrist and gave her a hard shove toward the stairs. *"Show me."*

She had promised Witch that she would play out this

game so that all the boys would be safe. But something wasn't right because this *foulness* was supposed to ask about the Mikal boy, not *her* boy.

Her boy would understand this confusion. He was playing Witch's game too.

"Show me where he is," the foulness whispered as it followed close behind her.

Tersa climbed the stairs and led him to the bedroom where her boy waited.

It took all the control Daemon had to stand still when that bastard shoved Tersa into the bedroom. The shadow Sceltie began barking, but Jaenelle had deliberately left out any commands to attack.

"You brat!" The Warlord's voice sounded hoarse, as if his vocal cords had been damaged at some point and didn't heal correctly.

Daemon stepped back, drawing the Warlord farther into the room and away from Tersa.

"You brat! When I'm through with you, even your own brother won't recognize you!"

Tersa jerked as if struck, but Daemon didn't have time to wonder why because the Warlord lunged, his hand reaching for where a boy's arm would be.

Instead of scrambling back, Daemon stepped forward and clamped a hand around the Warlord's wrist. As Jaenelle intended, contact with another male broke the illusion spell around Daemon. The release of her power in the spell also broke the illusion around the Warlord.

Scars on the throat. Hideous scars on the face. One cloudy eye.

A monster had begotten a monster. As Daemon looked into the man's clear eye, he felt a stir of pity—enough pity that he decided it would be a swift execution rather than the slow one a monster deserved.

"You came to hurt the boy," Tersa said, taking a step toward them.

Daemon glanced up and saw rage and a terrible kind of clarity in his mother's eyes. "It's done now."

"You want to hurt *my boy*."

"Tersa . . ." He was Black-shielded. There was nothing the Warlord could do to him and nothing the man could do to break free of him. But Tersa might still get hurt, especially now that she was standing directly behind the bastard.

"Jaenelle says it is like deboning chicken," Tersa said in a singsong voice. "Just hook two fingers around the spine and pull."

No time to say anything or do anything. One moment the Warlord was standing in front of him, caught in a bone-breaking grip. The next . . .

He felt the sharp tingle of Craft as the bones of hand and fingers passed under his grip. He tightened his hand to hold on to the man's wrist, but there was nothing but soft flesh, and the Warlord's hand swelled like a sausage casing when it gets squeezed.

Passing the bones through flesh and skin, Tersa whipped the skeleton free. Then witchfire, fueled by her fury, took the bones, charring them black.

For that moment, the blackened skeleton hung intact from her upraised arm. For that moment, the Warlord stood there, his good eye filled with horror and disbelief. Then the bones rained down on the floor like black hailstones, and the muscles and organs collapsed in on themselves, contained by a shapeless sack of skin.

Daemon stood there, holding one wrist, too stunned to let go.

The eyes lay on top of the fleshy sack, still staring at him.

He's demon-dead, so he's still in there, Daemon thought as his gorge rose. *His Self is still in there and his mind is still aware.*

Tersa dropped the spine on top of the rest of the bones and frowned. "Jaenelle doesn't cook. Why would she know about deboning a chicken?"

Daemon looked at his mother. Then he released his hold on the Warlord's wrist and ran for the bathroom.

"I'm sorry," Daemon stammered. "I didn't know what to do with it except bring it to you."

Saetan stared at the skin sack filled with organs and muscles—and the brain. Daemon had thought to put a bubble shield around the sack before bringing it to the Keep. That was fortunate because the contents were starting to drain from the orifices.

Considering what the Warlord had done to his victims, it shouldn't matter if the bastard heard them or not, but the man's mind had broken under the horror of the punishment, so Saetan added an aural shield over Daemon's bubble shield, and then hid it all in a mist so that neither of them had to look at it.

"I've walked the Realms for over fifty thousand years, and I've never seen this before," he said as he walked over to the end of the courtyard where Daemon stood.

"He told Tersa to show him the boy, not the Mikal boy." Daemon swallowed hard. "To her mind, he threatened me, not the illusion."

"And she reacted."

Daemon nodded.

"And Jaenelle told her how to do this?"

Another nod.

His boy was looking glassy-eyed and green, which matched how he was feeling. The speed with which it happened and the grotesque result would have unsettled both of them under any circumstances, but the feral natures and the tempers of the women involved scared the shit out of him. No matter what she'd told Tersa, Jaenelle had not learned to do this by deboning a chicken.

If the Darkness was merciful, he would never learn why or how his daughter had acquired this particular piece of Craft—and he hoped with all his heart that Daemon never learned why or how either.

"What do we do now?"

Linking his arm through Daemon's, he led his son back into the Keep. "You're going to go home, take a sedative, and get some sleep."

"Maybe I should—"

"You're the Warlord Prince of Dhemlan, not the High Lord of Hell." Saetan put enough bite in his voice to clear the glassy look from Daemon's eyes. "You did your part in this, Prince. Now it's time for me to do mine."

"And your part is?"

"To sift through what is left of his mind for the names of his victims before releasing him to the final death. I'll send you the list. I'm sure you'll know how to quietly pass on the information to the people who need it."

"What happens after that?"

"He is demon-dead," Saetan said gently. "After his Self returns to the Darkness, the meat will be left for the flora and fauna of Hell."

SEVEN

A week after No Face had been destroyed, Saetan walked into the sitting room where Sylvia was reading, and sat down in a ladder-back chair next to her wheeled chair.

"It's time for us to talk," he said.

She marked the page in her book and set it aside. She'd known this was coming, but she hadn't expected it to come this soon. Even with the heartache and worry about her sons, there had been comfort in his presence. She felt the drag of daylight as soon as the sun rose, and went to bed to avoid the drain in her power. She would wake for a moment when he joined her later in the morning, and then sleep again, cradled in his arms, until they both rose at sunset.

"It's hard for the living to let go of the dead, and it's hard for the dead to let go of the living. That's why my rules about interaction between the living and the demon-dead are so strict, and that's why I'm so harsh when those rules are broken."

"Did you live by your own rules, Saetan?" She knew the man, so she already guessed the answer.

"Everything has a price," he said softly. "When I became a Guardian, I made a choice. It wasn't prudent to let some things, like Dhemlan Kaeleer, leave my control, but the personal things . . ." He sighed. "I never met Mephis's wife. I never knew his children. I never held them or played with them or read them stories. I straddled the line between living and dead, so I didn't belong with them. I had contact with Mephis only here at the Keep. He was a grown man, and it was necessary because we were all waiting for the promised dream to become flesh. But I kept my distance from his family, asking no less of myself than I required of the other citizens of Hell."

"But you know Daemonar," she said.

He let out a pained laugh. "Yes. Well, Lucivar is not Mephis. When I gave Mephis an order, he obeyed it. When I give Lucivar an order, half the time he ignores it and pisses on my foot. When Daemonar was born, Lucivar told me he didn't give a damn about my rules. The boy was going to know his grandfather." He paused, then added, "And things changed after Jaenelle came into our lives. The boundaries didn't exist with the people she touched. That's why I know that while the rules I've set for the citizens of Hell must be strictly enforced most of the time, there can be exceptions."

She felt a *zing* that had nothing to do with her body and everything to do with her heart. "I can see my boys one more time?"

"If that's what you want," he replied. He leaned forward and took her hands, rubbing his thumbs over her knuckles. "Prince Sadi denied your father custody of your sons."

"Why?"

"For one thing, your father doesn't feel it's appropriate for the boys to see you anymore. You're dead. They need to accept that and rebuild their lives without you. Normally I would agree with him, but not this time. You are strong enough to let them go—and they will go, Sylvia. The day will come when they need you to be nothing more than a good memory. But for now, Daemon and I are willing to sanction, and chaperon, a visit twice a month here at the Keep in Kaeleer. You, Beron, and Mikal can spend the evening together. You'll have the reassurance that they're being taken care of."

By whom? she wondered. "Everything has a price."

"And this is no exception."

"What is your price, High Lord?"

"I want to show you something."

Using Craft, he floated her above the chair. She straightened her legs so that her long skirt just brushed the floor. Linking her arm through his, she floated beside him as he made his way through the Keep's corridors until they reached the Dark Altar. After he opened the Gate, he led her to a landing web, wrapped a shield around her, and caught the Black Winds.

When they dropped from the Winds to another landing web, she looked around. "This is SaDiablo Hall, but it's . . ."

"In the Dark Realm. At one time, I ruled in all three Realms, so I built the Hall in all three Realms."

"Mother Night." She couldn't imagine what it had cost to build *one* of the Halls, let alone three.

She'd expected the place to be empty. It was a hive of activity. She saw caution in every eye when the demon-dead spotted the High Lord, but there were also smiles and pleasantries. He held what was left of their lives in his hands, and they didn't forget that.

Just as he now held hers.

"Most of the demon-dead remain near the Gate closest to where they lived," Saetan said quietly. "Some go to specific territories that have been claimed by a particular group, like the Harpies or the *cildru dyathe*. And some have unfinished business—the novel they never found time to write or the dream of learning to paint that they gave up out of duty to family. Some want to learn to play a musical instrument. Unfinished business. Not with the living; with themselves. I provide a place for them to live, a modest amount of yarbarah for sustenance, and the materials they need. In turn, they take care of this place, and the stronger look after the weaker when it's needed."

"It's a community of artists," she said, wishing he would slow down so she could get a better look at the paintings. Some were hung out of kindness. Others were stunning and beautiful.

"This is what I wanted you to see." He opened a door and guided her inside.

The room was divided in half. There were scribbles and colored handprints and primitive drawings covering the set of folding panels that separated the room.

It's less frustrating than trying to clean the walls all the time, Saetan said.

Since he was clearly moving to keep them out of sight of whoever was on the other side of the panels, she stifled a laugh.

"It's a pretty nice place," a young male voice said. "There are toys and games and lots of books to read for fun. There are also chores and studies, but those are interesting too. Some of the time."

Sylvia smiled. That sounded so much like Mikal.

Saetan slipped his arm out of hers. After making sure she was steady, he stepped back. *Go ahead. Take a look.*

Taking hold of the edge of the panel, she eased herself into a position to see the room.

Thirty children, if not more. None of them had reached adolescence, whatever their race. Among them was a Dhemlan boy sitting on the floor, hugging a stuffed toy.

Sylvia looked back at Saetan. *Is that . . . ?*

Haeze's brother? Yes.

She listened for a minute as the boy in charge explained the rules everyone had to follow in order to be a resident of the Hall.

Pushing against the panel, she floated back to Saetan. *Who is the Keeper of the Rules?*

The first cildru dyathe to choose to live here instead of on their island. Daemon rescued him from the spooky house several years ago and brought him to me. In his way, he's made the same choice another cildru dyathe made long ago—to be the leader of this band of children and help the others adjust and survive and let go when they're ready.

She caught something the boy said, and looked more closely at the man. *You can't help the ones who don't trust adults enough to accept help, but you help these children, don't you? You're the one who comes to read them stories or listen to them or give them a hug. Aren't you?*

Some came from loving homes. Others never knew the comfort of a hug. Not from a father or a mother.

Everything has a price. Suddenly she knew what he was asking of her in exchange for spending time with her own sons—to be a maternal presence for the children who had never known any. To help them with their unfinished business. To give them a sense of family. With him.

Linking her arm with his, she tipped her head toward the door. He took them out of the room, then waited for her to indicate a direction. Instead she just looked at him.

"I asked you once, and I understand better now why you gave me the answer you did," she said. "But everything has changed, so I'm going to ask again. Will you marry me, Saetan?"

She saw shock in his eyes, swiftly followed by joy, which was just as swiftly followed by caution.

"Can you promise me that you won't stay one day longer than you truly want to?" he asked.

"I promise you that."

"Then I will be honored to be your husband for all the days that come before that day."

She threw her arms around him and held him as tightly as he held her.

"What kind of wedding would you like?" he asked.

She eased back enough to look at him. "A fast one."

EIGHT

Sylvia had to wait a week for her wedding because Jaenelle wouldn't allow Beron to travel to the Keep until every tiny part of his ears, eyes, and throat had healed completely. She chafed about the delay, but approved of the reason.

The Priestess from Riada came to the Keep to perform the marriage ceremony. The food for the living guests had been provided by Mrs. Beale from the Hall and Merry from The Tavern.

Sylvia's father and brother had been invited. They weren't able to smudge that line between the living and the dead and had refused to attend. But her sons were there, along with Marian and Lucivar, Daemonar, Jillian and Nurian, Tersa and Manny, Surreal and Rainier, Daemon and Jaenelle, and plenty of kindred who were also members of this pieced-together family.

Saetan slipped an arm around her waist and held out a ravenglass goblet of yarbarah. "How are you doing, Lady Sylvia?"

Accepting the goblet, she narrowed her eyes. "Mikal and Daemonar are about to get into some mischief. They've got that look."

"You think so?" he asked, laughing softly.

The boys had barely taken a step before they were flanked by Scelties and blocked by Kaelas. In that moment, Sylvia saw three male heads turn in that direction— Daemon, Lucivar, and Rainier.

She pressed her lips together to keep from laughing aloud, since Mikal looked so annoyed at having his fun stopped before it started.

She took a sip of the yarbarah, then handed back the goblet. "I appreciate the sentiment, and the dress is *gorgeous*, but Jaenelle shouldn't have harassed the dressmakers to get it made for the wedding." The wedding ring, a square-cut ruby with flanking diamonds, had come from Banard's shop. It wasn't custom-made like the dress, but it had been chosen with care.

"My darling, *Jaenelle* would never harass a dressmaker or be as demanding about fit and style."

Sylvia brushed a hand over the rich red fabric. "Then who . . . ?"

"Daemon, however, makes up for being demanding by knowing exactly what he wants—and being a very generous patron of some of Amdarh's more exclusive establishments."

She felt the room tip a little when she considered the rest of the wedding gift. "The lingerie? Jaenelle or Surreal chose that. Didn't they?"

Saetan just looked at her.

"Oh, Hell's fire."

"Has it occurred to you yet that Daemon and Lucivar are now your stepsons?"

"Don't threaten me on my wedding day, SaDiablo."

He burst out laughing.

A minute later, Jaenelle came up to them and gave Sylvia a bright smile that would have scared her right down to her toes if she'd still had any.

"I need to borrow your wife," Jaenelle told Saetan. "Lady Sylvia and I need to have a little chat."

NINE

Daemon picked up the first letter from the thick stack on his desk and swore softly. The swearing became more vigorous and creative as he worked his way through the stack. By the time Rainier walked into the study to go over the week's assignments, Daemon was one wrong word away from exploding.

"What in the name of Hell are these?" he roared, dropping the letters on the blackwood desk.

Rainier winced. "Ah. I was hoping to get here before you saw those."

"And they are?"

"Just what they seem—offers from District Queens all around Dhemlan to become the new Queen of Halaway. And the same offer from a few young Queens from other Territories."

"I know who rules in my Territory, Rainier. Some of these women rule towns or cities that are larger—and more profitable—than a small village, and others already rule a handful of villages. They're going to give up that income to rule *Halaway*?"

Rainier looked uncomfortable. "You read the letters? Of course you did."

"So I know that the letters addressed to the Province Queen, of which there are few, are sincere offers to add Halaway to the villages under the Ladies' rule because every village needs to be held by someone. But most of these . . ."

He stopped. Even after more than a decade of marriage, he still felt the raw fury of a vulnerable man whose reputation could be compromised. But that was his state of mind, and he had no right to whip Rainier with that fury.

"Why did we get these at all?" he asked through gritted teeth. "Shouldn't a committee from the village or the Province Queen sort through these and present me with a short list for final approval?"

"Normally it would be done that way," Rainier said. "But, Prince, your reaction to these letters—and they *are* only letters—is exactly why no one else is willing to make a choice. No one wants to be held responsible for whatever Queen ends up living on your doorstep—especially if she proves to be too friendly a neighbor."

Daemon took in a deep breath and blew it out.

"If I were you, I would put those aside," Rainier said. "When I spoke with Sylvia's First Circle yesterday, they said they had been talking to a particular Lady about becoming Halaway's Queen and were hopeful that she would accept. She's supposed to give them her answer today."

"She's one of these?" He pointed to the stack of letters.

"I don't know, but judging by how much care they were taking in what they said, they want this particular Queen."

"If they feel that strongly, I'll certainly make an effort not to interfere, as long as the Lady doesn't think ruling Halaway means having access to my bed," Daemon said as the study door opened and Jaenelle walked in.

"That might be a problem," she said cheerfully. "Rainier, the Prince and I need to talk."

Rainier looked at her, then at Daemon, and limped out of the room as fast as he could, closing the door behind him.

Jaenelle settled in the visitor's chair and smiled at Daemon. "Sit down, Prince."

His stomach clenched, but he obeyed.

"Sylvia's First Circle asked me to take her place as the

Queen of Halaway," Jaenelle said. "This morning I accepted and signed a five-year contract."

Daemon's jaw dropped. "But . . . you don't want to rule. I don't know how many times I've heard you say that over the years."

She looked embarrassed. "Apparently, what I say and what I do are not the same things, and I've been the only one who hasn't noticed that."

Oh, shit. Who was the fool who told her?

"Ladvarian says that Scelties and Queens are meant to herd. It is our nature, and denying our nature is foolish. When I ruled Kaeleer, that was a heavy burden, even with all the other Queens to help me. And after I was hurt, it took me a long time to heal, and my becoming well was the most important thing. And I had a mate, and it was also important that I spend a lot of time with him and play. But now it's time for me to work again, and officially ruling the small village right next to my home won't be much different from what I already do. Or so says the Sceltie."

He couldn't think of one thing he dared to say.

"As much as I'd like to kick his furry ass for what he said, Ladvarian was right. It's time for me to have my own flock again."

"A new court?" he asked.

She shook her head. "Sylvia's First Circle doesn't belong to me in the truest sense, but they're good men who are committed to Halaway, and we'll work well together to take care of the village and its people." She hesitated. "And they're willing to accommodate the things Sylvia and I want for Mikal and Beron."

Ah. Now he was hearing a reason that made sense. Then he remembered something about Sylvia's First Circle that made him brace involuntarily for pain. Jaenelle was a Queen—and no matter who their husbands might be, Queens had privileges.

"Consort?" he asked.

She gave him a sharp look. Her voice was equally sharp.

"The Warlord Prince of Dhemlan does *not* become the Consort of a District Queen and serve in her court—no matter who she is. Hopefully my *husband* will be willing to escort me to formal functions when required."

"Which will leave an opening in the Queen's Triangle." There would be plenty of men who would come sniffing around once Jaenelle became Queen, for ambition's sake if for nothing else.

She fluffed her hair. "I was thinking of asking Rainier to stand as First Escort to fill that side of the Triangle. I didn't think you would object, since you already treat him as your stand-in when you can't accompany me to an event."

He felt his face heat even as he felt the ache around his heart ease. "It's not that I don't trust you."

She smiled. "I know. For all the strength and power of your caste, Warlord Princes have their weak spots. On occasion, because you love so deeply, you will feel insecure. That is as much a part of your nature as ruling is a part of mine. As long as you remember that I love you, we'll be fine."

He nodded and searched for a way to step back from discussing her new court. "What about Mikal and Beron?"

"Ah. Mikal is easy. We're doing a little decorating of the guest bedroom in Tersa's cottage so that it will be Mikal's room."

"And Tildee's," he added.

"And Tildee's. In exchange for being allowed to live with Tersa, Mikal has promised to do his assigned chores and his schoolwork and not try to smudge the truth with Tersa the way he sometimes did with his mother, because doing that would upset Tersa's hold on the mundane world. Since you are the patriarch of the family and he is now officially family, he answers to you, and any discipline that may be required comes from you."

"Good to know," he muttered. "And Beron?"

"That's trickier," she hedged.

"Why? He can live here with us. There is plenty of room."

"He doesn't want to live here with us."

Daemon sat back, crossed his legs at the knees, steepled his fingers, and raised one eyebrow in polite query.

"I see," Jaenelle said. "The nervous husband is gone, and the Prince is back."

He waited.

"The Queen's residence is Beron's home. He doesn't want to leave it. Not yet. And there are advantages to letting him stay there. For one, I won't be living there—not most of the time, although I will have a suite of rooms and will stay overnight on occasion. With my husband."

Daemon's lips twitched.

"Having Beron stay there also means that I'll be able to justify keeping on the whole staff, since there will be someone in residence."

"A boy his age living alone? I don't think so."

"He's not a boy. He's an adolescent youth who is almost old enough to attend school on his own."

"Almost old enough isn't old enough."

She narrowed those sapphire eyes.

He tapped a finger against his chest. "Patriarch of the family, remember?"

"He'll be old enough in five years," she said tightly.

Which explained the length of her contract.

"Jaenelle . . ."

"The next five years will be a proving ground. The three of us will work out the rules and restrictions. If Beron violates any of the big rules, he'll be packed up and will have to live here with us and be held to a short leash. Since Surreal and Rainier live in the village half of the time, they can drop by and check on him, day or night."

"Not to mention that the court will be working in the other half of the residence most days." Daemon nodded.

"If he acts like a responsible young man, at the end of that five years, he'll be allowed to go to Amdarh and train in the work of his choice."

"Which is?"

She studied him, as if trying to judge how he would respond even before she said the words.

"He wants to be an actor. He wants to perform onstage. He's had a passion for it since the first time he was given a part in a school play. He's talked about this for as long as I've known him. It's what he wants to do, Daemon. A life dream."

That explained her fury when Jaenelle discovered how the Healer had damaged Beron, and why she had been so fierce about restoring his voice, hearing, and vision to exactly what they had been before the damage.

And it explained something else. "His grandfather disapproves?"

"It's not a profession suitable for a Queen's son. Beron should be training to serve in a court or apprentice for some other suitable occupation."

"Which is nothing Beron wants."

"No. That disapproval has caused a strain in the relationship between grandfather and grandson. While Sylvia was alive, she supported Beron's choice, encouraging him to audition for the plays performed in the village. With her gone, there would have been no buffer, especially if he had gone to live with Sylvia's father. Beron doesn't want to hurt anyone's feelings, but he wouldn't have backed down from what he wants. Eventually he would have rebelled and chosen a reckless path that would have done him irreparable harm."

Daemon sat forward. She sounded too certain, which meant she'd seen something in a tangled web. "Couldn't you have told me some of that when you asked me to deny Sylvia's father custody of her sons?"

"Did I need to?" Witch asked.

No. As wife or Queen, he was hers to command. "So I guess we're all settled."

"I guess we are." Jaenelle stood up, walked around the desk, and gave him a kiss that narrowed his focus to just one thing: sex.

"I'm going to talk to Rainier and explain his new duties," she said. "Why don't you apply yourself to the paperwork so that we can take a long nap after the midday meal? You can warm up my feet."

"I'll warm up anything you want," he purred.

Laughing, she eased back and picked up the stack of letters. "I'll answer these for you. Just to save you some time."

"You do that."

When she closed the study door, he blew out a breath. "Get your mind out of your pants, boyo," he muttered. Although his pants weren't exactly where his mind was fixed right now. It was more on the things he wanted to taste. . . .

He shifted in his chair and pulled a stack of reports to the center of his desk. Before he'd read the first page, there was an enthusiastic scratching on the door.

Daemon?

daemondaemondaemondaemondaemon.

Sighing, he used Craft to open the door. Shuveen, Boyd, and Floyd rushed over to him. Shuveen was the first to jump into his lap, giving him time to put a shield over his crotch before Boyd and Floyd scrambled to join her. One Sceltie on his lap, he could handle. Three Scelties? Someone was going to plant a paw on his balls.

Easy enough to tell them he had to work and they needed to leave him alone—and he almost did. Then he thought about family. What would have happened to Mikal if Tildee hadn't been with the boy, hadn't received her training here at the Hall?

There was no black-haired, blue-eyed daughter to climb in his lap and ask for a story, but he and Jaenelle had raised quite a few kindred youngsters over the past few years, and now there were Beron and Mikal, who would need help and guidance and love.

He looked at the three Scelties, at the brown eyes filled with happy expectation. Whose lives would they change one day because of what he and Jaenelle taught them?

"One story," he said. "Then I have to work."

He waited for them to carefully turn around so they were all facing the desk. Then he put his arms around them, called in the storybook, and began reading *Sceltie Saves the Day*.

THE HIGH
LORD'S
DAUGHTER

A story that spans decades . . .

ONE

In the dream, Daemon opened his eyes and knew three things: He was lying on a beach, he was naked, and he was dead.

There was pain in his chest. Huge, terrible pain. It had dulled to an ache now, but the memory of that pain was reason enough to keep his eyes focused on the gray metal sky above him and not allow his fingers to explore the flesh around the ache.

Shifting position, he climbed stiffly to his feet, careful to keep his eyes focused beyond his body. He wasn't ready to see the damage, wasn't ready to face the truth.

Promise me.

He spotted the tent, the loosely woven fabric billowing in the early-morning breeze. He'd seen that tent before, more than seventy years ago. It had held a treasure then, a promise, a dream. Now it held . . .

When he reached the tent, he slipped inside. Nothing there except a washstand in one corner. A small towel and a full jug of water sat next to the basin. He poured water in the basin and washed his face. As he raised his head, he saw the edge of the framed mirror now floating above the washstand.

Daemon closed his eyes and straightened up. Then he opened his eyes and looked in the mirror. Looked at the hole in his chest where his heart had been.

How was a man supposed to survive a wound like that? How was he supposed to pretend it wasn't there?

Promise me.

He tried to speak, but his throat closed, preventing him from saying the words. Protecting him for a little while longer. Because once he said the words . . .

Daemon opened his eyes. Early morning from the look of the sky. Groaning, he sat up, scrubbed his fingers through his hair, and looked around.

Brandy bottles were lined up on the wooden seat nearby, except for the last one, which lay on the damp ground next to him, almost empty. That explained why his shirtsleeve was wet and smelled. Just as the number of empty bottles on the wooden seat explained how he'd ended up sleeping outside—again.

Outside, he thought as he climbed to his feet, but still within the Hall. The sunken garden, that place of peace and power that his father had made for private meditations, was protected by the imposing structure Saetan had built as the SaDiablo family seat.

He found no peace in this garden—at least, not while he was sober—but he ended up here on the nights when his sleep was haunted by dreams, or on the nights when he couldn't sleep at all.

Raised flower beds bordered all four sides except where the stone steps led down into the garden. A raised stone slab and the wooden seat were positioned between the two statues that dominated the space.

As he brushed at his clothes, Daemon kept his eyes fixed on the grass. He couldn't look at the female statue, couldn't look at that face. Not today. So he turned to the other statue, as he'd often done over the past year. The crouched male that was a blend of human and animal. A feline head supported by massive shoulders. Teeth bared in a snarl. One paw/hand braced on the ground near the body of a small, sleeping woman while the other was raised above her, its claws unsheathed. Glittering, green stone eyes stared at him.

Honor, cherish, and protect. It was the male's duty, and his privilege, to honor, cherish, and protect. To serve.

He had one last duty to perform for the woman who had been his Queen—and his wife.

Vanishing the brandy bottles, Daemon left the sunken garden and returned to his suite. The conspicuous absence of servants in the corridors meant Beale had known where he was and had made sure no one would see him before he chose to be seen.

When he reached his suite, he turned the physical lock on the door. That simple request for privacy wouldn't alarm anyone, even today.

A fresh set of clothes was laid out for him—his typical black jacket and trousers and a white silk shirt.

He stripped out of his clothes and left them on the clothes stand for Jazen to deal with. Naked, he stepped in front of the dresser and looked in the mirror. No torn flesh. No gaping hole in his chest. He saw the visual evidence of his pain only when dreaming.

Promise me.

Tears filled his eyes as he looked at his gold wedding ring. His right hand trembled. His left hand closed into a fist so tight that his nails broke the skin in his palm. Protective. Resisting the need to obey that last command just a little while longer.

A year to grieve, because your heart won't ever let go if I ask for less. So take your year to grieve, and when that year is over, promise me you'll take up your life again. Promise me, Daemon.

They'd had seventy years together. Seventy rich and wonderful years. Jaenelle had been healthy and vibrant right up to the afternoon when she had kissed him and gone to her room for her usual nap, leaving him in his study with a mound of paperwork.

She lay down to take a nap—and never woke up.

Dreams made flesh did not become demon-dead. She had slipped away from him without warning, without a chance to say a final good-bye—or hold on to her for a while longer. But a few months earlier, during a quiet evening of the last Winsol they'd shared, Jaenelle had asked for a promise that amounted to her last command.

One year. She had been dead one year, and it was time to keep his promise.

He called in a small, beautifully carved jewelry box and used Craft to open the lid. Inside was her wedding ring.

Forcing his left hand open, he removed his wedding ring, placed it next to hers, closed the lid, and vanished the box.

Then he went into the bathroom to shower away the grief—and hide the last tears.

Comfortably settled in a small, sunny breakfast room, Surreal ate a solitary meal and waited. Sadi would be down soon, dressed as elegantly as usual—a contrast to the gold eyes that had been dulled by grief for the past year.

She almost hoped those eyes, and Daemon's highly intelligent brain, would remain dulled by grief for one more day. She would prefer having this particular fight after the fact.

The door opened. Daemon walked into the room, followed by Beale, who set a fresh pot of coffee on the table and retreated.

Daemon took a seat and poured a cup of coffee for himself. "Surreal."

"Sadi." She topped off her own coffee, debated for a moment about the wisdom of scratching his temper, then leaned back in her seat and stared at him.

Grief had dimmed the beauty of his face, but that wasn't a permanent change. Seventy years was nothing to someone from the long-lived races, and since he was only eighteen hundred years old, he still looked like a well-toned Warlord Prince in his prime—seductive, sensual, washing the room with sexual heat just by passing through. She had spent the past few years discouraging idiot women who looked at Jaenelle and figured Sadi *had* to be looking for sex outside of the marriage bed because how could a man who looked like *that* want to bed an old, white-haired woman in her nineties?

Jaenelle had gotten old in years, but she was never *old*,

and whether those idiot women wanted to believe it or not, Jaenelle Angelline had been more than able to handle Daemon Sadi in bed and out.

Surreal just hoped she had done her job as second-in-command sufficiently well that Sadi hadn't been aware of those women. He wouldn't have done anything while Jaenelle lived because that would have called attention to why those women were sniffing around him. And he hadn't been interested in doing anything for the past year. But now? Had any of them come to his attention enough that he would hone his temper and go hunting?

"Something wrong?" Daemon asked, sounding edgy and brittle.

"You look like shit."

"You do know how to flatter me."

The silence that followed was uneasy on her part and chilly turning toward predatory on his. That was why she wanted to jump up and hug Beale when he entered the room and set a covered dish in front of Daemon.

Beale lifted the cover. Daemon looked at the simple breakfast and swallowed hard.

None of them knew if Daemon's refusal to eat anything before the midday meal was a personal gesture of mourning or an inability to keep down food during the first few hours after waking up alone, but they had all known he would be at the breakfast table today whether he could keep the food down or not.

Daemon said, "Thank you, Beale," picked up his fork, and began to eat his first breakfast in a year.

Surreal finished her own breakfast, glad of the delay, however fleeting, before she told him about the day's task.

"What are you doing here?" Daemon asked. "I thought you would be in Amdarh for . . . something Holt had mentioned."

"It's a celebration for Lady Zhara, and it's next week." She swallowed some coffee, then added, "You'll also be attending."

He put down his fork. "No, I will not."

"Zhara is the Queen of Amdarh, the capital city of Dhemlan, and you are the Warlord Prince of Dhemlan. So, yes, you will be attending."

The room chilled, and Daemon said too softly, "No, I will not."

She waited. He'd regained enough of himself that his face and eyes didn't betray the vicious internal struggle she knew had to be going on—just as she knew the decision had been made for him and who had made it.

"So you'll be there as my companion?" Daemon asked coldly.

The moment he appeared at a social event, everyone would know he'd ended his year of mourning, and there would be women drooling over the chance to ride his cock—and make use of anything else they could squeeze from the Warlord Prince of Dhemlan. There were also women who believed they were in love with him and wanted to gain his attention.

And there was a woman who had loved him for a lot of years and would continue to do her best to hide it because that was still the only way to help him.

"Actually, sugar, I'll be there as your guard, but I have a thigh sheath for my stiletto, so I'll still be wearing a dress."

Daemon blinked. The chill faded from the room. "You'll have a knife?"

"I'll have several. I usually do. But at least one will be visible, so no one can say they didn't have sufficient warning if things get messy."

His lips twitched. He picked up his fork and took another bite of his breakfast. "So you came to the Hall this morning to tell me about this celebration?"

Shit. "No, I came to clean out Jaenelle's suite. Helene will help me."

Daemon set down the fork again. "No," he crooned, "you will not."

She'd sometimes wondered if, with the right provocation, he would kill her without hesitation. She didn't have to wonder anymore. The answer was in those glazed, murderously sleepy gold eyes.

She gave a pointed look to the bare ring finger of his left hand. "You made your promise, Sadi, and I made mine. Today I'm going to keep that promise. Jaenelle wanted her suite cleaned out after the year of mourning ended. There are specific things she wanted saved and taken to the Keep. The rest are to be given away or sold."

He snarled at her, but it was a sound of pain rather than anger. Unfortunately, being driven by pain made him more dangerous.

She pointed a finger at him. "And that right there is the reason why I'm doing this and you're not." She wanted to get out of this room before her bowels loosened past controlling, but she didn't want to spend the next few decades wondering if the Sadist would pay her a visit. "You would never disobey your Queen. Why do you think I would disregard a request from her?"

He looked away.

"If there is something particular you would like to keep and it's not on the list of items Jaenelle wanted stored at Ebon Askavi, I'll set it aside for you," Surreal said gently.

Daemon hesitated, then shook his head.

"Will you be around if I need to ask you about something?"

"I'll be in my study at least for the morning," he replied. "I expect Holt has a long list of items he wants to review with me." He pushed back from the table. "Keep your promise, Surreal. I won't interfere."

She waited until he left the room before she allowed herself to sag for a moment. Then she straightened up and took a last sip of coffee. The sooner she and Helene cleaned out Jaenelle's suite, the better it would be for all of them.

TWO

The Arachnian Queen, the Weaver of Dreams, delicately touched one thread of the web spun by Witch before the living myth became a song in the Darkness. This web had slept many years because the dreams it held had been too unshaped to become flesh. But something had changed, and now the golden spider could sense the whisper of wishes, of longings.

Specific dreamers. Most unusual to tie threads to specific dreamers when the shaping had not yet begun. Too much chance that the dream would never be flesh if one of the dreamers stopped wishing, stopped wanting. But that was why Witch had made the web this way—because these dreamers had to wish long enough, had to want hard enough, even if they weren't aware of the wanting.

As long as the dreamers gave her something to work with, the Weaver would keep her promise and add to the web Witch had begun. And someday, another Arachnian Queen would add the last strand to this dream.

ᴄHᴙᴇᴇ

Standing in the family parlor of Lucivar's eyrie, Daemon grinned like a fool and didn't give a damn. He looked at the Eyrien baby girl in his arms and purred, "Hello, beautiful."

She studied him with solemn eyes. Then she broke into a grin.

"Hell's fire," Lucivar said. "She's barely out of the womb, and she's already half-seduced by your voice."

"As she should be," Daemon replied, loosening the blanket enough to get a better look at his niece. "Look at those perfect little fingers and those perfect little toes."

"She is a darling."

Daemon tucked the blanket around the baby. "Does Surreal know you named your daughter Titian?"

"Not yet. I have to go up to the northern camp tomorrow and most likely will be gone overnight. Surreal is coming here in the morning and will stay with Marian until I get back."

Had Surreal told him she would be staying in Ebon Rih? Or would he find a note on his desk when he returned to the Hall? Sometimes he had the feeling that she was trying to avoid him, but he didn't know why. Did she have a lover she didn't want catching his attention, or was she still pissed off about the woman he'd bedded one night a few weeks ago? Damned hard to tell with her lately.

"Is there trouble?" Daemon asked.

"No, but I've already postponed this visit twice while waiting for the witchling to be born." Lucivar reached for the baby. "Let me have her."

Daemon took a step back. "Why?"

"Since I helped make her, I get to hold her."

"You're sharing."

Lucivar narrowed his eyes. "Fine. But if she messes her diaper, you're not handing her back until you clean her up."

Daemon looked at Titian, who began grinning again the moment she had his full attention. "*Tch*," he said. "You have a silly papa. He thinks I'm going to be scared off by a little poop."

Lucivar snorted. "Suit yourself."

Daemonar bounded into the parlor. "I get to hold her now."

"No," they said.

"Yes, I can," Daemonar insisted. "Mother said I can."

"No," they said.

"Why not?"

"Because we're older than you, and we outrank you," Lucivar said. "So we get to hold her."

"Neither of those things are true about me," Saetan said as he walked into the parlor. "Hand her over."

Daemon hesitated, but the gleam in his father's eyes warned him not to start this particular pissing contest. So he transferred Titian into Saetan's arms.

"Come on, boyo," Saetan said to Daemonar. "You can sit over there with me, and we'll both admire your sister."

Daemonar gave his father and uncle a surly look that was just shy of an actual challenge. Then he turned his back on them and followed his grandfather.

Daemon held his breath while he watched Saetan cross the room. He didn't realize Lucivar had done the same thing until he heard his brother's careful sigh.

"Coffee?" Lucivar asked.

Daemon nodded, then said, "We'll be in the kitchen if you need us."

"We'll be here," Saetan replied dryly enough to tell them both they had been dismissed.

They retreated to the kitchen.

Plenty of food, Daemon noted as he eyed the various dishes on the counters. "Anything you need?"

"Besides help eating all this before it spoils?" Lucivar asked, letting out a huff of laughter. He poured coffee into two mugs. "No, we have plenty, even if we're feeding a young male who claims to be hungry again before the dishes from the previous meal leave the table."

"Judging by the look he gave us, he's clearly left childhood behind within the past few weeks," Daemon said, accepting the mug of coffee.

"Yeah, he's in the 'push until he gets his ass kicked' stage, so I can look forward to a couple of decades of continuous pissing contests while he's making the transition from boy to youth. Once his brain starts working again and he's allowed the privileges of a young adult male, the pissing contests should lessen to one a week instead of several times a day. Or so I'm told. At first Marian sympathized with him about getting into an argument with me about every damn little thing, but she's feeling less generous now that she finds herself dealing with a young Warlord Prince trying to fuss over her and give her orders instead of being around a son who takes orders."

Laughing, they both leaned back against the counter.

"Marian is all right?" Daemon asked. He'd arrived at the eyrie an hour ago and he hadn't seen her yet.

"She's fine. Tired, but that's to be expected. No reason for her not to get some sleep when we're all here to watch the baby."

"No reason at all." Daemon studied Lucivar. "But something is wrong."

Lucivar turned his head toward the window that looked out over Marian's garden. "How long are we supposed to pretend, old son?"

"Pretend what?"

"That we don't know there is something wrong with Father."

He knew Lucivar would be the one to ask the question, to finally say the words.

"He's old, Prick."

"Yeah, I know that, Bastard. He's old. But it's showing now. Has been for the past few months."

"I don't feel him at the level of the Black anymore," Daemon said quietly. "I'm not sure if that's significant or not, but when I was with him at the Keep's library a few weeks ago, I realized I was the only one standing in the abyss at the depth of the Black."

Lucivar looked at him, a silent question.

"I'll talk to him," Daemon said.

Daemonar bounded into the kitchen. "Mother is going to feed Titian. Want to watch?"

"No," Lucivar said firmly, "and neither do you."

"Yes, I do!"

Lucivar stared at his son until Daemonar hunched in on himself.

"Another time," Lucivar said, "but not today."

"Yes, sir." The subdued posture lasted until Daemonar focused on the covered dishes on the counter. "If I can't watch Mother feed Titian, can I have a nutcake instead? And milk?"

"Fine. We'll all have something. Sit down, puppy."

Daemonar pulled out a chair at the big kitchen table and sat—and looked much too innocent.

He wasn't interested in watching his sister have a meal, was he? Daemon asked Lucivar.

Sure, he was. Lucivar set his mug down and began pulling plates out of the cupboard. *But he's smart enough to realize he could negotiate getting a treat for himself if I wouldn't let him watch.*

Daemon held the coffee in his mouth until he was sure he could swallow without choking. Then he looked at the archway and noticed Saetan. The hint of sadness in the old man's eyes was hidden the moment Saetan realized he was being watched.

I'll be back, Daemon told Lucivar. Setting his mug in the sink, he looked at Saetan. "You're leaving?"

"I think our Ladies could use some quiet time," Saetan replied.

"In that case, I'll go with you."

A raised eyebrow to indicate a father knew an excuse when he heard one. But there was wariness now in Saetan's gold eyes.

They left the eyrie and rode the Red Wind back to the Keep.

Daemon made no comment about the choice of Winds. He said nothing at all while he followed Saetan to one of the sitting rooms. He watched his father like a predator coming to some conclusions about the prey.

"Do you need fresh blood?" Daemon asked.

"No," Saetan replied.

"Yarbarah?"

"No. Why do you ask, Prince?"

"Because the daylight hours are draining you in a way they didn't before. Because you need the support of a cane more often than not these days."

"I'm a Guardian," Saetan said testily. "The daylight hours have always been draining. And I've had a bad leg for a lot of years."

Watching. Studying. And then knowing.

"When was the last time you drank a glass of yarbarah, Prince SaDiablo?" Daemon asked softly.

Saetan tensed at the choice of title but didn't correct it.

"When was the last time you had any fresh blood?"

Saetan turned to face him. "I haven't had yarbarah or fresh blood since the day after my daughter died."

"That was seventeen years ago." A chill went through Daemon, but he couldn't tell if it was temper or fear. "You haven't drunk yarbarah or fresh blood *for seventeen years*?"

It began making sense—the slow decline, the absence of

the Black Jewels that Saetan no longer wore, his seldom being available anymore during daylight hours.

"You're changing from Guardian to demon-dead, aren't you? *You've lied to us for seventeen years?*"

Saetan's eyes glazed with temper. "I don't have to explain myself to you."

"Oh, yes, you do. And we both know why, don't we, *Prince SaDiablo?*"

"Yes, we both know why," Saetan replied with a snarl. "But I'm not the only one who has kept a secret, am I, *High Lord?*"

Daemon rocked back on his heels. Then he glided from one end of the sitting room to the other, too restless to stand still.

"I didn't want that for you," Saetan said quietly. "I didn't expect that from you. To manage the family estates, yes. But not that."

"I am my father's son," Daemon said just as quietly as he glided past. "Is that why you've let yourself decline? Because I intruded?"

"No, Daemon. No. Witch was the daughter of my soul. She was the reason I became a Guardian and extended my years for so long. I never intended to live beyond her."

When he reached his father again, Daemon stopped. "But it's different now. You have children who still need you, *grandchildren* who need you."

"The same can be said for every father who loves his children. We all die—and we all have to let go, both the dead and the living."

It's not fair! But that was a boy's cry, a response to losing someone he loved. The man who had been cautiously exploring Hell for the past few decades understood why the dead needed to be kept away from the living most of the time.

"How long before you make the transition to demon-dead?" Daemon asked.

"A few months."

"And how long after that before the final death?"

Saetan hesitated. "A few years."

"A dozen or more?"

"A handful or less."

So damn hard to breathe. Why was it so hard to breathe? "Are you going to tell Lucivar?"

Saetan closed his eyes for a moment. "And confirm what he's already guessed? If you think it will help him accept it, then I will."

"Whether he accepts it or not, you owe it to him." Daemon took another turn around the room. "Why didn't you tell us?"

"Do you want the truth?"

"Of course I want the truth!"

"I didn't tell Lucivar because I didn't want to spend a couple of decades fighting with him over a choice that is mine to make—and that is as much a part of living as every other choice. I wanted to enjoy the time I could have with him and Marian and Daemonar."

"And me?" Daemon asked. "Why didn't you tell me?"

Saetan took a deep breath, then let it out slowly. "Because you are your father's son. You put aside mourning, as Jaenelle wanted you to, but you didn't let her go enough to take up your life."

Cold rage whispered in his blood. "Be careful, old man."

Saetan smiled. "Yes. That look in your eyes. That's why I didn't tell you. You weren't ready to accept another loss because her absence still haunts you, still hurts you."

"I've 'taken up my life,' as you put it," Daemon snarled.

"You've given in to your body's needs and had sex with a woman on occasion, but you haven't had a lover," Saetan countered. "When loneliness eats at you enough, you respond to an invitation that offers more companionship than sex—at least for a while. You might even feel some affection for the woman once you do get to the bedding stage. But she's still not a lover. Not to you. Then one day she stops drinking the contraceptive brew and comes to you ripe and fertile—and you can scent it in her body and in her emotions. That's the day you walk away from her without a second thought. Because you don't—can't—love her, and while you trust a few women enough to have sex with them, you don't trust them with the possibility of having your child. And some part of you is afraid that if you ever do trust a woman that much, she will be the wrong woman, and you'll end up betrayed just as I was."

Daemon said nothing.

"I knew that when you were ready to face my leaving, we would have this conversation," Saetan said gently.

"And now we have." The words came out colder than he'd intended. He had escorted many women over the past few years while fulfilling his obligations as the Warlord Prince of Dhemlan. But he'd bedded damn few of them, far fewer than Saetan assumed. He could get physical relief well enough without a partner, so he'd given in to the craving to touch another body only a handful of times since he'd last kissed his wife. And the last invitation he'd accepted, the one that seemed to offend Surreal for some inexplicable reason, had scratched at memories of being a pleasure slave. Instead of bringing some comfort, the sex had left him feeling dangerously mean. Because he knew too well what the Sadist wanted to do to that woman, Beale now had strict orders to keep the bitch out of the Hall, and Holt, his secretary, now checked the guest list for her name before accepting any invitations on behalf of his Prince.

Pushing aside his personal life, Daemon considered his duties. "When you decided to retire from the living Realms, you taught me what I needed to know to take over the family estates and fortune. Are you going to teach me what I need to know about Hell, or is that something I'm expected to learn for myself?"

Saetan studied him for a long moment. "I'll teach you. It's the least I can do for my heir."

FOUR

"Would you like to hold her?" Marian asked.

"No," Surreal said quickly. *Maybe.* Where was this yearning to hold a baby coming from? "I think my mother would have been flattered that you named your daughter Titian."

"And you?"

"I'm . . ." She sighed. "As the Shaladoran people say, my heart is too full for words."

Marian smiled at Surreal. Then she looked at Titian. "This little bundle is asleep, and Daemonar will be in school for a couple more hours. Why don't we go into the kitchen? I seem to be outeating my men since the birth. It's a little scary."

Surreal laughed softly as they walked from the parlor to the kitchen. Having arrived in time to help clean up the carnage Lucivar and Daemonar called breakfast, she didn't think anyone could outeat those two, but she'd been told to encourage any desire Marian had for food.

Setting the baby's basket at one end of the kitchen table, Marian rummaged in the cold box.

"Looks like there's a couple good servings left of this vegetable casserole. And there's a beef soup, and . . ." Marian looked over her shoulder. "Just tell me what you have a taste for. I can probably find it in one of these dishes."

Surreal looked at the overflowing counters and the cold

box that didn't have room left in it for a spoon. "Is it traditional to provide this much food to a new mother's family? Seems a little excessive."

"How many dishes did you bring with you this morning?" Marian asked.

She set her teeth in a smile. "I suggested waiting a week to send the offerings from the Dea al Mon, the Hall, and my house. I was overruled—and anyone who thinks hearth witches are gentle, fuzzy-hearted women has never dealt with Mrs. Beale."

"Mrs. Beale is an excellent cook, but she isn't a hearth witch," Marian countered.

"I don't care."

Chuckling, Marian pulled covered dishes out of the cold box. "We'll have the vegetable casserole and some of that crusty bread."

"Suits me."

"And after we eat, you can tell me what's wrong."

"Nothing is wrong. Hey hey hey! You're not supposed to be using Craft yet!"

"Keep your voice down," Marian warned, glancing at Titian's basket. Then she raised the dish. "It's just a warming spell. Basic Craft. Nothing that requires power on the level of my Jewels, or any Jewel for that matter. Even Lucivar doesn't fuss about me using this much Craft, and he fussed about *everything* through the whole of this pregnancy."

"I don't care if he'd fuss about it—you're not doing it while he's gone." Surreal took the casserole dish, set it above the counter, and put a warming spell on the dish to heat up the food in a few minutes.

"Is it all right if I make the coffee?" Marian asked too sweetly.

"I'm not being unreasonable about this."

"Yes, you are. But that's because something is wrong, and you won't talk about it."

"Nothing is wrong," Surreal growled.

"I saw your face this morning when Daemon's name came up."

She had learned the hard way that emotions left to fester could turn into a poison, so she moved to the other end of the kitchen, away from the table and the baby.

"For most of the years he and Jaenelle were married, I shielded Sadi from bitches who wanted to see how seriously he took his marriage vows, especially during the later years of Jaenelle's life. Some of us have not forgotten what happened when Lektra tried to take Jaenelle's place—or that Daemon threatened to kill all the Dhemlan witches if anyone tried to get between him and his wife again. I've made a particular effort to keep one bitch away from him, even after he began escorting women to social events. I can't tell you her real name because I've been calling her 'Dorothea' since the day I met her."

"Mother Night," Marian whispered.

"I protected him *for years*. And the first time I spend a few days with the Dea al Mon and he's in Amdarh on his own for some social obligations, *he ends up sleeping with the bitch*." Surreal raked her fingers through her hair. "I don't know what that says about him—if he's become that lonely or that unaware of the intentions of the women who are all but stripping down in public to get his attention—but I do know the family history, and I do know Sadi is his father's son. Anyone who knows those things has good reason to be afraid of what could happen if his temper snaps the wrong way. The purge in Dhemlan would be devastating."

"Do you think he'd ...?" Marian cleared her throat. "Of course he would. What happened to the Dorothea woman?"

"Nothing as far as I can tell. I think she was hoping to keep him interested long enough to get pregnant, but it appears that something about her repulsed him once she got him into bed, and he's avoided her since then."

"So she's not pregnant?" Marian asked.

Surreal shook her head. "No. Thank the Darkness." Then she sighed. "He needs someone, Marian. He would deny it with his last breath, but he needs someone to cuddle and fuss over."

"If he and Jaenelle had had children . . ." Now Marian sighed.

"Yeah. But they didn't."

"Not all the women who are interested in being with him are calculating bitches, are they?"

"No, some of them are young, starry-eyed, and love the Prince they see at social functions with all their hearts. But they haven't seen the cold side of him. They haven't seen the Sadist. And they think if he made any kind of commitment to them, he would love them the way he loved Jaenelle."

"She was the love of his life," Marian said. "He'll never love another woman the way he loved her."

"No, he won't. And sooner or later, any of those starry-eyed girls would break and become bitter under the truth of that. And when they became bitter, he would become colder and more distant—and less capable of giving any woman any kind of affection." And that would be a waste of a good man.

Marian's eyes filled with tears. She waved a hand when Surreal touched her shoulder. "Just moods. Happens for a while after the birth. I feel too much." She looked toward the counter. "And you'd better get that casserole out of the dish while it's still edible."

"Shit." For the next few minutes they busied themselves with putting the food on the table and getting themselves settled.

Marian cut a piece of the crusty bread and handed it to Surreal. "Do you think it's foolish to wish that Daemon finds someone to love again someday?"

"No," Surreal said, looking at Titian asleep in her basket. "I don't think wishing is foolish."

As the Weaver of Dreams tended the tangled web that Witch had left in the golden spiders' care, she listened to longings, yearnings, and wishes that resonated with that web—and added more threads.

FIVE

Daemon had known for three years that this day was coming, but he still wasn't ready. Week by week, he'd watched his father's gentle decline—the body getting more frail, the power fading. But the mind was still sharp and strong. That was why Saetan had chosen this day to say his good-byes.

Why is Grandfather going to leave us?

How were they supposed to answer Daemonar's question? What were they supposed to say to Mikal and Beron about the man who had loved their mother and protected them after her physical death—and had had the strength to let Sylvia go when she was ready to become a whisper in the Darkness?

Daemon knew what Saetan would say: They were supposed to answer the questions and take care of the living just like every other man who faced this day and all the tomorrows that would come after.

He looked at Lucivar. They were the last ones left in Saetan's bedroom at the Keep.

Lucivar looked at him. Resistance, denial, and then acceptance flashed in those gold eyes.

"Tell your brother what you know about me," Saetan told Lucivar.

Lucivar hesitated, then nodded. "I will." Then to Daemon, "I'll be nearby."

Daemon waited until Lucivar left the room before sitting on the edge of the bed.

"You have the letters I wrote to Mikal and Beron?" Saetan asked.

"And the ones for Daemonar and Titian. I also have the ones Sylvia wrote to her sons. I'll abide by the instructions she gave you and see that the boys get the letters at the appropriate times."

"Good." Saetan shifted against the pillows. Then he smiled. "We've said our good-byes. I want you to go now and not come back until it's done."

"Your body?"

"Most often, the husks of the demon-dead end up nourishing the Dark Realm, but Draca and Geoffrey—and even Lorn—didn't think that was appropriate for me. So the empty vessel will go to the fire, and the ashes will be mixed with the soil in one of the courtyard gardens here at the Keep."

"In the same garden as Jaenelle's ashes?"

"Yes. Sylvia chose a garden at the Hall in Hell, but . . ."

"Your place is here, with the daughter of your soul."

"Yes."

Show some balls, old son, and do this for him. "We're not going to let you linger here alone for a few more days."

"I don't want you here, Daemon. I want a clean break from the family."

"I know." He held out his right hand, his Black Jewel glowing with its reservoir of power. "You're the one who taught me that the High Lord is sometimes merciful." *And that there can be a price for that mercy.*

Saetan looked at Daemon's hand, then looked into his eyes. "Can you live with this?"

He needed a moment to be sure his voice would be steady. "Yes, Father, I can."

Saetan closed his eyes and held out his hand.

Daemon closed his hands around his father's. So little power left sustaining that flesh, that mind. So little holding the Self to this life.

The Black absorbed that power between one breath and the next, and Saetan Daemon SaDiablo, Prince of the Darkness and High Lord of Hell, became a whisper in the Darkness.

After tucking Saetan's hand under the covers, Daemon left the bedroom and went to the sitting room where the others waited.

Daemonar was cuddled up with Surreal. Little Titian was dozing on Marian's lap. Lucivar stood close to them.

He'd told Saetan the truth. He could live with that particular duty, but he would deal with the grief of that choice in private. The family patriarch took care of his family first and his own heart second.

Lucivar shifted, just enough to catch Surreal's attention and then Marian's.

Daemon looked at the women and children, but it was his brother's eyes that he met and held, "He's gone."

Alone in the passenger compartment of the small Coach, Surreal shifted restlessly in her seat. Part of her wished that Sadi had stayed in the compartment with her, distracting her from the grief she wanted to keep at bay a little while longer; the other part was glad he'd chosen to drive the Coach, since riding the Black Winds would get them back to the Hall faster.

It also meant she needed to make some decisions faster.

There was something wrong with Sadi, something more than the grief they were all feeling. That *something* had begun three years ago, shortly after they'd learned that Saetan had stopped drinking yarbarah and was allowing his power to fade—and, with it, the body that had been sustained by that power for more than fifty thousand years. Since then, Daemon had become increasingly withdrawn. Not from the family. He played with Daemonar and Titian, responded to Marian with warmth and love, and seemed the same as he'd always been with Lucivar. But she'd noticed he'd become colder and more calculating when he escorted a woman to a social event—and more often than not, the woman didn't get as much as a good-night kiss, let alone anything more intimate.

At first she'd worried that the coldness was her fault. After some internal debate, and with Marian's encouragement, she'd told Sadi why she'd been so pissed off with him about the bitch he'd bedded shortly before Titian was born. He'd accepted her explanation, even said he understood. But he began withdrawing from physical contact with everyone but the family.

She had been available whenever he needed a companion for a social obligation, and that had kept the bitches who lusted for ambition away from him. Had her presence also kept away the women who lusted for *him*?

Sadi hadn't had sex in three years? Well, neither had she. That wasn't the point. The point was he'd begun building a wall between himself and everyone else since the day he knew his father was leaving them, and she was worried about what would happen to him if that wall became so thick that no one could reach him.

But right now, there wasn't anything she could do. Daemon was closed off with the Warlord who was supposed to be their driver, and she didn't want to think about anything except her own aching heart and the man who had been a wonderful father to all of them.

He had managed the SaDiablo family's wealth and estates for close to a century. He had been the Warlord Prince of Dhemlan for almost as long. And he had explored a Realm that few among the living had seen—and fewer still could survive. But until a few hours ago, he had still been a son, had still been the heir, had still had the illusion that he could hand all the duties and responsibilities back to the man who had shouldered them for a very, very long time.

Now the illusion was gone and it was time to officially shoulder two other titles: patriarch of the SaDiablo family—and High Lord of Hell.

*   *   *

Daemon escorted Surreal to the large sitting room in the family wing of the Hall. He thought she'd been steady enough when they'd left the Keep, but maybe he shouldn't have left her alone in the Coach. Maybe she'd been pushing grief away as fiercely as he'd been.

This sitting room had a lived-in shabbiness seen nowhere else in the Hall, a kind of broken-in comfort. Only family and close friends were invited to this room. Bookshelves held the books of immediate interest, cupboards held toys for Titian and games for Daemonar and Mikal, and there were separate cupboards for the Scelties' toys and chewies. There was a hodgepodge of sofas, chairs, lamps, and tables, and a round table that served as a game table as well as a place to have a light meal.

It was a private room that wasn't meant to be seen by any but the most trusted.

"Beale is bringing up something to eat," Daemon said, watching Surreal weave around the room, barely avoiding the furniture. The last time he'd seen her this way, the last time he'd spent time with her in this room while she'd cried and sworn and ripped a chair to pieces before she'd fallen into an exhausted sleep, was the night after Rainier died and was taken to the Keep to make the transition to demon-dead.

"I'm not hungry." Her voice was stripped of emotion.

"I'm not either, but we should both try to eat."

She moved as if she were drunk, but that lack of grace was caused by exhaustion and the grief finally breaking through her control.

"Do you remember the first time the High Lord kicked you out of his study?" Daemon asked.

"He kicked you out too," she grumbled as tears slid down her face.

"Because of you."

"It wasn't my fault Kaelas helped Graysfang get past the shields I'd put around my bedroom."

"You didn't see Saetan's face when you said you'd rather have a wolf in your bed than a man because a wolf could lick his own balls."

She laughed a little and wiped at the tears, but they kept flowing. "He let me be family. I wasn't, not by birth or blood, but he didn't care about that. He treated me like family, hugging and scolding and . . ."

The effort to hold back a sob seemed to break her completely.

"Surreal." Daemon gathered her up and held her close. Not a child who needed protection. Not anymore. If he'd protected her at times in her life, she had also protected him. And Jaenelle. They had circled around it for a lot of years, but he recognized that he and Surreal had developed a partnership committed to Jaenelle.

"That stupid bastard!" Surreal cried. "I want to kick his ass for dying on us!"

"So do I," he said, holding her tighter as his eyes filled with tears. "So do I. But it was time for him to go."

"That's not the point."

That little bit of snarl helped her regain some emotional balance. When she eased back, he let her go—and felt strangely hollow.

"Surreal . . ."

She scooted around him, heading for the bathroom adjoining the sitting room. "I'm going to wash my face. If Beale hears me sniffling, he'll have ten Healers up here trying to listen to my chest. My lungs healed decades ago, but if I so much as sneeze, he's there with sweaters and blankets. And Helton is even worse about . . ."

Whatever else she said was lost when she closed the bathroom door.

Calling in a handkerchief, Daemon wiped his own face and was sufficiently tidy when Beale brought in the tray.

"It's done?" Beale asked.

"Yes, it's done. Saetan is a whisper in the Darkness."

"Then please accept our condolences."

"Thank you, Beale. And please tell Mrs. Beale that I appreciate her preparing something for Lady Surreal and me so late in the evening."

"I'll tell her. Holt is staying with your mother and Mikal tonight. Lady Tersa has been . . . distracted . . . today, and since there is no journeymaid staying with her at the moment, we thought it best if someone was at the cottage."

"I agree. I should have thought of it myself when Tersa decided not to come with us." Daemon glanced at the clock on the mantel. "There's no point disturbing them tonight. I'll talk to Tersa and Mikal tomorrow. And Manny." He'd have to walk carefully around his chat with Manny. She'd been feeling her years lately and had begun fussing about what would happen to the Blood who became demon-dead when Saetan no longer ruled Hell. "Do you agree?"

If Beale was surprised to be asked the question, he didn't show it. "Yes . . . Prince. I agree."

High Lord. The title hung in the air between them, proving that Beale had been aware of a great many things these past years and had kept his own counsel.

"For now, it will remain Prince Sadi," Daemon said, then added silently, *At least in public and in this Realm.*

"Understood."

Surreal emerged from the bathroom a moment after Beale left the sitting room, making Daemon suspect that she'd waited in order to avoid the butler.

"Any better?" he asked gently.

She shook her head. "Sadi? Could I stay here with you tonight?"

He'd been reaching for one of the covers on the dishes. He stopped and looked at her. "Of course you can stay. Your suite is always ready for you."

She swallowed hard. "No. Could I stay with you tonight?"

He stared at her, sure he'd misunderstood.

"I don't want to be alone." She let out a watery laugh as the tears started again. "There are probably a hundred people in this house, so it's not like being *alone* . . ."

Yes, it is, he thought. He'd been surrounded by those people too, but he'd still felt painfully alone after Jaenelle died. And still felt alone most of the time—and still sometimes had the dream where he looked in a mirror and saw the hole in his chest where his heart had been.

"Surreal." He put his arms around her, wanting to give her some measure of the comfort she was seeking—and found some comfort when she wrapped her arms around him.

My father is dead.

The two people who had truly understood him in ways no one else ever could were gone.

He brushed his lips over her temple and felt something inside him stir. It had been so long since he'd held someone, and even longer since he'd dared hold someone when he was feeling vulnerable.

His lips traveled down her cheek, and he tasted tears. When he started to pull back, she kissed his jaw, then his mouth. A soft kiss, asking for nothing but contact.

Then her mouth warmed, moved, asked for more. And he gave her more because it felt so good to hold someone again.

With each brush of their bodies, something in him stirred, wanted, needed, *yearned*. But he started to pull away because she'd asked for comfort and not . . .

"Daemon." Surreal took his face in her hands. "Freely given, freely taken. Just for tonight. So neither of us will be alone tonight. All right?"

She wasn't a child, and the dream he'd waited for had come and gone.

My father is dead.

He allowed himself a moment to consider nothing except what he needed tonight.

"Come with me." Clasping her hand, he led her out of the sitting room, not sure where he was going, not caring where he was going as long as they ended up in a room with a bed.

Except when he reached the first available room, he hesitated, and then bared his teeth in a snarl before he moved on, searching for something because now it was more than a desire for comfort and sex driving him, and that *something* was tangled around this particular woman.

By the time he found the room that felt right, he didn't know where he was in the Hall and he didn't care. It had a bed, and it had her. Heat pulsed in his veins, but it burned in her too because she tore at his shirt in order to touch skin, and her purr of satisfaction as she ran her hands over his chest and shoulders tripped something inside him. A moment before, he'd been pulling at her clothes too. Now he became savagely gentle, letting her strip him down before he used Craft to cuff her hands behind her back.

"Sadi," she snarled.

Using Craft, he pulled back the covers and plumped up the pillows.

"Want me?" he purred.

Aroused past prudence, she tried to bite him.

He laughed, but he said, "Do that again, and the only thing you'll get is a cold shower."

She swore at him but let him coax her into bed. Then she swore some more while he played with her, stroking, petting, kissing, and licking until she was too caught up in sensation to form words. He gave her small climaxes that eased the need without eliminating the need, and enjoyed the slow emergence of her skin as he removed her clothing piece by piece.

Finally he released her hands and slid into her, relishing each moan and plea for more. So he gave her more. And then, when he couldn't hold back his own need for release, he gave her everything.

Surreal drifted up to awareness. For the first time in weeks, maybe longer, she felt relaxed, easy. There was some soreness, but that was to be expected since she hadn't had a man inside her for three years. She suspected she would find a few bruises from the times when Sadi had edged into rough play, but nothing she hadn't asked for—and he probably had a few bruises of his own from her hands and teeth.

She hoped he wasn't going to get pissy when he saw them.

She wanted to float a while longer, keeping her thoughts confined to the delicious feel of the bed and Daemon's hand resting on her belly, warm and heavy. But when she opened her eyes . . .

Her vision had been so tear-blurred last night, and Sadi had taken them through so many corridors to find a discreet bedroom, she hadn't known where they ended up. And last night the room hadn't mattered, as long as it had a bed or sofa. Hell's fire, last night she wouldn't have cared if they'd ended up on the floor. But now . . .

His psychic scent was much too prominent for this to be a seldom-used bedroom. Maybe this was the bedroom he used when a woman stayed overnight for sex? The thought cut, but she'd asked for something they both needed last night, and she'd told him it was freely given. So she couldn't quibble now if he hadn't seen it differently from the other sex he'd had since he'd been anyone's lover. Even if those other women hadn't recognized the difference, she'd lived around him long enough to know that Daemon as a sex partner, even when he was giving great sex, paled in comparison with Daemon as a lover.

That thought added a wash of sadness over her contentment. Better to slip out now and go back to her suite to clean up and maybe get another hour of sleep. She would meet him at the breakfast table as if they'd parted company in the family sitting room and spent the night in their own beds.

She started to shift, to slide out from under his hand. Except the fingers suddenly pressed down on her belly and the nails pricked in warning.

"Going somewhere?" Daemon crooned as he rose up on one elbow and looked down at her.

It was still too dark to see his face, his eyes. But that particular timbre in the deep voice had her heart racing. She knew the Sadist's voice when she heard it.

His hand didn't actually press down on her belly, but it felt heavier, more . . . possessive.

Then he turned back the covers for her at the same time a light appeared through a half-closed door on the opposite side of the room. Enough light to see the room—and to see his eyes.

Not quite the Sadist. But not Daemon either. He was riding a side of his nature that was somewhere between the two.

She slipped out of bed and walked into the bathroom, too aware that a predator watched her and was considering if she too was a predator and required careful handling or if she was prey.

She used the toilet, then let water run in the sink to wash her face and stall for time.

They weren't in a guest room. She'd seen enough to realize the room was too personal to be any kind of guest room. His bedroom, then, The Consort's suite, since he hadn't moved out of the room next to Jaenelle's. A swift, careful probe confirmed he'd put Black shields in the walls and Black locks on the doors. No way for her to get out of this room until he let her go.

Mother Night.

A Warlord Prince's bedroom is his private place, and he tends to be more possessive when he's there. So if you're invited into his bedroom, you want to be more careful in how you deal with him.

At the time, Surreal had thought Jaenelle's mind had begun wandering because of old age, especially because those kinds of comments had usually come when they were alone and working on some chore not even remotely related to the subject matter.

Which was why all those comments had stuck in her mind.

"Hell's fire," Surreal whispered as she dried her face. Jaenelle's mind hadn't wandered. She'd been giving lessons in a way that wouldn't be resisted—and wouldn't be forgotten.

*   *   *

Damned if he understood why they had ended up here, except that he'd needed to have her in this room, in this bed.

You're only eighteen hundred years old, Daemon. You are not going to spend the rest of your life celibate.

You don't think I can? he'd crooned.

I know you can. That's why I want you to promise me that you won't. No one will think you're being unfaithful if you find another lover after the year of mourning. You're not going to spend the rest of your life without that kind of companionship or comfort. If you're not comfortable accepting that as a request from your wife, consider it a command from your Queen.

Cornered. He hadn't liked making that promise, and he hadn't liked the sex much. Even when he'd enjoyed it physically, he hadn't liked it much because of the expectations that always seemed to shroud the bed. And because he usually dreamed about Hekatah and Dorothea afterward. He didn't need more of a reminder than that of what could happen if a man got careless and had sex with a woman who rode a cock in order to ride ambition.

Besides, something had been missing from the bed with the women he'd pleasured that had made even the best sex a disappointment for him.

That elusive something wasn't missing last night, though.

The water in the bathroom shut off, and his attention sharpened.

He'd have to think about why last night was different. Later.

Daemon hadn't moved at all during her time in the bathroom.

"It's early," he crooned. "Come back to bed."

Not a lot of choices.

She slipped into bed, not sure what to expect. Arousal was dominant in his psychic scent, so she wouldn't have been surprised if he'd rolled on top of her. After all, he was the dominant male in Kaeleer, and that much power had privileges no other male could claim.

Instead, he pulled the covers up high enough to cover her breasts. Then his fingers lightly stroked her hair, combing it away from her face.

"How are you?" he asked, his voice still in that dangerous croon.

"All right."

"Sore?"

"A little." She didn't dare so much as tweak the truth. Not with him. Not now.

His fingers drifted to her temple, down her jaw, over her neck and shoulders. So light. So delicate.

Her heart stopped racing as she relaxed under that delicate touch. When he eased the covers down to her hips, she didn't protest, barely noticed because those fingers kept drifting along her skin, making her float.

A brush of thumb over hard nipple made her whimper—and whimper even louder because he stopped touching.

"Pain?" he asked. Then his mouth closed over that nipple, and what he did with his tongue stopped just shy of pain. "Stop?"

She curled her fingers in his hair to hold him in place. "Not if you want to live." It was meant as a growl but came out a different kind of whimper.

After he gave her breasts sufficient attention, he kissed her mouth, hot and full. Then he said, "Do you want more, or do you want to leave?"

It took her a moment to realize she understood the words. He could sense her arousal, psychic and physical, but if she said she wanted to leave, he would release the lock on the door and let her go with no protest, no show of temper or disappointment. When a man belonged to the most dangerous caste of male, a display of temper in bed could be seen as coercion far too easily.

It took her even less than a moment to realize he would

probably never make this invitation again, and while she'd had some men who were good lovers—and a few who had been excellent in bed—she had never been with anyone who could make a woman feel like he did.

"I want more," she said.

He slid over her, slid into her as she opened for him.

As the sun slowly brightened the room, he rode her delicately, lazily, and so thoroughly he made her feel things she hadn't ever dreamed were possible.

SIX

Four days after her night with Daemon, Surreal caught the Gray Wind and headed for Amdarh, intending to spend a few days at the family's town house. She had barely reached the town beyond Halaway when she felt a pain in her abdomen—a pain more severe than the worst moontime cramps she'd ever experienced. A pain so severe she almost tumbled from the Gray Web.

Shaken, she dropped from the Winds and waited for the pain to subside. Then she continued on to Amdarh, riding the Green Winds.

A day after that, just wearing her Gray Jewels caused her the same kind of pain as trying to use her Gray power during her moontime, and even wearing her Birthright Green made her queasy.

A day after that, she used Craft without thinking and threw up on the sitting room rug—and became so weak and dizzy, Helton found her lying in her own vomit a few minutes later.

Helton panicked, along with the rest of the town house's staff, and Healers converged on the SaDiablo residence, including Lady Zhara's personal Healer.

She answered all their questions truthfully, except one.

Despite her protests that it couldn't have happened, every single Healer assured her that it had.

So she stayed in bed resting for a day, putting up

with Helton's fussing to make up for scaring the man so badly.

For herself, she was excited—and she was scared.

And she was terrified of what would happen when she told Sadi.

e. She wasn't sure of anything where he was con-
She'd expected him to be upset or pissed or defen-

t now, she was afraid he would kill her—or just kill
.

be it wasn't smart to have sex that night," she said,
ds tumbling over one another in her haste to ex-
hadn't been drinking a contraceptive brew, but
re, I haven't been with anyone in years, so why
keep drinking the stuff? And it shouldn't have
y fertile time. Not that I thought about that—or
g else—that night, but it shouldn't have been my
me."

yet you got pregnant."
dn't do it alone," she snapped. "And maybe you
thinking clearly that night either, but you were the
o initiated the other three times the following
,"

aid nothing for a long moment. Just studied her.
ldn't tell if his eyes held affection or hate.
ou don't want to marry me, that is your choice,"
n crooned. "I won't force you, although you should
r the advantages of being my wife. But regardless
you decide, you'll stay here until the baby is born.
at, you can leave. The child, however, stays with
er my roof and under my protection. Is that clear?"
nt to leave now." She hated that her voice shook.
Your suite is ready for you, as always. Beale and
will retrieve your clothing and other personal
om your house."
n stay in my own house! It's just down the road."
"

should have run to the Keep, should have asked
for sanctuary until she'd reached some kind of
ent with Sadi. No chance to do that now.
n't feel well," she whispered. "I need to rest."
offer of marriage stands. Consider it."
eached behind her and turned the door handle. As

SEVEN

Surreal walked into the Hall early the next morning and
gave Beale a bright smile. "Good morning, Beale."

The flash of alarm on Beale's face before he regained
control confirmed that her mirror hadn't lied—she looked
as washed-out and sickly as she felt, and she was becoming
more fragile with every hour that passed. That was why she
had to act before she lost the reason to act.

"I need to see Sadi," she said, tipping her head toward
the study door at the back of the great hall. "Is he there?"

"Yes." Beale hesitated. "Should I send for the village
Healer? Or your personal Healer in Amdarh?"

"Saw my Healer yesterday. Today I need to talk to
Sadi." Now it was her turn to hesitate, but she had to consider the tempers she would be dealing with today. "Prince
Yaslana is supposed to see me this morning. I left a message at my house that I would be here. You know how early
he can arrive, and I didn't want him getting snarly if he
didn't find me at home, so . . ."

"I'll be certain to let him know your whereabouts the
moment he arrives," Beale said.

Maybe he meant to sound reassuring, but as she walked
to Sadi's study, she thought Beale's words sounded more
like a threat.

Daemon didn't look up when she entered the room, but he
said, "Good morning. Beale said you were here. I don't

think there is anything today that requires my second-in-command's attention, but you can check with Holt if you like. Let me finish this up, and then I can join you for a quick meal in the breakfast—"

He looked up at that moment. He dropped the pen back in its holder and pushed away from the desk.

"I need to talk to you." She hated feeling so fragile—and hated even more how much that fragility scared her, because all the Healers had warned her that it would take so little right now to destroy the life beginning to grow inside her.

"What's wrong?" He moved toward her with a speed that had her backing up against the door. "Are you ill? Have you seen a Healer?"

"No, I'm not ill. Yes, I've seen a Healer. Sadi, I'm—"

"Come over here and sit down. You're—"

"—pregnant."

He jerked to a stop, then took a step back.

Not Daemon anymore, she thought as she watched his eyes change. *May the Darkness have mercy on me, whatever he is right now is more—and worse—than the Sadist.*

"Pregnant." His voice was cold and viciously gentle. He took another step back and slipped his hands in his trouser pockets.

"I don't expect anything from you," she said quickly. "That's not why I'm here. I just wanted you to know that I won't deny that you're the baby's father. When it's time for the Birthright Ceremony, I won't deny paternity. You have my word, Sadi. I won't do that to you."

"You're not leaving with my child," he said too softly.

"Well, it's a little small to be staying here without me," she snapped.

"You're not leaving with my child," he said again.

Now he approached her. Stalked her. She wasn't sure he was sane.

"We'll be married a week from tomorrow," he said.

"I didn't agree to marry you!"

"You're not leaving with my chil

"Well, as sure as the sun doesn't keep me locked away here."

He raised his right hand. The B flashed as he unleashed some of Hall shook as his power rolled thr snapped into place within all the ou locks on the doors and windows turl ily home into a prison.

He smiled at her.

"Sadi, don't," she whispered, shiv

"What are the Healers going to te Surreal?" he crooned. "You're alread able. You can't use any of your Je you're pregnant without destroying t you can't protect yourself or the chil be drained on a regular basis for th order for the baby to grow healthy il

"Lucivar could drain the Jewels."

"Instead of the baby's father? I moved closer.

She couldn't back away from hir ready pressed against the door.

"I didn't tell you about the preg something from you," she said. He w touching her, but he was much too c

"Your heart is pounding, and yo fear," he crooned. "That isn't good f

Then back off. But she didn't dar

"Your Jewels need to be drained.

"Lucivar will be here soon."

"So you told him and not me?"

"No! I sent a message, said I ne morning, and it was urgent. But I di before I told you. I didn't tell *anyo* child, and I won't if you don't want a

He studied her. She wasn't sure h

he pulled the door open, the movement nudged her against him. She turned to avoid feeling him pressed against her belly, but he still held the handle, and his left arm blocked her escape, so she felt the heat of him on her back and buttocks. And felt his breath on her cheek as he leaned into her.

"While you're considering whether you would enjoy being the wife of the Warlord Prince of Dhemlan, also consider if you could tolerate being the wife of the High Lord of Hell."

She half turned. "I'm not going to be marrying Uncle—"

She saw it in his eyes, and now understood why he felt different, felt even more dangerous. The Sadist was now the High Lord.

May the Darkness have mercy on me.

"I'd like to go to my room now."

"Think about my offer," he whispered. Then he stepped back and let her go.

She bolted out of Daemon's study. Beale was waiting for her in the great hall. At first, she was grateful to hook her arm in his for light support, but by the time they climbed the stairs and were walking toward her suite, she was clinging to him to stay on her feet, and Holt came at a run to support her on the other side. Helene met them at the suite and tucked her on the sofa when she got stubborn about being put to bed. After admitting that she had left the tonic the Healer had made up for her at her house in the village, Jazen dashed to Halaway to retrieve it. She didn't ask what else Sadi's valet intended to retrieve while he was there.

She let them fuss over her because she needed some help. Mostly, she let them fuss as a way to keep all of them from thinking about the cold temper that waited for them behind the study door.

Daemon stood in his study, staring at nothing.

The vision he had seen in a tangled web last night: a beautifully wrapped gift being offered to him by someone he trusted. He hadn't seen the woman, only the hands holding the gift. And today . . .

A child. A baby. *His.*

The *wanting* was suddenly, brutally fierce. He wanted this baby with everything in him and would do whatever it took to keep it. He hoped for her sake that Surreal understood that. He didn't want to hurt her, but if he had to choose between them, he wouldn't hesitate to destroy her in order to protect the child.

There were times when the pain of missing Jaenelle almost crushed him. He wanted her back. Sweet Darkness, how he wanted her back!

Jaenelle wasn't coming back, but now there was a chance to give his heart to someone else without betraying the love of his life. He wasn't sure if the limited affection he could give a woman would be enough to keep a wife content, but he *knew* he could love the child.

He hoped for all their sakes that Surreal understood that too.

Lucivar hovered over the Hall and swore softly. When he received Surreal's note last night, he'd known something was wrong, but based on her saying, "It's urgent, but don't come until tomorrow morning," he hadn't expected to arrive and find the Hall locked down as if prepared for an attack. Black shields. Black locks. The only partial access was the double front doors, which had a Red lock— probably because Beale would be the one granting access and could release, and restore, a Red lock.

He made a fast descent, then backwinged to land lightly on the gravel drive. The door opened before he reached it, and he was right—Beale *was* guarding the only potential way into the Hall.

"The Prince is in his study, waiting to speak to you," Beale said.

"I'm here to see Surreal," Lucivar replied.

"She is resting."

"Resting? At this hour? Is she ill?"

"The Prince will explain."

He didn't like the sound of that. He liked it even less when he walked into Daemon's study and found his brother standing in the middle of the room, watching him with glazed, sleepy eyes.

"Is Surreal ill?" Lucivar asked, shoving the door closed.

"She's pregnant," Daemon replied softly.

He rocked back on his heels. There hadn't been a man in Surreal's life in quite some time, so her unexpected pregnancy explained Daemon locking down the Hall against outsiders, and it explained why Surreal was here and not at her own house. It also explained the chill in Daemon's temper and those glazed eyes.

Lucivar settled into a fighting stance, his wings half spread for balance—an instinctive response. "Am I here to help her drain her Jewels or to help you have a chat with the cock who danced with her?"

"I am the cock who danced with her," Daemon crooned.

His lungs locked, and for a moment he couldn't breathe. "You?"

Daemon smiled.

Lucivar shuddered. "I'd like to talk to Surreal."

"You don't need my permission."

"Today I do."

Daemon's smile became more gentle—and more terrifying. "Yes, today you do."

Would I have walked out of this room intact if I hadn't known that? He didn't need to ask the question when he already knew the answer.

The study door opened, Daemon's invitation for him to leave.

Turning his back on the Sadist was playing with suicide, but he did it. When he reached the door, Daemon said, "Lucivar? I want this baby."

Lucivar looked over his shoulder. "I'll talk to Surreal. And then you and I will talk."

He walked out of the study. Beale stood in the great hall at the doorway leading to the informal receiving room and the staircase that led to the family wing.

"Anything I need to know?" he asked the butler.

"Lady Surreal saw her Healer in Amdarh and was given a tonic to help her body adjust to . . ." Beale fumbled, clearly reluctant to speak of something so personal when it pertained to the SaDiablo family—especially when none of them knew if Daemon would take offense at someone talking about Surreal.

Lucivar nodded so that Beale didn't have to continue. "I'm going up now to talk to her—with the Prince's permission."

"I don't believe Lady Surreal's Jewels have been drained yet," Beale said.

Not something I can do for her now, Lucivar thought as he strode through the corridors that led to Surreal's suite.

Blood was the living river, and the body was the vessel for the power that made the Blood who and what they were. But everything had a price. When a witch wore darker Jewels, her moontimes were more uncomfortable and the pain of doing more than basic Craft during the first three days was fierce. That was the reason they drained their Jewels before a moontime—to let the body rest. And when they were pregnant, they submitted to someone else draining the reserve power in their Jewels so that their power didn't try to fill the child in the womb—and destroy it.

He rapped once on Surreal's sitting room door and went in before she answered. One look at her had him yanking back his temper because she didn't need a man yelling at her, but he couldn't stop himself from going up to the windows where she stood and opening his wings halfway to look more intimidating.

"Get off your feet," he snarled.

"Take a piss in the wind," she snarled back.

Relieved that she didn't sound as sick as she looked, he took a step back to give her some room.

"Aren't you going to ask how this happened?" Surreal said.

"I have two children. I know how it happened. What I don't know is what you want to do about it."

"Do about it? I'm keeping it! How could you think I would . . ." She burst into tears.

"Ah, Surreal." He put his arms around her and cuddled her while she cried. "That isn't what I meant."

"I'm not upset," she said, still crying. "My body is doing strange things, and it's making me weepy. And being weepy because I can't help it is *not* the same as being upset."

Lucivar rubbed his cheek against her hair. "It will be all right. In a couple of days, you'll swing over to bitchy and that will feel more normal to you."

She punched him. He laughed.

When she seemed settled again, he called in a handkerchief and let her mop her face.

"What I meant was, what do you want to do about Sadi? Talk to me, Surreal."

"I'd rather you talk to *him*."

"After you tell me what you want. I thought Daemon had this place locked down to keep everyone out, but that's not all of it, is it?"

"He says I can't leave with his child."

"Well, the baby can't go anywhere without you for quite some time, and he can't seriously expect you to stay inside the Hall for the next ten months."

"I wouldn't bet on that, sugar." Surreal sniffled once more, then vanished the handkerchief. "He offered to marry me. *Told* me, more like it. A week from tomorrow."

He loved his brother, but he wasn't sure Daemon was emotionally ready to be anyone's husband yet—if ever.

"What did you say?" he asked.

"I haven't given him an answer yet." She looked sad and wistful. "But I am going to marry him."

"Why?" When she didn't answer, he swore softly. "I know you care for Daemon. And he cares for you. But I'm not sure he can give you the kind of love a wife deserves from a husband."

"I do have some conditions that he'll have to agree to, and if he agrees, I think we can do well enough together."

"You don't have to settle for 'well enough.'"

She turned away to stare out the window. "I want this baby, Lucivar. Not just *a* baby; *this* baby. And I want this chance at a marriage. I haven't shared my life with anyone since Rainier, and we were never lovers, never had that kind of bond. Plenty of men since then have been willing to entertain a short-term liaison, especially if it got them an invitation to sit at a dinner table with Daemon and talk about whatever grand idea they had that needed a *little* financial backing. But men from the short-lived races didn't want to have children who wouldn't reach true adulthood in their lifetime, and men from the long-lived races saw their offspring's lives cut short if I was the mother. I never fit in to either place. Sadi knows all that, but he wants this child too, regardless of whatever life span it may have. And I have the feeling that if he doesn't have someone soon who can make a claim on his heart, he'll become so cold and distant we'll all lose him. Or he'll become so lonely, he'll accept the illusion of love and end up like his father, with a woman who loves ambition more than him. Well, I do love him, and I know he probably will never love me. But I can keep him from being alone, and I can give him a family of his own."

"And what will you get?" Lucivar asked.

"I'll get a family too."

"Is that enough?"

"I'll find out."

"Then I guess I should talk to him about the wedding."

"I need to talk to him first. Could you stay around for a little while?"

"All right."

"Lucivar? Did you know Sadi is the High Lord now?"

Her words froze Lucivar's heart. He'd suspected that Daemon had begun absorbing that side of Saetan's duties years ago—Sadi was, after all, Saetan's true heir—but he hadn't wanted to see the evidence, hadn't wanted to acknowledge what had been unspoken until now. He'd been afraid that once he admitted that Daemon was the High Lord, he would lose the man who was his brother.

He understood Surreal's decision now. The Realms couldn't afford to let Daemon slide into an isolated, lonely existence. None of them wanted to see Daemon repeat the mistakes in Saetan's life—or see the rise of someone like Hekatah because of those mistakes. The new High Lord of Hell needed to be kept tethered to the living because the simple truth was he was more dangerous than his predecessor.

"Go on and talk to him," Lucivar said. "Get things settled between you." He paused. "And then get off your feet."

He thought her answer landed squarely on the side of bitchy, which pleased him because it meant she was feeling a little better—and he'd take bitchy over tears any day.

Surreal found Daemon standing in the middle of his study, watching her with those glazed gold eyes.

"I have some conditions," she said. "If you can agree to them, I'll marry you."

"I'm listening," he crooned.

Her throat closed up. She was dancing on the knife's edge by making any demands of him, but now was the only time such things could be said—if she could get her voice working again.

He moved toward her slowly. He probably thought his movements weren't threatening. Unfortunately, until things were settled between them, there was *nothing* about him that wasn't threatening.

"Let me tell you what I think are some of your concerns," he said as he stepped close enough to touch her. "The wife of the Warlord Prince of Dhemlan has to make a commitment to be faithful to her husband and take no lovers. Naturally, she would want the same commitment from her husband. Yes?"

"Yes," Surreal whispered, staring at the Black Jewel peeking through the unbuttoned opening of his white silk shirt.

"But I don't think you want to be married and celibate," Daemon continued, his voice becoming a soothing caress. "And I think you enjoyed the pleasure I gave you in bed. Yes?"

"Yes," she whispered.

"So one of your conditions is that I be a husband to my wife in every way? That I don't deny you the pleasure and comfort of sex?"

She nodded, still not daring to look into his eyes.

"I was aware of that when I made the offer, Surreal," he said gently. "I can't promise you a husband's love, because I don't know if I have that in me anymore. But I can promise you all of the social courtesies, all of the physical courtesies. That much I can, and will, give you."

He lifted her chin with one finger, a silent command to look at him. "Is there anything else?"

"No. Yes. I don't want to be locked up here for the next ten months!"

"If I agree to that, you, in turn, will try to tolerate occasional bouts of rabid protectiveness?"

She heard amusement in his voice and felt the slightest release of tension in his body.

"If you turn rabid, I'll turn bitchy."

He smiled. "Fair enough. One question. Is there a particular stone you would like for your wedding ring? Or a particular kind of setting?"

She shook her head. "Surprise me."

"In that case, Lady . . ."

His lips touched hers, a soft kiss that remained soft but grew warmer. She floated on the sensation of being wrapped in the softest blanket. So soft, so deliciously warm. She felt light and heavy, and there was nothing in the world but his mouth so soft on hers and his hands lightly brushing her back under her shirt.

She wanted to snuggle down into that soft warmth and doze for hours, safe and content.

She didn't know how much time had passed before Daemon raised his head and said, "Feel better?"

Her head began to clear, but the warm, sleepy feeling remained—and the sharp discomfort in her abdomen was gone.

"You drained my power," she said. "Gray and Green."

"Yes." He kissed her temple.

"You going to kiss me like that every time you drain me?" She felt him smile.

"I'm going to kiss you like that simply to kiss you like that. And I'll do it often if it pleases you."

Mother Night.

She felt the pull of desire between her legs, but the soft warmth wrapped around her again, and she didn't want to do anything about that pull. Not right now.

"Once I drain your Jewels to give you an unfilled reservoir, your body will channel its power to them naturally, the same as it does during your moontime," Daemon said. "I thought you would be more comfortable if I took a direct path this first time."

She was pretty sure he'd wrapped some spells around her while kissing her, but she felt too comfortable and lazy and soft to care.

"Why don't you snuggle down on the sofa in here and take a nap?" he said.

She nodded. She'd do anything to keep that voice stroking over her, petting her. And maybe tomorrow—or next month—she'd figure out why feeling that way should piss her off. For now, she let him settle her on the leather sofa in his study and tuck a light blanket around her.

"Rest, Surreal," he said quietly as he ran a hand over her hair.

Rest, he'd said. So she obeyed.

EIGHT

Happy to have a few minutes when she wasn't required to smile at women she wanted to knife, Surreal sat alone at a table near the ballroom windows, watching her husband partner one of the Province Queens in a dance.

Sadi hadn't insulted anyone's intelligence by pretending—or implying—that the reason the marriage had been planned with such speed was that he had suddenly fallen in love with his second-in-command. Besides, no one, male or female, who had participated in a pregnancy and saw the way Sadi and Yaslana responded whenever anyone came near her had any doubts about why Daemon was getting married again.

Some of the Province Queens who attended the brief ceremony and were now staying for the afternoon-long reception resented Surreal for standing between them and Sadi all those years, certain she'd done it so that she would be in position to snag the coveted title of lover or the more lucrative title of wife at a time when Sadi might be emotionally vulnerable—like, for example, the day his father finally became a whisper in the Darkness. Other Ladies were noticeably relieved that Daemon had remarried and had chosen someone whose temper and ambitions weren't likely to give anyone unpleasant surprises. A few were genuinely happy for her.

All the Queens' Consorts were hearty in their congratulations since her new title of "wife" meant their Ladies would no longer dare look in Sadi's direction—which meant their own positions in the courts were secure at least for the duration of their contracts.

But whether they resented her, were relieved for themselves, or were happy that the Warlord Prince of Dhemlan had a steady sexual companion, they had all been careful of how they approached her.

Not because they felt threatened by *her*, Surreal thought with a dollop of resentment, but because the consequences of pissing off Daemon or Lucivar right now were bound to be painful—and messy.

"Am I interrupting?"

Surreal smiled at Lady Zhara. "Not at all. Please join me." She and the Queen of Amdarh had had their share of disagreements over the years, but despite that, they had become friendly and worked well together.

Zhara set a plate on the table. "I thought you might be feeling up to a little nibble now that the ceremony is over and your nerves have settled. When I was pregnant with my first child, I found that a bite or two every couple of hours was easier to handle than a meal, especially in the early stages." She studied Surreal. "But if seeing or smelling food makes you queasy, I'll remove the plate right now. *Is* that why you're sitting so far away from the feast?"

Surreal selected a triangle of toast that held a bit of chopped beef. "I wasn't sitting away from the food; I was sitting close to the windows and fresh air. And, actually, I *could* use a bit of food now. Breakfast didn't stay down this morning."

Zhara made a sympathetic face. "It will get better." She selected a slice of fruit from the plate and tipped her head toward the center of the room. "I'm surprised Prince Sadi isn't dancing attendance on you instead of dancing with the guests. Especially since you weren't feeling well this morning."

Snarling, Surreal selected a cube of cheese. "After the wedding ceremony and well-wishing were completed, I went to the bathroom to pee. Just to pee. And he followed

me inside the room and intended to stay so that I
wouldn't—I don't know—fall over in a faint and crack my
skull or some other such nonsense. After I tried to punch
him, I told him if he didn't stop fussing and give me some
breathing room, he would have the distinction of being
married and divorced on the same day. Which is why he's
currently over there and I'm over here."

Zhara swallowed hard. Surreal couldn't tell if the
woman was appalled or amused.

"Mother Night," Zhara finally said. "But he did respect
your wishes."

"You think so? The bastard sicced the Scelties on me!"

He did not sic us. The duet of voices came from under
the table. *We volunteered.*

Zhara pressed her lips together and stared at the ceiling.
Her shoulders shook.

Surreal pondered the plate of food. That flash of temper
seemed to clear up the last of the morning wobbles, so she
began eating with more enthusiasm.

Holt wandered by, set two wineglasses on the table, and
wandered off.

Zhara picked up a glass and sniffed. "I'm guessing this
one has water." She set that one in front of Surreal, then
took a sip from the other glass and nodded her approval.
"Your ring is lovely. The design looks like something
Banard would do, but I've never seen a stone like that."

"It's called earth's moonlight," Surreal said, holding out
her hand so that Zhara could get a better look. The stone
was a translucent dove gray that looked like it held streams
of light. The ring, made of yellow and white gold, swirled
around the center stone and had small diamonds.

"The design is like the moon and stars," Zhara said.

Surreal felt a funny little twitch in her chest. "The stone
is only found in Dea al Mon, which is why most people
have never seen one." Which meant Daemon had gone to
the Dea al Mon, her mother's people, to purchase that
stone for her ring.

"None of your kinsmen are here today?" Zhara asked.

Nothing sly about the question, no digging for gossip. She heard delicate concern in the older Queen's voice.

"We decided to do three small gatherings instead of one large one," Surreal said. "The Queens from Kaeleer's other Territories will be coming next week for an informal afternoon, and the following week, Daemon and I will spend a day with my mother's clan."

"And for your honeymoon?"

"A week in Amdarh."

"That's not . . ." Zhara stopped. She shook her head. "Forgive me, but . . ."

Surreal grinned. "The *Queen of Amdarh* is about to tell me her city isn't romantic enough for a honeymoon?"

"No, of course not. I love the city, but . . ." Flustered, Zhara stopped again.

"But you thought the Prince would choose someplace else?" When Zhara nodded, Surreal smiled, feeling a little misty about the other woman's concern. "Amdarh was my choice. Shopping. Concerts. The theater. I won't be able to stay in the city without Sadi or Yaslana as escort until after the baby is born—and I won't put everyone at risk by trying to defy that request and provoke their protective instincts."

Zhara knew how sharp Sadi's protective instincts could be. She had been there when Daemon had threatened to purge Dhemlan the next time someone tried to harm Jaenelle Angelline.

Anyone who remembered that threat and learned Daemon was the High Lord of Hell now would be scared witless.

"I'm going to indulge myself in the shops and let him fuss over me while I do it," Surreal continued. "That should please both of us."

Zhara laughed. "Yes, it should. Ah. I think your husband has sent a negotiator."

Surreal looked over her shoulder and saw Lucivar walking toward her.

Lucivar greeted Zhara, then held out his hand to Surreal. "We're dancing."

"Do you know how to negotiate?"

"Sure. You want to lead?"

Surreal looked at Zhara, who shrugged. Then she looked back at Lucivar. "Why are we dancing?"

"I think your husband figured if you didn't kick me in the balls, you were ready to suffer a dance with him."

Suffer a dance. That didn't sound like words from a husband who hoped for a warm welcome on his wedding night.

"He's really upset that I wouldn't let him stay and watch me pee?"

She wasn't sure Zhara was still breathing. She wasn't sure Lucivar was breathing either until he said, "Well, shit. Come on. I'll dance with you and knock some sense into his head afterward."

"You'd have more luck knocking sense into a stone wall."

"Don't push it, witchling."

So she danced with Lucivar, then was handed off to Holt. And she watched a roomful of Dhemlan's Queens and their aristo companions stand there with their mouths hanging open when Lucivar grabbed his brother and almost yanked Daemon off his feet as he hauled Sadi out of the ballroom.

When they returned, both looking a little rumpled but otherwise unscathed, Daemon asked her for a dance—a request she granted.

"Lucivar says I'm being an ass," Daemon said.

"He could have been looking in a mirror when he said it," she replied sweetly.

He let out a startled laugh. "I like the suggestion, but he was right. I can't protect you from morning sickness or the other physical discomforts that will come, but I do want to protect you. I don't want you to hurt."

"Everything has a price, Sadi." She smiled at him. "But it eases the discomfort some to know you're suffering with me in your own way."

"Really?"

"Shit, no."

Chuckling, he drew her closer. "All right, Lady. I will try to behave and be reasonable."

"So will I, Prince. So will I."

"Do you think Daemon and Lucivar have tossed the last of the guests out the door?" Surreal asked Marian hours later. Pleading fatigue halfway through the festivities, she had come up to the family sitting room, and Marian and the children had come with her.

"Don't encourage Lucivar by saying things like that," Marian said. "We live on a mountain. When someone gets tossed out of our house, there's a long drop after the first step."

Surreal set her dinner tray on the table in front of the sofa. "How did we end up playing hawks and hares by ourselves?"

"We let Daemonar and Titian go up to the playroom with the Scelties. They ran around until they all fell asleep. I didn't want to run around, and you're not allowed to run around. So we ended up here, playing hawks and hares, eating dinner off a tray, and not having to be polite." Marian looked at the clock. "Shouldn't you get ready for your wedding night?"

"Do you think there will be one?" She tried to smile, but her eyes filled with tears.

"Why would you say that?" Marian asked as she reached over and held one of Surreal's hands.

"He flinched when I slipped the wedding ring on his finger."

"I didn't see that, and I was standing right next to you."

"I doubt anyone saw it, but I felt it. He'd been steady until that point, but he flinched when it came time to wear a wedding ring again."

Marian looked alarmed. "It's not the same ring, is it?"

"No. He had a new one made, but what it stands for . . ." Surreal sighed. "He'll never get over Jaenelle. She will always be the love of his life."

"That doesn't mean he won't love you."

"I didn't ask him to." She rested her head on the back of the sofa and looked at the ceiling instead of at Marian. "When the conditions for the marriage were set, that was something he couldn't promise, so it's nothing I can expect."

She sat up, brushed her hair back, and stood up. "Enough melancholy. I hope this baby is in a better mood once it's outside the womb. If these moods are an indication of its temperament, this is going to be one blubbery child."

"Get some rest," Marian said gently. "We'll see you in the morning."

She walked to her old suite. At Daemon's request, she'd chosen another suite of rooms as their private living quarters within the Hall. It was still in the family wing, but away from the rooms Jaenelle and Saetan used to occupy. Her new bedroom connected with Daemon's but also had access to the baby's room, making it a family suite until the child was old enough to have a suite of its own.

That suite was still being renovated. Daemon could be subtle about visiting his new wife's bed, but she wondered how often he would force himself to make the walk while his bedroom was still distant from hers.

As she began to wonder if tonight would be one of the nights when he chose his own bed, he knocked on the door.

"Come in."

She'd bought a deep green gown and robe shot with gold threads for this night. It took effort to pretend a calm she couldn't feel, especially when he leaned back against the door and did nothing but look at her.

Just when she started to fidget, he pushed away from the door and walked up to her. His gold eyes stared at her lips until they started feeling kiss-swollen. She felt the room do one slow spin when one fingertip finally brushed over her lower lip.

Seduction spells. Or maybe it was just his presence when he didn't try to leash all that sexual heat.

With his hands on her shoulders, he backed her up to one of the bedposts. Removing her robe, he raised her arms just above her head and guided her hands around the post.

"Hold on," he said.

Be passive. Don't push me.

She heard those silent commands. He would walk away if she couldn't give him what he needed tonight—and he might not come back, despite his promise that she wouldn't spend her marriage being celibate.

He touched her face, her neck, her chest, her belly. Butterfly caresses that whispered over her skin. Heat that reached her through the gown. A touch. A kiss. Sometimes just his breath against her skin. But he didn't touch her breasts until her nipples hardened from wanting him. Then he touched, kissed, bit just enough to keep her still while his fingers drifted up her thighs and began teasing her until she moaned out of need. Her nightgown vanished as he sank to his knees and used his mouth to finish what his fingers had begun.

She didn't remember him tucking her into bed, didn't remember him getting undressed. By the time her brain started working again, he was suckling her breasts and playing with her until she was desperate to have him. That was when he mounted her, pinning her hands over her head as he moved with a lazy rhythm.

Was he moving like that because he was afraid he might hurt the baby? No, she realized in the last moments before her body surrendered to him completely and she couldn't think at all. He played like this because he liked it—and making her mindless with pleasure was one of the things he liked.

NINE

The birthing room was ready, the adjoining room where the family could wait was ready, and the Healer and her assistant had arrived. Beale was guarding the Hall's front door from any premature well-wishers; Helene was giving the family suite another quick cleaning and the crib a last polish, and making sure there were plenty of linens, diapers, blankets, towels, and whatever else a newborn might need. Holt was sorting through the correspondence and business papers so that the new father could make the most efficient use of his available time. And he, the about-to-be new father, was apparently doing nothing but being a pain in the ass.

"I don't need to sit," Surreal snarled as she waddled around the birthing room.

She most certainly did need to sit, Daemon thought, but he couldn't shove her into a chair. Not in her condition. "You're not comfortable standing," he pointed out in a soothing voice.

"Whose fault is that?" She grabbed the back of a chair and pressed the other hand to her belly, her face tight with pain.

"Remember what the Healer said about breathing," Daemon said.

"Go take a piss in the wind."

He slipped his hands out of his trouser pockets and made an effort to unclench his teeth as he took a step toward her, one hand extended. "Let me help you."

"You and your cock have done quite enough already," she snarled as she moved away from him.

"Surreal . . ."

Lucivar walked into the room and gave Surreal a lazy, arrogant smile. "Want to shred something, darling?"

"Yes," she snapped, "but since he likes his balls, I doubt he'd stand still for it."

"Surreal . . . ," Daemon soothed.

"Stop hovering over me!" she shouted. "This baby will come when it wants to come, and your pushing at me isn't going to make it come any faster!"

"I'm not pushing. . . ."

"You prick-assed son of a bitch, *get out of here*!"

Daemon looked at Lucivar. "I was told she'd be bitchy, but is it normal for her to sound insane?"

"Insane?" Surreal shrieked. "You think I sound *insane*?"

"Yes," Lucivar said to Daemon. "Right now, she doesn't like you much, old son, so come into the next room and give her some peace."

"Why are you taking my side?" Surreal demanded.

"When Marian was in labor with Daemonar, she wanted the birthing room clear of males on occasion, and when I got stubborn about it, she threatened to cook up the afterbirth and feed it to me."

Daemon felt like something stringy and greasy was stuck in his throat. He swallowed hard and looked at Surreal.

She looked at him and said, "I'll stab you before I cook anything."

"Thank you," he said faintly. "I appreciate it."

"Then get out!"

Lucivar hauled him into the adjoining room, closing the door to the birthing room most of the way. That gave Surreal sufficient privacy but made it easy to hear her.

Daemon let out a shaky sigh. "She's hurting."

"She's in labor, old son. Having a baby hurts like a wicked bitch. Or so I've been told."

"There has to be something the Healer can do. Something *I* can do. Hell's fire, Lucivar. If I can drain the power from Surreal's Jewels to make her more comfortable, why can't I take some of the pain?"

"The Healer has spells to dull the pain. You have to let her take care of that part," Lucivar said. "You trust her, don't you?"

"Yes, I trust her but—" Daemon tensed as he heard another voice in the birthing room.

"It's Marian," Lucivar said. "She'll keep Surreal company until your presence is requested."

"Will it be requested?" Daemon asked softly. "She's hurting, and it's my fault. She's having my baby, and she kicked me out of the room."

"Like I said, she doesn't like you much right now and doesn't want you around every minute, but that doesn't mean—"

"Sadi!" Surreal shouted. "If you want to keep that over-rated cock of yours, get your ass back in here!"

"—she wants you to go too far away," Lucivar finished.

Daemon rocked back on his heels and stared at the partially open door. "So she's going to keep flipping from wanting me with her to wanting me gone? For how long?"

Lucivar put both hands on Daemon's back and gave him a light shove. "For as long as it takes to birth this baby."

"Mother Night."

"And may the Darkness be merciful. Show some balls, boyo."

"That's what got me into this in the first place," Daemon muttered. But he went into the birthing room and found Surreal looking teary-eyed and vulnerable—and ready for a few hugs and cuddles.

Lucivar wandered over to the window farthest away from the door. Moments after Daemon walked into the birthing room, Marian walked out and closed the door between the rooms.

"How are they?" he asked when Marian wrapped her arms around his waist and leaned against him.

"They'll be fine, but your brother is going to need you today," she replied. "Surreal is focused on having the baby, but Daemon seems . . . shakier, more vulnerable."

"Until the Birthright Ceremony, the child isn't legally his. He'll spend years raising that child and loving that child, but it won't be his until that day."

Marian leaned back enough to look at him. "You've never worried about that, have you?"

He brushed her hair away from her face. "No, but that's you and me. It's not going to be as easy for Daemon to trust."

"That's not fair to Surreal."

"No, it's not, but that's how it is."

Marian hesitated. "Have you ever wondered . . . ?"

He sighed. Then he nodded. "I don't know if Jaenelle wasn't able to have children or if it just never happened for them."

"I think there was a concern—a fear—that she wouldn't survive childbirth," Marian said quietly. "Nothing was ever said; I just had that impression the couple of times her moontime was late. It seemed like Daemon was relieved when the moon's blood started."

"Could be. It would have destroyed him if she had died that way." He huffed out a breath. "Maybe that's why it never happened. Hell's fire, I was able to make myself infertile for centuries and did it so thoroughly I *know* I never sired a child until the night we made Daemonar. And Daemon had suppressed his sexuality and fertility even more than I did for most of his life."

"He wasn't unreceptive to having a child," Marian said. "At least, not until Jaenelle got hurt."

"Not until Jaenelle's body was healed and remade through a tangled web," Lucivar corrected. "After she came back to him, he had a hard time dealing with her being in any kind of pain—and took care of whatever was causing the problem." *And maybe had taken care of more things than he'd intended to.*

Lucivar kissed Marian's forehead. "Doesn't matter why things happened the way they did. Today we focus on helping Surreal get through childbirth without killing her husband."

Marian froze for a moment, then looked at him with wide eyes. "Someone did remember to take away all her knives. Don't you think?"

Lucivar released his wife and headed for the birthing room door. "I think I'll slip in and take a quick look around."

She felt frightened, feral, and more than a little possessive. Ignoring Helene and the Healer's assistant as they cleaned her up, Surreal kept her eyes on the man who stood too far away from the bed, cradling *her* child in his arms. She wanted to tear the baby out of his arms—and tear off his arms in the process.

"Drink this," the Healer said, holding a cup to her lips. "You need to drink this now."

"Trying to drug me?" She flicked her eyes to the woman's startled face, then focused again on the man *who wouldn't even look at her.*

"It's a tonic to provide you with some quick nourishment. A couple of swallows is all. Your body will use it all up; it won't get to your milk."

Milk. The baby needed milk.

"A couple of swallows, Lady," the Healer said.

She took the cup and drained it.

"There," Helene said as she smoothed the bedcovers. "You should be able to rest easy now."

The man immediately looked up, looked at her, and she realized he hadn't been ignoring her; he'd been giving her privacy while they cleaned her and the bed. Now he watched her as she watched him, but there was wariness in his eyes.

What had she done to make him so wary?

Warlord Prince. Husband. Daemon.

With each word that identified *who* he was, her head cleared a little more and images and sounds flashed by in memory, jumbled and distorted—the pain, the Healer's encouraging voice, a male voice promising it wouldn't hurt much longer, the thin cry of a baby, the man lowering her to the pillows and moving toward the child a woman lifted from between her legs, and her sudden attack to keep him, and everyone else, away from her baby. Hands holding her down while she fought and screamed—and the woman, the Healer, rushing to the far side of the room and handing *her* baby to . . .

Surreal raised a hand, touched her shoulder, and flinched.

"You're going to have a few bruises," the Healer said quietly. "Prince Yaslana wasn't trying to hurt you, but you had to be restrained for your own safety and the child's."

She stared at Daemon. "Was anyone hurt?"

"No," he said quietly. "But we all learned some things about the Dea al Mon side of your nature."

He was lying. She could feel it. Someone *had* gotten hurt, but she knew he wouldn't tell her if she asked him. At least, not right now.

"I'll be back in a little while to answer any questions you may have," the Healer said. "For now, why don't the three of you get acquainted?"

Helene and the Healer's assistant left through the outer room while the Healer went into the adjoining room, no doubt to report to Lucivar and Marian.

"I guess I must have gone a little insane?" she asked.

"Something like that." He sat on the edge of the bed near her knees, still wary of her and ready to move out of reach. He also had a shield around himself and the baby so she couldn't touch either one.

She scraped her fingers through sweat-damp hair. "Hell's fire, Sadi. What do you want me to say? Things got fuzzy toward the end."

"Sometimes you're a scary woman, Surreal." Daemon studied her. "Still feeling fuzzy?"

"No." Now she felt scared as she realized how badly she'd unnerved him. He was keeping the baby away from her. Was he going to take her child? Had she done something that made him think she would hurt the child? *Mother Night.* "The baby?"

"She's fine."

She. Daughter. "She has the right number of fingers and toes?"

He smiled. "Yes, she does. I didn't have a chance to look at everything, but I saw that much."

We're both afraid, she thought. *Both afraid of being shut out by the other. And I don't know what I did to make him so wary of letting me near my own baby.*

"I hadn't decided on a name for a boy, but I know the name I'd like to give our daughter—with your consent," she said.

"Unless it's outlandish, I doubt I'll have a problem with any name you choose," he replied.

"Jaenelle Saetien. I would like to name her Jaenelle Saetien in honor of two people who meant a great deal to me."

Shock. Pain. And then, gratitude. "Are you sure?"

Surreal smiled. "I'm sure."

She watched his shoulders relax as he studied his daughter.

"Jaenelle say-tee-ehn," he said, pronouncing the name as she had. Then he gave his girl a loving smile. "Hello, witch-child."

The right choice, Surreal decided as she watched Daemon relax enough to unwrap the blankets and get a better look at his baby. She wanted to touch them both, and she couldn't until he trusted her enough to drop his shield.

His eyes wandered leisurely over that small body that had come from hers. Then he studied the head and his expression became bemused.

"Her ears are pointed," he said softly.

Suddenly self-conscious, Surreal pulled her hair over her own delicately pointed ears.

Daemon's smile turned soft and silly. He shifted position, moving up so that she could finally see her daughter and share this discovery.

She reached out to move the blanket to get a better look—and couldn't touch it. He tensed, but he dropped the shield. When she did nothing more than touch the blanket, he relaxed and shifted his body to include her.

"Look," he said, sounding enchanted. "Her little ears are pointed. She's going to be beautiful, like you."

A prick of tears. She blinked them back before he noticed.

Jaenelle began crying. Surreal saw Daemon change in a heartbeat from a soft man to a predator ready to protect his own.

"What's wrong?" Daemon's gold eyes were cold and glazed as he raised his head and looked at her.

The temper wasn't aimed at her, she realized. If he couldn't deduce what was wrong with his child quickly enough, he expected *her* to point out the problem so that he could take care of it—permanently.

That was the moment she understood that her part of the job wasn't so much to protect the child as to push Sadi back the necessary half step that would give his girl some breathing room from the instincts that would be honed to a lethal edge from now on.

Uncle Saetan hadn't had the leash of a partner when he'd raised Jaenelle and stood as the coven's protector. Looking at Daemon now, she began to appreciate just how formidable the old man's self-control had been.

"I think she's hungry," Surreal said.

A heartbeat. Two. Then Daemon blinked and looked around as if expecting to find a table of food that would appeal to his girl.

Surreal touched his sleeve. When he focused on her, she

tapped her chest. "For the next few months, her kitchen is right here."

He looked at her chest and blinked again. "Oh."

She held out her arms and waited.

Hesitation. Reluctance. But he finally settled the baby in her arms.

When he sat there, waiting, she turned shy. "I know you've seen my breasts before, but this is different."

Another heartbeat. Two. "You want me to leave?"

She nodded. "Could you ask Marian to come in?"

That request melted whatever resistance he had for leaving her alone with the child. He brushed a finger over the baby's hand, then leaned over and kissed Surreal with a tenderness that made her heart ache.

"Thank you," he said.

She grinned. "She is pretty wonderful, isn't she?"

"She's her mother's daughter. How could she be anything else?"

She sat there, stunned by the words, as Daemon slipped out of the room and Marian slipped in.

The moment Daemon stepped into the adjoining room, Lucivar caught him in a hard hug and held on while his brother shook with the effort to control his emotions—and probably control the pain he'd been hiding.

"Is Surreal all right now?" Lucivar asked.

"Yes," Daemon replied. He eased back enough to rest his forehead against Lucivar's. "What in the name of Hell happened?"

"Damned if I know. Marian got bitchy during labor, but she settled down once the baby was born. Surreal acted like a wild she-cat, and we were the bad humans trying to take her kitten." He paused. "How's the arm?"

"Not bad. The bleeding stopped." Daemon looked down at his right jacket sleeve. The illusion spell hid the tears and the blood.

"Liar. Come over here and strip down. I'll wash the arm, and then we'll have the Healer take care of it."

"I don't need—"

"Bastard, what part of that sounded like a choice?"

Daemon stared at him. Lucivar matched the look.

"I'm fine."

"She ripped your arm open and scared the shit out of you and everyone else in the room. Everyone was focused on taking care of her and keeping the baby safe, and no one's had a look at how badly you're hurt. So you're not fine. Not yet."

"She won't hurt the baby," Daemon said as he followed Lucivar to the table where a basin of steaming water sat beside basic healing supplies.

"She was never going for the baby, old son. She was going for your throat."

Daemon stripped off his jacket and swore vigorously as Lucivar helped him remove the shirt where it had stuck to the wounds in his upper right arm.

"What did she rip me with?" he asked as he sank into a chair next to the table.

Lucivar looked at the slices in Daemon's arm. They were deep enough that he wanted the Healer to take care of them and make sure the arm healed properly, but he could clean the wounds to give Daemon time to settle. "An open metalwork glove that had talons honed almost as sharp as my war blade. That must have been something she always kept with her, stored by Craft. I made sure she hadn't hidden any weapons in the room, but I hadn't expected her to use Craft so soon after birthing or have something that lethal that she could call in. And I didn't expect her to attack you."

"Why did she do that? I haven't given her a reason to feel hostile toward me. Have I?"

"Surreal didn't have an easy childhood or a soft life afterward. She saw as much blood, pain, and cruelty as we did in Terreille. Everything has a price, and the price strong witches pay for wearing dark Jewels is more painful moontimes and harder births. I'm guessing the pain and the smell of blood pushed her to someplace in her memories, mixing things up in the end. I don't think she knew who was with her; you were just a male reaching for her baby. As sure as the sun doesn't shine in Hell, she didn't know who I was when I was holding her down to give you and the Healer time to get the baby away from the bed so it wouldn't get hurt."

"You don't think it was just me she wanted to keep away?"

Since they were going to talk, Lucivar smeared a cleansing ointment over Daemon's wounds. "Nah. I told you. A witch who wears Gray Jewels has to be more careful and work a lot harder to keep a baby in the womb. Surreal has been feeling shaky and protective since the first morning she threw up. During the past few hours, she gave up everything civilized in order to birth this child."

"Her name is Jaenelle Saetien," Daemon said.

Lucivar froze for a moment. "Good name. What does Surreal think of it?"

"It was her choice."

Daemon was starting to sound drunk stupid. Lucivar thought it was a good sign that he was finally, and fully, relaxing. Of course, sounding drunk stupid could indicate that he'd lost more blood than was obvious, and that *wouldn't* be good.

Stepping into the corridor, Lucivar summoned the Healer to deal with Daemon's arm while he checked in with Beale, Jazen, and Holt to confirm that nothing needed Daemon's immediate attention—or his attention, since he figured he'd be handling any problems for the next day or so. They had nothing to tell him except that Tersa, Manny, Mikal, and Beron were now in the family sitting room with Daemonar and Titian. Once everyone had a little time to settle and he was sure Surreal was steady enough to tolerate the rest of the family meeting its newest member, they would all have a chance to coo before he nudged them out to enjoy the celebration dinner.

*   *   *

Surreal didn't ask the question until Jaenelle finished nursing. Cradling her baby girl, she looked at Marian. "Who did I hurt, and how bad is it?"

Marian turned her head toward the adjoining room's door. Surreal's stomach flipped.

"Lucivar?" she asked. "Did I hurt Lucivar?"

"No." Marian laid a hand on her arm, just above where the baby's head rested. "Lucivar is fine."

Surreal stared at the woman who was a sister through marriage. "Daemon."

Marian hesitated, then nodded. "But he'll be fine. The Healer's taking care of him."

"What did I do? *Marian, tell me.*"

"Hush, now. Don't upset the baby."

They waited until the baby stopped fussing. Then Marian said, "I've been here with you since Daemon left, so I haven't talked to Lucivar to get all the details. What I do know is you called in some kind of metal glove and ripped up Daemon's arm when the Healer picked up the baby. You attacked without warning. Daemon got between you and the Healer to protect her and the baby. Then Lucivar rushed in to restrain you until you were thinking clearly enough again to allow the women to take care of you."

"Where is it now, the metal glove?"

"Lucivar has it."

"When he's willing, I'd like it back. It was a Winsol gift from Rainier."

"I'll tell him." Marian hesitated. "The talons weren't poisoned, were they? I'm not sure anyone thought to check."

No wonder Sadi had been so wary of getting near her or letting her near the baby. "No poison. Not even a possibility of residual poison."

"That's good."

"Are you sure Daemon will be all right?"

"Yes. He'll be fine. Are you feeling up to letting the rest of the family see the baby? Just for a few minutes? Mrs. Beale has a meal ready for you. Are you hungry?"

"Yes, I'm hungry, and yes, they can come in."

A minute later, Lucivar walked in, and Surreal could hear excited voices in the other room.

"Daemon has gone to his suite to wash up and change into fresh clothes," Lucivar said.

"Are you pissed off at me?" Surreal asked. She heard tears in her voice.

"No, I'm not pissed off at you," Lucivar said. "Neither is Daemon. We want to do whatever you need to feel safe and easy."

"I'll stay and have a bite to eat with Surreal," Marian said quickly, looking from one to the other. "Daemon could come back a little later."

Surreal studied Lucivar's face, his eyes. "He doesn't want to see me?"

Lucivar met her look, made some decision, and sighed. "You caught him in the ribs as well as the arm. Bastard managed to hide that from me even while I was cleaning the arm. It wasn't until the Healer stepped in the blood that had pooled under the chair and I pushed to break the illusion spell that we discovered the other wounds and realized how much blood he'd lost."

"Mother Night," Surreal whispered.

"After she closed the wounds, we got him a clean shirt and let him receive congratulations from the family before taking him to his suite. Right now, the Healer is pouring some potent healing brews down his throat, and Jazen and the Scelties are under orders to make sure he stays down for a couple of hours. Then, if he's steady enough, he can come back and see you."

Tears filled her eyes and spilled over. "I'm sorry. I wasn't trying to hurt him. I'm not sure what I was trying to do."

"You thought you needed to protect your baby. He doesn't fault you for that, Surreal. Neither do I. But I need to know you're steady before I let him back in this room. He's in no condition to defend himself right now. Not from you."

"He doesn't have to."

Marian went into the small bathroom and returned with a damp cloth. "Here. Wipe your face so the children can come in and meet their new cousin."

Surreal did as she was told. She had a feeling Tersa knew why Daemon wasn't present, but the others were more interested in the baby and didn't notice the absence of the father.

When Lucivar decided they'd all had sufficient chance to coo, he herded them out, reminding them that there was a celebratory feast in the dining room.

"I'll tell Beale we're ready for some food and be back in a minute," Marian said.

Finally alone, Surreal looked at the baby girl sleeping in her arms and sighed. "Your birthing day turned out to be a lot more exciting than I'd intended. I figure your papa and uncle will start forgetting about that around the time we're planning your wedding. Of course, getting your papa to agree to let a boy have that first kiss could be a problem, but I'll work on it. I promise I will."

As soon as the rest of the family was out of sight, Lucivar wrapped his arms around Marian.

"Is Daemon really hurt that bad?" she asked.

"Yeah, he's hurt that bad," Lucivar replied. "He was bleeding all that time and hid it."

"To protect the baby."

"And so that Surreal wouldn't know, wouldn't feel the weight of blame for something done when she wasn't thinking clearly." He sighed. "But he will be all right."

"Did he tell you the baby's name?"

He nodded. "And that Surreal chose it."

"Lucivar?"

"Hmm?"

"Do you think either of them has realized yet that Jaenelle Saetien has the same birthday as Jaenelle Angelline?"

*   *   *

Later that evening, Surreal looked up from watching the baby sleep to find Daemon standing in the doorway.

"May I come in?" he asked.

"Sure."

He moved slowly, stiffly, as he approached the bed and came around to the side that held the baby basket.

"Hell's fire, Sadi, you look like shit."

"You flatter me, as always."

"I'm not playing," she said sharply, then lowered her voice when the baby stirred. "Sit down before you fall down." How much blood had he lost? And why had the fool allowed himself to keep bleeding like that?

Because he wouldn't leave the baby. And *she* wouldn't have calmed down if he'd left the room with the baby. So he'd stayed, hiding the wounds and the blood soaking into his clothes.

They were going to have a little chat about his taking care of himself so that he'd be able to take care of the child. On the other hand, she appreciated his restraint in not hurting her today.

"Daemon, sit down."

He used Craft to move a chair next to the bed. When that didn't give him a good view of his daughter, he sat on the edge of the bed, wincing as he shifted position. One finger touched a tiny hand.

He's already in love with her, Surreal thought as she watched him watch Jaenelle. The baby had a fuzz of black hair, gold eyes, and light brown skin. The delicately pointed ears were the only sign that she wasn't purely from the long-lived races.

"Are you disappointed that she's not a Queen?" Surreal asked.

The Healer had said it might take a few days for a psychic scent to become strong enough to identify a caste, but the words had been said to ease possible disappointment. Surreal had known within minutes of holding her baby that Jaenelle Saetien wasn't a Queen. Lucivar had known just by being in the same room with the girl, so she figured Daemon also knew.

Daemon looked at her, surprised. "Disappointed? No." His eyes went back to the baby. "Queens are the Blood's moral center and the heart of the land. Their will is the law, and every single person who lives in their territory is held by their whims. But for all that, their lives are set from the day they're born, and their lives are never truly their own. We need the Queens, but I'm relieved that my daughter will be spared the weight of those duties. She can become whatever she chooses to be."

"I'll remind of you of that when she announces a new course of study that's so outrageous just hearing about it makes you snort coffee out your nose."

He let out a startled laugh. Then his breath caught from the pain.

Surreal sighed. "Daemon, we both need to get some sleep before she wakes up and wants another meal."

He nodded, clearly unhappy.

This should have been a wonderful day for both of them, and he shouldn't have been exhausted from pain and blood loss because of her.

She snugged the baby basket up against her. "Come on, Sadi. Stretch out here and get some sleep."

He studied her, and she couldn't tell what he was thinking.

"There's not much room," he finally said.

And if she called in a knife, his throat would be in easy reach.

"There's enough." She thought for a moment. "But it would be smart to put a light shield along the sides so neither of us accidentally rolls off the bed."

He stretched out on his left side, the head of the baby basket brushing his chest, and put up the shields as she requested. It hurt her heart to see him moving so carefully because of the wounds and the pain. When the Healer came back tomorrow to check on her, she would make sure she knew what he was supposed to do to heal fully—and she would make sure he did it.

She looked at him, intending to ask if he'd taken the healing brew he was supposed to before bedtime. But Daemon was already sound asleep, his body curved protectively around the basket holding his daughter.

TEN

Daemon looked up when the study door opened, and watched Surreal walk toward the blackwood desk. Judging by that particular expression on her face, he knew he was in trouble. He just didn't know why.

"You're the parent on duty this morning," he pointed out.

"I'm aware of that, Sadi." Surreal pressed her hands on the desk and leaned toward him. "Before I decide if you deserve to have your ass kicked, I want to know one thing: Did you give Jaenelle permission to ride the horsie all by herself?"

Why was she pissed off about that? "The wheeled toy horse in the playroom?"

"No, the big live one outside."

He blinked. Sat back. "What, exactly, are we talking about?" Because she couldn't mean what she said. Jaenelle was much too young to mount a horse and ride alone.

"A black horse showed up this morning. When Jaenelle went outside to play, they made friends. Now they're cantering around the backyard, having a grand time."

"A groom put her up in front of him?" He couldn't approve of that, since the man hadn't asked permission from him or Surreal first, but Jaenelle loved the horses and she could be a persuasive little witchling. Of course, a groom being present didn't fit with Jaenelle being "all by herself."

"There's no groom," Surreal said. "There's no saddle or

bridle. And he's not from our stables. His name is Nightwind, he comes from the Isle of Scelt, and he's an Opal-Jeweled Warlord Prince."

Daemon shot to his feet. Seeing the look in Surreal's eyes, he sank back down. She hadn't called in a weapon—yet—but he knew better than to push her when she was in a riled-mother frame of mind.

"She's riding an unfamiliar horse—," he began.

"Who is an Opal-Jeweled Warlord Prince," she added.

"*—bareback?*"

"Yes. The grooms tried to approach him, but every time they got close, he took off—with her. The humans have retreated because they're afraid he'll bolt or try to jump something in his path. No one is sure how she's keeping her seat, although the stable master assures me that she's riding as if she'd been born knowing how to ride. Fhinn and Sorca are watching her, since the horse doesn't mind Scelties running along with him. So Jaenelle is fine for the moment, which is why we have time to discuss this."

He shot to his feet again. "Hell's fire, Surreal! Why haven't you done something?"

"Like I said, I wanted to make sure you hadn't given her permission."

"Why would you think I would give my permission?"

"Because you have a firm *no* and a soft *no*, and I had the feeling that Jaenelle heard whatever you said about the horsie as a soft *no*."

"There was no *no*, and there was no *yes*," Daemon snarled. "I didn't know about him!"

"Now you do. This one isn't about who's on duty, Sadi. This is about a pissing contest between two Warlord Princes and establishing *now* that Prince Nightwind gets his orders from you and not Jaenelle."

Daemon narrowed his eyes. Surreal didn't need him for this. She wore the Gray. She could slap that horse from one end of the estate to the other if that was what it took to convince Nightwind that he had to follow the rules they set for their daughter. Convincing the daughter, on the other hand . . .

"Why do you want me to be the strict parent who draws the line?" he asked.

"Because a line has to be drawn and held. She's too young to be galloping off without supervision. When that line gets drawn, there are going to be tears. She's having a wonderful time right now, so you know there will be tears. And we both know you tend to buckle when there are tears."

"I don't buckle," he snarled.

Surreal just looked at him.

"Not always." Actually, it wasn't the tears that gave him trouble; it was his fascination with how her little mind worked that usually tangled him up. He'd been stumbling over Jaenelle's logic since the day she figured out how to string words into complete sentences adults could understand. "All right. Fine. I'll draw the line."

"And I'll back you up all the way," she said sweetly.

He came around the desk and headed for the door. "You owe me."

Surreal laughed.

As he entered the great hall, he noticed Beale and Holt, but they didn't try to talk to him, so he kept going. If Jaenelle *was* having a grand time with the horsie, she was going to be one unhappy little witch when he put a stop to her playing with her new friend. And wouldn't that be pleasant to deal with?

He would be calm but firm with horse and child. After all, it wasn't *that* long ago that his little witchling had needed to hold on to him in order to walk. Of course, now she was running all over the place, and the Scelties were the only ones besides himself and Surreal who could keep track of her. But that didn't mean she could go riding by herself. No, it did not.

He stepped out on the back terrace, saw his little girl and the young black stallion, and thought, *Shit.*

They looked beautiful together—and they reminded him of another young girl and a horse named Dark Dancer who had looked just as beautiful as they flew over the ground.

But it wasn't the same. Jaenelle Angelline had been twelve at the time, not a *little* girl like Jaenelle Saetien. Still, he had to admit Surreal was right—he'd have a much harder time holding this particular line if he wasn't the one drawing it.

"Papa!" Jaenelle raised a hand and waved at him—and wobbled on that bare back so dreadfully far above the ground.

Daemon's heart bounced down to his knees and back up to his throat, but he kept his movements smooth and easy as he approached the horse, who had slowed to a walk and kept an eye on him.

"Papa! Look at me!"

"I see you, witch-child." But he was watching the stallion. "Come on, now. Let me help you down so you can introduce your new friend properly." And once he got her down, he would decide if she was ever getting near the horse again.

"Go over to Papa now," she said. "We'll get hugs!"

A Warlord Prince was a Warlord Prince, whether he walked on four legs or two. And this youngster was feeling just as possessive and territorial as Daemon.

Well, that wasn't quite true. *No one* could feel as possessive and territorial about his daughter as he did.

He waited, letting the stallion move toward him, giving Opal a chance to show respect for the Black—and remain among the living.

Once Daemon had his girl safely in his arms, he looked into those gold eyes shining with excitement. It wasn't the thought of tears that defeated him. It was the thought of how dull those eyes would be if he didn't allow the boundaries of her world to keep expanding.

Sighing, he looked at the horse and got down to the delicate business of negotiating the rules.

*　　*　　*

Surreal stepped out of Daemon's study and found Holt and Beale in the great hall, waiting for her.

Holt shook his head. "You're both so strict about the on-duty rule, I didn't think you could talk the Prince into going out there, not when you could deal with a kindred visitor."

"You just have to know the right thing to say," Surreal replied. *And knowing when Daemon needs to set the boundaries for his daughter doesn't hurt either—especially when being the one to set those boundaries is as much for his sake as for hers.*

"You talked him into handling it," Holt said, still shaking his head.

"I did—which means I win the bet." She grinned and held out a hand. "That will be ten silver marks each, gentlemen. Pay up."

ELEVEN

Surreal walked down the steps to the sunken garden that held two statues. She'd built her own little garden for quiet reflection, and came to this one only once a year on this particular day. Daemon came here often, and it held so much of his sorrow and grief she wondered how the groundskeepers could stand tending the flower beds and trimming the lawn—and cleaning the fountain where a woman with an achingly familiar face rose out of the water.

She glanced at the statue of the male, then looked away. She couldn't help the male, so she went over to the other statue and lifted the mug she'd brought with her.

"I brought you coffee." She poured the contents on the grass near the fountain. "Daemon's gone to your cottage in Ebon Rih, like he does every year on the anniversary of your death. He'll stay for a day or two, remembering you. When he comes home, he'll sleep in his own bed for a few days while he wrestles with the question of whether having sex with me is being unfaithful to you or if still loving you is somehow being unfaithful to me. I think he'll always wrestle with that question at this time of year. It's not easy being the second wife, not when you were the first. I wouldn't give it up, though."

She vanished the mug, then stuffed her hands in the pockets of her coat. "Jaenelle Saetien is a lot like you. I think that helps Daemon. I know it helps me, because watching him deal with her reminds me of you and Uncle

Saetan. Hell's fire, you should have seen him the first time he said *no* and she tried to negotiate to get parts of that *no* turned into a *yes*. I can't laugh *at* him when he's losing ground, because I need him to back me when I make rules, but it is fun to watch him deal with her. And not just fun for me. Beale and Holt are often in prime position to watch our little dramas. She's not shy the way you were. I blame her uncle Lucivar for that. I think she absorbed some of his Eyrien arrogance while she was in the womb, just by my being around him. She throws herself at the world and is confident the world will catch her. And maybe it always will."

A tear suddenly spilled over. Surreal wiped it away. "I know you're gone and can't hear me, but I'll ask anyway. You were Kaeleer's Heart, and you were Daemon's heart. Your death left a hole in him, and I don't know if it will ever heal."

"It will."

Surreal jolted, then looked toward the stairs. "Tersa."

Daemon's mother joined her and smiled at the statue that wore Jaenelle Angelline's face. "She knew Daemon's rise out of the Twisted Kingdom needed to be a slow journey in order for his mind to heal. The same is true of his heart. A slow journey, Surreal. Be patient. It will take time, but the hole inside him is filling—and you're one reason why it can."

Surreal licked her lips and asked the question that had been circling in her mind ever since Nightwind showed up a few months before. "Has Jaenelle Angelline come back as Jaenelle Saetien?"

Tersa shook her head. "No. Of that I am sure."

"But they're so alike in some ways."

"Yearnings can be strange things. What kind of daughter did you yearn for in the long hours of lonely nights?"

The question made her uneasy, but she answered it. "Someone like the golden-haired child I once knew, without the pain."

"Then you have the daughter of your heart. And isn't

she also exactly the kind of daughter Daemon needs in order to heal?"

Surreal didn't know how to answer that.

"You worry without reason," Tersa said. "One is like the other but is not the other."

"How can you be sure?"

Tersa brushed her fingers along Surreal's cheek. "Witch told me."

Daemon closed the cottage door and pressed his forehead against the wood. Most days the pain was a dull ache in the background of his life, a constant and faithful lover. Most days he barely noticed it while he was busy taking care of his family and the SaDiablo estates, and the Territory of Dhemlan.

Most days. But not on the anniversary of the day he lost his Queen, his lover, his heart. Then the pain roared back, sharp and cutting. It wasn't fair to Surreal, but he couldn't be around her on this day. Couldn't even be around Jaenelle Saetien, mostly because he didn't want to explain the tears and the hurting to his little girl.

Being invited to Jaenelle's private place had been special, a pocket of time when they could be nothing more than a man and woman in love. He cherished those memories, just as he cherished the memories of the time they took for themselves each Winsol. He tried not to think about them too much during the rest of the year. He'd made a promise to Surreal to be a husband, and he did his best to keep that promise. But on this day, he wandered the acre of land that belonged to the cottage or sat in the front room and let the memories flow—the ones that made him laugh, the ones that made him cry.

Later in the evening, he ate the food Marian left for him in the cold box. Then he lay down on the bed and closed his eyes. The dream would come—the one where he was dead and had a hole in his chest where his heart had been. It didn't plague him as often anymore, but it would come tonight.

Except it didn't. Instead, he dreamed he was stretched out on the altar in the Misty Place, comfortable and passive, lulled by the steady beat of his heart.

He opened his eyes and rolled onto his back, bumping against someone else on the altar—except she was propped up on one elbow, watching him out of ancient sapphire eyes.

"Jaenelle," he whispered.

She tapped a cat claw lightly against his chest. "Stubborn, snarly male. But I guess that's not surprising, since you always were."

The steady beat of his heart.

He looked down. The hole was still there, a gaping wound. But not completely empty anymore. Half a heart now beat in his chest.

"You taking that much back is progress," Witch said. "I'll keep the rest of it safe until you're ready to take it back."

"I want you to have it."

"No, Daemon. I had all of it for a lifetime. Eventually you'll take the rest of your heart back in order to share it again." She gave him a long, gentle kiss. "Sleep. I'll watch over you tonight."

He closed his eyes. As he drifted into an easy sleep, he heard her singing. He couldn't make out words or even a melody, but the song drifted through the Darkness and wrapped him in peace.

He woke up just after dawn, alone. But he could have sworn her scent was on his skin and he could feel the lingering warmth of her next to him in bed.

TWELVE

Daemon jolted awake when his bundle of witch landed on his back.

"Papa! I have something wonderful to show you!" Jaenelle gave his bare shoulder a smacking kiss.

He grunted, raised his head, and got his eyes open enough to look out the window. Then his head dropped back down on the pillow. "Witch-child, *nothing* is wonderful before the sun comes up, and the sun is still sleeping. Don't you want to sleep for another hour?"

"Tch."

Daemon groaned. What reasonable child *wanted* to get up before the sun?

"Papa."

Reaching out, he groped for the other adult who should have been in the bed. ★Surreal?★

★I'm in the bathroom. I'll be back in a minute.★

★Are you well?★

★Needing to pee first thing in the morning doesn't mean I'm ill. And being in the bathroom doesn't mean my moontime has started yet, so back off, Sadi.★ Defensive temper sizzled in the psychic link before Surreal broke the connection, a sure sign there was nothing wrong with *his* ability to read a calendar.

Fine. Wonderful. The sun wasn't up, he was barely awake, and he already had one female snarling at him and the other prepared to keep jumping on him until he saw whatever wonderful thing she wanted to show him.

He turned on the bedside lamp, its candle-light still set to the soft light he preferred for sex, and tried to force his brain into believing he should be awake at this hour of the morning. "All right, witch-child. Let me up."

Jaenelle slid off the bed, bouncing with excitement. "Come *on*, Papa." She started to yank the sheet off him.

He grabbed the sheet before she pulled it below his waist, and snarled softly, a sound that would have frightened everyone else and just made his daughter pause.

"Get out of here," he said. "Let me get dressed."

"I can wait for you," she protested. "If I leave, you'll take *forever*."

"I'm not wearing anything, so I'm not getting out of bed until you're gone."

"Oh, *tch*," she said with a dismissive wave of her hand. "I've seen boy parts before."

He didn't remember moving, but his hand was suddenly locked around her wrist. His temper had turned feral and cold and was rising to the killing edge, and he knew by the way her eyes widened that his eyes were glazed.

"Explain, witch-child," he crooned.

"I'm sorry." She tried to pull away from him, but his hold, while gentle, was unyielding. "We didn't mean to cause trouble."

"Jaenelle Saetien."

Daemon? Surreal asked.

He shut out his wife and stared at his trembling daughter. *"Explain."*

"Uncle Lucivar said it was all right!"

He saw the room through a red veil. With effort, he released Jaenelle's wrist. "Get out of here. *Now.*"

She ran. The moment she was out of the room, he flung the sheet aside, sprang out of bed, and strode to his own adjoining bedroom to get dressed. He could hear Jaenelle yelling for her mother, felt the crackle of Gray power in response. No doubt Surreal had used Craft to pass through the wall and meet Jaenelle in the corridor. Better that way. Right now he couldn't get past the rage to deal with the girl in any gentle way.

He was dressed and striding for his bedroom's door when Surreal rushed in from her room.

"Jaenelle's practically in hysterics," she said. "What in the name of Hell is going on?"

"I don't know yet." His hand closed on the door's handle.

"Where are you going?"

He turned his head and looked at her—and watched her freeze because she recognized the difference between dealing with the Warlord Prince of Dhemlan and the High Lord of Hell.

But she swallowed hard and pushed, because Surreal wouldn't do anything less. "Daemon, where are you going?"

He yanked on the handle and ripped the door off its hinges. Letting it fall, he snarled, "I'm going to have a chat with my brother."

All the way to Ebon Rih, Daemon worked to keep his temper chained—at least until he had some kind of explanation from Prince Yaslana.

"Oh, tch. I've seen boy parts before. . . . Uncle Lucivar said it was all right!"

Memories swam too close to the surface. Memories of a place called Briarwood and men who were called uncles—men who violated little girls. Memories of Jaenelle Angelline's body torn from a savage rape. And blood. So much blood. That terrible night had been the first time he'd seen Witch in the Misty Place after he'd fallen too far in the abyss and shattered his mind.

He dropped from the Black Wind to the landing web below Lucivar's eyrie. The air around him turned frigid, and the green leaves of the nearby plants frosted as he climbed the steps to the flagstone courtyard.

He walked into his brother's home without knocking,

then twisted the chain on his temper a little more when he heard Daemonar and Titian chattering in the kitchen—and heard Lucivar answer some question that had been inserted in the chatter.

Maybe it was better this way, with the children here. If Lucivar had been alone ...

He walked into the kitchen. Titian looked up and gave him a cheerful, "Hi, Uncle Daemon," before she picked up his mood and hunched in her seat.

Lucivar gave him one measuring look, then continued cooking breakfast.

Daemonar stood up, a young Warlord Prince prepared to die defending his father and sister. The boy swallowed hard and said, "It wasn't Jaenelle's fault."

"It wasn't anyone's fault," Lucivar said with such dismissive certainty the tone pierced Daemon's cold rage, leaving behind a moment's doubt.

"But something did happen," Daemon said too softly.

Lucivar shrugged, then filled two of the plates on the counter with eggs and bacon, adding slices of toast and a bowl of summer berries. Calling in a tray, he stacked it with the plates, silverware, the butter dish, and a jar of Marian's jam. He took two glasses from a cupboard and filled them with milk.

"Daemonar, take the tray into the dining room. You and your sister have breakfast in there. Titian, can you carry the milk?"

"We're supposed to eat where?" Daemonar asked as Lucivar handed him the tray.

"Dining room," Lucivar replied. "You know. The place you only see on special occasions. Now go."

"But, Papa."

"Go."

Daemonar glanced at Daemon, fear in his eyes. "Come on, Titian."

Daemon said nothing, did nothing except assess every move and every sound Lucivar made. When the children were in the other room, he wrapped a Black shield around the kitchen, then added an aural shield. Whatever they said to each other would remain private—providing they were both still alive when the discussion was done.

Lucivar took two white mugs from the cupboard. "Coffee?"

"Not yet." He didn't eat with an enemy. Refusing the coffee right now was a warning that while he and Lucivar would always be brothers, they might no longer be friends.

Lucivar filled one mug, then set the coffeepot back on the stove. "I'm surprised you didn't show up sooner. And frankly, Bastard, I'm surprised you're this pissed off about it."

"My daughter was exposed to a naked male. You knew and didn't tell me. You're damn right I'm pissed off about it."

"I told her to tell you." Lucivar sighed. "I guess she didn't."

"Now you will," he said coldly. "And the first thing you're going to tell me is who displayed himself to a girl her age."

Lucivar took a slow swallow of coffee. "Me."

It crushed his heart. He suspected that would be the answer and had hoped he was wrong.

Then he considered Daemonar's words and Lucivar's dismissive response. Jaenelle had been equally dismissive about whatever had happened. *Was* he wrong?

"Explain." He could barely force out the word.

"Do you want the short version or all the details?"

"Oh, I want all the details, Prick. I do want the details."

"All right." Lucivar huffed out a breath and told him.

Lucivar rested in the small pool that was one of his favorite places in Ebon Rih, lulled by the twitter of birds, the easy fall of water, and the voices of young girls doing happy girl things. He'd checked the area before setting up a perimeter shield that allowed Titian and Jaenelle Saetien to have a feeling of independence while never being beyond his awareness.

After a quick dip to cool off from the summer heat, they'd said they wanted to pick wildflowers so that Marian could teach them . . . something. Since he and Daemonar had the pool to themselves, they stripped completely and settled into water he considered sun-warmed to perfection, since it was still first-gasp cool.

Through half-closed eyes, he watched his son trying to act relaxed and lazy, but the boy was too focused on the sound of the girls' voices to be either.

No. Daemonar still acted like a boy at times, but he was well into the adolescent stage, both physically and emotionally, and the aggressive temper of a Warlord Prince was now added to the possessive, protective side of their caste.

Daemonar sighed and ducked under the water. When he surfaced, he sighed again. "They giggle a lot. Especially when they're together. Why do they giggle like that?"

"Because they're girls."

"That's not much of an answer."

"It's the only one I've got, boyo. Young females are still females, and their minds are wondrous, strange, and confusing."

Daemonar rolled his eyes. "It makes Titian and Jaenelle sound dumb, like some of the older girls in school. Except Jillian. *She* wouldn't act dumb."

Quick to defend, Lucivar thought. "Anything I need to know about?"

"No, sir."

And a little too quick with that answer. Might be nothing, but Lucivar wouldn't dismiss it until he'd had a chat with Jillian and *knew* it was nothing. Daemonar saw Jillian as an older sister, which meant she was his to protect and defend. So the boy would never admit to an adult that she was doing something dumb even if he thought she was doing something dumb.

Looked like it was time for a reminder talk about the difference between doing something dumb but not dangerous and doing something that put one of them in the position of needing the intervention of an adult—namely, him.

"They're going to pick *all* the flowers," Daemonar said.

Lucivar studied his son. "If you want to do something

for your mother, you can help her weed the garden this evening. Then you can have some time alone with her. She'll like that just as much as picked flowers."

Big sigh. "The girls will push in."

"I'll keep the girls out of the way."

"Yeah?" Daemonar climbed out of the pool, looking happier.

"Hey." Lucivar waited until Daemonar met his eyes. "Do not start teasing them."

"I won't."

Lucivar stared at him. "They're having a good time. Let them be."

"I'm not going to do anything. Not with Jaenelle here."

"Because she's younger than you and Titian?"

Daemonar grinned. "No, because she hits a lot harder than Titian."

His sigh turned into a chuckle. "Go on, then."

Daemonar grabbed his clothes and darted over to the bushes where he would have privacy dressing.

Lucivar pushed away from the edge of the pool and floated on his back, his wings spread.

Didn't get much quiet time these days, not since Marian had given birth to their third child, a boy they named Andulvar in honor of the Demon Prince. A hard birthing, and it was taking Marian longer to recover. Because she needed more rest and her time and strength were being given to the baby, he made sure Daemonar and Titian had a little time alone with her each day. And he made sure she had a little time for herself. Like today when he took the children for an afternoon at the pool and Jillian was at the eyrie to help out and watch the baby so that Marian could have a couple of hours to sleep or read in peace.

With all the children nearby but occupied, he could have a few minutes of peace himself.

The girls' shrieks had him snapping upright, but he stayed in the pool, listening while he sent out psychic probes to search for the problem. They weren't yelling for help, and those shrieks weren't telling him much. The sound could be for anything—bug, snake, weird formation of bark on a tree. Granted, the girls weren't prone to shrieking, since they'd learned early how their fathers responded to the sound, but they *were* young girls of a certain age, so . . .

Daemonar's voice. Angry. Distressed. Close to panic.

It didn't matter if he couldn't sense anything wrong. If all three of them were upset, there *was* a problem.

Lucivar surged out of the water, calling in his war blade as he strode toward their voices. He used Craft to pass through the bushes in his way, never breaking stride. Nothing should have been able to slip through his perimeter shield. *Nothing!* But if something had and the children were under attack . . .

He burst in on them, his temper rising to the killing edge as he scanned the clear, grassy area where Jaenelle and Titian stood, then probed the bushes behind Daemonar—and found nothing.

"What in the name of Hell is going on?" he roared.

Daemonar and Titian began talking so fast they were barely coherent, their words a cacophony of tripping sounds full of accusations, justifications, denials, and explanations. But it was Jaenelle's expression—baffled and a bit disappointed—that caught his attention and made him uneasy.

A sharp whistle silenced his children. Daemonar clutched his clothes to cover himself. Titian twisted her fingers. Jaenelle remained focused on . . . whatever.

Then, sounding apologetic, she said, "It looks like baby Andulvar's stuff."

Daemonar made a strangled noise. Titian glanced at her father, blushed fiercely, and looked away. Jaenelle cocked her head and continued to ponder.

"What?" He looked down to figure out what the witchling found so interesting—and swore silently but with great sincerity. And suddenly all the accusations, justifications, denials, and explanations made sense.

After making one more swift probe to be sure there was

no danger, Lucivar vanished his war blade and called in the loin wrap he usually wore as a morning cover-up in the summer. As he secured the wrap, he said, "Before I decide whose ass gets kicked, let me see if I understand this. Some of the older girls at school have gotten curious about what a boy has tucked in his pants, and they've been teasing Titian, saying she's too young to know about such things."

"They made it sound all mysterious, and I wanted to know!" Titian wailed.

"So when you heard Daemonar in the bushes, Jaenelle tried to sneak up on him and get a look at what the older girls were talking about."

"I tried to be quiet, but Daemonar heard me right away," Jaenelle said.

No, he didn't, Lucivar thought. *Otherwise, he would have started yelling before the shrieking started.* But he found it interesting that Jaenelle was trying to give Daemonar credit for catching her—and even more interesting that she *had* been able to sneak up on an Eyrien boy who already had a few years of formal training. Of course, that boy was still naked and nowhere near the bushes where he'd gone to get dressed, which meant he'd decided to sneak up on the girls and see what they were doing and had been so intent on that he'd forgotten the reason he was still carrying his clothes— until Jaenelle sneaked up on him and he realized how much trouble he'd be in for being naked in front of his young cousin.

Lucivar said, "So now you've seen the mysterious boy parts that are making the older girls act silly."

"Really?" Jaenelle asked doubtfully.

"Darling, if someone is male and human, this is what he's got in his pants."

"Oh."

He quivered with the effort not to laugh at the keen disappointment held in that single word. Apparently boy parts weren't mysterious after all. In fact, they weren't even interesting. At least, not for a good many years.

Thank the Darkness for that.

"Papa?" Titian said after a long moment of feet-shuffling silence. "Can we go back to picking flowers?"

"Not yet." Lucivar gave all the children a lazy, arrogant smile. "First, we're going to discuss some new rules."

"That's it," Lucivar said, setting his coffee mug on the counter.

Daemon stood still, saying nothing, trying to find his balance. Jaenelle Saetien hadn't seen a strange man intent on doing her harm in any way. And he couldn't fault Lucivar for choosing the war blade over pants when it sounded like the children were in trouble. He would have made the same choice of weapons over modesty.

His head throbbed and his stomach churned, no doubt from holding in all that rage that now had no target.

He watched Lucivar pick up the coffeepot and refill one mug. "Is there enough in there for another cup?"

Lucivar gave him that measuring look, understanding the message. He filled the other mug and handed it to Daemon.

"I don't know what to say." Daemon sipped the coffee. "I know too much, Lucivar. I heard too many nightmares while Jaenelle and I were married, and I never want my little girl to know the things my Queen knew."

"I know about those nightmares too." Lucivar took two plates out of the cupboard and divided the rest of the food. "Jaenelle Saetien didn't say anything about her visit here until this morning?"

"Oh, she was a bundle of information about the visit, talking about the baby, and Auntie Marian teaching her and Titian to make wildflower wreaths, and getting to do practice routines with you using the sparring sticks, and playing with the wolf pack who lives on the mountain with you, and shopping in Riada with Titian and Jillian and the three of them stopping at The Tavern for the midday meal. She said you had some new rules, but that was thrown in with the rest, and she didn't elaborate, so it sounded like they were boundaries that just applied to her when she was with you in Ebon Rih." Daemon took a long swallow of cool coffee. "She didn't say anything about seeing a man's body until she wanted to show me something wonderful and tried to drag me out of bed."

"What was it?" Lucivar asked.

Daemon sighed. "I don't know. The conversation ended once she mentioned boy parts."

Lucivar looked out the kitchen window. "Hell's fire. What time did she jump on you that you got here so early?"

"Before sunup."

Lucivar huffed out a laugh. "No wonder you arrived here looking like you were skating the border of the Twisted Kingdom."

"Prick, I know you better than to think what I was thinking. For that, I'm sorry."

"Don't be. If Titian had hit me with that bit of information before I was awake, I would have landed on your doorstep wondering the same thing. The only difference is I would have pinned your ass to the wall before we started talking."

He meant it. All of it.

Lucivar picked up one of the plates and held it out. "You want this?"

"Yes, I do." Taking his plate and mug to the kitchen table, he sat down.

Lucivar tossed him a fork, then joined him.

"Tell me about these rules," Daemon said.

"I kept it simple." Lucivar spread jam on his toast. "Look equals tell. Touch equals tell. Permission before action. No exceptions."

"Is that supposed to make sense?"

"The long version of the rules is, if any male tries to show them his stuff or tries to talk them into showing him their bodies, the first thing they do is shield. The second thing they do is holler for you or me, and we will decide what needs to be done. If anyone tries to touch them or tries to make them touch body parts—"

"They shield and holler for one of us."

Lucivar nodded. "If they want to spend private time with a friend, male or female, they get our permission first. I won't refuse any reasonable request and will set whatever boundaries I feel are necessary, but permission comes before action."

"And the consequences of disobeying your rules?"

Lucivar looked him in the eyes. "I'll destroy the enemy, regardless of gender or age. And unless there is permission beforehand, I will regard any person who tries to sneak off with one of my children as an enemy."

Daemon sat back. "There might be mitigating circumstances."

"Not if I find out about it afterward instead of beforehand."

"That's a hard line." One he knew Lucivar would hold. "Do these rules apply to Daemonar too?"

"Yes. And Jillian."

Daemon stiffened. "Has someone been bothering Jillian?"

Lucivar shook his head. "No—and I intend to keep it that way." He paused. "Look, Bastard, you may think those rules are harsh, and maybe you want to soften them for Jaenelle Saetien. But when it comes to my children, when they stay with you, I expect you to hold that line."

He polished off the eggs. "I don't have any trouble with your rules or holding that line for any of the children—including Mikal."

"And Beron?"

Daemon shook his head. "Beron has his own residence and is apprenticing in his chosen profession, so he's old enough to choose his own company." But it wouldn't hurt to remind the young Warlord that being given that much independence didn't mean the family patriarch wasn't aware of *all* of his activities.

"The theater group he belongs to is performing a play in Riada next month. We're looking forward to seeing him."

And Uncle Lucivar will keep an eye on him while Beron is in Ebon Rih, Daemon thought, working to hide a smile.

"You want more coffee?" Lucivar asked. "I'll make another pot."

"Sure. Where is Marian?"

"Sleeping in."

Something in the tone, in the way Lucivar moved around the kitchen. "Is she all right?"

"Just slow coming back from this birthing. It's taking longer for her to regain her strength and energy. She'll be fine."

"But . . . ?" Daemon asked gently.

Lucivar filled the coffeepot and put it on the stove to heat before replying. "Nurian is an excellent Healer, and I trust what she says. But I wish Jaenelle Angelline was still here to tell me Marian will be fine. I'd feel a lot easier if she was still here to tell me that."

Daemon walked into his study and found Surreal waiting for him, comfortably settled on the long leather sofa. She had a book in her lap and a crossbow aimed at his groin.

"Is that necessary?" he asked politely.

"You tell me." Her tone was a few steps short of polite.

He slipped his hands in his trouser pockets and waited. When Surreal began a discussion by pointing a weapon at a man, it was wise to yield as much as possible.

"I upset Jaenelle." The crossbow didn't waver, so he considered the other half of his offense. "And I left you to deal with it without giving you any idea of what you were facing."

"Which is something you won't do again. Agreed?"

Was there a choice? "Agreed."

Surreal vanished the crossbow, then shifted so that he could sit beside her.

"Jaenelle Saetien is very sorry that she forgot to tell you about Uncle Lucivar's new rules—which you will explain to me in detail by the end of the day," she said. "A new friend showed up early this morning, and she needed to tell you about him before she totally broke the rules instead of just bending the rules by waiting for you to wake up before she told you about her new friend, since he was in her room, but you didn't wake up, which is why she woke you, but then she mentioned the boy parts, which Uncle Lucivar had also told her to tell you about, and before she could explain, you cat-puffed, kicked her out of the room, and left to yell at Lucivar."

"I what? Cat-puffed? What in the name of Hell is that?"

"I'm guessing it's what a pissed-off feline does."

"Well, that makes me sound scary."

"No, it makes you sound like a rolly ball of fur. Regardless . . ." Surreal grabbed a fistful of his shirt and pulled him closer. "I'll give you a choice. You can go up there and settle things with your daughter and her new friends, or you can take the second part of the discussion about why boy parts wiggle."

He felt all the blood drain out of his head. "Why would there be a second part if the two of you already discussed this?"

"Because with Jaenelle Saetien, there is always a second part to a discussion."

That was a frightening truth. "All right. I'll meet these new friends."

"One of them is in her room. The other is in the stables."

"I take it these new friends have boy parts?"

Surreal released his shirt and leaned back. "Trust me, Sadi. Their boy parts are the least of your problems."

Once Daemon was on his way to meet his daughter's new friends, Surreal breathed out a shuddery sigh. No sign or scent of blood or wounds, so it wasn't likely that he and Lucivar had done more than yell at each other.

If it had been anyone other than Lucivar, even if the man's actions had been innocent or unintentional . . .

Sadi hadn't looked like a man who had shattered the family by maiming or killing his brother. No, her sense of him when he'd walked into the study was that of a man who knew it would take some work to clean up the emotional mess he'd left behind when he'd thundered out of the Hall.

She called in her favorite stiletto and studied its edge.

She'd been twelve when she was raped, but the man hadn't been strong enough to take more than her virginity. She'd come away from that bed with her Birthright Green Jewels and her power still intact.

Jaenelle Angelline had been twelve when she was raped. No one could have taken away Witch's power—she stood too deep in the abyss for anyone to do *that*—but she had abandoned her body for almost two years, traveling roads in the Twisted Kingdom, and maybe even the Darkness itself, that no one else could walk. And what had been done to her in Briarwood had left emotional scars that had haunted her all her life.

Daemon had married two women who had been scarred by rape, and he wasn't without scars himself—not with what she guessed had been done to him as a child and what he'd endured as a pleasure slave. So any hint that his daughter might be at risk of having the same kind of scars was enough to have his temper turn cold and brutal and committed to slaughter.

That was the mess Daemon had left her with this morning—trying to find a way to explain to a frightened girl why her darling papa had been so angry about the boy parts. Jaenelle Saetien had been more worried about getting Uncle Lucivar into trouble than whatever punishment she might face for failing to tell her father about the incident at the pool—and she'd been worried that she had somehow hurt her papa's heart.

Which was true.

Surreal vanished the stiletto, grabbed two fistfuls of hair, and pulled gently to ease some of the ache around her skull.

Old memories were bound to start surfacing now that they were this close to Jaenelle Saetien's Birthright Ceremony.

But old memories weren't the only things surfacing now, and she didn't know what to think about that.

Jaenelle Saetien's new friend was a half-grown Arcerian cat named Kaele. A Warlord Prince who wore a Green Birthright Jewel.

May the Darkness have mercy on me, Daemon thought as the cat put himself between man and girl.

Kaele looked at Daemon and snarled.

Daemon looked at Kaele and snarled—and let his Black power thunder softly through the room, leaving no doubt about who was the dominant male.

"No no no," Jaenelle said, throwing herself on the cat and clamping both arms around his neck. "Do *not* snarl at Papa! He won't let us play if you snarl at him."

Why are you here? Daemon asked on a spear thread.

To be friends with your kitten, Kaele replied. *And with you. The Weavers said it was time.*

Mother Night.

There were rules for the wilder kindred to follow when they stayed at the Hall. He just couldn't remember any of them.

Well, there was the most important one.

"Do not swat anyone or eat anyone without asking me first," he said.

I could ask the dogs, Kaele said, clearly preferring to communicate with other kindred.

"No, you'll ask me." He trusted the Scelties for the most part, but the ones who lived at the Hall came from the Sceltie school Jaenelle Angelline and Ladvarian had begun and that he now co-owned with Ladvarian's descendants. So these dogs were loyal to his family and very protective of his wife and daughter. Usually he was grateful for that, but with the presence of an Arcerian cat, he could see Morghann and Khary happily pointing out a human they didn't like and putting the label of "dinner" on the fool.

"Are you mad at Uncle Lucivar?" Jaenelle asked in a small voice.

Daemon shook his head. "No, we got that sorted out. But I wish you had told me about it when I was more awake to understand what had happened."

"I know." She hugged Kaele's neck hard enough to produce a grunt from the cat.

Daemon went down on one knee. "Come here, witch-child."

She released the cat and came to him. Of course, the cat, being a Warlord Prince, came too.

He rested his hands on her shoulders, giving Kaele time to accept that *he* could touch his own daughter.

"Uncle Lucivar is going to hold you to his rules—and so am I. Do you understand that?"

"Yes, Papa."

"I've seen too many bad things, Jaenelle, and I'm afraid of what I would do if someone hurt you."

"That's what Mama said."

"Your mother is a very smart woman."

Jaenelle smiled. "She said that too."

He kissed her cheek and hugged her, as much to reassure her as to comfort himself. As he held her, he sent out a delicate psychic probe. It wouldn't invade her mind or thoughts, but it would give him a sense of her emotions, of whether she was as easy about seeing a naked man as she seemed to be.

And found something he hadn't expected.

His daughter was keeping secrets from him.

He eased back and looked at her. Nothing haunted those gold eyes, but *something* was there. Something, he suddenly realized, that had been there on and off for the past few years—and more so in the past year as she got closer to her Birthright Ceremony.

"I guess I should introduce myself to your other friend," he said as he rose gracefully.

"You'll like him." She gave him an unsure but game smile that made him tremble.

He wasn't sure he would like this friend, but unless he

hated the male on sight, he'd let things slide. At least for today. But before he met this second friend, he wanted to have a word with his wife.

Surreal was still sitting on the sofa in his study, so he didn't have to hunt for her.

"Hell's fire," she said, grinning. "If your father could see the look on your face, he'd laugh himself silly."

He sank down beside her, feeling boneless. "There is an Arcerian cat in the Hall again."

"I know. I met him. You need to put strengthening spells on Jaenelle's bed—and think about getting her a bigger bed if he's intending to be a frequent visitor."

"Since he's in the stables, I'm assuming her other friend has fur and boy parts?"

"He does. He also has a spiral horn—and his name is Moondancer. He can trace his bloodlines back to a Warlord Prince named Kaetien."

Daemon heard the wobble in her voice. He turned his head and studied her, seeing enough in her eyes before she looked away.

He cupped her face in his hands. "Talk to me, Surreal. What do you know?"

"About what?"

Shaky. Of course, this whole day must have stirred up memories for her too.

"Jaenelle Saetien is keeping secrets. Even if she had a reason for not telling me, she might have told you."

"Let it go, Sadi."

"I can't. Not today."

Surreal pulled away. He released her face but closed one hand around her wrist.

"Surreal," he said gently. He could see her struggling to decide what to tell him.

"A special friend," she finally said. "A secret friend. Someone she's known 'forever,' which I take to mean these past few years."

"How could someone have slipped into the Hall without our being aware of it?"

"No one could. But she doesn't see this friend here at home. She meets this friend in dreams."

Daemon forgot how to breathe. "Have you asked . . . ?"

Surreal shook her head. "She was upset about telling me. She didn't want to break Lucivar's rules, especially now that she knew how upset it would make you, but she didn't want to tell me because it wasn't time for us to know about this friend. So I told her it was all right to keep the secret for a while longer."

She meets this friend in dreams.

He didn't know what to think, didn't know what to feel.

"Daemon?" Surreal wrapped her hand around his other wrist. "Aren't you wondering?"

He felt dizzy, off balance. "About something in particular? I've wondered about too much already today."

"The wild kindred races withdrew from most human contact decades ago. Even most of the wolves don't talk to us directly; they maintain contact with the two packs who have stayed connected to the family. Now there's an Arcerian cat descended from Kaelas visiting here. There is a unicorn descended from Kaetien. The Scelties who live with us now are named Morghann and Khary, and we didn't name them. Are a tiger and dragon going to show up in the next few weeks?"

He rested his forehead against hers. "You think this has something to do with Jaenelle's special friend?"

"I don't know, but what I'm wondering is this: What do the kindred know that we don't?"

THIRTEEN

The Birthright Ceremony. A rite of passage. One of the most important days in a child's life.

And in a father's life.

A dozen aristo families gathered at a Sanctuary in a central Dhemlan Province to witness the children who would be gifted with their Birthright Jewels—and to witness the fathers who would be legally gifted with their children.

Because one of those children was the daughter of Prince Daemon Sadi and Lady Surreal SaDiablo, the Sanctuary grounds were packed with Queens, both District and Province, and aristos from every Province in Dhemlan as well as the whole SaDiablo family.

Surreal stood apart from the rest of the parents, ignoring the nervous glances being cast her way by the Queens and other adults. Sometimes several children went through the Birthright Ceremony on the same day. Sometimes only one child stood at the altar and resonated in the Darkness, drawing the particular Jewel that matched who and what she was.

They had decided to let Jaenelle Saetien participate at the same time as other children—which meant the second part of the Ceremony would also be public. That was the reason everyone was keeping their distance from her. There was one father who was a danger to them all if *anything* went wrong today.

"And they still brought their children here," she growled.

"Did you really think they wouldn't want to watch the spectacle?" Lucivar asked as he came up beside her.

"If I were them, I would stay far away from this place today."

"Is that why we're doing this at a Sanctuary near one of the family's estates instead of in Halaway?"

"This was Sadi's choice. I think . . ." Because it was Lucivar, she slipped an arm through his and voiced the worry that had gnawed at her ever since Daemon announced where the Birthright Ceremony would take place. "I think he chose this Sanctuary and this estate so that he would have someplace to run to if anything went wrong. There won't be memories of this day at the Hall."

"Is something going to go wrong?" Lucivar asked, giving her a sharp look.

Surreal shook her head. "No, I made my choice the first time I saw Daemon's face when he looked at his daughter. I'm just not sure what *his* choice will be after today." She tried to smile in response to Lucivar's unspoken question. "After today, when his daughter is irrevocably his, he may not feel the need to stay married."

"Is that your way of warning me that you're leaving him?"

"No," she said softly. "I'm not leaving him." *Don't do this. Not today.* "I did want to warn you about something else."

"Oh?"

"Has Titian said anything about the incident this summer when you and the children were at the pool?"

"She said something to Marian."

It was obvious he wasn't thrilled about what was said, but he was accepting it—and maybe even felt a little relieved.

"Do I need to call in my crossbow to get the details?" she asked.

"I overheard Titian tell Marian that the older girls had been making a fuss about boy stuff just so the younger girls would think they knew about something interesting, and it was all a big tease."

"Oh, dear." She bit her lower lip and told herself to behave. Then she thought, *Ah, shit, he deserves this.* "Jaenelle has been doing a lot of thinking about the day she saw your boy stuff."

"Is she upset?" Lucivar asked with a hint of alarm.

"Noooo. But she did come to a different conclusion than Titian. Jaenelle Saetien has decided that, for the most part, boy stuff is not interesting and it looks funny when it wiggles."

He made a pained sound, but since he was managing to keep a straight face, she went on. "However, she also concluded that when someone is *special*, his stuff becomes special too. Like, your stuff becomes special when you're around Auntie Marian. Otherwise, she wouldn't have let you help her make the baby."

She felt him shake. She wasn't sure if he was about to start laughing hysterically or just become hysterical.

"Having come to that conclusion about her darling uncle Lucivar—"

He whimpered.

"—she has decided the same must be true of her darling papa. He's shyer than you so she hasn't been able to confirm that, but she's certain it's true because Daemon is her papa and he's wonderful."

"Mother Night." Lucivar swallowed hard. "What did Daemon say?"

"He doesn't know about this yet. She decided that he's been so nervous about the party we're having after the Ceremony that it wasn't the time to tell him about her conclusions regarding boy stuff."

"Then why in the name of Hell did you tell me?"

"Because one of these days he's going to be standing at your door looking like he'd gotten kicked in the head, and I thought you should have some idea about why so you can comfort him."

"Why can't *you* comfort him?"

"Because, sugar, I tend to agree with her—especially when boy stuff wiggles."

He walked away, weaving a little. Within moments, Marian came up to her, the baby asleep on her shoulder.

"I want to know what you said to put that look on his face," Marian said. "I think it will come in handy someday."

"Oh, don't worry. You have a daughter too. I'm sure you'll see that look again."

Marian laughed softly as she rubbed the baby's back, but her eyes remained serious. "Are you concerned about today? About Jaenelle?"

"A little. I don't care what Jewels she wears. Neither does Daemon. But I should have sensed something at this point, should have some idea of what Jewel Jaenelle will wear, and I don't. Based on how quickly she picks up basic—and not-so-basic—Craft, she should be strong enough to need a reservoir for her power."

"Daemon isn't sensing anything either?"

Surreal shook her head. "I wear the Gray; Daemon wears the Black. If her power is so weak she comes away from the Ceremony without a Jewel . . ."

"She'll feel like an outsider within her own family," Marian concluded. "Especially because Titian wears Birth-right Summer-sky and Daemonar wears the Green."

Surreal shivered at the thought. Wasn't that how so many things had gone wrong with Jaenelle Angelline's life? She had been the outsider in her family, with her special friends and abilities no one had wanted to understand until Saetan had recognized her as the daughter of his soul.

Well, Jaenelle Saetien was *never* going to feel like an outsider whether she wore a Jewel or not.

"You look so fierce," Marian said. "Where did you go?"

"Nowhere. Too far." She tried to smile. "Daemon is going through the steps with Jaenelle. Want to make a bet on who is lecturing who?"

"Do you remember—," Daemon began.

"I remember!" Jaenelle huffed out a breath. "Papa! We've gone over this forever-many times!"

He went down on one knee to be closer to her. "I know, but—"

"*Papa!*" She cat-puffed and jumped back. "Don't put your knee on the ground. You'll get dirty! Stand up!"

He obeyed. She immediately closed in on him and began whacking at his knee to clean off flecks of dirt.

"We have to stay neat and tidy because this is an important day," Jaenelle said.

"Yes, Lady."

She gave him a narrow-eyed look to see if he was making fun of her. Then she got a look in her eyes that was much too old for her young years—and scared the shit out of him.

"You're afraid, aren't you?" she asked.

Terrified, actually. "A little."

She grabbed his hand in both of hers and gave him a sweet smile. "Don't worry, Papa. Everything will be fine. I already know what Jewel I'm supposed to pick. My friend told me."

His stomach lurched. There had been no mention of the special friend over the past few weeks. "Witch-child, you can't choose a Jewel just because you like its color."

"*Tch.* I *know* that. I *know* all this stuff, Papa." She looked past him. "I'm supposed to stand with the other children now, and you're supposed to stand with Mama."

She hauled him over to where Surreal stood with Marian, then ran off to join the other children who were going through the Ceremony.

Marian looked at him, then looked at Surreal and sighed. "I'll pay you later." She wandered off.

"Problem?" Surreal asked.

"Apparently, it's now your responsibility to keep me neat and tidy," he replied dryly. "And if you're going to place bets about me, do I get a share of the winnings?"

She gave him a sharp smile. "No."

His heart raced and the need to move was almost unbearable. But he stood still because he wasn't willing to let anyone know how much effort it was taking to stay in control and appear no more anxious than any other father waiting to be told his fate with regard to his child.

Surreal slipped her arm through his. Then she looked at the children and sighed. "She's at the end of the line."

"Maybe we should have had a private Ceremony," he muttered.

"You're the Warlord Prince of Dhemlan. Even if she had been the only child acquiring a Birthright Jewel today, it wouldn't have been a private Ceremony."

A hard truth. If nothing else, all the Dhemlan Queens would have come to witness the second half of the Ceremony.

"We should move up with the families who are participating today," he said. When she started to withdraw her arm, he pressed his hand over hers, holding her in place. "There's no reason to be formal. Is there?"

She studied his face and shook her head. "No reason."

Her mood seemed bittersweet, and he suspected he was the cause of whatever bitterness dimmed her pleasure in this special day. She had been his partner, his friend, his lover. They had laughed together and worried together and, sometimes, fought with each other.

He hadn't been the husband she deserved. He had taken care of her body and enjoyed doing it, and he'd made an effort not to deliberately hurt her heart. He cared for her, deeply, but he'd never said the words that matter most to a woman.

And yet, she had stayed—and he wanted her to stay because he wanted to be with her, wanted to share his life with her.

Maybe, once this day was behind them, the tension that had been building between them would go away, along with the unspoken questions and doubts.

Maybe.

Or maybe, like the previous patriarch of the SaDiablo family, he would find himself surrounded by people he loved and yet always feel alone.

His heart ached with love and pride as he looked at the people who were his family. Sylvia's boys, Beron and Mikal. Manny, who had taken care of him when he'd been a child. Tersa, his mother. Jillian. Marian and the children. Lucivar. And Surreal.

Giving his arm a squeeze, Surreal slipped away to talk to Manny. Lucivar shifted to fill the space.

"How did you survive this twice?" Daemon asked.

Lucivar shrugged. "Nothing I could do about it. A child will wear the Jewels a child will wear. I figure it's my job to teach them to live up to their own potential instead of trying to match someone else—including me."

"That's not what I meant."

"If you don't know the answer to that, old son, then you haven't been paying attention to the woman you've lived with these past fifteen years," Lucivar said quietly, turning enough to make the words private. "She loves you. You know that, don't you? And she's as committed to her daughter as you are."

"I know." Daemon sighed. "I know." But was that commitment enough?

"Boys," Tersa said.

He and Lucivar immediately looked toward the Sanctuary where the first girl was coming out with her new Jewel.

"Oh," Marian said with warm pleasure. "She has a Summer-sky."

The next child in line, a boy, went into the Sanctuary with his chosen witness while the girl stood beside her mother, who proceeded with the formal granting of paternity.

Another child went in, and another man was granted legal rights to the child he had made.

Daemon called in chairs for the women and spread a blanket for the children so that they could sit on the ground and play hawks and hares. Lucivar called in a jug of water and let Daemonar take a glass to Jaenelle while he poured water for the rest of them.

By the second hour, Manny was dozing in her chair, and

Surreal had gone off with Marian, who needed to feed and change the baby.

"A dozen children is too many," Daemon said, accepting the glass of wine Lucivar poured for him. "We should have been split up into smaller groups throughout the day, like they did in Ebon Rih when your children went through the Ceremony." When Lucivar said nothing, he felt like a fool. "I should have insisted on this group being split into smaller groups."

"Maybe. Not that it would have made any difference. Not today. They are here to watch you and your daughter."

"Isn't that delightful?"

"Everything has a price."

By the time they reached the third hour, children were getting whiny, adults were getting restless, and Daemon was ready to exile every Queen and aristo present. He'd had enough of the speculative looks and the whispers behind their hands. He also made note of the ones, like Lady Zhara, who had remained gracious and friendly during the long wait, and didn't appear to be there for any other reason than to offer her good wishes.

Then, finally, Jaenelle was the only one waiting her turn.

He held out his hand, palm side down. Surreal placed her hand over his, standing on his left. They walked up to the Sanctuary, where the Priestess waited for them.

The Priestess looked at Jaenelle. "Who will stand as your witness?"

Daemon tensed and felt Surreal do the same. How was Jaenelle supposed to choose one parent over the other in public?

Before he could insist on both of them going in with her, Tersa walked up to them and held out her hand. "Come with me, little Sister."

Jaenelle took her grandmother's hand and followed the Priestess to the room where her Birthright strength would be acknowledged and made apparent by the Jewel that would be both warning and reservoir for the power she wielded.

Surreal's hand trembled on his, but she gave no other sign of surprise or distress.

Is that possible? she asked. *Have you seen signs that Jaenelle might be a natural Black Widow?*

She's too young for there to be any sign that she belongs to that caste. I don't think Tersa meant to indicate that Jaenelle was another Sister of the Hourglass. But she could have meant exactly that. With Tersa, it was hard to tell. *Besides, Tersa stood as your witness too, didn't she?*

Yes, she did, Surreal replied softly. *Yes, she did.*

Five minutes later, Tersa and Jaenelle walked out of the Sanctuary. Jaenelle held nothing in her hands, and there was no Jeweled pendant around her neck.

Daemon's heart sank, but he smiled at his girl—and the happy smile she gave him in return almost broke him.

Daemon . . . , Surreal said.

"My Jewel hasn't arrived yet," Jaenelle said. "My friend said it might come late because its presence would confuse the other children."

"Finish the Ceremony," Tersa said.

Daemon looked at the Priestess. "I don't understand what—"

"Prince," Tersa said. "You will have no answers until the last choice is made."

He moved away from Surreal until he stood in the spot where the other men had stood.

"Come here, Jaenelle," Surreal said. She placed her hands on the girl's shoulders and looked at him.

"I, Surreal SaDiablo, acknowledge Prince Daemon Sadi as the father of Jaenelle Saetien SaDiablo. I grant him all paternal rights from this day forward."

Surreal raised her hands. Jaenelle walked the distance between them and took the hand he held out to her. Even though his hand closed around the child's, his eyes never left the woman's.

She's yours now, Surreal said on a psychic Gray thread.

Thank you.

Let's hear you say that the next time she asks an 'interesting' question.

He huffed out a quiet laugh. *Smart-ass.*

That made *her* smile.

"Well," Daemon said, as he led Jaenelle back to the rest of the family. "Let's finish up here so we can go to the estate and have our party."

"We can't go yet," Jaenelle protested. "We have to wait for my Jewel!"

"Witch-child . . ."

Jaenelle and Tersa turned at the same moment, looked in the same direction. Jaenelle pulled away from him and ran off. Before he could take off after her, Tersa froze him in place with three words.

"She has come."

He stared at his mother, a Black Widow who walked the roads of the Twisted Kingdom. She had changed his life centuries ago with those same three words.

"Daemon." Surreal looked stricken, but she squared her shoulders and said, "Go."

Not sure how much pain he was leaving behind him, he ran after his daughter.

She was walking back to him when he caught up to her, her smile brilliant as she clutched a pendant, its gold chain spilling over her hands.

"Look at my Jewel, Papa! Isn't it wonderful?"

He looked at the Jewel in her hands and sank to his knees.

"I *told* the Priestess that I would have a Rose and a Summer-sky and a Purple Dusk and an Opal and a Green as my Birthright, but she said I could only have one, and I *knew* that wasn't right because the Lady had shown me this Jewel and said it used to be hers but now it would be mine. It even has a name! It's called—"

"Twilight's Dawn," he whispered.

"Yes." She beamed at him. "She said you would understand and teach me how to use it."

His mind was spinning. His heart was in turmoil. "Who said this, witch-child?"

"My special friend. The Lady in the Misty Place. The one who's called the Song in the Darkness."

He swallowed a sob. Pain? Joy? He couldn't tell. "Where . . . ?"

"She's over there." Jaenelle turned and pointed. "She's waiting for you. She said I should wait for you here." She rolled her eyes. "And that I should let you put a shield around me."

"She always was a wise Lady."

Jaenelle hesitated. "She said, when you were ready, you would tell me stories about her. About when she lived in the Realms. She said Uncle Lucivar and Mama could tell me stories too."

"They can. They will."

He stood up. After a moment's hesitation, he put a Red shield around his darling witch-child, since Lucivar or Surreal could break it and get her out. Just in case he didn't come back.

He walked over to the place where she had pointed. One moment he felt nothing. The next . . .

Not the Misty Place, but not the grounds of the Sanctuary either.

And there she was. Witch. The living myth. His love and his heart.

"Prince," Witch said, smiling.

"Jaenelle," he whispered, reaching for her.

His hand went through hers, but when she reached up and rested that same hand against his face, he felt the warmth of her, breathed in the familiar scent of her. She had chosen to show him the Self that lived in the Misty Place deep in the abyss, to show him the dream that had lived within the human flesh.

She was showing him his Queen rather than his former wife.

"How can you be here?"

"This is a shadow, an illusion."

"I know, but . . ."

She looked at him with those haunted, ancient sapphire eyes. One hand still rested against his face; the other now rested against his chest, over his heart.

"Jaenelle Saetien . . ."

"Is the daughter of your blood, the daughter of your heart, and the daughter of your dreams. She is those things to Surreal as well. Two dreamers, Daemon, yearning for the same dream."

His brain felt sluggish. He couldn't get past that he was seeing her again, feeling her touch—but he had to try because his daughter waited for him.

His daughter. And Surreal's.

"You know about me and Surreal?"

Her cat claws pricked his chest. "The Arachnian Queens tended the web until it was ready to be more than dreams, but I'm the one who first gave it shape because of what I saw in a tangled web years before I became a song in the Darkness. You could have married someone else, and you might have had children. But not this child, Daemon. Not this one. This one needed a mother who had known you before you came to Kaeleer, who had known me."

"This one?" Words tumbled through his mind. Webs. Visions. Dreams.

He turned his head and looked toward the spot where he'd left his little girl—and suddenly it made sense. "Jaenelle Saetien is . . . ?"

"Dreams made flesh." Witch smiled. "Your dreams. Surreal's dreams. And my dreams for both of you."

Like Jaenelle Angelline, but not the same.

"Daemon."

He turned back to her. "I don't know what to do."

"Don't you? It's simple, Prince. Listen to your heart. It's healed. It's whole. You loved me as a wife with all your heart for the whole of my life. You will love me as your Queen for the whole of *your* life. But there is someone else you love now, Daemon, and it's time for you to share your heart with more than your daughter."

He closed his eyes and said nothing.

"Stubborn snarly male. Do you need my permission to love the woman who is now your wife, to acknowledge what you feel for her?"

"I don't love Surreal the way I loved you. I'll never love anyone the way I loved you."

"I know. But you do love her, Daemon."

"Yes. I do."

Her voice softened. "Then it's time you told her."

She stepped back, and the loss of her touch raked his heart.

He opened his eyes and studied her, drinking in her face. "Will I see you again?"

She hesitated, then said, "Your daughter will, when she needs to, but you need to let go of the past. However, you won't be alone. No one understands what it's like to stand so deep in the abyss. No one understands what it's like to know there is no one who can touch the most private part of your Self. Saetan was the strongest protector the Realms had ever known, but he also made mistakes because even Andulvar's presence at the depth of the Ebon-gray wasn't enough to keep him from feeling isolated and alone. You're not alone there, Daemon."

"How can I not be . . ."

What had Jaenelle Saetien called the Lady in the Misty Place? The Song in the Darkness. He'd heard it when he stood in the abyss at the full depth of his power, when he knew, with absolute certainty, that he was alone. But that song had been there, a voice that wrapped around him down where it wasn't possible for anyone else to be. He thought he imagined it being Jaenelle's voice because he missed her so much, but she'd been with him all along.

"You won't be alone," she said again.

"For how long?"

Witch smiled. "Long enough."

He thought about that web of power that spiraled from the Misty Place down into the Darkness. Enough power to keep her with him in this one way, to keep him balanced for a lifetime.

And because he had this assurance that she was still with him in some way, he began letting go of what could no longer be.

"May I tell Lucivar about any of this?"

"He's your brother. You can tell him anything." She took a step back and began to fade away. "It's time for you to go."

"Your will is my life."

He closed his eyes. When he opened them, she was gone.

"Papa?"

And there was his other dream, waiting for him. She'd put the chain over her neck and was holding the Jewel, shifting it this way and that to look at the colors.

He walked over to her, sank to his knees, wrapped his arms around her, and pressed his face against her shoulder.

"Papa?" Jaenelle put her arms around him. "Why are you crying? Weren't you happy to see the Lady?"

"Yes. Yes, I was. She gave me a gift. Such a wonderful gift. For your mother too."

Fighting for control, he sat back on his heels, took out a handkerchief, and cleaned up.

Jaenelle Saetien studied him. "Maybe if we go to our house and have the party, you'll feel better."

Laughing, he vanished the handkerchief. "Maybe I will."

He stood up, brushed off his knees before she could comment about the dirt, and held out his right hand.

"Papa! I'm supposed to stand on your *left*. Those are the *rules*."

His Jaenelle Saetien was a stickler for Protocol. Much like his father had been.

"Indulge your papa. Just for today. We'll go back to following the rules tomorrow."

She looked skeptical, but she put her left hand over his

right and let him escort her back to where the rest of the family waited.

Most of the families had left for their own celebrations, but the Queens and aristos who had come to witness the spectacle, as Lucivar called it, were still milling around when he walked by. So they saw Lucivar's stunned look and the way Surreal pressed a hand against her chest and began to laugh and cry when she realized what Jewel her daughter wore.

He walked up to Surreal and said softly, "We need to talk."

"You saw her?" she whispered. "You actually saw *her*?"

"Yes."

Pain. Confusion. Unhappy acceptance.

"It will be all right," he said. "I swear by all that I am, it will be all right."

"Can we go now?" Daemonar asked. "I'm *starving*."

"Shall we go?" he asked Surreal.

She nodded.

He dropped his hand from under Jaenelle's, tacit permission for her to race after her cousins. Then he slipped an arm around Surreal's waist and guided her to the Coach.

Surreal gulped a mouthful of sparkling wine as she watched the children run around. As soon as they reached the estate, Jillian had herded the younger children to their rooms to change out of their formal clothes.

Good thing, Surreal thought. She wasn't sure what game they were playing, but it was a good bet that at least one of them was going to end up with scraped knees or a bloody nose.

"Enough!"

Unless Lucivar roared them into a decision to find a less rambunctious game.

Twilight's Dawn. Jaenelle Saetien wore Twilight's Dawn—a Jewel no one thought would be seen again.

"Are you brooding or just getting drunk?" Lucivar

asked as he reached from behind her, took her glass, and drained it in one long swallow.

"I guess I'm not getting drunk," she replied, looking at the empty glass. She followed the sound of laughter, and there was Daemon standing next to Tersa and Manny, looking as beautiful as the first time she saw him. "I don't know what to do, Lucivar. I don't know what he wants me to do now. She's come back to him."

He handed her the empty glass and gave her a lazy smile. "If you believe that, you're drunker than you look."

"Mean-hearted prick," she muttered. But since she suspected he was right, at least about the being drunk part, she didn't try to walk over to the terrace and refill her glass.

"Who's a mean-hearted prick?" Daemon's arm wrapped around her waist. "Do you want more wine?"

"I think I've already had a bit too much."

He pressed his lips gently against her temple. "Me too. It's been quite a day."

The sexual heat that usually poured out of him was banked to a sensual warmth. She leaned into him, more comforted than aroused.

She wasn't sure how long they stood there with the light fading around them and the autumn air turning cool. She would stand there with him forever if that was what he wanted.

"Surreal?" he said quietly.

"Hmm?"

He took the glass from her and vanished it. "You know that small table in the sitting room that you're so fond of?"

"Uh-huh."

"It now has a vase in it."

"You mean on it."

"No, in it."

She was suddenly a lot more sober. "There isn't one of them old enough or with sufficient training to try to pass one object through another." And she had a bad feeling she knew exactly which child had tried it. "They shouldn't be—"

He pressed a finger against her lips. She narrowed her eyes and raised his hand. "If I have to deal with this tonight when I'm on the shaky side of sober, *you* have to answer the next sex question."

There was the expected glint of panic, but there was also laughter in his eyes. "Or the table could just disappear and we could scratch our heads and wonder where it went."

Playful. She hadn't expected that from him. Not tonight. "We could do that."

He brushed a finger over her lips. "Surreal . . ."

I love you.

He didn't say it. Not quite. But when he cupped her face in his hands and kissed her, she *felt* the words.

And that night, when he made love to her and said her name, it sounded like a promise, like a lovely caress.

The *New York Times*
bestselling
Black Jewels Series

by Anne Bishop

This is the story of the heir to a dark throne, a magic
more powerful than that of the High Lord of Hell,
and an ancient prophecy. These books tell of a
ruthless game of politics and intrigue, magic and
betrayal, love and sacrifice, destiny and fulfillment.

Daughter of the Blood
Heir to the Shadows
Queen of the Darkness
The Invisible Ring
Dreams Made Flesh
Tangled Webs
The Shadow Queen
Shalador's Lady